The Vampire Diaries novels

VOL. I: THE AWAKENING
VOL. II: THE STRUGGLE
VOL. III: THE FURY
VOL. IV: DARK REUNION
THE RETURN VOL. 1: NIGHTFALL
THE RETURN VOL. 2: SHADOW SOULS
THE RETURN VOL. 3: MIDNIGHT
THE HUNTERS VOL. 1: PHANTOM

Stefan's Diaries novels

VOL. I: ORIGINS
VOL. 2: BLOODLUST
VOL. 3: THE CRAVING
VOL. 4: THE RIPPER

The Secret Circle novels

THE INITIATION AND THE CAPTIVE PART I
THE CAPTIVE PART II AND THE POWER

CREATED BY

L. J. Smith

The Vampire Diaries

THE HUNTERS

VOL. 1

PHANTOM

An Imprint of HarperCollinsPublishers

HarperTeen is an imprint of HarperCollins Publishers.

Produced by Alloy Entertainment
151 West 26th Street, New York, NY 10001
www.alloyentertainment.com

Library of Congress Cataloging-in-Publication Data is available.
ISBN 978-0-06-211958-2

Typography by Jennifer Heuer
11   12   13   14   15   GPAU   10 9 8 7 6 5 4 3 2 1
❖
First Edition

lena Gilbert stepped onto a smooth expanse of grass, the spongy blades collapsing beneath her feet. Clusters of scarlet roses and violet delphiniums pushed up from the ground, while a giant canopy hung above her, twinkling with glowing lanterns. On the terrace in front of her stood two curving white marble fountains that shot sprays of water high into the air. Everything was beautiful, elegant, and somehow familiar.

This is Bloddeuwedd's palace, a voice in her head said. But when she had been here last, the field had been crowded with laughing, dancing partygoers. They were gone now, although signs of their presence remained: empty glasses littered the tables set around the edges of the lawn; a silken shawl was tossed over a chair; a lone high-heeled shoe perched on the edge of a fountain.

Something else was odd, too. Before, the scene had been lit by the hellish red light that illuminated everything in the Dark Dimension, turning blues to purples, whites to pinks, and pinks to the velvety color of blood. Now a clear light shone over everything, and a full white moon sailed calmly overhead.

A whisper of movement came from behind her, and Elena realized with a start that she wasn't alone after all. A dark figure was suddenly *there*, approaching her.

Damon.

Of course it was Damon, Elena thought with a smile. If anyone was going to appear unexpectedly before her here, at what felt like the end of the world—or at least the hour after a good party had ended—it would be Damon. God, he was so beautiful. Black on black: soft black hair, eyes black as midnight, black jeans, and a smooth leather jacket.

As their eyes met, she was so glad to see him that she could hardly breathe. She threw herself into his embrace, clasping him around the neck, feeling the lithe, hard muscles in his arms and chest.

"Damon," she said, her voice trembling for some reason. Her body was trembling, too, and Damon stroked her arms and shoulders, calming her.

"What is it, princess? Don't tell me you're afraid." He smirked lazily at her, his hands strong and steady.

"I *am* afraid," she answered.

"But what are you afraid of?"

That left her puzzled for a moment. Then, slowly, putting her cheek against his, she said, "I'm afraid that this is just a dream."

"I'll tell you a secret, princess," he said into her ear. "You and I are the only real things here. It's everything else that's the dream."

"Just you and me?" Elena echoed, an uneasy thought nagging at her, as though she were forgetting something—or someone. A fleck of ash landed on her dress, and she absently brushed it away.

"It's just the two of us, Elena," Damon said sharply. "You're mine. I'm yours. We've loved each other since the beginning of time."

Of course. That must be why she was trembling—it was joy. He was hers. She was his. They belonged together.

She whispered one word: "Yes."

Then he kissed her.

His lips were soft as silk, and when the kiss deepened, she tilted her head back, exposing her throat, anticipating the double wasp sting he'd delivered so many times.

When it didn't come, she opened her eyes questioningly. The moon was as bright as ever, and the scent of roses hung heavy in the air. But Damon's chiseled features were pale under his dark hair, and more ash had landed on the shoulders of his jacket. All at once, the little doubts that had been niggling at her came together.

Oh, no. Oh, no.

"Damon." She gasped, looking into his eyes despairingly as tears filled her own. "You can't be here, Damon. You're . . . dead."

"For more than five hundred years, princess." Damon flashed his blinding smile at her. More ash was falling around them, like a fine gray rain, the same gray ash Damon's body was buried beneath, worlds and dimensions away.

"Damon, you're . . . dead now. Not undead, but . . . gone."

"*No*, Elena . . ." He began to flicker and fade, like a dying lightbulb.

"Yes. Yes! I held you as you died. . . ." Elena was sobbing helplessly. She couldn't feel Damon's arms at all now. He was disappearing into shimmering light.

"Listen to me, Elena. . . ."

She was holding moonlight. Anguish caught at her heart.

"All you need to do is call for me," Damon's voice said. "All you need . . ."

His voice faded into the sound of wind rustling through the trees.

Elena's eyes snapped open. Through a fog she registered that she was in a room filled with sunlight, and a huge crow was perched on the sill of an open window. The bird tilted its head to one side and gave a croak, watching her with bright eyes.

A cold chill ran down her spine. "Damon?" she whispered.

But the crow just spread its wings and flew away.

"**D**ear Diary,
    I AM HOME! I can hardly dare to believe it, but here I am.

I woke with the strangest feeling. I didn't know where I was and just lay here smelling the clean cotton-and-fabric-softener scent of the sheets, trying to figure out why everything looked so familiar.

I wasn't in Lady Ulma's mansion. There, I had slept nestled in the smoothest satin and softest velvet, and the air had smelled of incense. And I wasn't at the boardinghouse: Mrs. Flowers washes the bedding there in some weird-smelling herbal mixture that Bonnie says is for protection and good dreams.

And suddenly, I knew. I was home. The

Guardians did it! They brought me home.

Everything and nothing has changed. It's the same room I slept in from when I was a tiny baby: my polished cherry-wood dresser and rocking chair; the little stuffed black-and-white dog Matt won at the winter carnival our junior year perched on a shelf; my rolltop desk with its cubbyholes; the ornate antique mirror above my dresser; and the Monet and Klimt posters from the museum exhibits Aunt Judith took me to in Washington, DC. Even my comb and brush are lined up neatly side by side on my dresser. It's all as it should be.

I got out of bed and used a silver letter opener from the desk to pry up the secret board in my closet floor, my old hiding place, and I found this diary, just where I hid it so many months ago. The last entry is the one I wrote before Founder's Day back in November, before I . . . died. Before I left home and never came back. Until now.

In that entry I detailed our plan to steal back my other diary, the one Caroline took from me, the one that she was planning to read aloud at the Founder's Day pageant, knowing it would ruin my life. The very next day, I drowned in Wickery Creek and rose again as a vampire. And then I died again and returned as a human, and traveled to the Dark Dimension, and had a thousand adventures. And my old diary has been sitting right here where I left it under the closet floor, just waiting for me.

The other Elena, the one that the Guardians planted in everyone's memories, was here all these months, going to school and living a normal life. That Elena didn't write here. I'm relieved, really. How creepy would it be to see diary entries in my handwriting and not remember any of the things they recounted? Although that might have been helpful. I have no idea what everyone else in Fell's Church thinks has been happening in the months since Founder's Day.

The whole town of Fell's Church has been given a fresh start. The kitsune destroyed this town out of sheer malicious mischief. Pitting children against their parents, making people destroy themselves and everyone they loved.

But now none of it ever happened.

If the Guardians made good on their word, everyone else who died is now alive again: poor Vickie Bennett and Sue Carson, murdered by Katherine and Klaus and Tyler Smallwood back in the winter; disagreeable Mr. Tanner; those innocents that the kitsune killed or caused to be killed. Me. All back again, all starting over.

*And, except for me and my closest friends—
Meredith, Bonnie, Matt, my darling Stefan, and
Mrs. Flowers—no one else knows that life hasn't
gone on as usual ever since Founder's Day.*

*We've all been given another chance. We did it.
We saved everyone.*

*Everyone except Damon. He saved us, in the
end, but we couldn't save him. No matter how
hard we tried or how desperately we pleaded,
there was no way for the Guardians to bring him
back. And vampires don't reincarnate. They don't
go to Heaven, or Hell, or any kind of afterlife.
They just . . . disappear.*

Elena stopped writing for a moment and took a deep
breath. Her eyes filled with tears, but she bent over the
diary again. She had to tell the whole truth if there was
going to be any point to keeping a diary at all.

*Damon died in my arms. It was agonizing to
watch him slip away from me. But I'll never let
Stefan know how I truly felt about his brother. It
would be cruel—and what good would it do now?*

*I still can't believe he's gone. There was no one
as alive as Damon—no one who loved life more
than he did. Now he'll never know—*

At that moment the door of Elena's bedroom suddenly flew open, and Elena, her heart in her throat, slammed the diary shut. But the intruder was only her younger sister, Margaret, dressed in pink flower-printed pajamas, her corn-silk hair standing straight up in the middle like a thrush's feathers. The five-year-old didn't decelerate until she was almost on top of Elena—and then she launched herself at her through the air.

She landed squarely on her older sister, knocking the breath out of her. Margaret's cheeks were wet, her eyes shining, and her little hands clutched at Elena.

Elena found herself holding on just as tightly, feeling the weight of her sister, inhaling the sweet scent of baby shampoo and Play-Doh.

"I missed you!" Margaret said, her voice on the verge of sobbing. "Elena! I missed you so much!"

"What?" Despite her effort to make her voice light, Elena could hear it shaking. She realized with a jolt that she hadn't seen Margaret—*really* seen her—for more than eight months. But Margaret couldn't know that. "You missed me so much since bedtime that you had to come running to find me?"

Margaret drew slightly away from Elena and stared at her. Margaret's five-year-old clear blue eyes had a look in them, an intensely *knowing* look, that sent a shiver down Elena's spine.

But Margaret didn't say a word. She simply tightened

her grip on Elena, curling up and letting her head rest on Elena's shoulder. "I had a bad dream. I dreamed you left me. You went *away.*" The last word was a quiet wail.

"Oh, Margaret," Elena said, hugging her sister's warm solidity, "it was only a dream. I'm not going anywhere." She closed her eyes and held on to Margaret, praying her sister had truly only had a nightmare, and that she hadn't slipped through the cracks of the Guardians' spell.

"All right, cookie, time to get a move on," said Elena after a few moments, gently tickling Margaret's side. "Are we going to have a fabulous breakfast together? Shall I make you pancakes?"

Margaret sat up then and gazed at Elena with wide blue eyes. "Uncle Robert's making waffles," she said. "He *always* makes waffles on Sunday mornings. Remember?"

Uncle Robert. Right. He and Aunt Judith had gotten married after Elena had died. "Sure, he does, bunny," she said lightly. "I just forgot it was Sunday for a minute."

Now that Margaret had mentioned it, she could hear someone down in the kitchen. And smell something delicious cooking. She sniffed. "Is that *bacon?*"

Margaret nodded. "Race you to the kitchen!"

Elena laughed and stretched. "Give me a minute to wake all the way up. I'll meet you down there." *I'll get to talk to Aunt Judith again,* she realized with a sudden burst of joy.

Margaret bounced out of bed. At the door, she paused

and looked back at her sister. "You really are coming down, right?" she asked hesitantly.

"I really am," Elena said, and Margaret smiled and headed down the hall.

Watching her, Elena was struck once more by what an amazing second chance—third chance, really—she'd been given. For a moment Elena just soaked in the essence of her dear, darling home, a place she'd never thought she'd live in again. She could hear Margaret's light voice chattering away happily downstairs, the deeper rumble of Robert answering her. She was so *lucky*, despite everything, to be back home at last. What could be more wonderful?

Her eyes filled with tears and she closed them tightly. What a *stupid* thing to think. What could be more wonderful? If the crow on her windowsill had been Damon, if she'd known that he was out there somewhere, ready to flash his lazy smile or even purposely aggravate her, now *that* would have been more wonderful.

Elena opened her eyes and blinked hard several times, willing the tears away. She couldn't fall apart. Not now. Not when she was about to see her family again. Now she would smile and laugh and hug her family. Later she would collapse, indulging the sharp ache inside her, and let herself sob. After all, she had all the time in the world to mourn Damon, because losing him would never, ever stop hurting.

he bright morning sun shone on the long, winding drive that led to the garage behind the boardinghouse. Puffs of white cloud scudded across the light blue sky. It was such a peaceful scene that it was almost impossible to believe that anything bad had ever happened in this place.

The last time I was here, thought Stefan, putting on his sunglasses, *it was a wasteland.*

When the kitsune had held sway in Fell's Church, it had been a war zone. Children against parents, teenage girls mutilating themselves, the town half-destroyed. Blood on the streets, pain and suffering everywhere.

Behind him, the front door opened. Stefan turned quickly to see Mrs. Flowers coming out of the house. The old woman wore a long black dress, and her eyes were shielded by a straw hat covered with artificial flowers. She looked tired and worn, but her smile was as gentle as always.

"Stefan," she said. "The world is here this morning, the way it should be." Mrs. Flowers stepped closer and gazed up into his face, her sharp blue eyes warm with sympathy. She looked as if she were about to ask him something, but at the last minute seemed to change her mind and instead said, "Meredith called, and Matt, too. It seems that, against all the odds, everyone has survived unscathed." She hesitated, and then squeezed his arm. "Almost everyone."

Something twisted painfully in Stefan's chest. He didn't want to talk about Damon. He couldn't, not yet. Instead, he bowed his head. "We owe you a great debt, Mrs. Flowers," he said, choosing his words with care. "We never could have defeated the kitsune without you—you were the one who held them at bay and defended the town for so long. None of us will ever forget that."

Mrs. Flowers's smile deepened, an unexpected dimple flickering in one cheek. "Thank you, Stefan," she said with equal formality. "There is no one I would have rather fought alongside than you and the others." She sighed and patted his shoulder. "Although I must be getting old at last; I feel the need to spend most of today dozing in a chair in the garden. Fighting evil takes more out of me than it used to."

Stefan offered his arm to assist her down the porch steps, and she smiled at him once more. "Tell Elena that I'll make those tea biscuits she likes whenever she's ready to leave her family and come visit," she said, then turned toward her rose garden.

Elena and her family. Stefan imagined his love, her silky blond hair tumbling about her shoulders, little Margaret in her lap. Elena had another shot at a real human life now, which was worth everything.

It had been Stefan's fault that Elena lost her first life— he knew that with a hard certainty that gnawed at his insides. He had brought Katherine to Fell's Church, and Katherine had destroyed Elena. This time he would make sure Elena was protected.

With one last glance at Mrs. Flowers in her garden, he squared his shoulders and walked into the woods. Birds sang at the sun-dappled edges of the forest, but Stefan was headed much deeper in, where ancient oaks grew and the underbrush was thick. Where no one would see him, where he could hunt.

Stopping in a small clearing several miles in, Stefan took off his sunglasses and listened. From nearby came the soft crackle of something moving beneath a bush. He concentrated, reaching out with his mind. It was a rabbit, its heart beating rapidly, looking for its own morning meal.

Stefan focused his mind on it. *Come to me*, he thought,

gently and persuasively. He sensed the rabbit stiffen for a moment; then it hopped slowly out from under a bush, its eyes glassy.

It came toward him docilely and, with an extra mental nudge from Stefan, stopped at his feet. Stefan scooped it up and turned it over to reach the tender throat, where its pulse fluttered. With a silent apology to the animal, Stefan gave himself over to his hunger, allowing his fangs to click into place. He tore into the rabbit's throat, drinking the blood slowly, trying not to wince at the taste.

While the kitsune had threatened Fell's Church, Elena, Bonnie, Meredith, and Matt had insisted he feed on them, knowing human blood would keep him as strong as possible for the fight. Their blood had been almost otherworldly: Meredith's fiery and strong; Matt's pure and wholesome; Bonnie's sweet as dessert; Elena's heady and invigorating. Despite the foul taste of the rabbit in his mouth, his canines prickled with remembered hunger.

But now he wouldn't drink human blood, he told himself firmly. He couldn't keep crossing that line, even if they were willing. Not unless his friends' safety was at risk. The change from human to animal blood would be painful; he remembered that from when he had first stopped drinking human blood—aching teeth, nausea, irritability, the feeling that he was starving even when his stomach was full—but it was the only option.

When the rabbit's heartbeat stopped altogether, Stefan gently disengaged. He held the limp body in his hands for a moment, then set it on the ground and covered it with leaves. *Thank you, little one,* he thought. He was still hungry, but he had already taken one life this morning.

Damon would have laughed. Stefan could almost hear him. *Noble Stefan,* he would scoff, his black eyes narrowing in half-affectionate disdain. *You're missing all the best parts of being a vampire while you wrestle with your conscience, you fool.*

As if summoned by his thoughts, a crow cawed overhead. For a moment, Stefan fully expected the bird to plummet to earth and transform into his brother. When it didn't, Stefan gave a short half laugh at his own stupidity and was surprised when it sounded almost like a sob.

Damon was never coming back. His brother was gone. They'd had centuries of bitterness between them and had only just started to repair their relationship, joining together to fight the evil that always seemed drawn to Fell's Church and to shield Elena from it. But Damon was dead, and now Stefan was the only one left to protect Elena and their friends.

A latent worm of fear squirmed in his chest. There was so *much* that could go wrong. Humans were so *vulnerable*, and now that Elena had no special powers, she was as vulnerable as any of them.

The thought sent him reeling, and immediately he took off, running straight toward Elena's house on the other side of the woods. Elena was his responsibility now. And he would never let anything hurt her again.

The upstairs landing was almost the same as Elena remembered it: shining dark wood with an Oriental carpet runner, a few little tables with knickknacks and photographs, a couch near the big picture window overlooking the front drive.

But halfway to the stairs, Elena paused, glimpsing something new. Among the silver-framed photos on one of the small tables was a picture of herself and Meredith and Bonnie, faces close together, grinning widely in caps and gowns and proudly brandishing diplomas. Elena picked it up, holding it close. She had graduated from high school.

It felt odd to see this *other* Elena, as she couldn't help thinking of her, her blond hair pulled back in an elegant French twist, creamy skin flushed with excitement, smiling with her best friends, and not remember a thing about it. And she looked so carefree, this Elena, so full of joy and hope and expectations for the future. This Elena knew nothing of the horror of the Dark Dimension or the havoc the kitsune had caused. This Elena was *happy*.

Glancing quickly among the photos, Elena located a few more she hadn't seen before. Apparently this other Elena had been queen of the Snow Ball, though Elena remembered Caroline had won that crown after Elena's death. In this picture, however, Queen Elena was resplendent in pale violet silk, surrounded by her court: Bonnie fluffy and adorable in shiny blue taffeta; Meredith sophisticated in black; auburn-haired Caroline looking aggrieved in a tight silver dress that left very little to the imagination; and Sue Carson, pretty in pale pink, smiling straight into the camera, very much alive. Tears stung Elena's eyes once more. They had saved her. Elena and Meredith and Bonnie and Matt and Stefan had saved Sue Carson.

Then Elena's gaze landed on another photograph, this one of Aunt Judith in a long, lacy wedding dress, Robert standing proudly beside her in a morning suit. With them was the other Elena, clearly the maid of honor, in a dress the color of green leaves, holding a bouquet of pink roses. Beside her stood Margaret, shining blond head ducked shyly, grasping Elena's dress with one hand. She was wearing a full-skirted white flower girl's dress tied with a wide green sash, and she clutched a basket of roses in her other hand.

Elena's hands shook a little as she put this picture down. It looked as if a good time had been had by all. What a pity she hadn't actually been there.

Downstairs, a glass clinked against the table, and she heard Aunt Judith laugh. Putting aside all the strangeness of this new past she'd have to learn, Elena hurried down the stairs, ready to greet her future.

In the dining room, Aunt Judith poured orange juice from a blue jug while Robert spooned batter onto the waffle iron. Margaret was kneeling behind her chair, narrating an intense conversation between her stuffed rabbit and a toy tiger.

A great surge of joy filled Elena's chest, and she grabbed Aunt Judith in a tight hug and spun her around. Orange juice spilled across the floor in a wide arc.

"Elena!" scolded Aunt Judith, half laughing. "What's the matter with you?"

"Nothing! I just I love you, Aunt Judith," Elena said, hugging her tighter. "I really do."

"Oh," said Aunt Judith, her eyes soft. "Oh, Elena, I love you, too."

"And what a beautiful day," Elena said, pirouetting away. "A wonderful day to be alive." She dropped a kiss on Margaret's blond head. Aunt Judith reached for the paper towels.

Robert cleared his throat. "Are we to take it that you've forgiven us for grounding you last weekend?"

Oh. Elena tried to figure out how to respond, but after she'd been living on her own for months, the whole concept of being grounded by Aunt Judith and Robert seemed ridiculous. Still, she widened her eyes and put on an appropriately contrite expression. "I'm truly sorry, Aunt Judith and Robert. It won't happen again." *Whatever* it *is.*

Robert's shoulders relaxed. "We'll say no more about it, then," he said with obvious relief. He slid a hot waffle onto her plate and handed her the syrup. "Do you have anything fun planned for today?"

"Stefan is picking me up after breakfast," Elena said, then paused. The last time she had talked to Aunt Judith, after the disastrous Founder's Day pageant, Aunt Judith and Robert had been seriously anti-Stefan. They, like most of the town, had suspected him of being responsible for Mr. Tanner's death.

But apparently they had no problem with Stefan in this world, because Robert simply nodded. And, she reminded herself, if the Guardians had done what she asked, Mr. Tanner was alive, so they couldn't have suspected Stefan of killing him. . . . Oh, it was all so *confusing*!

She went on: "We're going to hang out in town, maybe catch up with Meredith and the others." She couldn't wait to see the town back to its old, safe self and to be with Stefan when, for once, they weren't battling some horrible evil but could just be a normal couple.

Aunt Judith grinned. "So, just another lazy day, hmm? I'm glad you're having a nice summer before you go off to college, Elena. You worked so hard all last year."

"Mmm," said Elena vaguely, cutting into her waffle.

She hoped the Guardians had gotten her into Dalcrest, a small college a couple hours away, as she'd requested.

"Come on up, Meggie," Robert said, buttering the little girl's waffle. Margaret scrambled up onto her chair, and Elena smiled at the obvious affection on Robert's face. Margaret was clearly his darling little girl.

Catching Elena's eye, Margaret growled and thrust the toy tiger across the table toward her. Elena jumped. The little girl snarled, and her face was momentarily transformed into something savage.

"He wants to eat you with his big teeth," Margaret said, her little-girl voice hoarse. "He's coming to *get* you."

"Margaret!" Aunt Judith scolded as Elena shuddered. Margaret's briefly feral look reminded her of the kitsune, of the girls they had driven mad. But then Margaret gave her a huge grin and made the tiger nuzzle Elena's arm.

The doorbell rang. Elena crammed the last bite of waffle into her mouth. "That's Stefan," she mumbled around it. "See you later." She wiped her lips and checked her hair in the mirror before opening the door.

And there was Stefan, as handsome as ever. Elegant Roman features, high cheekbones, a classical straight nose, and sensually curving mouth. He held his sunglasses loosely in one hand, and his leaf green eyes caught hers with a gaze of pure love. Elena broke into a wide, involuntary smile.

Oh, Stefan, she thought to him, *I love you, I love you. It's so wonderful to be home. I can't stop missing Damon and wishing we could have done* something *differently and saved him—and I wouldn't want to stop thinking of him—but I can't help being happy, too.*

Wait. She felt like someone had slammed on the brakes and she'd been thrown against a seat belt.

Though Elena was sending the words, and a huge wave of affection and love with them, toward Stefan, there was no response, no return of emotions. It was as if there were an invisible wall between her and Stefan, blocking her thoughts from reaching him.

"Elena?" Stefan said aloud, his smile faltering.

Oh. She hadn't realized. She hadn't even thought about this.

When the Guardians took her powers, they must have taken *everything.* Including her telepathic connection to Stefan. It had lingered. . . . She was sure she had still heard him, and reached his mind, after she had lost her connection to Bonnie. But now it was gone completely.

Leaning forward, she grasped his shirt, pulled him to her, and kissed him fiercely.

Oh, thank God, she thought, as she felt the familiar, comforting sense of their minds entwining. Stefan's lips curled into a smile beneath hers.

I thought I'd lost you, she thought, *that I wouldn't be able*

to reach you like this anymore, either. Unlike with the telepathic connection they'd shared, she knew the thoughts
weren't reaching Stefan as words but as images and emotions. From him, she felt a wordless, steady stream of
unfailing love.

A throat was cleared pointedly behind them. Elena
reluctantly released Stefan and turned to see Aunt Judith
watching them.

Stefan straightened with an embarrassed blush, the
slightest look of apprehension in his eyes. Elena grinned.
She loved that he'd been through hell—literally—but was
still scared to upset Elena's aunt. She put her hand on
his arm, trying to send a message that Aunt Judith now
accepted their relationship, but Aunt Judith's warm smile
and greeting said it for her.

"Hello, Stefan. You'll be back by six, won't you, Elena?"
Aunt Judith asked. "Robert's got a late meeting, so I
thought you, Margaret, and I could go out for a girls' night
together." She looked hopeful yet hesitant, like someone
knocking on a door that might be slammed in her face.
Elena's stomach knotted with guilt. *Have I been avoiding
Aunt Judith this summer?*

She could imagine that, if she hadn't died, she might
have been eager to move on with her life and chafed at the
family that wanted to keep her home and safe. But this
Elena knew better—knew how lucky she was to have Aunt

Judith and Robert. And it seemed that this Elena had a lot of making up to do.

"Sounds like fun!" she said cheerfully, pasting a bright smile on her face. "Can I invite Bonnie and Meredith? They'd love a girls' night." And it would be nice, she thought, to have friends around who were as clueless about what had been going on in this version of Fell's Church as she was.

"Wonderful," Aunt Judith said, looking happier and more relaxed. "Have a good time, kids."

As Elena headed out the door, Margaret ran out of the kitchen. "Elena!" she said, wrapping her arms tightly around Elena's waist. Elena bent and kissed the top of her head.

"I'll catch you later, bunny rabbit," she said.

Margaret motioned for Elena and Stefan to kneel down, then put her lips right next to their ears. "Don't forget to come back this time," she whispered before retreating inside.

For a moment, Elena just knelt there, frozen. Stefan squeezed her hand, pulling her up, and even without their telepathic connection, she knew they were having the same thought.

As they headed away from the house, Stefan took her by the shoulders. His green eyes gazed into hers, and he bent forward to brush a light kiss upon her lips.

"Margaret's a little girl," he said firmly. "It could just be that she doesn't want her big sister to leave. Maybe she's worried about you going off to college."

"Maybe," Elena murmured as Stefan wrapped his arms around her. She inhaled his green, woodsy scent and felt her breathing slow and the knot in her stomach loosen.

"And if not," she said slowly, "we'll work it out. We always do. But right now I want to see what the Guardians gave us."

4

It was the little changes that surprised Elena the most. She had expected the Guardians to bring Fell's Church back. And they had.

The last time she'd seen the town, probably a quarter of the houses had been rubble. They'd been burned or bombed, some fully destroyed, some only half-gone, with police tape dangling dismally across what was left of their entrances. Around and above the ruined houses, trees and bushes had grown and stretched strangely, vines draping over the debris, giving the streets of the small town the look of an ancient jungle.

Now Fell's Church was—mostly—the way Elena remembered it. A picture postcard–perfect small Southern town of deep-porched houses surrounded by carefully tended flower gardens and big old trees. The sun was shining and the air was warm with the promise of a hot and humid Virginia summer day.

From a few blocks away came the muted roar of a lawn mower, and the smell of cut grass filled the air. The Kinkade kids in the house on the corner had dragged out their badminton set and were batting the birdie back and forth; the youngest girl waved to Elena and Stefan as they passed. Everything took Elena back to the long July days she'd known all the previous summers of her life.

Elena hadn't asked for her old life back, though. Her exact words had been: *I want a new life, with my real old life behind me.* She'd wanted Fell's Church to be the way it would have been now, months later, if evil had never come to town back at the beginning of her senior year.

But she hadn't realized how jarring all the little changes would be. The small colonial-style house in the middle of the next block had been painted a surprising shade of pink, and the old oak tree in its front lawn had been cut down and replaced with a flowering shrub.

"Huh." Elena turned to Stefan as they passed the house. "Mrs. McCloskey must have died, or moved to a nursing home." Stefan looked at her blankly. "She never would have let them paint her house that color. There must be new people living there," she explained, shivering slightly.

"What is it?" Stefan asked instantly, as attuned to her moods as ever.

"Nothing, it's just . . ." Elena tried to smile as she tucked a silky lock of hair behind her ear. "She used to feed me cookies when I was a kid. It's strange to realize she might have died of natural causes while we've been gone."

Stefan nodded, and the two walked silently to Fell's Church's small downtown. Elena was about to point out that her favorite coffee shop had been replaced by a drugstore, when she grabbed Stefan's arm. "Stefan. *Look*."

Coming toward them were Isobel Saitou and Jim Bryce.

"Isobel! Jim!" Elena shouted joyfully, and ran toward them. But Isobel was stiff in her arms, and Jim was looking at her curiously.

"Uh, hi?" Isobel said hesitantly.

Elena instantly stepped back. *Oops*. In *this* life, did she even know Isobel? They'd been in school together, of course. Jim had gone out with Meredith a couple of times before he and Isobel started dating, although Elena hadn't known him well. But it was possible she had never even spoken to quiet, studious Isobel Saitou before the kitsune came to town.

Elena's mind worked busily, trying to figure out how to get out of this without seeming crazy. But a warm buzz of happiness kept rising up in her chest, keeping her from taking the problem too seriously. Isobel was *okay*. She'd suffered so much at the hands of the kitsune: She'd pierced herself in horrible ways and slit her own tongue so severely that even after she'd recovered from the kitsune's thrall, she'd spoken in a soft slur. Worse, the kitsune goddess had been in Isobel's house the whole time, pretending to be Isobel's grandmother.

And poor Jim . . . Infected through Isobel, Jim had torn himself apart, eating at his own flesh. Yet here he was, as handsome and carefree—albeit mildly confused—as ever.

Stefan smiled broadly, and Elena couldn't stop giggling. "Sorry, guys, I'm just . . . so happy to see familiar faces from school. I must miss good old Robert E. Lee High School, you know? Who would have thought?"

It was a pretty weak excuse, but Isobel and Jim smiled and nodded. Jim cleared his throat awkwardly and said, "Yeah, it was a good year, wasn't it?"

Elena laughed again. She couldn't help herself. *A good year.*

They chatted for a few minutes before Elena casually asked, "How's your grandmother, Isobel?"

Isobel looked at her blankly. "My grandmother?" she said. "You must be confusing me with someone else. Both my grandmothers have been dead for years."

"Oh, my mistake." Elena said good-bye and managed to contain herself until Isobel and Jim were out of earshot. Then she took Stefan by the arms, pulled him toward her, and gave him a resounding kiss, feeling delight and triumph passing back and forth between them.

"We *did* it," she said when the kiss had ended. "They're fine! And not just them." More solemn now, she gazed up into his green eyes, so serious and kind. "We did something really important and wonderful, didn't we?"

"We did," Stefan agreed, but she couldn't help but notice something hard in his voice as he said it.

They walked hand in hand, and without discussing it, they headed for the edge of town, crossing Wickery Bridge and climbing the hill. They turned into the cemetery, past the ruined church where Katherine had hidden, and down into the little valley below that held the newer part of the graveyard.

Elena and Stefan sat down on the neatly trimmed grass by the big marble headstone with "Gilbert" carved into the front.

"Hi, Mom. Hi, Dad," Elena whispered. "I'm sorry it's been so long."

Back in her old life, she had visited her parents' graves often, just to talk to them. She'd felt like they were able to hear her somehow, that they were wishing her well from whatever higher plane they'd ended up on. It had always made her feel better to tell them her troubles, and before her life had gotten so complicated, she had told them everything.

She put out one hand and gently touched the names and dates carved on the tombstone. Elena bent her head.

"It's my fault they're dead," she said. Stefan made a soft noise of disagreement, and she turned to look at him. "It *is*," she said, her eyes burning. "The Guardians told me so."

Stefan sighed and kissed her forehead. "The Guardians wanted to kill *you*," he said. "To make you one of them. And they accidentally killed your parents instead. It's no more your fault than if they had shot at you and missed."

"But I distracted my father at the critical moment and made him crash," Elena said, hunching her shoulders.

"So the Guardians say," Stefan replied. "But they wouldn't want it to sound like their fault. They don't like to admit they make mistakes. The fact remains that the accident that killed your parents wouldn't have happened if the Guardians hadn't been there."

Elena lowered her eyes to hide the tears swimming in them. What Stefan said was true, she thought, but she couldn't stop the chorus of *myfaultmyfaultmyfault* in her head.

A few wild violets were growing on her left, and she picked them, along with a patch of buttercups. Stefan joined her, handing her a sprig of columbine with yellow bell-shaped blossoms to add to her tiny wildflower bouquet.

"Damon never trusted the Guardians," he said quietly. "Well, he wouldn't—they don't think much of vampires.

But beyond that . . ." He reached for a tall stalk of Queen Anne's lace growing beside a nearby headstone. "Damon had a pretty finely tuned sense for detecting lies—the lies people told themselves and the ones they told other people. When we were young we had a tutor—a priest, no less—who I liked and my father trusted, and Damon despised. When the man ran off with my father's gold and a young lady from the neighborhood, Damon was the only one who wasn't surprised." Stefan smiled at Elena. "He said that the priest's eyes were wrong. And that he spoke too smoothly." Stefan shrugged. "My father and I never noticed. But Damon did."

Elena smiled tremulously. "He always knew when I wasn't being totally honest with him." She had a sudden flash of memory: of Damon's deep black eyes holding hers, his pupils dilated like a cat's, his head tilting as their lips met. She looked away from Stefan's warm green eyes, so different from Damon's dark ones, and twisted the thick stalk of the Queen Anne's lace around the other flowers. When the bouquet was tied together, she placed it on her parents' grave.

"I miss him," Stefan said softly. "There was a time when I would have thought . . . when his death might have been a relief. But I'm so glad we came together—that we were brothers again—before he died." He put a gentle hand beneath Elena's chin and tilted her head up so that her eyes met his again. "I know you loved him, Elena. It's okay. You don't have to pretend."

Elena gave a little gasp of pain.

It was like there was a dark hole inside her. She could laugh and smile and marvel at the restored town; she could love her family; but all the time there was this dull ache, this terrible sense of loss.

Letting her tears loose at last, Elena fell into Stefan's arms.

"Oh, my love," he said, his voice catching, and they wept together, taking comfort in each other's warmth.

Fine ash had fallen for a long time. Now it settled at last and the small moon of the Nether World was covered with thick, sticky piles of dust. Here and there, opalescent fluid pooled against the charred blackness, coloring it with the rainbow of an oil slick.

Nothing moved. Now that the Great Tree had disintegrated, nothing lived in this place.

Deep below the surface of the ruined moon was a body. His poisoned blood had stopped flowing and he lay unmoving, unfeeling, unseeing. But the drops of fluid saturating his skin nourished him, and a slow thrum of magical life beat steadily on.

Every now and then a flicker of consciousness rose within him. He had forgotten who he was and how he had died. But there was a voice somewhere deep inside him, a light, sweet voice he knew well, that told him, *Close your eyes now. Let go. Let go. Go.* It was comforting, and his last spark of consciousness was holding on for a moment longer, just to hear it. He couldn't remember whose voice it was, although something in it reminded him of sunlight, of gold and lapis lazuli.

Let go. He was slipping away, the last spark dimming, but it was all right. It was warm and comfortable, and he was ready to let go now. The voice would take him all the way to . . . to wherever it was he would go.

As the flicker of consciousness was about to go out for the last time, another voice—a sharper, more command-ing voice, the voice of someone used to having his orders obeyed—spoke within him.

She needs you. She's in danger.

He couldn't let go. Not yet. That voice pulled painfully at him, holding him to life.

With a sharp shock, everything shifted. As if he'd been ripped out of that gentle, cozy place, he was suddenly freezing cold. Everything hurt.

Deep within the ash, his fingers twitched.

5

"Are you excited for Alaric to arrive tomorrow?" Matt asked. "He's bringing his researcher friend Celia, right?"

Meredith kicked him in the chest.

"Oof!" Matt staggered backward, knocked breathless despite the protective vest he had on. Meredith followed up with a roundhouse kick to Matt's side, and he fell to his knees, barely managing to raise his hands and block a straight punch to his face.

"Ow!" he said. "Meredith, time-out, okay?"

Meredith dropped into a graceful tiger stance, her back leg supporting her weight while her front foot rested lightly on her toes. Her face was calm, her eyes cool and watchful. She looked ready to pounce if Matt showed any sign of sudden movement.

When he'd arrived to spar with Meredith—to help her keep her hunter-slayer skills in top-notch shape—Matt had wondered why she had handed him a helmet, mouth guard, gloves, shin guards, and vest, while she wore only sleek black workout clothes.

Now he knew. He hadn't even come close to hitting her, while she'd pummeled him mercilessly. Matt eased a hand up under the vest and rubbed ruefully at his side. He hoped he hadn't cracked a rib.

"Ready to go again?" Meredith said, her eyebrows raised in challenge.

"Please, no, Meredith," Matt said, raising his hands in surrender. "Let's take a break. It feels like you've been punching me for hours."

Meredith walked over to the small fridge in the corner of her family's rec room and tossed Matt a bottle of water, then sank down next to him on the mat. "Sorry. I guess I got carried away. I've never sparred with a friend before."

Looking around as he took a long, cool drink, Matt shook his head. "I don't know how you managed to keep this place secret for so long." The basement room had been converted into a perfect place to train: throwing stars, knives, swords, and staves of various kinds were mounted on the walls; a punching bag hung in one corner, while a padded dummy leaned in another. The floor was lined with mats, and one wall was completely mirrored. In the middle of the opposite wall hung *the* fighting stave: a special weapon for battling the supernatural that had been handed down through generations of Meredith's family. It was deadly but elegant-looking, the hilt covered with jewels, the ends spiked with silver, wood, and white ash, and the needles steeped in poison. Matt eyed it warily.

"Well," said Meredith, looking away, "the Suarez family has always been good at keeping secrets." She began to move through a tae kwon do form: back stance, double fist block, left front stance, reverse middle punch. She was graceful as a slim black cat in her workout gear.

After a moment, Matt capped his water bottle, climbed to his feet, and began to mirror her movements. Left double front kick, left inside block, double-handed punch. He knew he was half a beat behind and felt shambling and awkward next to her, but frowned and concentrated. He'd always been a good athlete. He could do this, too.

"Besides, it's not like I was bringing my prom dates down here," Meredith offered after a cycle, half smiling. "It wasn't that hard to hide." She watched Matt in the mirror. "No, block low with your left hand and high with your right hand, like this." She showed him again, and he shadowed her movements.

"Okay, yeah," he said, only half concentrating on his words now, focused on the positions. "But you could have told *us*. We're your best friends." He moved his left foot forward and mimicked Meredith's backward elbow blow. "At least, you could have told us after the whole thing with Klaus and Katherine," he amended. "Before that, we would have thought you were crazy."

Meredith shrugged and dropped her hands, and Matt followed before he realized that the gestures weren't part of the tae kwon do form.

Now they stood side by side, staring at each other in the mirror. Meredith's cool and elegant face looked pale and pinched. "I was brought up to keep my heritage as a hunter-slayer a deep, dark secret," she said. "Telling *anybody* wasn't something I could consider. Even Alaric doesn't know."

Matt turned away from Meredith's mirror image to gape at the real girl. Alaric and Meredith were practically *engaged*. Matt had never been that serious with anyone—the girl he'd come closest to loving was Elena, and obviously that hadn't worked out—but he'd sort of figured that, if you committed your heart to somebody, you told them everything.

"Isn't Alaric a paranormal researcher? Don't you think he would understand?"

Frowning, Meredith shrugged again. "Probably," she said, sounding irritated and dismissive, "but I don't want to be something for him to study or research, any more than I want him to freak out. But since you and the others know, I'll have to tell him."

"Hmm." Matt rubbed his aching side again. "Is that why you're pounding on me so aggressively? Because you're worried about telling him?"

Meredith met his eyes. The lines of her face were still tense, but a mischievous glimmer shone in her eyes. "Aggressive?" she asked sweetly, falling back into the tiger stance. Matt felt an answering smile tug at the corners of his mouth. "You haven't seen anything yet."

Elena surveyed the restaurant Judith had picked with a kind of bemused horror. Beeping video game machines vied for attention with old-fashioned arcade games like Whac-A-Mole and Skee-Ball. Bouquets of brightly colored balloons bobbed over every table, and a cacophony of song rose from various corners as singing waiters delivered pizza after pizza. What seemed like hundreds of children ran loose across the floor, shrieking and laughing.

Stefan had walked her to the restaurant, but, eyeing the neon paint job with alarm, he'd declined to come in.

"Oh, I shouldn't intrude on girls' night," he'd said vaguely, and then disappeared so quickly Elena suspected he'd used vampiric speed.

"Traitor," she'd muttered, before warily opening the bright pink door. After their time together in the grave-yard, she felt stronger and happier, but she would have liked some support here, too.

"Welcome to Happytown," chirped an unnaturally cheery hostess. "Table for one, or are you meeting a party?"

Elena repressed a shudder. She couldn't imagine anyone choosing to come to a place like this by themselves. "I think I see my group now," she said politely, catching sight of Aunt Judith waving to her from a corner.

"This is your idea of a fun girls' night out, Aunt Judith?" she asked when she reached the table. "I was picturing something more like a cozy bistro."

Aunt Judith nodded toward the other side of the room. Peering over, Elena spotted Margaret, happily whacking away at toy moles with a mallet.

"We're always dragging Margaret to grown-up places and expecting her to behave," Aunt Judith explained. "I thought it was time she got a turn to do something she enjoyed. I hope Bonnie and Meredith won't mind."

"She certainly *looks* like she's enjoying herself," Elena said, studying her little sister. Her memories of Margaret from the last year were of strain and anxiety: During the fall Margaret had been upset by Elena's fighting with Judith and Robert and by the mysterious happenings in Fell's Church, and then, of course, devastated by Elena's death. Elena had watched her through the windows afterward and seen her sobbing. She'd suffered more than any five-year-old should, even if she didn't remember any of it now.

I'll take care of you, Margaret, she promised fiercely and silently, watching the studious concentration on her sister's face as Margaret practiced a little old-fashioned carnival violence. *You won't have to feel like that again in this world.*

"*Are* we waiting for Bonnie and Meredith?" Aunt Judith prompted gently. "Did you end up inviting them to join us?"

"Oh," said Elena, jarred out of her reverie. She reached for a handful of popcorn from the basket in the middle of the table. "I couldn't get ahold of Meredith, but Bonnie's coming. She'll love this."

"I absolutely, totally do love this," a voice agreed from behind her. Elena turned to see Bonnie's silky red curls. "Especially the expression on your face, Elena." Bonnie's wide brown eyes were dancing with amusement. She and Elena shared a look that was full of all the *we're back, we're back, they did what they said and Fell's Church is the way it should be again* that they couldn't say in front of Aunt Judith, then fell into each other's arms.

Elena squeezed Bonnie tightly, and Bonnie buried her face in Elena's shoulder for a moment. Her petite body quivered slightly in Elena's arms, and Elena realized that she wasn't the only one walking a fine line between delight and devastation. They'd gained so much—but it had come at a very high price.

"Actually," said Bonnie with careful cheer as she

released Elena, "I had my ninth birthday at a place very much like this. Remember the Hokey-Pokey Grill? That was *the* place to be when we were in elementary school." Her eyes held a bright sheen that might be tears, but her chin stuck out determinedly. Bonnie, Elena thought with admiration, was going to have fun if it killed her.

"I remember that party," Elena said, matching Bonnie's lightness. "Your cake had a big picture of some boy band on it."

"I was mature for my age," Bonnie told Aunt Judith merrily. "I was boy crazy way before any of my friends were."

Aunt Judith laughed and waved Margaret over toward their table. "We'd better order before the stage show starts," she said.

Elena, eyes wide, mouthed, *Stage show?* at Bonnie, who smirked and shrugged.

"Do you girls know what you want?" Aunt Judith asked.

"Do they have anything besides pizza?" Elena asked.

"Chicken fingers," answered Margaret, climbing into her chair. "And hot dogs."

Elena grinned at her sister's tousled hair and expression of delight. "What are you going to have, bunny?" she asked.

"Pizza!" Margaret answered. "Pizza, pizza, pizza."

"I'll have pizza, too, then," Elena decided.

"It's the best thing here," Margaret confided. "The hot dogs are weird-tasting." She squirmed in her chair. "Elena, are you coming to my dance recital?" she asked.

"When is it?" Elena asked.

Margaret frowned. "The day after tomorrow," she said. "You *know* that."

Elena glanced quickly at Bonnie, whose eyes were wide. "I wouldn't miss it for the world," she told Margaret affectionately, and her sister nodded firmly and stood up on her chair to reach the popcorn.

Under cover of Aunt Judith's scolding and the semimelodious sound of their singing waiter approaching, Bonnie and Elena exchanged a smile.

Dance recitals. Singing waiters. Pizza.

It was good to live in *this* kind of world for a change.

he next morning was clear and hot again, another beautiful summer day. Elena stretched lazily in her comfy bed, then pulled on a T-shirt and shorts and padded down to the kitchen for a bowl of cereal.

Aunt Judith was braiding Margaret's hair at the table.

"Morning," Elena said, pouring milk into her bowl.

"Hi, sleepyhead," said Aunt Judith, and Margaret gave her a big smile and a finger-wiggling wave. "Keep still, Margaret. We're about to leave for the market," she told Elena. "What are you doing today?"

Elena swallowed her mouthful of cereal. "We're going to pick up Alaric and his friend at the train station and just hang out and catch up," she said.

"Who?" Aunt Judith asked, her eyes narrowing.

Elena's mind spun. "Oh, uh, you remember, he subbed for Mr. Tanner teaching history last year," she said, wondering if that was in fact true in this world.

Aunt Judith frowned. "Isn't he a little old to be socializing with high school girls?"

Elena rolled her eyes. "We're not in high school anymore, Aunt Judith. And he's only about six years older than us. And it's not just girls. Matt and Stefan are coming, too."

If this was Aunt Judith's reaction to the news of their spending time with Alaric, Elena could tell why Meredith was hesitant to tell people about their relationship. It made sense to wait a couple of years, until people thought of her as a grown-up. Since no one here knew all that Meredith had seen and done, she seemed like any other eighteen-year-old to them.

It's a good thing Aunt Judith doesn't know Stefan's five hundred years older than I am, Elena thought with a secret smirk. *She thinks* Alaric's *too old.*

The doorbell rang.

"That's Matt and everybody," Elena said, rising to put her bowl in the sink. "See you guys tonight."

Margaret widened her eyes at Elena in silent appeal, and Elena detoured on her way to the door to squeeze the little girl's shoulder. Was Margaret still worried Elena wouldn't come back?

Out in the foyer, she ran her fingers through her hair

before opening the door.

Standing in front of her was not Stefan, though, but a perfect stranger. A really good-looking stranger, Elena noted automatically, a boy about her age with curly golden hair, sculpted features, and bright blue eyes. He was holding a deep red rose in one hand.

Elena stood a little straighter, unconsciously pulling her shoulders back and pushing her hair behind her ears. She adored Stefan, but that didn't mean she couldn't *look* at other boys, or talk to them. She wasn't dead, after all. *Not anymore*, she thought, smiling at her private joke.

The boy smiled back. "Hey, Elena," he said cheerfully.

"Caleb Smallwood!" Aunt Judith said, coming into the hall. "There you are!"

Elena felt herself recoil, but she kept the smile on her face. "Any relation to Tyler?" she said, outwardly calm, and ran her eyes over him, trying to be subtle, checking for . . . for what? For signs of his being a werewolf? She realized she didn't even know what those would be. Tyler's good looks had always had a flavor of an animal about them, with his large white teeth and broad features, but had that been a coincidence?

"Tyler's my cousin," Caleb answered, his smile beginning to turn to a quizzical frown. "I thought you knew that, Elena. I'm staying with his folks while Tyler's . . . gone."

Elena's mind raced. Tyler Smallwood had run away

after Elena, Stefan, and Damon had defeated his ally, the evil vampire Klaus. Tyler had left his girlfriend—and sometimes hostage—Caroline pregnant. Elena hadn't discussed Tyler and Caroline's fate with the Guardians, so she had no idea what had happened with them in this reality. Was Tyler even a werewolf now? Was Caroline pregnant? And if she was, was it with werewolf or human babies? She shook her head slightly. Brave new world, indeed.

"Well, don't leave Caleb out on the porch. Let him in," Aunt Judith instructed from behind her. Elena stood aside, and Caleb moved past her into the hall.

Elena tried to reach out with her mind and sense Caleb's aura, to read him to see if he was dangerous, but once again came up against that brick wall. It would take some time to get used to being a normal girl again, and suddenly Elena felt horribly vulnerable.

Caleb shifted from foot to foot, looking uncomfortable, and she quickly composed herself. "How long have you been in town?" she asked, and then kicked herself for treating this boy she obviously was supposed to know like a stranger again.

"Well," he said slowly, "I've been in town all summer. Did you hit your head over the weekend, Elena?" He grinned teasingly at her.

Elena lifted a shoulder, thinking of all she *had* suffered over the weekend. "Something like that."

He held out the rose. "This must be for you."

"Thank you," said Elena, confused. A thorn pricked her finger as she took it by the stem, and she stuck the finger in her mouth to stanch the blood.

"Don't thank me," he said. "It was just sitting on the front steps when I got here. You must have a secret admirer."

Elena frowned. Plenty of boys had admired her through school, and if this had been nine months ago, she could have made a good guess at who would leave her a rose. But now she didn't have a clue.

Matt's battered old Ford sedan pulled up outside and honked. "I've got to run, Aunt Judith," she said. "They're here. Nice seeing you, Caleb."

Elena's stomach twisted as she walked toward Matt's car. It wasn't just the strangeness of meeting Caleb that was affecting her, she realized, turning the rose's stem absently between her fingers. It was the car itself.

Matt's old Ford was the car she had driven off Wickery Bridge back in the winter, panicked and pursued by evil forces. She'd died in this car. The windows had shattered as she hit the creek, and the car had filled with icy water. The scratched steering wheel and the dented hood of the car, covered with water, had been the last things she'd seen in that life.

But here the car was—as whole again as she was.

Pushing the memory of her death from her mind, she waved at Bonnie, whose eager face was visible through the passenger window. She could forget about all those old tragedies, because now they had never happened.

Meredith perched elegantly on the swing on her front porch, pushing herself gently back and forth with one foot. Her strong, tapered fingers were still; her dark hair fell smoothly across her shoulders; her expression was as serene as ever.

There was nothing about Meredith that might show how tensely and busily her thoughts were churning, worries and contingency plans whirring away behind her cool facade.

She had spent yesterday trying to figure out what the Guardians' spell had changed for her and her family—particularly her brother, Christian, who Klaus had kidnapped over a decade ago. She still didn't understand it all, but it was dawning on her that Elena's bargain had more far-reaching consequences than any of them had imagined.

But today her thoughts were occupied with Alaric Saltzman.

Her fingers tapped anxiously against the arm of the swing. Then she schooled herself into stillness again.

Self-discipline was where Meredith found her strength, and if Alaric, her boyfriend—or at least, he had been her boyfriend . . . actually her perhaps engaged-to-be-engaged, sort of almost fiancé, before he left town—turned out to have changed toward her in the months they'd been apart, well, no one, not even Alaric, would see how that would hurt her.

Alaric had spent the past several months in Japan, investigating paranormal activity, a dream come true for a doctoral student in parapsychology. His study of the tragic history of Unmei no Shima, the Island of Doom, a small community where children and parents had turned against one another, had helped Meredith and her friends to understand what the kitsune were doing to Fell's Church, and how to fight it.

Alaric had been working at Unmei no Shima with Dr. Celia Connor, a forensic pathologist who, despite her full academic credentials, was the same age as Alaric, only twenty-four. So, clearly, Dr. Connor was brilliant.

From his letters and emails, Alaric had been having the time of his life in Japan. And he'd certainly found a lot of interests in common with Dr. Connor. Perhaps more so than with Meredith, who had only just graduated from a small-town high school, no matter how mature and intelligent she might be.

Meredith gave herself a mental shake and sat up straighter. She was being ridiculous, worrying about Alaric's relationship with his colleague. She was pretty sure she was being ridiculous, anyway. Fairly sure.

She gripped the arms of the swing more tightly. She was a vampire hunter. She had a duty to protect her town, and she *had*, with her friends, protected it well already. She wasn't just an ordinary teenager, and if she needed to prove that to Alaric again, she was confident she could, Dr. Celia Connor or no Dr. Celia Connor.

Matt's rattletrap of an old Ford sedan chugged up to the curb, Bonnie in front with Matt, Stefan and Elena sitting close together in the back. Meredith rose and crossed the lawn toward it.

"Is everything okay?" said Bonnie, round eyed, when she opened the door. "Your face looks like you're heading off to battle."

Meredith smoothed her features into impassivity and scrambled for an explanation that wasn't, *I'm worried about whether my boyfriend still likes me.* Quickly and easily, she realized there was another reason she was tense, a true one.

"Bonnie, I have a duty to help look out for everyone now," Meredith said simply. "Damon's dead. Stefan doesn't want to hurt humans, and that handicaps him. Elena's Powers are gone. Even though the kitsune were defeated, we still need protection. We'll always need to be careful."

Stefan tightened his arm around Elena's shoulders. "The things that make Fell's Church so appealing to the supernatural, the ley lines that have attracted all kinds of beings here for generations, are all still here. I can sense them. And other people, other *creatures*, will sense them, too."

Bonnie's voice rose in alarm. "So it's all going to happen *again*?"

Stefan rubbed the bridge of his nose. "I don't think so. But something else might. Meredith's right, we have to be vigilant." He dropped a kiss onto Elena's shoulder and rested his cheek against her hair. There was no question, Meredith thought wryly, why this particular supernatural being was drawn to Fell's Church, anyway, and it wasn't because of the ley lines running through the area.

Elena toyed with a single dark red rose, something Stefan must have brought her. "Is that the only reason you're worried, Meredith?" she asked lightly. "Your duty to Fell's Church?"

Meredith felt herself flush a little, but her voice was dry and calm. "I think that's reason enough, don't you?"

Elena grinned. "Oh, it's reason enough, I suppose. But could there be another one?" She winked at Bonnie, whose anxious expression lightened in response. "Who do we know who will be fascinated by all the tales you have to tell? *Especially* when he finds out that the story's not over yet?"

Bonnie turned all the way around in her seat, her smile growing. "Oh. *Oh.* I see. He won't be able to think of anything else, will he? Or anyone else."

Now Stefan's shoulders relaxed, and up in the driver's seat Matt let out a chuckle and shook his head. "You three," he said affectionately. "Us guys never stood a chance."

Meredith looked straight ahead and lifted her chin slightly, ignoring them all. Elena and Bonnie knew her too well, and the three of them had spent enough time scheming together that she should have known they'd see through her plan in a minute. But she didn't have to admit to it.

The solemn mood in the car had lifted, though. Meredith realized they were all doing it on purpose, reaching out gently and carefully with jokes and lighthearted teasing, trying to ease the pain Elena and Stefan must both be feeling.

Damon was dead. And while Meredith had developed a cautious, wary respect for the unpredictable vampire during their time in the Dark Dimension, and Bonnie had felt, Meredith thought, something warmer, Elena had *loved* him. Really loved him. And even though Damon and Stefan's relationship had been rocky, to say the least, for centuries, he had been Stefan's brother. Stefan and Elena were hurting, and everyone knew it.

After a minute, Matt's eyes flicked up to the rearview mirror to glance at Stefan. "Hey," he said, "I forgot to tell you. In this reality you didn't disappear on Halloween—you stayed the starting wide receiver and we took the football team all the way to the state championships." He grinned, and Stefan's face opened in simple pleasure.

Meredith had almost forgotten that Stefan had played with Matt on their high school football team before their history teacher, Mr. Tanner, died at the Halloween haunted house and everything went to hell. She had forgotten he and Matt had been real friends, playing sports and hanging out, despite the fact that they'd both loved Elena.

And maybe still do both love Elena? she wondered, and glanced quickly at the back of Matt's head from under her eyelashes. She wasn't sure how Matt felt, but he had always struck her as the kind of guy who, when he fell in love, stayed in love. But he was also the kind of guy who would always be too honorable to try to break up a relationship, no matter what he felt.

"And," Matt went on, "as the quarterback of the state champions, I guess I'm a pretty good prospect for colleges." He paused and broke out in a wide, proud smile. "Apparently, I have a full athletic scholarship to Kent State."

Bonnie squealed, Elena clapped, and Meredith and Stefan burst out with congratulations.

"Me, me now!" Bonnie said. "I guess I studied harder in this reality. Which was probably easier, since one of my best friends didn't *die* first semester and was available to help tutor me."

"Hey!" Elena said. "Meredith was always a better tutor than me. You can't blame it on me."

"Anyway," Bonnie continued, "I got into a four-year college! I didn't even bother to apply to any in our other life because my GPA was *not* high. I was going to take nursing classes at the community college like Mary did, even though I'm not sure I'm really cut out to be a nurse because, *yuck*, blood and other fluids. But, anyway, my mom was saying this morning that we should go shopping for my room at Dalcrest before Labor Day." She shrugged a little. "I mean, I know it's not Harvard, but I'm pretty excited."

Meredith joined in the congratulations quietly. *She* had, in fact, gotten into Harvard.

"Ooh. And! And!" Bonnie was bouncing in her seat with excitement. "I ran into Vickie Bennett this morning. She's definitely not dead! I think she was surprised when I hugged her. I forgot we weren't really friends."

"How is she?" asked Elena interestedly. "Did she remember anything?"

Bonnie tilted her head. "She seems fine. I couldn't exactly ask her what she remembered, but she didn't say anything about being dead or vampires or anything. I mean, she was always a little bit blah, you know? She did tell me she saw you downtown last weekend and you told her what color lip gloss she ought to buy."

Elena raised her eyebrows. "Really?" She paused and went on uncertainly, "Is anybody else feeling weird about all of this? I mean, it's wonderful—don't get me wrong. But it's weird, too."

"It's *confusing*," Bonnie said. "I'm grateful, obviously, that all the horrible things are gone and everybody's okay. I'm thrilled to have my life back. But my father blew up at me this morning when I asked where Mary was." Mary was one of Bonnie's older sisters, the last one living at home besides Bonnie. "He thought I was trying to be funny. Apparently she moved in with her boyfriend three months ago, and you can imagine how my dad feels about *that*."

Meredith nodded. Bonnie's dad was the protective paternal type, and pretty old-fashioned in his attitudes toward his daughters' boyfriends. If Mary was living with her boyfriend, he must be apoplectic.

"Aunt Judith and I have been fighting—at least, I think so. But I can't find out exactly why," Elena confessed. "I can't ask, because obviously I should already know."

"Shouldn't everything be perfect now?" Bonnie said wistfully. "It seems like we've been through enough."

"I don't mind being confused, as long as we can go back to real life," Matt said earnestly.

There was a little pause, which Meredith broke, reaching for something to take them out of their somber thoughts. "Pretty rose, Elena," she said. "Is that a gift from Stefan?"

"No, actually," Elena said. "It was sitting on my front stoop this morning." She twirled it between her fingers. "It's not from any of the gardens on our street, though. No one has such beautiful roses." She smiled teasingly at Stefan, who tensed up once more. "It's a mystery."

"Must be from a secret admirer," Bonnie said. "Can I see?"

Elena handed it up to the front seat, and Bonnie turned the stem around carefully in her hand, looking at the blossom from all angles. "It's gorgeous," she said. "A single, perfect rose. How romantic!" She pretended to swoon, lifting the rose to her forehead. Then she flinched. "Ouch! Ouch!"

Blood ran down her hand. Much more blood than ought to come from the prick of a thorn, Meredith noted, already reaching into her pocket for a tissue. Matt pulled off the road.

"Bonnie—" he began.

Stefan breathed in sharply and leaned forward, his eyes widening. Meredith forgot about the tissue, fearing the sudden sight of blood had caused Stefan's vampiric nature to take over.

Then Matt gasped and Elena said sharply, "A camera, quick! Someone give me your phone!" with such a tone of command that Meredith automatically handed Elena her phone.

As Elena pointed the camera phone at Bonnie, Meredith finally saw what had startled the others.

The dark red blood was running down Bonnie's arm, and as it ran, it had streamed into twists and curves from her wrist to her elbow. The trickles of blood spelled out a name over and over. The same name that had been haunting Meredith for months.

celiaceliaceliacelia

"**W**ho's Celia?" Bonnie said indignantly, as soon as they'd wiped off the blood. She'd put the rose down carefully in the middle of the front seat, between her and Matt, and they were all very consciously *not* touching it. Pretty as it was, it looked more sinister than beautiful now, Stefan thought grimly.

"Celia *Connor*," Meredith said sharply. "Dr. Celia Connor. You saw her in a vision once, Bonnie. The forensic anthropologist."

"The one who's working with Alaric?" Bonnie said. "But why would her name show up in blood on my arm? In *blood*."

"That's what I'd like to know," Meredith said, frowning.

"It could be some kind of warning," Elena proposed.

"We don't know enough yet. We'll go to the station, we'll meet Alaric and *Celia*, and then . . ."

"Then?" prompted Meredith, meeting Elena's cool blue eyes.

"Then we'll do whatever we have to do," Elena said. "As usual."

Bonnie was still complaining when they got to the train station.

Patience, Stefan reminded himself. Usually he enjoyed Bonnie's company, but right now, his body craving the human blood he'd become accustomed to, he felt . . . off. He rubbed his aching jaw.

"I'd really hoped we'd get at least a couple days of everything being normal," Bonnie moaned for what seemed like the thousandth time.

"Life's not fair, Bonnie," Matt said gloomily. Stefan glanced at him in surprise—Matt was usually the first to leap in and try to cheer up the girls—but the tall blond was leaning against the closed ticket booth, his shoulders drooping, his hands tucked into his pockets.

Matt met Stefan's gaze. "It's all starting up again, isn't it?"

Stefan shook his head and glanced around the station. "I don't know what's going on," he said. "But we all need to be vigilant until we can figure it out."

"Oh, that's comforting," Meredith muttered, her gray

eyes alertly scanning the platform.

Stefan folded his arms across his chest and shifted closer to Elena and Bonnie. All his senses, normal and paranormal, were on full alert. He reached out with his Power, trying to sense any supernatural consciousnesses near them, but felt nothing new or alarming, just the calm background buzz of ordinary humans going about their everyday business.

It was impossible to stop worrying, though. Stefan had seen many things in his five hundred years of existence: vampires, werewolves, demons, ghosts, angels, witches, all sorts of beings who preyed on or influenced humans in ways most people could never even imagine. And, as a vampire, he knew a lot about blood. More than he had cared to admit.

He'd seen Meredith's eyes flick toward him with suspicion when Bonnie began to bleed. She was right to be wary of him: How could they trust him when his basic nature was to kill them?

Blood was the essence of life; it was what kept a vampire going centuries after his natural life span should have ended. Blood was the central ingredient in many spells both benevolent and wicked. Blood had Powers of its own, Powers that were difficult and dangerous to harness. But Stefan had never seen blood behave in the way it had on Bonnie's arm today.

A thought struck him. "Elena," he said, turning to face her.

"Hmmm?" she answered distractedly, shading her eyes as she peered down the track.

"You said the rose was just lying there waiting for you on the porch when you opened the door this morning?"

Elena brushed her hair out of her eyes. "Actually, no. Caleb Smallwood found it there and handed it to me when I opened the door to let him in."

"Caleb Smallwood?" Stefan narrowed his eyes. Elena had mentioned earlier that her aunt had hired the Smallwood boy to do some work around the house, but she should have told him of Caleb's connection to the rose before. "Tyler Smallwood's cousin? The guy who just showed up out of nowhere to hang around your house? The one who's probably a *werewolf*, like the rest of his family?"

"You didn't meet him. He was perfectly fine. Apparently he's been around town all summer without anything weird happening. We just don't remember him." Her tone was breezy, but her smile didn't quite reach her eyes.

Stefan reached out automatically to speak to her with his mind, to have a private conversation about what she was really feeling. But he couldn't. He was so used to depending on the connection between them that he kept forgetting it was gone now; he could sense Elena's emotions, could feel her aura, but they could no longer communicate telepathically. He and Elena were separate again. Stefan hunched his shoulders miserably against the breeze.

Bonnie frowned, the summer wind whipping her strawberry ringlets around her face. "Is *Tyler* even a werewolf now? Because if Sue's alive, he didn't kill her to become a werewolf, right?"

Elena held her palms to the sky. "I don't know. He's gone, anyway, and I'm not sorry. Even before he was a werewolf, he was a real jerk. Remember what a bully he was at school? And how he was always drinking out of that hip flask and hitting on us? But I'm pretty sure Caleb's just a regular guy. I'd have known if there was something wrong with him."

Stefan looked at her. "You've got wonderful instincts about people," he said carefully. "But are you sure you're not relying on senses you don't have anymore to tell you what Caleb is?" He thought of how the Guardians had painfully clipped Elena's Wings and destroyed her Powers, the Powers she and her friends only half-understood.

Elena looked taken aback and was opening her mouth to reply when the train chugged into the station, preventing further discussion.

Only a few people were disembarking at the Fell's Church station, and Stefan soon spotted Alaric's familiar form. After stepping down to the platform, Alaric reached back to steady a slender African-American woman as she exited behind him.

Dr. Celia Connor was certainly lovely—Stefan would give her that. She was tiny, as small as Bonnie, with dark skin and close-cropped hair. The smile she gave Alaric as she took his arm was charming and slightly puckish. She had large brown eyes and a long, elegant neck. Stylish but practical in designer clothing, she wore soft leather boots, skinny jeans, and a sapphire-toned silk shirt. A long, diaphanous scarf was wrapped around her neck, adding to her sophisticated demeanor.

When Alaric, all tousled sandy hair and boyish grin, whispered familiarly in her ear, Stefan felt Meredith tense. She looked like she'd like nothing better than to try out a few of her martial arts moves on a certain gorgeous forensic anthropologist.

But then Alaric spotted Meredith, dashed over, and took her in his arms, pulling her off her feet as he swung her into a hug, and she visibly relaxed. In a few moments, they were both laughing and talking, and they didn't seem to be able to stop touching each other, as if they needed to reassure themselves that they were actually together again at last.

Clearly, Stefan thought, any worries Meredith had had about Alaric and Dr. Connor had been groundless, at least as far as Alaric was concerned. Stefan turned his attention to Celia Connor again.

His first wary tendrils of Power discovered a slight simmering resentment emanating from the anthropologist. Understandable: She was human, she was quite young despite her poise and her many professional achievements, and she had spent a great deal of time working closely with the very attractive Alaric. It wouldn't be surprising if she felt a bit proprietary toward him, and here he was being pulled away from her and into the orbit of a teenage girl.

But more important, his Power found no supernatural shadow hanging about her and no answering Power in her. Whatever the meaning of the name Celia written in blood, it seemed Dr. Celia Connor hadn't caused it.

"Somebody take pictures!" Bonnie called, laughing. "We haven't seen Alaric for *months*. We have to document his return!"

Matt got out his phone and took a couple of pictures of Alaric and Meredith, their arms around each other.

"All of us!" Bonnie insisted. "You too, Dr. Connor. Let's stand in front of the train—it's a terrific backdrop. You take this one, Matt, and then I'll take some with you in them."

They shuffled into various positions: bumping, excusing, introducing themselves to Celia Connor, throwing their arms around one another in a casually exuberant style. Stefan found himself pushed to the edge, Elena's arm through his, and he discreetly inhaled the clean, sweet scent of her hair.

"All aboard!" the conductor called, and the train doors closed.

Matt, Stefan realized, had stopped taking pictures and was staring at them, his blue eyes widening in what looked like terror. "Stop the train!" he shouted. "Stop the train!"

"Matt? What on *earth*?" Elena said. And then Meredith looked behind them, toward the train, with an expression of dawning comprehension.

"Celia," she said urgently, reaching out toward the other woman.

Stefan watched in confusion as Celia jerked away from them abruptly, almost as if an unseen hand had grabbed her. As the train began to move, Celia walked, then ran beside it with stiff, frantic motions, her hands pulling rapidly at her throat.

Suddenly Stefan's perspective shifted and he understood what was happening. Celia's diaphanous scarf had somehow been firmly caught by the closing door of the train, and now the train was pulling her along by the neck. She was running to keep from being strangled, the scarf like a leash yanking her along. And the train was beginning to pick up speed. Her hands pulled at the scarf, but both ends were caught in the door, and her tugging only seemed to tighten it around her neck.

Celia was approaching the end of the platform and the train was chugging faster. It was a flat drop from the platform to the scrub ground beyond. In a few moments, she would fall, her neck would be broken, and the train would drag her along for miles.

Stefan took all this in within the space of a single breath and sprang into action. He felt his canines lengthen as a surge of Power went through him. And then he took off, faster than any human, faster than the train, and sped toward her.

With one quick motion, he took her in his arms, relieving the pressure around her throat, and tore the scarf in half.

He stopped and put Celia down as the train sped up and left the station. The remnants of the scarf slipped from around her neck and fluttered onto the platform by her feet. She and Stefan stared at each other, breathing hard. Behind them, he could hear the others shouting, their feet pounding on the platform as they ran toward them.

Celia's dark brown eyes were wide and filled with tears of pain. She licked her lips nervously and took several short, gasping breaths, pressing her hands against her chest. He could hear her heart pounding, her blood rushing through her system, and he concentrated on pulling his canines back and resuming his human face. She staggered suddenly, and Stefan slipped his arm around her.

"It's okay," he said. "You're all right now."

Celia gave a short, slightly hysterical laugh and wiped at her eyes. Then she stood upright, straightening her shoulders, and inhaled deeply. Stefan could see her deliberately calming herself, although her heartbeat was reeling, and he admired her self-control.

"So," she said, holding out her hand, "you must be the vampire Alaric's told me about."

The others were coming up to them now, and Stefan glanced at Alaric in alarm.

"That's something I'd rather you kept private," Stefan told her, feeling a prick of irritation at Alaric for divulging his secret. But his words were almost drowned out by a gasp from Meredith. Her gray eyes, usually so serene, were dark with horror.

"Look," she said, pointing. "Look at what it says." Stefan turned his attention to the pieces of sheer fabric around their feet.

Bonnie gave a little whimper and Matt's eyebrows furrowed. Elena's beautiful face was blank with shock, and Alaric and Celia both appeared entirely confused.

For a moment, Stefan saw nothing. Then, like a picture coming into focus, his vision adjusted and he saw what everyone was looking at. The torn scarf had fallen into an elaborately twisted heap, and the supposedly random folds of fabric quite clearly formed letters that spelled:

meredith

8

"It was seriously creepy," said Bonnie. They had all bundled into Matt's car, Elena hopping onto Stefan's lap and Meredith onto Alaric's (which, Bonnie had noted, Dr. Celia had seemed less than thrilled by). Then they'd hurried back to the boardinghouse, looking for counsel.

Once there, they'd all crowded into the parlor and spilled out the story to Mrs. Flowers, talking over one another in their excitement. "First Celia's name—in my *blood*—appearing out of nowhere," Bonnie went on, "and then there's this weird accident that could have *killed* her, and then Meredith's name appears, too. It was all just really, really creepy."

"I'd put it a bit more strongly than that," Meredith said. Then she arched an elegant eyebrow. "Bonnie, this is no doubt the first time I've ever complained you weren't being dramatic enough."

"Hey!" Bonnie objected.

"There you go," Elena joked. "Keep looking on the bright side. The latest insanity is making Bonnie low-key."

Matt shook his head. "Mrs. Flowers, do you know what's happening?"

Mrs. Flowers, seated in a cozy corner chair of the parlor, smiled and patted him on the shoulder. She'd been knitting when they came in, but had laid the pink bundle of yarn aside and had fixed her calm blue eyes on them with her full attention as they told their story. "Dear Matt," she said. "Always straight to the point."

Poor Celia had been sitting on the couch by Alaric and Meredith, looking stunned since they'd arrived. It was one thing to study the supernatural, but the reality of a vampire, mysteriously appearing names, and a brush with death must have been a shock to her system. Alaric had a reassuring arm around her shoulders. Bonnie thought maybe the arm should have been around Meredith's shoulders. After all, *Meredith's* name had just shown up in the scarf's folds. But Meredith was just sitting there, watching Alaric and Celia, her face composed, her eyes unreadable.

Now Celia leaned forward and spoke for the first time.

"Pardon me," she said politely, her voice shaking a bit, "but I don't understand why we've brought this . . . this issue to . . ." Her voice trailed off as her eyes flickered to Mrs. Flowers.

Bonnie knew what she meant. Mrs. Flowers looked like the epitome of a sweet, dotty elderly lady: soft flyaway gray hair drawn back in a bun, a politely vague expression, a wardrobe that leaned toward pastels or shabby blacks, and a habit of muttering quietly, apparently to herself. A year ago, Bonnie herself had thought Mrs. Flowers was just the crazy old woman who ran the boardinghouse where Stefan lived.

But appearances could be deceptive. Mrs. Flowers had earned the respect and admiration of every one of them by the way she had protected the town with her magic, Power, and good sense. There was a lot more to this little old lady than met the eye.

"My dear," said Mrs. Flowers firmly, "you've had a very traumatic experience. Drink your tea. It's a special calming blend that's been passed down in my family for generations. We will do everything we can for you."

Which, Bonnie observed, was a very sweet and ladylike way of putting Dr. Celia Connor in her place. *She* was to drink her tea and recuperate, and *they* would figure out how to solve the problem. Celia's eyes flashed, but she sipped her tea obediently.

"Now," Mrs. Flowers said, looking around at the others, "it seems to me that the first thing to do is to figure out what the *intention* is behind the appearance of the names.

Once we do that, perhaps we will have a better idea of *who* might be behind their appearance."

"Maybe to warn us?" Bonnie said hesitantly. "I mean, Celia's name appeared, and then she almost died, and now Meredith . . ." Her voice trailed off and she looked at Meredith apologetically. "I'm worried you might be in danger."

Meredith squared her shoulders. "It certainly wouldn't be the first time," she said.

Mrs. Flowers nodded briskly. "Yes, it's possible that the appearance of the names has a benevolent intention. Let's explore that theory. Someone may be trying to get a warning to you. If so, who? And why do they have to do it in this way?"

Bonnie's voice was even softer and more hesitant now. But if no one else was going to say it, she would. "Could it be Damon?"

"Damon's dead," Stefan said flatly.

"But when Elena was dead, she warned me about Klaus," Bonnie argued.

Stefan massaged his temples. He looked tired. "Bonnie, when Elena died, Klaus trapped her spirit between dimensions. She hadn't fully passed away. And even then, she could only visit you in your dreams—not anyone else, just you, because you can sense things other people can't. She couldn't make anything happen in the physical world."

Elena's voice trembled. "Bonnie, the Guardians told

us that vampires don't live on after death. In any sense of the word. Damon's gone." Stefan reached out and took her hand, his eyes troubled.

Bonnie felt a sharp stab of sympathy for them both. She was sorry she'd brought Damon up, but she hadn't been able to stop herself. The thought that he might be watching over them, irascible and mocking but ultimately kind, had briefly lifted the weight from her heart. Now that weight came crashing back down. "Well," she said dully, "then I don't have any idea who might be warning us. Does anybody else?"

They all shook their heads, baffled. "Who even knows about us now that has this kind of power?" Matt asked.

"The Guardians?" said Bonnie doubtfully.

But Elena shook her head with a quick decisive motion, blond hair swinging. "It's not them," she said. "The last thing they'd do is send a message in blood. Visions would be more their style. And I'm pretty sure the Guardians washed their hands of us when they sent us back here."

Mrs. Flowers interlocked her fingers in her lap. "So perhaps there is some as yet unknown person or being looking after you, warning you of danger ahead."

Matt had been sitting ramrod straight in one of Mrs. Flowers's daintier chairs, and it creaked alarmingly as he leaned forward. "Um," he said. "I think the better question is, what's causing that danger?"

Mrs. Flowers spread her small, wrinkled hands. "You're perfectly right. Let's consider the options. On the one hand, it could be a warning for something that was naturally going to happen. Celia's—you don't mind if I call you Celia, do you, dear?"

Celia, still looking shell-shocked, shook her head.

"Good. Celia's scarf getting caught in the train doors could have been a natural accident. Forgive me for saying so, but those long, dramatic scarves can be very dangerous. The dancer Isadora Duncan was killed in just that way when her scarf caught in the wheel of a car many years ago. Perhaps whoever sent the message was simply raising a flag for Celia to be careful, or for the rest of you to take care of her. Perhaps Meredith merely needs to be cautious over the next few days."

"You don't think so, though, do you?" asked Meredith sharply.

Mrs. Flowers sighed. "This all feels rather malevolent to me. I think if someone wanted to warn you about the possibility of accidents, they could find a better way than names written in blood. Both of these names appeared as the results of rather violent incidents, correct? Bonnie cutting herself and Stefan ripping the scarf from Celia's neck?"

Meredith nodded.

Looking troubled, Mrs. Flowers continued. "And, of course, the other possibility is that the appearance of the names is itself malicious. Perhaps the names' appearance is an essential ingredient in or targeting method for some spell that is *causing* the danger."

Stefan frowned. "You're talking about dark magic, aren't you?"

Mrs. Flowers met his eyes squarely. "I'm afraid so. Stefan, you're the oldest and most experienced of us by far. I've never heard of anything like this, have you?"

Bonnie felt a bit surprised. Of course, she knew that Stefan was much older than even Mrs. Flowers—after all, he'd been alive before electricity, or running water, or cars, or anything they took for granted in the modern world, while Mrs. Flowers was probably only in her seventies.

But still, it was easy to forget how long Stefan had lived. He looked just like any other eighteen-year-old, except that he was exceptionally handsome. A traitorous thought flickered at the back of her mind, one she'd had before: How was it that Elena always got all the best-looking guys?

Stefan was shaking his head. "Nothing like this, no. But I think you're right that it may be dark magic. Perhaps, if you spoke to your mother about it . . ."

Celia, who was starting to take more of an interest in what was going on, looked at Alaric quizzically. Then she cast a glance toward the door, as if expecting a hundred-year-old woman to wander in. Bonnie grinned to herself, despite the seriousness of the situation.

They had all gotten so matter-of-fact about Mrs. Flowers's frequent conversations with the ghost of her mother that none of them blinked when Mrs. Flowers gazed off into space and started muttering rapidly, eyebrows lifting, eyes scanning unoccupied space as if someone unseen were speaking to her. But to Celia it must have seemed pretty strange.

"Yes," said Mrs. Flowers, returning her attention to them. "Ma*ma* says there is indeed something dark stirring in Fell's Church. But"—her hands lifted, palms empty—"she cannot tell what form it takes. She simply warns us to be careful. Whatever it is, she can sense that it's deadly."

Stefan and Meredith frowned, taking this in. Alaric was murmuring to Celia, probably explaining what was going on. Matt bowed his head.

Elena pushed on, already working on the next angle. "Bonnie, what about you?" she asked.

"Huh?" Bonnie asked. Then she realized what Elena meant. "No. Nuh-uh. I'm not going to know anything Mrs. Flowers's mother doesn't."

Elena just looked at her, and Bonnie sighed. This was important, after all. Meredith's name was next, and if there was one thing that was true, it was that she and Meredith and Elena had one another's backs. Always. "All right," she said reluctantly. "I'll see if I can find out anything else. Can you light me a candle?"

"What now?" Celia asked in confusion.

"Bonnie's psychic," Elena explained simply.

"Fascinating," Celia said brightly, but her eyes slid, cool and disbelieving, across Bonnie.

Well, whatever. Bonnie didn't care what she thought. She could assume that Bonnie was pretending or crazy if she wanted to, but she'd see what happened eventually. Elena brought a candle over from its spot on the mantel, lit it, and placed it on the coffee table.

Bonnie swallowed, licked her lips, which were suddenly dry, and tried to focus on the candle flame. Although she'd had plenty of practice, she didn't like doing this, didn't like the sensation of losing herself, as if she were sliding underwater.

The flame flickered and grew brighter. It seemed to swell and fill Bonnie's field of vision. All she could see was flame.

I know who you are, a cold, rough voice suddenly growled in her ear, and Bonnie twitched. She hated the voices, sometimes as soft as if they were coming from a distant television, sometimes right beside her, like this one. She somehow always managed to forget them until the next time she began to fall into a trance. A faraway child's voice began a wordless off-key humming, and Bonnie focused on making her breathing slow and steady.

She could feel her eyes slipping out of focus. A sour

taste, wet and nasty, filled her mouth.

Envy twisted, sharp and bitter, inside her. *It's not fair, not fair,* something muttered sullenly in her skull. And then blackness took over.

Elena watched apprehensively as Bonnie's pupils widened, reflecting the candle flame. Bonnie was able to sink into trances much more quickly now than when she had begun having them, which worried Elena.

"Darkness rises." A flat, hollow voice that didn't sound anything like Bonnie's came from her friend's mouth. "It's not here yet, but it wants to be. It's cold. It's been cold for a long time. It wants to be near us, out of the darkness and as warm as our hearts. It hates."

"Is it a vampire?" asked Meredith quickly.

The not-Bonnie voice gave a harsh, choking laugh. "It's much stronger than any vampire. It can find a home in any of you. Watch one another. Watch yourselves."

"What is it?" asked Matt.

Whatever it was that spoke through Bonnie hesitated.

"She doesn't know," said Stefan. "Or she can't tell us. Bonnie," he said intently, "is someone bringing this thing to us? Who's causing it?"

No hesitation this time. "Elena," it said. "Elena brought it."

onnie winced at the nasty metallic taste in her mouth and blinked several times, until the room around her came back into focus. "Ugh," she said. "I *hate* doing that."

Everyone was staring at her, their faces white and shocked.

"What?" she said uneasily. "What'd I say?"

Elena was sitting very still. "You said it was my fault," she said slowly. "Whatever is coming after us, I brought it here." Stefan reached out to cover her hand with his own.

Unbidden, the meanest, narrowest part of Bonnie's mind thought wearily, *Of course. It's always about Elena, isn't it?*

Meredith and Matt filled Bonnie in on the rest of what she'd said in her trance, but their eyes kept returning to

Elena's stricken face, and as soon as they finished telling her what she'd missed, they turned away from Bonnie, back to Elena.

"We need to make a plan," Meredith said to her softly.

"We'll all want some refreshment," Mrs. Flowers said, rising to her feet, and Bonnie followed her into the kitchen, eager to escape the tension of the room.

She wasn't really a plan girl, anyway, she told herself. She'd made her contribution just by being the vision girl. Elena and Meredith were the ones everyone looked to for making the decisions.

But it wasn't *fair*, was it? She wasn't a fool, despite the fact that her friends all treated her like the baby of the group. Everyone thought Elena and Meredith were *so clever* and *so strong*, but Bonnie had saved the day again and again—not that anyone ever remembered that. She ran her tongue along the edges of her teeth, trying to scrape off the nasty sour taste still in her mouth.

Mrs. Flowers had decided that what the group needed to soothe them was some of her special elder-flower lemonade. While she filled the glasses with ice, poured the drinks, and set them out on a tray, Bonnie watched her restlessly. There was a rough, empty feeling inside Bonnie, like something was missing. It wasn't *fair*, she thought again. None of them appreciated her or realized all she'd done for them.

"Mrs. Flowers," she said suddenly. "How do you talk to your mother?"

Mrs. Flowers turned to her, surprised. "Why, my dear," she said, "it's very easy to speak to ghosts, if they want to speak to you, or if they are the spirits of someone you loved. Ghosts, you see, have not left our plane but stay close to us."

"But still," Bonnie pressed on, "you can do more than that, a lot more." She pictured Mrs. Flowers, young again, eyes flashing, hair flying, fighting the kitsune's malevolent Power with an equal Power of her own. "You're a very powerful witch."

Mrs. Flowers's expression was reserved. "It's kind of you to say so, dear."

Bonnie twirled a ringlet of her hair around one finger anxiously, weighing her next words. "Well . . . if you would, of course—only if you have time—I'd like you to train me. Whatever you'd be willing to teach me. I can see things and I've gotten better at that, but I'd like to learn everything, anything else you can show me. Divining, and about herbs. Protection spells. The works, I guess. I feel like there's so much I don't know, and I think I might have talent, you know? I hope so, anyway."

Mrs. Flowers looked at her appraisingly for one long moment and then nodded once more.

"I will teach you," she said. "With pleasure. You possess

great natural talent."

"Really?" Bonnie said shyly. A warm bubble of happiness rose inside her, filling the emptiness that had engulfed her just moments ago.

Then she cleared her throat and added, as casually as she could manage, "And I was wondering . . . can you talk to anyone who's dead? Or just your mother?"

Mrs. Flowers didn't answer for a few moments. Bonnie felt like the older woman's sharp blue gaze was looking straight through her and analyzing the mind and heart inside. When Mrs. Flowers did speak, her voice was gentle.

"Who is it you want to contact, dear?"

Bonnie flinched. "No one in particular," she said quickly, erasing an image of Damon's black-on-black eyes from her mind. "It just seems like something that would be useful. And interesting, too. Like, I could learn all about Fell's Church's history." She turned away from Mrs. Flowers and busied herself with the lemonade glasses, leaving the subject behind for now.

There would be time to ask again, she thought. *Soon.*

"The most important thing," Elena was saying earnestly, "is to protect Meredith. We've gotten a warning, and we need to take advantage of it, not sit around worrying about where it came from. If something terrible—something *I* brought somehow—is coming, we'll deal with it when it gets here. Right now, we look out for Meredith."

She was so beautiful, she made Stefan dizzy. Quite literally: Sometimes he would look at her, catch her at a certain angle, and would see, as if for the first time, the delicate curve of her cheek, the lightest rose-petal blush in her creamy skin, the soft seriousness of her mouth. In those moments, every time, his head and stomach would swoop as if he'd just gotten off a roller coaster. *Elena.*

He belonged to her; it was as simple as that. As if for hundreds of years he had been journeying toward this one mortal girl, and now that he had found her, his long, long life finally had found its purpose.

You don't have her, though, something inside him said. *Not all of her. Not really.*

Stefan shook off the traitorous thought. Elena loved him. She loved him bravely and desperately and passionately and far more than he deserved. And he loved her. That was what mattered.

And right now, this sweet mortal girl he loved was efficiently organizing a schedule for guarding Meredith, assigning duties with the calm expectation that she would be obeyed. "Matt," she said, "if you're working tomorrow night, you and Alaric can take the daytime shift. Stefan will take over at night, and Bonnie and I will pick up in the morning."

"You should have been a general," Stefan murmured to

her, earning himself a quick smile.

"I don't need guards," Meredith said irritably. "I've been trained in martial arts and I've faced the supernatural before." It seemed to Stefan that her eye rested speculatively on him for a second, and he forced himself not to bristle under her scrutiny. "My stave is all the protection I need."

"A stave like yours couldn't have protected Celia," Elena argued. "Without Stefan there to intervene, she would have been killed." On the couch, Celia closed her eyes and rested her head against Alaric's arm.

"Fine, then." Meredith spoke in a clipped tone, her eyes on Celia. "It's true, out of all of us, only Stefan could have saved her. And that's the other reason this whole team effort to protect me is ridiculous. Do you have the strength and speed these days to save me from a moving train, Elena? Does *Bonnie?*" Stefan saw Bonnie, coming in with a tray of lemonade glasses, pause and frown as she heard Meredith's words.

He had known, of course, that with Damon dead and Elena's Powers gone, he was the only one left to protect the group. Well, Mrs. Flowers and Bonnie had some limited magical ability. Then Stefan amended the thought further. Mrs. Flowers was actually quite powerful, but her powers were still depleted from fighting the kitsune.

It came to the same thing, then: Stefan was the only

one who could protect them now. Meredith might talk about her responsibilities as a vampire hunter, but in the end, despite her training and heritage, she was just another mortal.

His eyes scanned the group, all the mortals, *his* mortals. Meredith, serious gray eyes and a steely resolve. Matt, eager and boyish and decent down to the bone. Bonnie, sunny and sweet, and with a core of strength perhaps even she didn't know she had. Mrs. Flowers, a wise matriarch. Alaric and Celia . . . well, they weren't *his* mortals the way the others were, but they fell under his protection while they were here. He had sworn to protect humans, when he could. If he could.

He remembered Damon saying to him once, laughing in one of his fits of dangerous good humor, his face gleeful, "They're just so fragile, Stefan! You can break them without even meaning to!"

And Elena, his Elena. She was as vulnerable as the rest of them now. He flinched. If anything ever happened to her, Stefan knew beyond a doubt that he would take off the ring that let him walk in the day, lie down in the grass above her grave, and wait for the sun.

But the same hollow voice inside that questioned Elena's love for him whispered darkly in his ear: *She would not do the same for you. You are not her everything.*

As Elena and Meredith, with occasional interjections

from Matt and Bonnie, continued to argue about whether
Meredith needed the efforts of the group to guard her,
Stefan closed his eyes and slipped into his memories of
Damon's death.

*Stefan watched, foolish and uncomprehending and just not
fast enough, as Damon, quicker than him till the last, dashed
toward the huge tree and flung Bonnie, light as dandelion fluff,
out of the reach of the barbed branches already plummeting
toward her.*

*As he threw her, a branch caught Damon through his chest,
pinning him to the ground. Stefan saw the moment of shock in
his brother's eyes before they rolled backward. A single drop of
blood ran from his mouth down his chin.*

*"Damon, open your eyes!" Elena was screaming. There was
a rough tone in her voice, an agony Stefan had never heard
from her before. Her hands jerked at Damon's shoulders, as if
she wanted to shake him hard, and Stefan pulled her away. "He
can't, Elena, he can't," he said, half sobbing.*

*Couldn't she see that Damon was dying? The branch had
stopped his heart and the tree's poison was spreading through
his veins and arteries. He was gone. Stefan had gently lowered
Damon's head to the ground. He would let his brother go.*

But Elena wouldn't.

*Turning to take her in his arms and comfort her, Stefan saw
that she had forgotten him. Her eyes were closed and her lips*

were moving soundlessly. All her muscles were taut, straining toward Damon, and Stefan realized with a dull shock that she and Damon were connected still, that a last conversation was being carried on along some private frequency that excluded him.

Her face was wet with tears, and she suddenly fumbled for her knife and with one swift, sure movement, nicked her own jugular vein, starting blood flowing across her neck. "Drink, Damon," she said in a desperate, prayerlike voice, prying his mouth open with her hands and angling her neck above it.

The smell of Elena's blood was rich and tangy, making Stefan's canines itch with desire even in his horror at her carelessness in cutting her own throat. Damon did not drink. The blood ran out of his mouth and down his neck, soaking his shirt and pooling on his black leather jacket.

Elena sobbed and threw herself on top of Damon, kissing his cold lips, her eyes clenched shut. Stefan could tell she was still in communion with Damon's spirit, a telepathic exchange of love and secrets private between them, the two people he loved most. The only people he loved.

A cold tendril of envy, the feeling of being the outsider looking in, the one who was left all alone, curled along Stefan's spine even as tears of grief ran down his face.

A phone rang, and Stefan snapped back to the present.

Elena glanced at her cell and then answered, "Hi, Aunt Judith." She paused. "At the boardinghouse with everybody. We picked up Alaric and his friend from the train." Another pause and she grimaced. "I'm sorry, I forgot. Yes, I will. In just a few minutes, all right? Okay. Bye."

She hung up and got to her feet. "Apparently at some point I promised Aunt Judith I would be home for dinner tonight. Robert's getting out the fondue set and Margaret wants me to show her how to dip bread in cheese." She rolled her eyes, but Stefan wasn't fooled. He could see how delighted Elena was to have her baby sister idolizing her again.

Elena went on, frowning, "I'm not sure I'll be able to get out again tonight, but someone needs to be with Meredith at all times. Can you stay here tonight, Meredith, instead of at home?"

Meredith nodded slowly, her long legs drawn up under her on the couch. She looked tired and apprehensive, despite her earlier bravado. Elena touched her hand in farewell, and Meredith smiled at her. "I'm sure your minions will take good care of me, Queen Elena," she said lightly.

"I'd expect nothing less," Elena answered in the same tone, turning her smile on the rest of the room.

Stefan got to his feet. "I'll walk you home," he said.

Matt rose, too. "I can drive you," he offered, and Stefan was surprised to find that he had to suppress the urge to shove Matt back into his seat. *Stefan* would take care of Elena. She was *his* responsibility.

"No, stay here, both of you," Elena said firmly. "It's only a few blocks, and it's still broad daylight out. You look after Meredith."

Stefan settled back in his chair, eyeing Matt. With a wave, Elena was gone, and Stefan stretched out his senses to follow her as far as he could, pushing his Power to sense whether anything dangerous, anything at all, lurked nearby. His Powers weren't strong enough, though, to reach all the way to Elena's house. He curled his hands into tight, frustrated fists. He had been so much more powerful when he allowed himself to drink human blood.

Meredith was watching him, gray eyes sympathetic. "She'll be okay," she said. "You can't watch her all the time."

But I can try, thought Stefan.

When Elena strolled up her walk, Caleb was clipping the glossy green leaves of the flowering camellia bushes in front of the house.

"Hi," she said, surprised. "Have you been here all day?"

He stopped trimming and wiped the sweat off his forehead. With his blond hair and healthy tan, he looked like a California surfer transplanted to a Virginia lawn. Elena thought Caleb seemed just right on a perfect summer day like this one, a lawn mower humming in the distance somewhere, the sky blue and high above them.

"Sure," he said cheerfully. "Lots to do. It looks good, right?"

"It really does," she said. And it did. The grass was mowed, the hedges were perfectly trimmed, and he had set out some daisies in the flower beds near the house.

"What've you been up to today?" Caleb asked.

"Nothing as energetic as this," Elena said, suppressing the memory of the desperate race to save Celia. "My friends and I just picked someone up at the train station and hung out inside for the rest of the day. I hope the weather holds, though. We want to take a picnic up to Hot Springs tomorrow."

"Sounds like fun," Caleb said agreeably. Elena was tempted for a moment to invite him along. Despite Stefan's reservations, he seemed like a nice guy, and he probably didn't know many people in town. Maybe Bonnie would hit it off with him. He was pretty cute, after all. And Bonnie hadn't really been interested in anyone for a while. *Anyone other than Damon*, a secret little voice said in the back of her mind.

But of course she couldn't invite Caleb. What was she thinking? She and her friends couldn't have outsiders around while they talked about what supernatural entity had it in for them now.

A little pang of longing hit her. Would she ever be a girl

who could have a picnic and swim and flirt and be able to talk to anyone she liked, because she had no dark secrets to conceal?

"Aren't you exhausted?" she asked, quickly changing the subject.

She thought she saw a flicker of disappointment in his eyes. Had he realized she was thinking of inviting him along on the picnic and then changed her mind? But he answered readily enough. "Oh, your aunt ran me out a couple of glasses of lemonade, and I had a sandwich with your sister at lunchtime." He grinned. "She's a cutie. And an excellent conversationalist. She told me all about tigers."

"She talked to you?" Elena said with surprise. "She's usually really shy around new people. She wouldn't talk to my boyfriend, Stefan, until he'd been around for months."

"Oh, well," he said, and shrugged. "Once I showed her a couple of magic tricks, she was so fascinated she forgot to be shy. She's going to be a master magician by the time she starts first grade. She's a natural."

"Really?" said Elena. She felt a sharp shift in her stomach, a sense of loss. She had missed so much of her little sister's life. She'd noticed at breakfast that she looked and sounded older. It was like Margaret had grown into a different person without her. Elena gave herself a mental shake: She needed to stop being such a whiner. She was unbelievably lucky just to be here now.

"Oh, yeah," he said. "Look, I taught her this." He held out a tanned fist, turned it over, and opened his hand to reveal a camellia blossom, waxy and white, closed his hand, then opened it again to reveal a tightly furled bud.

"Wow," said Elena, intrigued. "Do it again."

She watched intently as he opened and closed his hand several times, revealing flower then bud, flower then bud.

"I showed Margaret how to do it with coins, switching between a quarter and a penny," he said, "but it's the same principle."

"I've seen tricks like that before," she said, "but I can't figure out where you're hiding the one that isn't showing. How do you do it?"

"Magic, of course," he said, smiling, and opened his hand to let the camellia blossom fall at Elena's feet.

"Do you believe in magic?" she said, looking up into his warm blue eyes. He was flirting with her, she knew—guys *always* flirted with Elena if she let them.

"Well, I ought to," he said softly. "I'm from New Orleans, you know, the home of voodoo."

"Voodoo?" she said, a cold shiver going down her spine.

Caleb laughed. "I'm just playing with you," he said. "*Voodoo*. Jeez, what a load of crap."

"Oh, right. Totally," Elena said, forcing a giggle.

"One time, though," Caleb continued, "back before my parents died, Tyler was visiting, and the two of us went to the French Quarter to get our fortunes told by this old *voudon* priestess."

"Your parents died?" Elena asked, surprised. Caleb lowered his head for a moment, and Elena reached out to touch him, her hand lingering on his. "Mine did, too," she said.

Caleb was very still. "I know," he said.

Their eyes met, and Elena winced in sympathy. There was such pain in Caleb's warm blue eyes when she looked for it, despite his easy smile.

"It was years ago," he said softly. "I still miss them sometimes, though, you know."

She squeezed his hand. "I know," she said quietly.

Then Caleb smiled and shook his head a little, and the moment between them was over. "This was before that, though," he said. "We were maybe twelve years old when Tyler visited." Caleb's slight Southern accent got stronger as he went on, his tone lazy and rich. "I didn't believe in that stuff back then, either, and I don't think Tyler did, but we thought it might be kind of fun. You know how it's fun to scare yourself a little sometimes." He paused. "It was pretty creepy, actually. She had all these black candles burning and weird charms everywhere, stuff made of bones and hair. She threw some powder on the floor around us and looked at the different patterns. She told Tyler she saw a big change coming for him and that he needed to think carefully before he put himself in someone else's power."

Elena flinched involuntarily. A big change had certainly come for Tyler, and he had put himself in the vampire Klaus's power. Wherever Tyler was now, things hadn't turned out the way he'd planned.

"And what did she tell you?" she asked.

"Nothing much, really," he answered. "Mostly just to be good. Stay out of trouble, look out for my family. That kind of thing. Stuff I try to do. My aunt and uncle need me here now, with Tyler missing." He looked down at her again, shrugged, and smiled. "Like I said, though, it was mostly just a load of crap. Magic and all that nutty stuff."

"Yeah," Elena said hollowly. "All that nutty stuff."

The sun went behind a cloud and Elena shivered once more. Caleb moved closer to her.

"Are you cold?" he said, and reached a hand out toward her shoulder.

At that moment a raucous caw burst from the trees by the house, and a big black crow flew toward them, low and fast. Caleb dropped his hand and ducked, covering his face, but the crow angled up at the last minute, flapping furiously, and soared away over their heads.

"Did you see that?" Caleb cried. "It almost hit us."

"I did," Elena answered, watching as the graceful winged silhouette disappeared into the sky. "I did."

10

Elder blossoms can be used for exorcism, protection, or prosperity, Bonnie read, lying flopped down on her bed, chin propped on her hands. *Mix with comfrey and coltsfoot and bind in red silk during a waxing moon to make a charm bag for attracting wealth. Distill in a bath with lavender, feverfew, and motherwort for personal protection. Burn with hyssop, white sage, and devil's shoestring to create a smoke that can be used in exorcising bad spirits.*

Devil's shoestring? Was that really an herb? Unlike most of the others, it didn't sound like something she'd find in her mother's garden. She sighed noisily and skipped ahead a little.

The best herbs for aiding meditation are agrimony, chamomile, damiana, eyebright, and ginseng. They may be tossed together and burned to create smoke or, when picked at dawn, dried and sprinkled around the subject in a circle.

Bonnie eyed the thick book balefully. Pages and pages and pages of herbs and what their properties were in different circumstances, and when to gather them, and how to use them. All written as dryly and dully as her high school geometry textbook.

She had always hated studying. The best thing about the summer between high school and college was that no one could expect her to spend any time tucked up with a heavy book, trying to memorize excessively boring facts. Yet here she was, doing just that, and she'd totally brought it on herself.

But when she had asked Mrs. Flowers to teach her magic, she had expected something, well, *cooler* than being handed a heavy book on herbs. Secretly, she had been hoping for one-on-one sessions that involved casting spells, or flying, or summoning fantastical servants to do her bidding. Less reading quietly to herself, anyway. Shouldn't there be some way that magical knowledge could just implant itself in her brain? Like, well, magically?

She flipped forward a few more pages. Ooh, this looked a bit more interesting.

An amulet filled with cinnamon, cowslip, and dandelion leaves will help in attracting love and fulfilling secret desires. Gather the herbs in a gentle rain and, after drying, bind them with red velvet and gold thread.

Bonnie giggled and kicked her feet against the mattress, thinking that she could probably come up with some secret desires to fulfill. Did she need to pick the cinnamon, or would it be okay to just get it out of the spice cupboard? She turned a few more pages. Herbs for clarity of sight, herbs for cleansing, herbs that had to be gathered under the full moon or on a sunny day in June. She sighed once more and closed the book.

It was past midnight. She listened, but the house was quiet. Her parents were sleeping.

Now that her sister Mary, who'd been the last of Bonnie's three older sisters to leave home, had moved in with her boyfriend, Bonnie missed having her right down the hall. But there were also advantages to not having her nosy, bossy big sister so close.

She climbed out of bed as quietly and cautiously as she could. Her parents weren't as sharp-eared as Mary, but they would come and check on her if they heard her getting up in the middle of the night.

Carefully, Bonnie pried up a floorboard under her bed. She had used it as her hiding place ever since she was a little girl. At first she had kept a doll she'd borrowed from Mary without permission; a secret candy stash bought with her allowance; her favorite red silk ribbon. Later, she'd hidden notes from her first boyfriend, or tests she'd failed.

Nothing as sinister as what was hidden there now, though.

She lifted out another book just as thick as the volume on herbs Mrs. Flowers had lent her. But this one was older-looking, with a dark leather cover wrinkled and softened by time. This book was from Mrs. Flowers's library, too, but Mrs. Flowers hadn't given it to her. Bonnie had snuck it off the shelf while Mrs. Flowers's back was turned, sliding it into her backpack and projecting her most innocent face when Mrs. Flowers's sharp eyes lingered on her afterward.

Bonnie felt a bit guilty tricking Mrs. Flowers like that, especially after the old woman agreed to mentor her. But, honestly, no one else would have *had* to sneak the book out in the first place. Any reason Meredith or Elena gave for wanting it would have immediately been accepted by everybody as right and true. They wouldn't even *have* to give a reason, just say that they needed the book. It was only Bonnie who would be sighed at and patted on the head—*sweet, silly Bonnie*—and stopped from doing what she wanted.

Bonnie stubbornly set her chin and traced the letters on the book's cover. *Traversing the Boundaries Between the Quick and the Dead*, they read.

Her heart was pounding as she opened the book to the page she'd marked earlier. But her hands were quite steady as she removed four candles, two white and two black, from beneath the floorboard.

She struck a match, lit one of the black candles, and tilted it to drip wax on the floor beside her bed. When there was a little pool of melted wax, Bonnie pressed the bottom of the candle into it, so that it stood upright on the floor.

"Fire in the North, protect me," she intoned. She reached for a white candle.

Plugged into its charger on the bedside table, her phone rang. Bonnie dropped the candle and swore.

Leaning over, she picked up the phone to see who was calling. *Elena*. Of course. Elena never realized how late it was when she wanted to talk to somebody.

Bonnie was tempted to press "ignore," but thought better of it. Maybe this was a sign that she shouldn't perform the ritual after all, at least not tonight. Maybe she should do some more research first to make sure she was doing it right. Bonnie blew out the black candle and pushed the button to answer her phone.

"Hey, Elena," she said, hoping her friend didn't sense her irritation as she placed the book gently back under the floorboard. "What's up?"

The ash was unbearably heavy. He strained against it, pushing at the blanket of gray holding him down. He clawed frantically, a panicked part of him wondering whether he was even going upward at all, whether he might not instead be digging himself farther under the surface.

One of his hands was clutched tightly around something—something fine and fibrous, like thin petals. He didn't know what it was, but he knew he shouldn't let go of it, and despite the fact that it hampered his struggle, he did not question this need to hold on.

It seemed as if he were clawing at the thick ash forever, but finally his other hand broke through the crumbling layers and relief flooded his body. He'd been going the right way; he wasn't going to be buried forever.

He reached out blindly, searching for something he could use to lever himself out. Ash and mud slid under his fingers, giving him nothing firm, and he floundered until he found what felt like a piece of wood in his grasp.

The edges of the wood bit into his fingers as he clung to it as though it were a lifeline in a stormy ocean. He gradually maneuvered his way up, slipping and sliding in the slick mud. With one last great effort, he wrenched his body out of the ash and mud, which gave a thick sucking noise as his shoulders emerged. He climbed to his knees, his muscles screaming in agony, then to his feet. He shuddered and shook, nauseated but euphoric, and wrapped his arms around his torso.

But he couldn't see anything. He panicked until he realized something was holding his eyes shut. He scrubbed at his face until he detached sticky clumps of ashy mud from his eyelashes. After a moment, he was finally able to open his eyes.

A desolate wasteland surrounded him. Blackened mud, puddles of water choked with ash. "Something terrible happened here," he said hoarsely, the sound startling him. It was so profoundly quiet.

It was freezing, and he realized he was naked, covered with only the same muddy ash that was everywhere. He hunched over and then, cursing himself for his momentary weakness, painfully straightened himself up.

He had to . . .

He . . .

He couldn't remember.

A drop of liquid ran down his face, and he wondered vaguely whether he was crying. Or was it the thick, shimmering fluid that was everywhere here, mixing with the ash and mud?

Who was he? He didn't know that, either, and that blankness triggered a trembling in him that was quite separate from the shivering caused by the cold.

His hand was still clenched protectively around the unknown object, and he raised his fist and stared at it. After a moment, he slowly uncurled his fingers.

Black fibers.

Then a drop of the opalescent fluid ran across his palm,

over the middle of the fibers. Where it touched, they transformed. It was hair. Silky blond and copper hair. Quite beautiful.

He closed his fist again and held them against his chest, a new determination building inside him.

He had to go.

Through the haze, a clear picture of his destination sprang into his mind. He shuffled forward through the ash and mud, toward the castlelike gatehouse with high spires and heavy black doors that he somehow knew would be there.

lena hung up the phone. She and Bonnie had discussed everything that was going on, from the mysterious appearance of Celia's and Meredith's names to Margaret's upcoming dance recital. But she hadn't been able to bring up what she had really called to talk about.

She sighed. After a moment, she felt under her mattress and pulled out her velvet-covered journal.

> *Dear Diary,*
> *This afternoon, I talked with Caleb Smallwood*
> *on the front lawn of my house. I barely know him,*
> *yet I feel this visceral connection with him. I love*
> *Bonnie and Meredith more than life itself, but they*
> *have no idea what it's like to lose your parents,*

and that puts a space between us.

I see myself in Caleb. He's so handsome and seems so carefree. I'm sure most people think his life is perfect. I know what it's like to pretend to have it together, even when you're coming apart. It can be the loneliest thing in the world. I hope he has a Bonnie or a Meredith of his own, a friend he can lean on.

The strangest thing happened while we were talking. A crow flew straight at us. It was a big crow, one of the biggest I've ever seen, with iridescent black feathers that shone in the sun and a huge hooked beak and claws. It might have been the same one that appeared on my windowsill yesterday morning, but I wasn't sure. Who can tell crows apart?

And, of course, both the crows reminded me of Damon, who watched me as a crow before we even met.

What's strange—ridiculous, really—is this dawning feeling of hope I have deep inside me. What if, I keep thinking, what if somehow Damon's not dead after all?

And then the hope collapses, because he is dead, and I need to face that. If I want to stay strong I can't lie to myself. I can't make up pretty fairy tales where the noble vampire doesn't die, where the rules get changed because it's someone I care about.

But that hope comes sneaking up on me again: What if?

It would be too cruel to say anything about the crow to Stefan. His grief has changed him. Sometimes, when he's quiet, I catch a strange look in his leaf green eyes, like there's someone I don't know in there. And I know he's thinking of Damon, thoughts that take him somewhere I can't follow anymore.

I thought I could tell Bonnie about the crow. She cared about Damon, and she wouldn't laugh at me for wondering whether there were some way he might still, in some form, be alive. Not after she suggested the very same thing earlier today. At the last minute, though, I couldn't talk to her about it.

I know why, and it's a lousy, selfish, stupid reason: I'm jealous of Bonnie. Because Damon saved her life.

Awful, right?

Here's the thing: For a long time, out of millions, there was one human Damon cared about. Only one. And that one person was me. Everyone else could go to hell as far as he was concerned. He could barely remember my friends' names.

But something changed between Damon and Bonnie, maybe when they were alone in the Dark Dimension together, maybe earlier. She's always had a little crush on him, when he wasn't being cruel, but then he started to take notice of his little redbird. He watched her. He was tender with her.

And when she was in danger, he moved to save her without a second thought as to what it might cost him.

So I'm jealous. Because Damon saved Bonnie's life.

I'm a terrible person. But, because I am so terrible, I don't want to share any more of Damon with Bonnie, not even my thoughts about the crow. I want to keep part of him just for me.

Elena reread what she had written, her lips pressed tightly together. She wasn't proud of her feelings, but she couldn't deny they existed.

She leaned back on her pillow. It had been a long, exhausting day, and now it was one o'clock in the morning. She'd said good night to Aunt Judith and Robert a couple of hours ago, but she didn't seem to be able to make it into bed. She'd just puttered around after changing into her nightdress: brushing her hair, rearranging some of her possessions, flipping through a magazine, looking with satisfaction at the fashionable wardrobe she hadn't had access to in months. Calling Bonnie.

Bonnie had sounded odd. Distracted, maybe. Or perhaps just tired. It was late, after all.

Elena was tired, too, but she didn't want to go to sleep. She finally admitted it to herself: She was a little afraid to go to sleep. Damon had been so real in her dream the other night. His body had felt firm and solid as she held him; his silky black hair had been soft against her cheek. His smooth voice had sounded sarcastic, seductive, and commanding by turns, just like the living Damon's. When she had remembered, with a sickening horror, that he was gone, it had been as if he had died all over again.

But she couldn't stay awake forever. She was so tired. Elena switched off the light and closed her eyes.

She was sitting on the creaky old bleachers in the school gym. The air smelled of sweaty athletic shoes and the polish they used on the wooden floor.

"This is where we met," said Damon, who she now realized was sitting beside her, so close the sleeve of his leather jacket brushed her arm.

"Romantic," Elena replied, raising one eyebrow and looking around the big empty room, the basketball hoops hanging at each end.

"I try," Damon said, a tinge of a laugh coloring his dry voice. "But *you* chose where we are. It's your dream."

"*Is* it a dream?" Elena asked suddenly, turning to study his face. "It doesn't feel like one."

"Well," he said, "let me put it this way. We're not actually *here*." His face was serious and intent as he gazed back at her, but then he flashed one of his sudden, brilliant smiles and his eyes slid away. "I'm glad we didn't have gymnasiums like this when I did my studies," he said casually, stretching out his legs in front of him. "It seems so undignified, with the shorts and the rubber balls."

"Stefan said that you played sports then, though," Elena said, distracted despite herself. Damon frowned at Stefan's name.

"Never mind," she said hastily. "We might not have much time. Please, Damon, please, you said you're not here, but are you *anywhere*? Are you all right? Even if you're dead . . . I mean really dead, dead for good, are you *somewhere*?"

He looked at her sharply. His mouth twisted a little as he said, "Does it matter that much to you, princess?"

"Of course it does," Elena said, shocked. Her eyes were filling with tears.

His tone was light, but his eyes, so black she couldn't tell where the iris ended and the pupil began, were watchful. "Everyone else—all your friends—this town—they're all okay, though, aren't they? You have your world back. There are such things as collateral damages you have to expect if you're going to get what you want."

Elena could tell from Damon's expression that what she said next would matter dreadfully. And, in her heart of hearts, hadn't she admitted to herself the other day that, as much as she loved Damon, things were better now, that everything could be good again with the town saved and her returned to her old life? And that she wanted it that way, even if it meant Damon was dead? That Damon was what he said: *collateral damage?*

"Oh, Damon," she said at last, helplessly. "I just miss you so much."

Damon's face softened and he reached for her. "Elena—"

"Yes?" Elena murmured.

"Elena?" A hand was gently shaking her. "Elena?" Someone stroked her hair, and Elena nuzzled sleepily into the touch.

"Damon?" she said, still half dreaming.

The hand paused in its stroking and then withdrew. She opened her eyes.

"Just me, I'm afraid," said Stefan. He was sitting next to her on her bed, his mouth a straight, tight line, his eyes averted.

"Oh, Stefan," said Elena, sitting up and throwing her

arms around him. "I didn't mean—"

"It's all right," Stefan said flatly, turning away from her. "I know what he meant to you."

Elena pulled him toward her and looked up into his face. "Stefan. *Stefan.*" His green eyes had a distant expression. "I'm sorry," she said pleadingly.

"You have nothing to apologize for, Elena," he said.

"Stefan, I was dreaming about Damon," she confessed. "You're right, Damon was important to me, and I . . . miss him." A muscle twitched at the side of Stefan's face, and she stroked his jaw. "I will never love anyone more than I love you, Stefan. It would be impossible. *Stefan*," she said, feeling like she might cry, "you're my true love, you know that." If only she could reach out and show him with her mind, *make* him understand what she felt for him. She'd never fully explored her other Powers, never fully claimed them, but losing their telepathic connection felt like it might kill her.

Stefan's expression softened. "Oh, Elena," he said slowly, and wrapped his arms around her. "I miss Damon, too." He buried his face in her hair and his next words were muffled. "I've spent hundreds of years fighting with my only brother, with us hating each other. We *killed* each other when we were human, and I don't think either of us ever got over the guilt and the shock, the horror of that moment." She felt a long shudder go through his body.

He sighed, a soft, sad sound. "And when we finally started to find our way back to being brothers again, it was all because of you." His forehead still resting on her shoulder, Stefan took Elena's hand and held it between both of his, turning it over and stroking it as he thought. "He died so suddenly. I guess I never expected . . . I never expected Damon to die before I did. He was always the strong one, the one who truly loved life. I feel . . ." He smiled a little, just a sad twist of his lips. "I feel . . . surprisingly lonely without him."

Elena entwined her fingers with Stefan's and held his hand tightly. He turned his face toward hers, meeting her eyes, and she pulled back a little so she could see him more clearly. There was pain in his eyes, and grief, but there was also a hardness she had never seen there before.

She kissed him, trying to erase that hard edge. He resisted her for half a second, and then he kissed her back.

"Oh, Elena," he said thickly, and kissed her again.

As the kiss deepened, Elena felt a sweet, satisfying sense of rightness sweep through her. It was always like this: If she felt distanced from Stefan, the touch of their lips could unite them. She felt a wave of love and wonder from him, and held on to it, feeding the emotion back to him, the tenderness between them growing. With her Powers gone, she needed this more than ever.

She reached out with her mind and emotions, past the

tenderness, past the rock-solid love that was always waiting for her in Stefan's kiss, and delved deeper into his mind. There was a fierce passion there, and she returned it, their emotions twining together, as their hands held each other harder.

Beneath the passion, there was grief, a terrible, endless grief, and farther still, buried in the depths of Stefan's emotions, was an aching loneliness, the loneliness of a man who had lived for centuries without companionship.

And in that loneliness was the taste of something unfamiliar. Something . . . unyielding and cold and faintly metallic, as if she had bitten into foil.

There was something Stefan was holding back from her. Elena was sure of it, and she reached deeper into his mind as their kisses intensified. She needed all of him. . . . She started to pull back her hair, to offer him her blood. That always brought them as close as they could possibly be.

But before he could accept her offer, there was a sudden knock on the door.

Almost immediately it opened and Aunt Judith peeked in. Elena, blinking, found herself alone, her palms stinging from the speed with which Stefan had pulled away from her. She looked around hastily, but he'd vanished.

"Breakfast is on the table, Elena," Aunt Judith said cheerfully.

"Uh-huh," Elena said, distracted, peering at the closet, wondering where Stefan had hidden himself.

"Are you all right, dear?" her aunt said, her forehead creased with concern. Elena had a sudden picture of how she must look: wide-eyed, flushed, and disheveled, sitting in her rumpled bed and looking wildly around the room. It had been a long time since Stefan had needed to use his vampiric speed for anything as mundane as not getting caught in her bedroom!

She gave Aunt Judith a reassuring smile. "Sorry, I'm still half-asleep. I'll be right down," she said. "I'd better hurry. Stefan will be here to pick me up soon."

As Aunt Judith left the room, Elena finally caught sight of Stefan, waving from the lawn below her open window, and she waved back, laughing, the strange emotions at the bottom of Stefan's mind put aside for the moment. He gestured that he was going around to the front of the house and that he would see her in a minute.

She laughed again and jumped up to get ready for the picnic at Hot Springs. It was nice to be the kind of girl who worried about getting grounded. It felt . . . pleasurably normal.

A few minutes later, as Elena, now dressed in shorts and a light blue T-shirt, her hair pulled back in a ponytail, headed down the stairs, the doorbell rang.

"That'll be Stefan," she called as Aunt Judith appeared

in the kitchen doorway. Elena grabbed her beach bag and picnic cooler from the bench in the hall.

"Elena!" Aunt Judith scolded. "You have to eat something before you go!"

"No time," Elena said, smiling at the familiarity of the argument. "I'll grab a muffin or something on the way." She and Aunt Judith had exchanged these words, or similar ones, most mornings of Elena's years in high school.

"Oh, Elena," Aunt Judith said, rolling her eyes. "Don't move, young lady. I'll be right back."

Elena opened the door and smiled up into Stefan's eyes. "Why, hello there, stranger," she said softly. He kissed her, a sweet touch of his lips on hers.

Aunt Judith hurried back into the hallway and pressed a granola bar into Elena's hand. "There," she said. "At least you'll have something in your stomach."

Elena gave her a quick hug. "Thank you, Aunt Judith," she said. "I'll see you later."

"Have fun, but please don't forget Margaret's dance recital tonight," Aunt Judith said. "She's so excited about it." Aunt Judith waved good-bye from the doorway as Elena and Stefan strolled toward the car.

"We're meeting the others at the boardinghouse and caravanning to Hot Springs," Stefan said. "Matt and Meredith are both bringing their cars."

"Oh, good, we won't be as crowded as we were yesterday.

Not that I minded sitting on your lap, but I thought I might squish Celia in the middle," Elena said. She turned her face up and stretched like a cat in the sunshine. A breeze tossed her ponytail, and she closed her eyes and enjoyed the sensation. "It's a gorgeous day for a picnic," she said. The world was alive with birdsong and with the rustle of trees. A faint tracery of white clouds underscored the bright blue of the sky. "Would it be jinxing ourselves to say it feels like the kind of day where nothing could go wrong?" she asked.

"Yes, it absolutely would be jinxing ourselves to say that," Stefan said, straight-faced, unlocking the passenger-side door for her.

"Then I won't say it," Elena said. "I won't even think it. But I feel good. I haven't been to Hot Springs for ages." She grinned with pure pleasure, and Stefan smiled back at her, but Elena was struck once again by that certain something new—something troubling—in his eyes.

12

"It's going to be a lovely day—perfect for a picnic," Meredith observed calmly.

Bonnie had tactfully but firmly steered Celia into Matt's car instead of Meredith's, and so Meredith was alone with Alaric—at last!—for the first time since he'd arrived. Half of her just wanted to pull off the road, grab Alaric, and kiss him and kiss him, she was so glad that he was finally here. All through the insanity of the last few months, she'd wished that he were there to fight by her side, to depend on.

But the other half of her wanted to pull off the road, grab Alaric, and demand that he explain to her exactly what his relationship was with Dr. Celia Connor.

Instead, here she was, driving placidly, hands at ten and two on the steering wheel, making small talk about the weather. She felt like a coward, and Meredith Suarez was no coward. But what could she say? What if she was just paranoid, and making a ridiculous fuss about a strictly professional relationship?

She glanced at Alaric out of the corner of her eye. "So . . ." she said. "Tell me more about your research in Japan."

Alaric ran his hands through his already tousled hair and grinned at her. "The trip was fascinating," he said. "Celia's so intelligent and experienced. She just puts together all these clues about a civilization. It was a real eye-opener for me to watch her decipher so much from the evidence in the graves there. I never knew much about forensic anthropology before, but she was able to reconstruct an amazing amount about the culture of Unmei no Shima."

"Sounds like she's simply amazing," Meredith said, hearing the acid in her tone.

Apparently Alaric didn't notice it. He smiled a little. "It took quite a while for her to take my paranormal research seriously," he said ruefully. "Parapsychology isn't particularly well regarded by the experts in other scientific disciplines. They think people like me who choose to spend their lives studying the supernatural are charlatans, or naive. Or a little crazy."

Meredith made herself speak pleasantly. "You were able to convince her at last, though? That's good."

"Sort of," Alaric answered. "We got to be friends, anyway, so she stopped thinking I was a complete fraud. I think she's found it all a lot more believable after the one day she's spent here, though." He gave a wry smile. "She tried to hide it, but she was blown away yesterday when Stefan saved her. The existence of a vampire makes it clear that there's a lot conventional science knows nothing about. I'm sure she'll want to examine Stefan if he'll let her."

"I would imagine so," said Meredith dryly, resisting the urge to ask Alaric why he thought Stefan would cooperate when he had seemed so displeased that Alaric had told Celia about him.

Alaric slid a hand across the car seat until he was close enough to run a finger gently along Meredith's arm. "I learned a lot while I was gone," he said earnestly, "but I'm really more concerned about what's going on right now in Fell's Church."

"You mean this dark magic that is supposedly rising here?" Meredith asked.

"I mean the dark magic that seems to be targeting you and Celia," Alaric said forcefully. "I'm not sure either of you is taking it seriously enough."

Me and *Celia*, thought Meredith. *He's just as worried about her as he is about me. Maybe more.*

"I know we've faced danger in the past, but I feel

responsible for Celia," Alaric went on. "I brought her here, and I'd never be able to forgive myself if something happened to her."

Definitely more, Meredith thought bitterly, and shrugged off Alaric's hand.

She instantly regretted the motion. What was the matter with her? This wasn't who she was. She'd always been the calm, rational one. Now here she was feeling like, well, like a jealous girlfriend.

"And now it's threatening you, too," Alaric went on. He tentatively touched her knee, and this time Meredith let his hand stay. "Meredith, I know how strong you are. But it's terrifying to me that this doesn't seem to be the kind of enemy we're used to. How can we fight what we can't even see?"

"All we can do is be vigilant," Meredith said. Her training had been comprehensive, but even she didn't understand this new evil. Yet she knew how to protect herself much better than Alaric realized. She glanced at him out of the corner of her eye. His window was open a crack, and the breeze ruffled his sandy hair. They knew each other so well, yet he still didn't know her biggest secret.

For a moment she considered telling him, but then he turned to her and said, "Celia's putting on a brave face, but I can tell she's scared. She's not as tough as you are."

Meredith stiffened. No, this wasn't the right time to tell

Alaric that she was a hunter-slayer. Not when she was driving. Not when she was this angry. Suddenly his hand felt heavy and clammy on her knee, but she knew she couldn't push it off again without betraying her feelings. Inside, though, she was raging at how the conversation kept coming back to Celia. Alaric had thought of her first. And even when he was talking about the danger to Meredith, he couched it in terms of what had happened to Celia.

Alaric's voice became a buzz in the background as Meredith clutched the steering wheel so tightly her knuckles whitened.

Really, why was she surprised that Alaric had feelings for Celia? Meredith wasn't blind. She could be objective. Celia was smart, accomplished, beautiful. Celia and Alaric were in the same place in their lives. Meredith hadn't even started college yet. She was attractive—she knew that—and certainly intelligent. But Celia was all that and more: She was Alaric's equal in a way Meredith couldn't be just yet. Sure, Meredith was a vampire hunter. But Alaric didn't know that. And when he did know, would he admire her strength? Or would he turn away from her, scared of her abilities, and toward someone more academic, like Celia?

A black bubble of misery filled Meredith's chest.

"I'm beginning to think I should take Celia away from here if I can get her to leave." Alaric sounded reluctant, but Meredith could hardly hear him. She felt as cold as if she were being enveloped in a fog. "Maybe I should get her back to Boston. I think you should leave Fell's Church, too, Meredith, if you can convince your family to let you go away for the rest of the summer. You could come with us, or maybe there's a relative you could stay with if your family wouldn't like that. I'm worried that you aren't safe here."

"Nothing's happened to me yet," said Meredith, surprised by the calm of her own voice, when such dark emotions were boiling inside her. "And I have a responsibility to be here and protect the town. If you think Celia will be safer away from here, do what you and she think is best. But you know there's no guarantee that whatever's threatening us won't follow her somewhere else. And at least here there are people who believe in the danger.

"Besides," she added thoughtfully, "the threat to Celia may be over. Maybe once the attack is averted, it moves on to someone else. My name didn't appear until after Stefan saved Celia. If so, then the danger is only to me."

Not that you care, she thought viciously, and was surprised at herself. Of course Alaric cared.

It was just that he seemed to care about what happened to Celia more.

Her fingernails cut into her palms around the steering wheel as she carefully followed Stefan's car off the road and toward the parking lot for Hot Springs.

"Stop!" Alaric shouted, panic in his voice, and Meredith automatically slammed on the brakes. The car squealed to a halt.

"What?" Meredith gasped. "What is it?"

And then she saw her.

Dr. Celia Connor had gotten out of Matt's car to cross to the path up to the springs. Meredith had come speeding right toward her. Only inches from Meredith's front bumper, Celia was frozen, her pretty face gray with fear, her mouth a perfect O.

One more second, and Meredith would have killed her.

13

"I'm so sorry. I'm *so* sorry," Meredith said for the tenth time. Her usually composed face was flushed, and her eyes were bright with unshed tears. Matt didn't remember ever seeing her so upset about something, especially something that had ended up not being a big deal. Sure, Celia *could* have been hurt, but the car hadn't touched her.

"I'm fine, really I am, Meredith," Celia assured her again.

"I just didn't see you. I don't know how, but I didn't. Thank God for Alaric," Meredith said, throwing a grateful glance at Alaric, who was sitting close beside her and rubbing her back.

"It's okay, Meredith," he said. "It's all okay." Alaric seemed more concerned for Meredith than for Celia, and

Matt didn't blame him. Babbling was pretty out of character for Meredith. Alaric wrapped his arms tightly around Meredith, and she visibly relaxed.

Celia, on the other hand, tensed noticeably as Meredith leaned into Alaric's embrace. Matt traded a rueful glance with Bonnie.

Then Stefan reached out and stroked Elena's shoulder absently, and Matt was surprised to feel a jealous pang of his own. Wasn't he ever going to get over Elena Gilbert? It had been more than a year since they dated, and about a century in experience.

Bonnie was still watching him, now with a speculative gleam in her eyes, and Matt shot her a bland smile. He'd just as soon not know what Bonnie saw in his face when he looked at Elena and Stefan.

"Around this bend and up the slope is the Plunge," he said to Celia, ushering her forward along the trail. "It's a little bit of a hike, but it's the best place around here for a picnic."

"Abso*lute*ly the best," said Bonnie cheerily. "We can jump down the waterfall." She fell in on Celia's other side, helping him to herd her away from the two couples, who were murmuring to one another softly as they followed behind.

"Is that safe?" asked Celia dubiously.

"Totally," said Bonnie. "Everybody jumps the waterfall

here, and nobody's ever gotten hurt."

"Usually it's safe," said Matt, more cautiously. "You and Meredith might want to think about not swimming, Celia."

"I hate this," Bonnie said. "I hate having to be extra-careful because of some dark thing that we don't know anything about. Everything should be *normal*."

Normal or not, it was a magnificent picnic. They spread their blankets on the rocks near the top of the waterfall. The small falls plummeted down the side of the cliff and ended in a deep pool of effervescent water, making a sort of natural fountain that spilled into a clear bronze-green pool.

Mrs. Flowers had packed salads and breads and desserts for them, as well as meat and corn to grill on a hibachi Stefan had brought from the boardinghouse. They had more than enough food for a couple days of camping, let alone one lunch. Elena had stowed cold drinks in a cooler, and, after hiking up the trail in the Virginia summer heat, everyone was happy to crack open a lemonade or soda.

Even Stefan took a water bottle and drank as he started heating the grill, although it was automatically understood by everyone that he would not be eating. Matt had always found the fact that he never saw Stefan eating a little creepy, even before Matt knew he was a vampire.

The girls squirmed out of jeans and tops to display their bathing suits, like caterpillars transforming into butterflies. Meredith was tan and lean in a black one-piece.

Bonnie was wearing a petite mermaid-green bikini. Elena wore a soft gold bandeau that went with her hair. Matt watched Stefan watching her appreciatively, and felt that little twist of jealousy again.

Both Elena and Bonnie pulled their T-shirts back on over their bathing suits almost immediately. They always did: Their pale skin burned instead of tanned. Celia lounged on a towel, looking spectacular in a casual yet daringly cut white swimsuit. The effect of the pure white against Celia's coffee-colored skin was amazing. Matt noticed Meredith's eyes passing over her and then glancing sharply at Alaric.

But Alaric was too busy shucking down to a pair of red trunks. Stefan stayed out of the direct sunlight, remaining in his dark jeans and black T-shirt.

Wasn't that a little creepy, too? Matt thought. Stefan's ring protected him from the sun's rays, didn't it? Did he still have to stick to the shadows? And what was with the black clothing? Was he pretending to be Damon now? Matt frowned at the thought: One Damon had been more than enough.

Matt shook his head, stretched his arms and legs, turned his face toward the sun, and tried to get rid of his thoughts. He liked Stefan. He always had. Stefan was a good guy. *A vampire*, a dry voice in the back of his mind noted, *even a harmless one, can rarely be described as a good guy.*

Matt ignored the voice.

"Let's jump!" he said, and headed toward the waterfall.

"Not Meredith," said Stefan flatly. "Not Meredith, and not Celia. You two stay here."

There was a little silence, and he glanced up from the grill to see his friends staring at him. He kept his face neutral as he returned their gazes. This was a life-or-death situation. It was Stefan's responsibility now to keep them safe, whether they liked it or not. He looked at them each in turn, holding their eyes. He was not going to back down.

Meredith had risen to her feet to follow Matt to the falls' edge, and she hesitated for a moment, clearly unsure how to react. Then her face hardened, and Stefan saw that she had chosen to take a stand.

She stepped toward him. "I'm sorry, Stefan," she said, her voice level. "I know you're worried, but I'm going to do what *I* decide I want to do. I can look after myself."

She moved to join Matt, who was standing at the edge of the cliff, but Stefan's hand whipped out to grab her wrist, his fingers as strong as steel. "No, Meredith," he said firmly.

Out of the corner of his eye, he saw Bonnie's mouth drop open. Everyone was looking at him with puzzled, anxious faces, and Stefan tried to soften his tone. "I'm just trying to do what's best for you."

Meredith sighed, a long, gusty sound, and seemed to be making an effort to let go of some of her anger. "I know that, Stefan," she said reasonably, "and I appreciate it. But I can't go through the world not doing the things I usually do, just waiting for whatever this is to come get me."

She tried to move around him, but he sidestepped to block her way again.

Meredith glanced at Celia, who threw up her hands and shook her head. "Don't look at me," Celia said. "*I* have no urge to jump off a cliff. I'm just going to lie in the sunshine and let you all work this out yourselves." She leaned back on her hands and turned her face toward the sun.

Meredith's eyes narrowed and she whirled back to Stefan. As she was opening her mouth, Elena broke in.

"What if the rest of us go first?" she suggested placatingly to Stefan. "We can make sure there's nothing clearly dangerous down there. And we'll be near her at the bottom. Nobody's ever been hurt jumping here, not that I've heard of. Right, guys?" Matt and Bonnie nodded in agreement.

Stefan felt himself softening. Whenever Elena used her logical voice and her wide, appealing eyes, he found himself agreeing to plans that, in his heart of hearts, he thought were foolhardy.

Elena pressed her advantage. "You could stand right by the water below, too," she said. "Then, if there's any problem, you could dive in right away. You're so fast, you'd get there before anything bad could happen."

Stefan *knew* this was wrong. He hadn't forgotten that sick swoop of despair, of realizing he was *too slow* to save someone. Once again, he saw Damon's long, graceful leap toward Bonnie that had ended with Damon falling to earth, a wooden branch driven through his heart. Damon had died because Stefan was too slow to save him, too slow to realize the danger and save Bonnie himself.

He'd also been too late to save Elena when she had driven off the bridge and drowned. The fact that she now lived again didn't mean he hadn't failed her then. He remembered her pale hair floating like seaweed in the chilly water of Wickery Creek, her hands still resting on the steering wheel, her eyes closed, and shuddered. He had dived repeatedly before he found her. She had been so cold and white when he carried her to shore.

Still, he found himself nodding. What Elena wanted, Elena got. He would stand by and protect Meredith as best as he could, and he prayed, as far as a vampire could pray, that it would be enough.

The rest of the friends stayed at the top while, down at the bottom of the falls, Stefan surveyed the pool at his feet. The water sprayed up exuberantly from where the falls hit the surface. Warm, pale sand encircled the pool's edges, making a tiny beach, and the center of the pool seemed dark and deep.

Matt jumped first, with a long, wavering whoop as he plummeted. The splash as he hit the water was huge, and he seemed to stay submerged for a long time. Stefan leaned forward to watch the water. He couldn't see through the foam thrown up by the falls, and an anxious quiver shot through his stomach.

He was just thinking of diving in after him when Matt's sleek wet head broke the surface. "I touched the bottom!" he announced, grinning, and shook his head like a dog, throwing glittering drops of water everywhere.

He swam toward Stefan, strong tan limbs moving powerfully, and Stefan thought how easy everything seemed for Matt. He was a creature of sunlight and simplicity, while Stefan was stuck in the shadows, living a long half-life of secrets and loneliness. Sure, his sapphire ring let him walk in the sun, but being exposed to the sunlight for a long time, like today, was uncomfortable, as if there were some kind of itch deep inside him. It was worse now that he was readjusting to a diet of animal blood again. His unease was yet another reminder that he didn't really belong here. Not the way Matt did.

He shrugged off his sour feelings, surprised at their emergence in the first place. Matt was a good friend. He always had been. The daylight must be getting to him.

Bonnie jumped next, and surfaced more quickly, coughing and snorting. "Oof!" she said. "I got water up my nose! Ugh!" She pulled herself out of the water and perched on a rock near Stefan's feet. "You don't swim?" she asked him.

Stefan was struck with a flash of memory. Damon, tanned and strong, splashing him and laughing in one of his rare fits of good humor. It was hundreds of years ago now. Back when the Salvatore brothers had lived in the sunlight, back before even the great-grandparents of his friends had been born. "Not for a long time," he answered.

Elena jumped with the same casual grace as she did everything else, straight as an arrow toward the bottom of the falls, her gold bathing suit and her golden hair gleaming in the sunshine. She was underwater for longer than Bonnie had been, and again Stefan tensed, watching the pool. When she broke the surface, she gave them a rueful grin. "I couldn't quite reach the bottom," she said. "I was stretching and stretching down. I could see the sand, but the water pushed me back up."

"I didn't even try," Bonnie said. "I've accepted that I'm too short."

Elena swam away from the bottom of the falls and climbed onto the sand, settling next to Bonnie at Stefan's feet. Matt climbed out of the water, too, and stood near the falls, gazing up critically. "Just jump feetfirst, Meredith," he called teasingly. "You're such a show-off."

Meredith was poised at the edge of the falls. She saluted

them and then leaped into a perfect swan dive, arching swiftly toward the pool, disappearing smoothly beneath the water with barely a splash.

"She was on the swim team," Bonnie said conversationally to Stefan. "She has a row of ribbons and trophies on a shelf at home."

Stefan nodded absently, his eyes scanning the water. Surely Meredith's head would break the surface in a second. The others had taken about this long to reemerge.

"Can I jump yet?" Alaric called from above.

"No!" Elena shouted. She rose to her feet and she and Stefan exchanged a worried glance. Meredith had been down there too long.

Meredith surfaced, sputtering and pushing her wet hair out of her eyes. Stefan relaxed.

"I did it!" she called. "I—"

Her eyes widened and she began to shriek, but her scream was cut off as she was abruptly yanked under the water by something they couldn't see. In the space of a breath, she was gone.

For a moment, Stefan just stared at where Meredith had been, unable to move. *Too slow, too slow,* an internal voice taunted him, and he pictured Damon's face, laughing cruelly and saying again, *So fragile, Stefan.* He couldn't see Meredith anywhere under the clear, effervescent water. It

was as if she had been taken suddenly away. All of this
flew through Stefan's head in only a heartbeat, and then he
dived into the water after her.

Underwater, he couldn't see anything. The white water
from the falls bubbled up, throwing foam and golden sand
in front of him.

Stefan urgently channeled his Power to his eyes, sharpening his vision, but mostly that just meant that now he
could see the individual bubbles of the white water and
the grains of sand in sharp relief. Where was Meredith?

The bubbling water was trying to push him up to the
surface, too. He had to struggle to move forward through
the murky water, reaching out. Something brushed his
fingers and he grabbed at it, but it was only a handful of
slippery pondweed.

Where was she? Time was running out. Humans could
go without oxygen for only a few minutes before brain
damage set in. A few minutes after that, there would be no
recovery at all.

He remembered Elena's drowning once more, the frail
white shape that he had pulled from Matt's wrecked car,
ice crystals in her hair. The water here was warm, but
would kill Meredith just as surely. He swallowed a sob and
reached out frantically again into the shadowed depths.

His fingers found skin, and it moved against his hand.

Stefan grasped whatever limb it was, tight enough to
bruise, and surged forward. In less than a second more, he

could see that it was Meredith's arm. She was conscious, her mouth tight with fear, her hair streaming around her in the water.

At first he couldn't see why she hadn't come to the surface. Then Meredith gestured emphatically, reaching to fumble at long tendrils of pondweed that had somehow become entangled with her legs.

Stefan swam down, pushing against the white water from the falls, and tried to work his hand under the pond-weed to pull it off her. It was wrapped so tightly around Meredith's legs that he couldn't get his fingers beneath it. Her skin was pressed white by the strands.

Stefan struggled for a moment, then swam closer and let Power surge into him, sharpening and lengthening his canines. He bit, careful not to scratch Meredith's legs, and pulled at the pondweed, but it resisted him.

A little late, he realized that the resilience of the plants must be supernatural: His Power-enhanced strength was enough to break bones, tear through metal, and should have had no problem with a bit of pondweed.

And finally—so *slow*, he reprimanded himself, always just so damn slow—he realized what he was looking at. Stefan felt his eyes widen in horror.

The tight strands of pondweed against Meredith's long legs spelled out a name.

damon

14

here were they? Elena watched the water anxiously. If anything had happened to Meredith or Stefan, it was Elena's fault. *She* had convinced Stefan to let Meredith jump the falls.

His objections had been totally reasonable; she could see that now. Meredith had been marked for death. For God's sake, Celia had almost been killed simply getting off a train. What had Meredith been thinking, jumping off a cliff into water when she was in the same sort of peril? What had *Elena* been thinking of to let her? She should have been by Stefan's side, holding Meredith back.

And *Stefan*. She knew he ought to be fine; the rational part of her brain kept reminding her that Stefan was a *vampire*. He didn't even need to breathe. He could stay underwater for days. He was incredibly strong.

But not so long ago, she had thought Stefan was gone forever, stolen by the kitsune. Bad things *could* happen to him—vampire or not. If she lost him now through her own stupid fault, through her own stubbornness and insistence that everyone pretend that life could be the way it used to be—that they could have some simple fun without doom following them—Elena would lie down and die.

"Do you see anything?" Bonnie asked, a tremble in her voice. Her freckles stood out in dark dots against her pale face, and her normally exuberant red curls were plastered flat and dark against her head.

"No. Not from up here." Elena shot her a grim look, and before she even consciously made the decision, she dived into the pool.

Underwater, Elena's vision was clouded by the froth and sand thrown up by the falls, and she treaded water for a moment as she tried to peer around. She saw a patch of darkness that looked like it might be human figures off near the middle of the pool and struck out toward it.

Thank God, Elena thought fervently. When she got closer, the darkness resolved itself into Meredith and Stefan. They seemed to be struggling against something in the water, Stefan's face near Meredith's legs, Meredith's hands reaching desperately toward the surface. Her face was bluish from lack of oxygen, and her eyes were wide with panic.

Just as Elena came close to them, Stefan jerked sharply and Meredith shot upward. As if in slow motion, Elena saw Meredith's arm swing toward her as Meredith rose. A sudden blow sent Elena shooting backward toward the rocks behind the falls, the falls pushing her deeper underwater as she passed under them.

This is bad, she had just enough time to think, and then her head hit the rocks and everything went black.

When Elena awoke, she found herself in her room at home, still in her bathing suit. Sun shone through the window, but Elena was wet and shivering with cold. Water trickled from her hair and bathing suit, droplets winding down her arms and legs and puddling on the carpet.

She was unsurprised to see that Damon was there, looking as sleek and dark and poised as ever. He'd been perusing her bookshelf, as comfortable as if he were in his own home, and he wheeled around to stare at her.

"Damon," she said weakly, confused but, as always, so happy to see him.

"Elena!" he said, appearing delighted for a moment, and then he frowned.

"No," he said sharply. "Elena, *wake up*."

"Elena, wake up." The voice was frightened and desperate, and Elena fought the darkness that seemed to be holding her down and opened her eyes.

Damon? she almost said, but bit the word back. Because of course it was Stefan who was gazing worriedly into her eyes, and even sweet, understanding Stefan might object to her calling him by his dead brother's name twice in one day.

"Stefan," she said, remembering. "Is Meredith all right?"

Stefan wrapped her tightly in his arms. "She will be. Oh, God, Elena," he said. "I thought I was going to lose you. I had to pull you to shore. I didn't know . . ." His voice trailed off, and he hugged her even closer to his chest.

Elena did a quick self-inventory. She was sore. Her throat and lungs hurt, probably from breathing in water and coughing it out. There was sand all over her, coating her arms and bathing suit, and it was starting to itch. But she was alive.

"Oh, Stefan," Elena said, and closed her eyes for a moment, resting her head against him. She was so cold and wet, and Stefan was so warm. She could hear his heart beating beneath her ear. Slower than a human's, but there, steady and reassuring.

When she opened her eyes again, Matt was kneeling next to them. "Are you okay?" he asked her. When she nodded, he turned his gaze to Stefan. "I should have jumped in," he said guiltily. "I should have helped you save them. Everything seemed to happen so fast, and by the time I knew something was really wrong, you were bringing them back out of the water."

She sat up and touched Matt's arm, feeling a warm flood of affection for him. He was so *good*, and he felt so responsible for all of them. "Everyone's fine, Matt," she said. "That's what matters."

A few feet away, Alaric was inspecting Meredith as Bonnie hovered over them. Celia stood a little farther away, her arms wrapped around herself as she watched Alaric and Meredith.

When Alaric shifted away, Meredith caught Elena's eye. Her face was white with pain, but she managed to give her an apologetic smile.

"I didn't mean to hit you," she said. "And Stefan, I should have listened to you, or just had more sense and stayed on shore." She grimaced. "I think I might have sprained my ankle. Alaric's going to drive me to the hospital so they can tape it up."

"What I want to know," Bonnie said, "is whether this means it's all over. I mean, Celia's name appeared, and she was almost strangled in the train doors. And Meredith's name appeared, and she almost drowned. They both got saved—by Stefan, good job, Stefan—so does that mean they're safe now? We haven't seen any more names."

Elena's heart lightened with hope. But Matt was shaking his head.

"It's not that easy," he said darkly. "It's never that easy. Just because Meredith and Celia could be saved one time, it doesn't mean whatever it is isn't still after them. And even though her name wasn't called, Elena was in danger, too."

Stefan's arms were still around Elena, but they felt hard and unyielding. When she glanced up at his face, his jaw was set and his green eyes full of pain.

"I'm afraid it's not the end. Another name has appeared," he told them. "Meredith, I don't think you could have seen it, but the plants you were tangled in spelled it out against your legs." Everyone gasped. Elena clutched his arm, her stomach dropping. She looked at Matt, at Bonnie, at Stefan himself. They'd never seemed more precious to her. Which one of the people who she loved was in danger?

"Well, don't keep us in suspense," Meredith said wryly. Her color was better, Elena noted, and her voice sounded crisp and competent again, although she winced as Alaric touched her ankle gently. "Whose name was it?"

Stefan hesitated. His eyes darted to Elena and then quickly away. He licked his lips in a nervous gesture she'd never seen from him before. Taking a deep breath, he finally said, "The name the plants spelled out was Damon."

Bonnie sat down with a thump, as though her legs had given way. "But Damon's dead," she said, her brown eyes wide.

But for some reason the news didn't shock Elena to the core. Instead, a hard, bright feeling of hope flooded her. It would make sense. She had never believed someone like Damon could just be *gone*.

"Maybe he's not," she heard herself say, lost in thought as she recalled the Damon in her dreams. When she had passed out under the water, she had seen him again, and he had told her to wake up. Was that dreamlike behavior? It could have been her subconscious warning her, she supposed doubtfully, but his *name* had appeared underwater.

Could he be alive? He had died—she had no doubt about that. But he was a vampire; he had died before, and lived again. The Guardians had tried, they said, and they had said there was no way to bring Damon back. Was it a pointless hope? Was the eager beating of her heart at the thought that Damon might be alive just Elena fooling herself?

Elena snapped back to the present to find her friends staring at her. There was a moment of complete silence, as if even the birds had stopped singing.

"Elena," Stefan said gently. "We saw him die."

Elena gazed into Stefan's green eyes. Surely, if there was any reason to hope, he would feel it the same way she did. But his gaze was steady and sad. Stefan, she saw, had no doubt that Damon was dead. Her heart squeezed painfully.

"Who's Damon?" Celia asked, but no one answered.

Alaric was frowning. "If Damon's definitely dead," he said, "if you're sure about that, then whatever is causing these accidents might be playing on your grief, trying to hit you where it hurts. Perhaps there's an emotional danger here that it's trying to create as well as a physical one."

"If spelling out Damon's name is meant to upset us, then it's aiming at Stefan and Elena," Matt said. "I mean, it's no secret that Meredith and I didn't like him much." He crossed his arms defensively. "I'm sorry, Stefan, but it's true."

"I respected Damon," said Meredith, "especially after he worked so hard with us in the Dark Dimension, but it's true that his death didn't . . . affect me the way it did Elena and Stefan. I have to agree with Matt."

Elena glanced at Bonnie and noticed that her jaw was clenched and her eyes glistened with angry tears.

As Elena watched, Bonnie's bright eyes dulled and lost focus, gazing off into the distance. She stiffened and turned her face up toward the top of the cliff.

"She's having a vision," Elena said, jumping to her feet.

Bonnie spoke in a voice flatter and rougher than her own. "He wants you, Elena," she said. "He wants you."

Elena followed her gaze toward the cliff. For a wild moment, that hard, bright hope came bursting back into her chest again. She fully expected to see Damon up there, smirking down at them. It would be just like him, if he'd somehow survived death, to show up suddenly, make a grand entrance, and then pass off the miracle with a shrug and a dry quip.

And there *was* someone standing at the top of the cliff. Celia gave a little scream, and Matt swore loudly.

It wasn't Damon, though. Elena could tell that right away. The silhouetted figure was broader than Damon's lithe form. But the sun was so bright she couldn't make out the person's features, and she lifted her hand to shade her eyes.

Like a halo, blond curly hair gleamed in the sunlight. Elena frowned.

"I think," she said, recognition dawning on her, "that's Caleb Smallwood."

s soon as Elena spoke Caleb's name, the person on the cliff began to pull back out of their line of sight. After a moment of hesitation, Matt took off running pell-mell up the path toward where they'd seen him.

It should have been silly, Elena thought, the way they all reacted as if they'd been threatened. Anyone had a right to hike the trails at Hot Springs, and Caleb—if it was Caleb—hadn't *done* anything but peer down over the edge of the cliff at them. But nevertheless, there had been something ominous about the figure hovering so watchfully above them, and their reaction didn't *feel* silly.

Bonnie gasped and her body relaxed as she came out of the trance.

"What happened?" she asked. "Oh, gosh, not *again*."

"Do you remember anything?" Elena said.

Bonnie shook her head mournfully.

"You said, 'He wants you, Elena,'" said Celia, examining Bonnie with a clinically enthusiastic glint in her eye. "You don't remember who you were talking about?"

"I guess if he wanted Elena, it could have been *anyone*," Bonnie said, her eyes narrowing. Elena stared at her. Had there been an uncharacteristic catty edge to Bonnie's tone? But Bonnie grinned ruefully back at her, and Elena decided the comment had just been a joke.

A few minutes later, Matt came back down the path, shaking his head.

"Whoever it was just vanished," he said, his forehead crinkled in confusion. "I couldn't see anyone on the trail in either direction."

"Do you think he's a werewolf, like Tyler was?" Bonnie asked.

"You're not the first person who's asked me that," Elena said, glancing at Stefan. "I just don't know. I don't think so, though. Caleb seems totally nice and normal. Remember how wolfy Tyler was even before he became a werewolf? Those big white teeth and his sort of animalness? Caleb's not like that."

"Then why would he spy on us?"

"I don't know," Elena said again, frustrated. She couldn't think about this now. Her mind was still swimming with the question: Could Damon be alive? What did Caleb matter, compared to that? "Maybe he was just hiking. I'm not even sure it was Caleb. It could have been some other guy with curly blond hair instead. Just a random hiker who got scared off when Matt went charging up the hill toward him."

Their discussion went in circles until eventually Alaric took Meredith off to the hospital to have a doctor check out her ankle. The rest of them adjourned to the top of the falls to gather up the picnic stuff.

They all nibbled at the chips and brownies and fruit, and Matt made himself a hot dog on the hibachi grill, but the joy had gone out of the day.

When Elena's phone rang, it was a welcome relief. "Hey, Aunt Judith," she said, forcing a cheerful note into her voice.

"Hi," Aunt Judith said hurriedly. "Listen, I have to go to the auditorium to help do all the girls' hair and makeup, and Robert already will have to leave work early to get to the recital on time. Would you do me a favor and pick up some flowers for Margaret on your way over? Something sweet and ballerinaish, if you know what I mean."

"No problem," Elena said. "I know exactly what you mean. I'll see you there." She wanted to forget for a while: forget mystery hikers and near-drownings and her constant alternating feelings of hope and despair about the appearance of Damon's name. Watching her little sister twirl around in a tutu sounded just about right.

"Terrific," said Aunt Judith. "Thank you. Well, if you are all the way up at Hot Springs, you'd better start heading home soon."

"Okay, Aunt Judith," Elena said. "I'll get going now."

They said good-bye, and Elena hung up and started gathering her things together. "Stefan, can I take your car?" she asked. "I need to get to Margaret's dance recital. You can give him a ride back, right, Matt? I'll call you guys later and we'll work on figuring this out."

Stefan got to his feet. "I'll come with you."

"What?" said Elena. "No, you need to stay with Celia and get to the hospital to take care of Meredith, too."

Stefan took her arm. "Don't go, then. You shouldn't be alone now. None of us are safe. There's something out there hunting us, and we need to all stick together. If we don't let each other out of our sight, then we can all protect one another."

His leaf green eyes were clear and full of anxiety and love, and Elena felt a pang of regret as she tugged her arm gently out of his grasp. "I need to go," she said quietly. "If I spend all my time being scared and hiding, then the Guardians might as well have let me stay dead. I need to be with my family and live as normal a life as I can."

She kissed him gently, lingering for a moment against

the softness of his lips. "And you know they haven't targeted me yet," she said. "Nothing's spelled out my name. But I promise I'll be careful."

Stefan's eyes were hard. "What about what Bonnie said?" he argued. "That he wants you? What if that means Caleb? He's hanging around at your house, Elena! He could come after you at any time!"

"Well, I'm not going to be there. I'll be at a dance recital with my family beside me," Elena pointed out. "Nothing will happen to me today. It's not my turn yet, is it?"

"Elena, don't be stupid!" Stefan snapped. "You're in danger."

Elena bristled. *Stupid?* Stefan, no matter how stressed or anxious, had never treated her with less than total respect. "Excuse me?"

Stefan reached for her. "Elena," he said. "Let me come with you. I'll stay with you until nightfall and then keep watch outside your house tonight."

"It's really not necessary," Elena said. "Protect Meredith and Celia instead. They're the ones who need you." Stefan's face fell, and he looked so devastated that she relented a little, adding, "Please don't worry, Stefan. I'll be careful, and I'll see you all tomorrow."

His jaw clenched, but he said nothing more, and she turned to make her way down the trail, not looking back.

* * *

Once they were back at the boardinghouse, Stefan couldn't relax.

He couldn't remember ever, in all his long life, feeling so edgy and uncomfortable in his own body. He itched and ached with anxiety. It was as if his skin were fitted too tightly over his bones, and he moved irritably, tapping his fingers against the table, cracking his neck, shrugging his shoulders, shifting back and forth in his chair.

He wants you, Elena. What the hell did that mean? *He wants you.*

And the sight of that dark, hulking figure up on the cliff, a shadow blotting out the sun, those golden curls shining like a halo above the figure's head . . .

Stefan knew he should be with Elena. All he wanted to do was to protect her.

But she had *dismissed* him, had—metaphorically, at least—patted him on the head and told him to stay, faithful guard dog that he was, and watch over someone else. To keep someone else safe. No matter that she was clearly in danger, that someone—some *he*—wanted her. Still she didn't want Stefan to be with her right now.

What *did* Elena want? Now that Stefan stopped to think about it, it seemed that Elena wanted a host of incompatible things. To have Stefan as her loyal knight. Which he would always, always be, he asserted to himself, clenching his fist tightly.

But she also wanted to hold on to the memories of Damon, and to keep that part of her she had shared with him private and pristine, separate from everyone else, even from Stefan.

And she wanted so much more, too: to be the savior of her friends, of her town, of her world. To be loved and admired. To be in control.

And to be a normal girl again. Well, that normal life she had lived had been destroyed forever when she met Stefan, when he made the choice to let her into his world. He knew it was his fault, all of it, everything that followed after that, but he couldn't be sorry that she was with him now. He loved her too much to have any room for regret. She was the center of his world, but at the same time, he knew it wasn't the same for her.

A hole inside him gaped with longing, and he moved restlessly in his chair. His canine teeth lengthened in his mouth. He couldn't remember the last time he had felt so . . . wrong. He couldn't get the image of Caleb out of his head, looking down at them from the top of the cliff, as if checking to see whether whatever violence he'd hoped to cause had come to pass.

"More tea, Stefan?" Mrs. Flowers asked him softly, breaking into his furious thoughts. She was leaning forward over a little table with the teapot, her wide blue eyes watching him from behind her glasses. Her face was so compassionate that he wondered what she could see in him. This elderly, wise woman always seemed to perceive so much more than anyone else; perhaps she could tell how he was feeling now.

He realized she was still waiting politely for his answer, the teapot suspended in one hand, and he nodded automatically. "Thank you, Mrs. Flowers," he said, offering forth his cup, which was still half-full of cold tea.

He didn't really like the taste of normal human drinks; he hadn't for a long time now, but sometimes drinking them made him fit in, made the others relax a bit more around him. When he didn't eat or drink at all, he could sense Elena's friends prickling, the hairs on the back of their necks rising, as some subconscious voice in them noted that he was not like them, adding it to all the other little differences he couldn't control, and thereby concluding he was *wrong*.

Mrs. Flowers filled his cup and sat back, satisfied. Picking up her knitting—something pink and fluffy—she smiled. "It's so nice to have all you young people gathered together here," she commented. "Such a lovely group of children."

Glancing at the others, Stefan had to wonder whether Mrs. Flowers was being gently sarcastic.

Alaric and Meredith had returned from the hospital, where her injury had been diagnosed as a mild sprain and taped up by the emergency room nurse. Meredith's usually serene face was tight, probably at least partially because of the pain and her irritation at knowing she'd have to stay off her foot for a couple of days.

And partially, Stefan suspected, because of where she was sitting. For some reason, when Alaric had helped her hobble into the living room and over to the couch, he had parked her directly next to Celia.

Stefan didn't consider himself an expert on romance—after all, he'd lived for hundreds of years and fallen in love only twice, and his romance with Katherine had been a disaster—but even he couldn't miss the tension between Meredith and Celia. He wasn't sure whether Alaric was as oblivious to it as he seemed or whether he was pretending obliviousness in the hope that the situation would blow over.

Celia had changed into an elegant white sundress and sat flipping through a journal titled *Forensic Anthropology*, looking cool and composed. Meredith was, in contrast, unusually grimy and smudged, her beautiful features and smooth olive skin marred by tiredness and pain. Alaric had taken a chair next to the couch.

Celia, ignoring Meredith, leaned across her toward Alaric.

"I think you might find this interesting," she said to him. "It's an article on the dental patterns in mummified bodies found on an island quite near Unmei no Shima."

Meredith shot Celia a nasty look. "Oh, yes," she said quietly. "Teeth, how fascinating." Celia's mouth flattened into a line, but she didn't reply.

Alaric took the magazine with a polite murmur of interest, and Meredith frowned.

Stefan frowned, too. All the tension humming between Meredith, Celia, and Alaric—and now that he was watching, he could tell that Alaric knew exactly what was going on between the two young women and was flattered, irritated, and anxious in equal parts—was interfering with Stefan's Powers.

While he'd sat and sipped his first cup of tea, reluctantly following Elena's command to "stay," Stefan had been sending out tendrils of Power, trying to sense whether Elena had made it home, whether anything had stopped her on her way. Whether Caleb had stopped her.

But he hadn't been able to find her, even with his senses extended to their utmost. Once or twice, he'd caught what felt like a fleeting impression of what might be the very specific sound, scent, and aura that unmistakably meant *Elena*, but then it slipped away from him.

He'd blamed the fact that he couldn't locate her on his weakening Powers, but now it was clear to him what was keeping him from finding her. All the emotion in this room: the pounding hearts, the flushes of anger, the acrid scent of jealousy.

Stefan pulled himself back, tried to quell the rage rising within him. These people—his *friends*, he reminded
himself—were not purposely interfering. They couldn't
help their emotions. He took a swig of his rapidly cooling
tea, trying to relax before he lost control, and winced at
the taste. Tea wasn't what he was craving, he realized. He
needed to get out to the forest soon and hunt. He needed
blood.

No, he needed to find out exactly what Caleb Smallwood
was up to. He stood up so abruptly, so violently, the chair
rocked unsteadily beneath him.

"Stefan?" Matt asked in an alarmed voice.

"What is it?" Bonnie's eyes were enormous.

Stefan glanced around the circle of distracted faces,
now all watching him. "I have to go." Then he turned on
his heels and ran.

16

e walked for a long, long time, though it seemed his surroundings never changed. The same dim light filtered through a constant cloud of ash. He plodded on through grime, through mud, through ankle-deep pools of dark water.

Occasionally, he unclenched his fist and gazed again at the locks of hair. Each time, the magic liquid cleaned them a little more, changing a scrap of fibrous blackness to two locks of shining hair, red and gold.

He walked on.

Everything hurt, but he couldn't stop. If he stopped he would sink back below the ash and mud, back to the grave—back to death.

Something whispered around the edges of his mind. He didn't know quite what had happened to him, but words and phrases spun in his head.

Words like *abandoned*, words like *alone*.

He was very cold. He kept walking. After a while, he realized he was mumbling. "Left me all alone. They'd never have left *him* here." He couldn't remember who this *him* was, but he felt a sick sort of satisfaction from the glow of resentment. He held on to it as he continued his march.

After what felt like an unchanging eternity, something happened. Ahead of him he could see the gatehouse he had imagined: spired like a fairy-tale castle, black as night.

He walked faster, his footsteps shuffling through the ash. And then the earth opened suddenly beneath his feet. In the space of a heartbeat, he was falling into nothingness. Something inside him howled, *Not now, not now*. He grabbed and clawed at the earth, his arms holding him afloat, his feet swinging into the emptiness below him.

"No," he moaned. "No, they can't . . . Don't leave me here. Don't leave me again." His fingers slipped, mud and ash sliding beneath his hands.

"*Damon?*" an incredulous voice roared. A great muscular figure stood above him, silhouetted against the moons and planets in the sky, his chest bared, long, spiraling tangles of hair spilling over his shoulders. This statue of a man reached down and grasped him by the arms, lifting him up.

He yelped in pain. Something beneath the earth had latched onto his legs and was pulling him back down.

"Hold on!" The other man grunted, muscles rippling. He strained and *heaved* against whatever was clinging onto Damon—*Damon*, the man had called him, and that felt right, somehow. The other man gave a great tug, and finally the force below released him, and he shot out of the earth, knocking his rescuer backward.

Damon lay panting on the ground, spent.

"You are supposed to be dead," the other man told him, climbing to his feet and holding out a hand to steady Damon. He pushed a long lock of hair away from his face and gazed at Damon with serious, troubled eyes. "The fact that you are not . . . well, I am not as surprised as I should be."

Damon blinked at his savior, who was watching him attentively. He wet his lips and tried to speak, but his voice wouldn't come.

"Everything has been disturbed here since your friends left," the man said. "Something essential has shifted in this universe. Things are not right." He shook his head, his eyes troubled. "But tell me, *mon cher*, how does it come to be that you are here?"

Finally Damon found his voice. It came out rough and quavering. "I . . . don't know."

The man immediately was all courtesy. "I think the situation calls for some Black Magic, *oui*? And some blood, perhaps, and a chance to clean up. And then, Damon, we must talk."

He gestured toward the dark castle ahead of them. Damon hesitated for a moment, glancing at the emptiness and ash around them, then trudged after him toward the open doors.

After Stefan swept out of the room so suddenly, everyone could only stare after him as the front door banged, signaling that he had left the house just as quickly. Bonnie hugged her arms around herself, shivering. A little voice in the back of her head told her that something was very, very wrong.

Celia finally broke the silence. "Interesting," she said. "Is he always so . . . intense? Or is it a vampire thing?"

Alaric chuckled dryly. "Believe it or not, he's always seemed very low-key and practical to me. I don't remember him being so volatile." He ran a hand through his sandy hair and added thoughtfully, "Maybe it was the contrast with his brother that made him seem so reasonable. Damon was pretty unpredictable."

Meredith frowned thoughtfully. "No, you're right. This isn't the way Stefan usually acts. Maybe he's emotional because Elena's threatened? But that doesn't make sense . . . she's been in danger before. Even when she *died*—he was heartbroken, but, if anything, it made him more responsible, not wilder."

"But when Elena was dead," Alaric reminded her, "the

worst thing he could imagine had already happened. It's possible that what's making him so jumpy is that he doesn't know where the threat's coming from this time."

Bonnie took a sip of tea, zoning out as Meredith *hmmm*ed thoughtfully, and Celia raised one skeptical eyebrow. "I still don't understand what you mean when you say Elena *died*. Are you suggesting she actually rose from the dead?"

"Yes," said Meredith. "She was turned into a vampire, then she was exposed to sunlight and physically died. They buried her and everything. Later—months later— she returned. She's human again, though."

"I find all that very hard to believe," said Celia flatly.

"Honestly, Celia," said Alaric, throwing up his hands in exasperation. "With everything you've seen since we got here—your scarf nearly choking you, then spelling out a name, Bonnie having a vision, Stefan practically flying to save you—I don't know why you're drawing the line now and saying you don't believe a girl could come back from the dead." He paused and took a breath. "I don't mean to sound harsh, but really."

Meredith smirked. "Believe it or not, it's true. Elena came back from the dead."

Bonnie wrapped one long red curl around her finger. She watched as her finger turned white and red against the strand of hair. Elena. Of course they were talking about

Elena. Everyone was always talking about Elena. Whether she was with them or not, everything they did or thought centered on Elena.

Alaric turned to address the whole group. "Stefan seems convinced that 'he wants you' means Caleb, but I'm not sure that it does. From what I've seen of Bonnie's visions, and what you guys have told me, they're hardly ever about what's right in front of her. Caleb's appearance—if it even *was* Caleb—could have been a coincidence. Don't you think so, Meredith?"

Oh, don't bother to ask me about the visions, Bonnie thought bitterly. *I'm only the one who has them.* Wasn't that the way it always was, though? She was the one everyone overlooked.

"It *could* be a coincidence," Meredith said doubtfully. "But if it's not Caleb she was talking about, who is it? Who wants Elena?"

Bonnie glanced under her eyelashes at Matt, but he was staring out the window, apparently completely detached from the conversation. She could tell that Matt still loved Elena, even if no one else knew. It was too bad: Matt was awfully cute. He could date anyone, but it was taking him a long time to get over her.

But then, no one ever seemed to get over Elena. Half the boys at Robert E. Lee High School had gone around gazing wistfully after her, as if she might suddenly turn around and fall into their arms. Certainly most of the boys Elena had dated had stayed a little bit in love with her, even after Elena had more or less forgotten their names.

It isn't fair, Bonnie thought, twirling her hair more tightly around her finger. Everyone always wanted Elena, and Bonnie had never even had a boyfriend for more than a few weeks at a time. What was wrong with *her?* People always told her how cute she was, how adorable, how fun . . . and then they looked past her to Elena, and it was like they couldn't see Bonnie anymore.

And while Damon, amazing, sexy Damon, had been *fond* of her, sometimes, when she wasn't trying to kid herself, she knew he hadn't really seen her, either.

I'm just the sidekick, that's my problem, Bonnie thought glumly. Elena was the star; Meredith was a hero; Bonnie was a sidekick.

Celia cleared her throat. "I have to confess I'm intrigued by the appearance of the names," she said stiffly. "It does seem like they point to some kind of threat. Whether or not Bonnie's purported vision comes to anything"—Bonnie shot her best nasty look at Celia, but Celia ignored it—"we should definitely investigate any background or context we can find for the unexplained appearance of the names. We should find out if there's a recorded history of this kind of thing happening before. The writing on the wall, if you will." She gave a thin-lipped smile at her own joke.

"But what would we investigate?" Bonnie said, finding herself unwillingly responding to Celia's teacherlike manner. "I wouldn't even know where to start looking for something like this. A book on curses, maybe? Or omens? Do you have anything like that in your library, Mrs. Flowers?"

Mrs. Flowers shook her head. "I'm afraid not, dear. My library, as you know, is mostly herbals. I have a few more specialized books, but I can't recall anything that might be helpful with this problem."

When she mentioned "more specialized books," Bonnie's cheeks got hot. She thought of the grimoire on communication with the dead, still tucked under the floorboards in her bedroom, and hoped Mrs. Flowers hadn't noticed it was missing.

After a few seconds, her cheeks had cooled enough that she dared to glance around, but only Meredith was looking at her, one elegant eyebrow raised. If Meredith thought something was up, she wouldn't rest until she got the whole story from Bonnie, so Bonnie gave her a bland smile and crossed her fingers behind her back for luck. Meredith raised her other eyebrow and looked at her with deep suspicion.

"Actually," Celia said, "I have a contact at the University of Virginia who studies folklore and mythology.

She specializes in witchcraft, folk magic, curses, all that kind of thing."

"Do you think we could call her?" said Alaric hopefully.

Celia frowned. "I think it would be better if I went up there for a few days. Her library isn't as well organized as it could be—I suppose it's symptomatic of the kind of mind that studies stories rather than facts—and it might take a while to discover if there's anything useful there. I think it would be just as well for me to get out of town for a while, anyway. After two brushes with death in two days"—she sent a pointed glance toward Meredith, who blushed—"I'm beginning to feel that Fell's Church isn't the healthiest place for me." She looked at Alaric. "You might find her library of interest, if you'd like to come with me. Dr. Beltram is one of the best-known experts in her field."

"Uh . . ." Alaric looked startled. "Thanks, but I'd better stay here and help Meredith. With her sprained ankle and everything."

"Mmm-hmmm." Celia glanced at Meredith again. Meredith, who had been looking steadily more delighted every second since Celia had announced she was leaving, ignored her and smiled at Alaric. "Well, I suppose I should give her a call and get my things together. No time like the present."

Celia stood up, smoothed her sundress, and walked out

the door, head high. As she passed, she brushed against the table near Mrs. Flowers's chair, sending her knitting to the floor.

Bonnie let out a breath as Celia left the room. "Well, really!" she said indignantly.

"Bonnie," said Matt warningly.

"I *know*," said Bonnie angrily. "She could have at least said 'excuse me,' right? And what was that with asking Alaric to come with her to UVA? He just got here, practically. He hasn't seen you for months. Of course he's not going to leave again with her right now."

"*Bonnie*," said Meredith, in a strangely choked voice.

"What?" said Bonnie, catching the oddness in her tone and looking around. "Oh. *Oh.* Oh, no."

Mrs. Flowers's knitting had fallen from its table, and the skein of yarn had rolled across the floor, unwinding as it went. Now, in the curls of soft pale pink, they could all clearly read one word written across the carpet:

bonnie

nce he got outside, Stefan remembered that Elena had taken his car. Turning into the woods, he began to run, using his Power to speed his pace. The pounding of his feet seemed to thud, *Guard her, Guard her.*

He knew where Tyler Smallwood had lived. After Tyler had attacked Elena at a dance, it had made sense to keep an eye on him. Stefan burst from the woods at the edge of the Smallwoods' property.

They owned an ugly house, in Stefan's opinion. An inaccurate portrayal of an old Southern manor estate, it was too big for the lawn it sat on and bulged with unnecessary columns and twisting rococo decorations. Just looking at it, Stefan had been able to tell that the Smallwoods had more money than taste, and that the architects who'd designed it weren't educated in true classical forms.

He rang the bell at the front door, then froze. What if Mr. or Mrs. Smallwood answered the bell? He would have to Influence them to give him as much information as they could about Caleb, and then to forget Stefan had been there. He hoped he had the Power to do it: He hadn't been eating enough, not even of animal blood.

But no one came. After a few seconds, Stefan sent questing tendrils of Power through the house. It was empty. He couldn't go in, couldn't search Caleb's room like he wanted to. Without an invitation, he was stuck out here.

He wandered around the house, peering through the windows, but finding nothing out of the ordinary other than entirely too many gilded frames and mirrors.

Behind the house he found a small white shed. Sending Power toward it, he felt something slightly . . . off. Just the slightest tinge of darkness, a feeling of frustration and ill intent.

The shed was padlocked, but the lock was easy enough to snap. And as no one lived here, he didn't need an invitation to enter.

The first thing he saw was Elena's face. Newspaper clippings and photos were tacked all over the walls: Elena, Bonnie, Meredith, himself. On the floor was a pentagram with more pictures and roses.

Stefan's certainty that something was wrong solidified. Elena was in danger. Sending Power before him, searching desperately for any trace of her, he took off running again.

* * *

As she drove away from the florist's, Elena turned the conversation with Stefan over and over in her mind.

What was going on with him since they'd come back to Fell's Church? It felt like there was part of him that he was holding back, hiding from her. She remembered the loneliness, the sinking, dizzy feeling of isolation that she had sensed when she kissed him. Was it Damon's loss that was changing Stefan?

Damon. Just the thought of him was enough to cause an almost physical pain in her. Mercurial, difficult, beautiful Damon. Dangerous. Loving, in his own way. The thought of his name, written in water plants across Meredith's legs, floated through her mind.

She didn't know what it meant. But there was no hope. She needed to stop lying to herself about that. She had seen Damon die. Yet it seemed impossible that someone as complex and strong and seemingly undefeatable as Damon could be gone so quickly and so simply. But that was the way it happened, wasn't it? She should know that death didn't often come with a grand show, that it usually came when you were least expecting it. She had known that before all this . . . all this *stuff* with vampires and werewolves and evil mysterious opponents. She had known all about the suddenness and simplicity of death for years, back when she was just normal Elena Gilbert, who didn't believe in anything supernatural, not even horoscopes or fortune-telling, much less monsters.

She glanced at the passenger seat next to her, where there lay the bouquet of pink roses she had picked up to give to Margaret. And, next to them, a simple bunch of forget-me-nots. *Like I'd ever forget*, she thought.

Elena remembered riding in the car toward home with her parents and baby Margaret on an ordinary Sunday afternoon. It had been a beautiful sunny fall day, the leaves of the trees by the roadside just beginning to be painted with red and gold.

They'd gone to lunch at a little inn out in the country. Margaret, who was teething, had been cranky at the restaurant, and they'd taken turns walking her up and down on the porch of the inn for a few minutes at a time while the others ate. But in the car she was quiet, half drowsing, her light golden lashes fluttering down to rest for longer and longer periods against her cheeks.

Elena's father had been driving, she remembered, and the radio had been tuned to the local station so he could catch the news. Her mother had twisted to look at Elena in the backseat, her sapphire blue eyes so like Elena's own. Her golden hair, touched with a little gray, was pulled back in a French braid, elegant and practical. Smiling, she had said, "Do you know what I think would be nice?"

"What?" asked Elena, smiling back at her. Then she saw a strange glitter, high in the sky, and leaned forward without waiting for a reply. "Daddy, what's that?" She'd pointed upward.

Elena never found out what her mother had thought would be nice. Her father never answered what *that* was.

The last things Elena remembered were sounds: her father's gasp and the screech of the car's tires. Everything after that was blank, until Elena had woken up in the hospital, Aunt Judith by her bedside, and learned that her parents were dead. They had died before the paramedics had even pried them out of the car.

Before they restored Fell's Church, the Guardians had told Elena that she should have died in that accident, and that her parents should have lived. The glitter had been their air car, and Elena had distracted her father at the worst possible moment, causing all the wrong people to die.

She could feel the weight of it now, the guilt at surviving, her anger at the Guardians. She glanced at the dashboard clock. There was still plenty of time before she had to be at Margaret's recital. Turning off the highway, she pulled into the cemetery's parking lot.

Elena parked the car and walked briskly through the newer part of the cemetery, carrying the forget-me-nots. Birds were chirping gaily overhead. So much had happened in this cemetery in the last year. Bonnie had seen one of her first visions among these tombstones. Stefan had followed her here, watching her secretly when she thought he was just the gorgeous new guy at school. Damon had nearly drained an old tramp under the bridge. Katherine had chased Elena out of the cemetery with fog and ice and a far-reaching, far-seeing evil. And, of course, Elena had driven off a bridge to her death here by the cemetery, at the end of that first life, the one that seemed so long ago now.

Elena picked her way past an ornate marble memorial to Fell's Church's Civil War veterans and down to the shady glen where her parents were buried. The tiny wildflower bouquet she and Stefan had left two days before had withered, and Elena threw it away and put the forget-me-nots in its place. She picked a bit of moss off her father's name.

The lightest crunch of gravel sounded from the path behind her, and Elena whirled around. There was no one there.

"I'm just jumpy," she muttered to herself. Her voice sounded oddly loud in the quiet of the cemetery. "Nothing to worry about," she said more firmly.

She settled in the grass by her parents' graves and traced the letters on her mother's headstone with one hand.

"Hi," she said. "It's been a while since I've actually sat here and talked to you, I know. I'm sorry. An awful lot has happened. . . ." She swallowed. "I'm sorry, too, because I found out that you weren't supposed to die when you did. I asked the Guardians to . . . to bring you back, but they said you had moved on to a better place and they couldn't reverse that. I wish . . . I'm glad you're happy wherever you are, but I still miss you."

Elena sighed, lowered her hand from the gravestone, and trailed it through the grass by her knees. "Something's after me again," she continued unhappily. "After all of us, I guess, but Bonnie said *I* brought it here when she was in a trance. And later she said he wants me. I don't know if it's two different people—or whatever—after us, or just one. But it's always me the bad things focus on." She twisted a blade of grass between her fingers. "I wish things could be simpler for me, the way they are for other girls.

"Sometimes . . . I'm so glad to have Stefan, and glad I could help protect Fell's Church, but . . . it's hard. It's really hard." A sob was building in her throat and she swallowed it back. "And . . . Stefan's always been there for me, but I feel like I don't know all of him anymore, especially because I can't read his thoughts. He's so tense, and it's like he needs to be in control all the time. . . ."

Something shifted behind her, just the slightest hint of movement. She felt a warm, damp breeze like a breath on the back of her neck.

Elena whipped her head around. Caleb was crouching behind her, so close they were almost nose-to-nose. She screamed, but Caleb slapped his hand over her mouth, muffling her cry.

aleb's hand was hot and heavy against her lips, and Elena scrabbled against it with her nails. He gripped her tightly with his other hand, holding her still, his fingers digging into her shoulder.

Elena struggled fiercely, flailing her arms and landing a firm blow in Caleb's stomach. She bit down hard on the hand he had over her mouth. Caleb jerked backward, quickly letting go of her and pulling his bitten hand to his chest. As soon as her mouth was uncovered, Elena screamed.

Caleb stepped away from her, holding his hands up in surrender. "Elena!" he said. "Elena, I'm so sorry. I didn't mean to scare you. I just didn't want you to scream."

Elena eyed him warily, breathing hard. "What are you doing here?" she asked. "Why were you sneaking up behind me if you didn't want to scare me?"

Caleb shrugged and looked a little embarrassed. "I was worried about you," he confessed, stuffing his hands in his pockets and hanging his head. "I was hiking up by Hot Springs earlier and I saw you and your friends. They were pulling you out of the water, and it looked like you weren't breathing." He peeked up at her through his long golden lashes.

"You were so worried about me you decided to grab me and cover my mouth to keep me from screaming?" Elena asked. Caleb ducked his head further and scrubbed at the back of his neck in an embarrassed way.

"I wasn't thinking." Caleb nodded solemnly. "You looked so pale," he said. "But you opened your eyes and sat up. I was going to come down and see if you were okay, but your friend saw me and started running up the path toward me like he was going to jump me, and I guess I just freaked out." He grinned suddenly. "I'm not usually such a wuss," he said. "But he looked *mad*."

Elena found herself feeling unexpectedly disarmed. Her shoulder still ached where Caleb had grabbed her. But he seemed so sincere, and so apologetic.

"Anyway," Caleb continued, gazing at her out of candid light blue eyes, "I was driving back to my aunt and uncle's place, and I recognized your car in the cemetery parking lot. I just came in because I wanted to talk to you and make sure you were okay. And then, when I got close to you, you were sitting down and talking, and I guess I was embarrassed. I didn't want to interrupt you, and I didn't want to barge in on something personal, so I just waited." He ducked his head sheepishly again. "And instead I ended up assaulting you and scaring you to death, which sure wasn't the better way to go. I'm really sorry, Elena."

Elena's heartbeat was returning to normal. Whatever Caleb's intentions, he obviously wasn't going to attack her again now. "It's all right," she said. "I hit my head on an underwater rock. I'm fine now, though. It must have looked pretty weird to see me just sitting here and muttering. Sometimes I come here to talk to my parents, that's all. This is where they're buried."

"It's not weird," he said quietly. "I find myself talking to my parents sometimes, too. When something happens and I wish they were with me, I start telling them about it and it makes me feel like they're there." He swallowed hard. "It's been a few years, but you never stop missing them, do you?"

The last bits of anger and fear drained out of Elena when she saw the sadness in Caleb's face. "Oh, Caleb," she said, reaching out to touch his arm.

She caught a sudden motion out of the corner of her eye and then, seemingly out of nowhere, Stefan appeared, running incredibly fast, straight toward them.

"Caleb," he growled, grabbing him by the shirt and throwing him to the ground. Caleb let out a grunt of surprise and pain.

"Stefan, no!" shouted Elena.

Stefan spun to look at her. His eyes were hard and his fangs were fully extended. "He's not what he says he is, Elena," he said in an eerily calm voice. "He's dangerous."

Caleb slowly pulled himself to his feet, using a gravestone as a support. He was staring at Stefan's fangs. "What's going on?" he asked. "What *are* you?"

Stefan turned toward him and, almost casually, slapped him back down.

"Stefan, stop it!" Elena yelled, unable to contain the note of hysteria in her voice. She reached out for his arm, but missed. "You're going to hurt him!"

"He *wants* you, Elena," Stefan growled. "Do you understand that? You can't trust him."

"Stefan," Elena pleaded. "Listen to me. He wasn't doing anything wrong. You *know* that. He's a human." She could feel hot tears gathering in her eyes and she blinked them away. Now was not the time to weep and wail. Now was the time to be cool and rational and to keep Stefan from losing control.

Caleb staggered to his feet, grimacing with pain, and this time charged clumsily at Stefan, his face flushed. He got one arm around Stefan's neck and yanked him to the side, but then Stefan, with an easy strength, tossed Caleb to the ground once more.

Stefan loomed over him threateningly as he stared up at him from the grass. "You can't fight me," Stefan growled. "I'm stronger than you. I can drive you out of this town, or kill you just as easily. And I will do either if you make me think it's necessary. I won't hesitate."

Elena grabbed Stefan's arm. "Stop it! Stop it!" she shouted. She pulled him toward her, trying to turn him so she could look into his eyes, so she could get through to him.

Breathe, she thought desperately. She had to calm things down here, and she tried to steady her voice, to sound logical. "Stefan, I don't know what you think is going on with Caleb, but just stop for a minute and think."

"Elena, look at me," Stefan said. His eyes were dark with emotion. "I *know*, I'm absolutely sure, that Caleb is evil. He's dangerous to us. We have to get rid of him before he gets a chance to destroy us. We can't give him the opportunity to get the better of us by waiting for him to make his move."

"Stefan . . ." Elena said. Her voice was shaking, and an oddly rational, detached part of her noted that this must be what it felt like when the person you loved most lost his mind.

She didn't know what she was going to say next, but before she could even open her mouth, Caleb had risen again. There was a long scratch down the side of his face, and his blond hair was tangled and full of dirt.

"Back off," Caleb said grimly, coming toward Stefan. He was limping a little bit, and clutched a fist-size rock in his right hand. "You can't just . . ." He raised the rock threateningly.

"Stop it, both of you," Elena yelled, trying for a fierce general's voice that would command their attention.

But Caleb just hoisted the rock and threw it straight at Stefan's face.

Stefan dodged the rock, moving almost too quickly for Elena to see, grabbed Caleb by the waist, and, in one graceful motion, flung him into the air. For a moment, Caleb was suspended, seemingly as light and boneless as a scarecrow tossed from the back of a pickup truck, and then he hit the side of the marble Civil War monument with a sickening crunch. With a thud, he fell to the ground at the foot of the statue and was still.

"Caleb!" Elena screamed in horror. She ran toward him, shoving her way between the bushes and clumps of grass that encircled the monument.

His eyes were closed and his face was pale. Elena could see the light blue veins in his eyelids. There was a spreading pool of blood on the ground beneath his head. A streak of dirt ran across his face, and that dirt and the long red scratch on his cheek suddenly seemed like some of the most heartbreaking things she had ever seen. He wasn't moving. She couldn't tell whether he was breathing.

Elena dropped to her knees and felt for Caleb's pulse, fumbling at his neck. As she found the steady thrum of a heartbeat beneath her fingers, she gasped in relief.

"Elena." Stefan had followed her to Caleb's side. He put his hand on her shoulder. "Please, Elena."

Elena shook her head, refusing to look at him, and shrugged his hand away. She felt in her pocket for her phone. "My god, Stefan," she said, her words clipped and tight, "you could have killed him. You have to get out of here. I can tell the police I found him like this, but if they see you, they're going to know you two were fighting." She swallowed hard as she realized the streak of dirt staining Caleb's shirt was Stefan's handprint.

"Elena," Stefan pleaded. At the anguish in his tone, she finally turned toward him. "Elena, you don't understand. I had to stop him. He was a threat to you." Stefan's leaf green eyes beseeched her, and Elena had to steel herself to keep from crying.

"You have to leave," she said. "Go home. I'll talk to you later." *Don't hurt anyone else*, she thought, and bit her lip.

Stefan stared at her for a long moment, then finally backed away. "I love you, Elena." He turned and disappeared into the trees, through the older and wilder part of the cemetery.

Elena took a steadying breath, wiped her eyes, and dialed 911. "There's been an accident," she said, her voice panicky, when the operator picked up. "I'm in the Fell's Church Cemetery off Route Twenty-three, over by the Civil War monument near the edge of the newer section. I've found someone. . . . It looks like he was knocked unconscious somehow. . . ."

19

"Honestly, Elena," Aunt Judith said, shaking her head as she adjusted the car's rearview mirror. "I don't know why these kinds of things always seem to happen to you, but you find yourself in the strangest situations."

"Tell me about it," Elena said, slumping down in the passenger seat of her aunt's car and resting her head in her hands. "Thank you for picking me up, Aunt Judith. I just felt too shaky to drive after being at the hospital with Caleb and everything." She swallowed. "I'm sorry I missed Margaret's dance recital after all."

Aunt Judith patted Elena's knee with one cool hand without taking her eyes off the road. "I told Margaret that Caleb got hurt and you had to take care of him. She understood. Right now I'm worried about you. It must have been a shock to find him like that, especially when you realized it was someone you knew. What exactly happened?"

Elena shrugged and repeated the lie she'd told the police. "I just found him lying there when I went to visit Mom and Dad." Elena cleared her throat before continuing. "The hospital's keeping him for a couple of days. They think he's got a bad concussion and they want to watch and make sure his brain doesn't swell. He woke up a little bit in the ambulance but was really groggy and didn't remember what had happened." Which was lucky, Elena thought. What if he'd said he was attacked by Elena Gilbert's boyfriend, who had something weird going on with his teeth? What if he'd said her boyfriend was a monster? It would be last fall all over again.

Aunt Judith frowned sympathetically and shook her head. "Well, Caleb's lucky you came along. He could have been lying there for days before anyone went looking for him."

"Yeah, lucky," said Elena hollowly. She rolled the bottom of her T-shirt between her fingers and was startled to realize she still had her bathing suit on under her clothes. The picnic that afternoon seemed like it had taken place a million years ago.

Then something Aunt Judith said struck her. "What do you mean, he could have been lying there for days before anyone looked for him? What about his aunt and uncle?"

"I tried calling them after you called me, but it seems that Caleb's been fending for himself for quite a while.

When I reached them, they were out of town on vacation, and frankly they didn't seem like they were too concerned about their nephew, even when I told them what had happened." She sighed heavily. "I'll go visit him tomorrow and bring him some of the flowers from our garden he's been working so hard on. He'll like that."

"Huh," said Elena slowly. "I thought he told me he came here to stay with his aunt and uncle because they were so upset about Tyler being missing."

"Maybe so," Aunt Judith said dryly, "but the Smallwoods seem to be doing pretty well now. They said that in their opinion, Tyler will come home when he's good and ready. That boy was always a little out of control. It sounds like Caleb is more worried about Tyler than they are."

She pulled into the driveway of their house, and Elena followed her inside to where Robert was reading his newspaper at the kitchen table.

"Elena, you look exhausted," he said, folding the paper and looking up at her in concern. "Are you all right?"

"I'm okay," she said numbly. "It's just been a long day." She thought she had never made more of an understatement in her life.

"Well, Margaret's gone to bed, but we saved you some dinner," Aunt Judith said, making a move toward the refrigerator. "It's a chicken casserole, and there's some salad. You must be starving."

But suddenly Elena felt sick. She'd been suppressing

all her feelings about Stefan and his attack on Caleb, keeping the images tamped down so she could get on with the
business of dealing with the police and the staff at the hospital and her own family. But she was tired and her hands
were shaking. She knew that she couldn't keep everything
under control for much longer.

"I don't want anything," she said, backing away. "I
can't . . . I'm not hungry, Aunt Judith. Thank you, though.
I just want to take a bath and go to bed." She turned and
hurried out of the kitchen.

"Elena! You have to eat something," she heard Aunt
Judith cry exasperatedly behind her as she hurried up the
stairs.

The solid-sounding murmur of Robert's voice broke in:
"Judith, let her go."

Elena ducked into the bathroom and closed the door
behind her.

She and Margaret shared the hall bathroom, and she
busied herself with emptying Margaret's bath toys from
the tub, keeping her mind carefully blank: a pink rubber
ducky, a pirate ship, a stack of gaily colored plastic cups.
A goofily smiling purple seahorse looked up at her with
painted blue eyes.

Once the tub was empty, Elena ran the water as hot
as she could stand and poured in a generous dollop of
apricot-scented bubble bath from a bottle that promised
to soothe her spirit while rejuvenating her skin. Soothing

and rejuvenating sounded good, although Elena had her doubts about how much she could reasonably expect from a bottle of bubble bath.

When the tub was full and frothy with a thick layer of bubbles, Elena quickly undressed and stepped into the steaming water. It stung at first, but she eased herself in bit by bit, gradually getting accustomed to the temperature.

Once she was comfortable, she lay back in the water, her hair floating out like a mermaid's, the sounds of the house muffled by the water over her ears, and let the thoughts she'd been avoiding come at last.

Tears overflowed her eyes and trickled down her cheeks to join the bathwater. She had believed that everything was going to be normal now that they were back home, that things were going to be good again. When she and her friends had gotten the Guardians to send them back and to change things, to reverse the deaths, to fix the broken, to make everything the way it would have been if nothing dangerous had touched the little town of Fell's Church, she had thought that it would make her life simple and easy. She would have her family, her friends, her Stefan.

But it wasn't going to work, was it? It wasn't ever going to be that way, not for Elena.

As soon as she'd come back to town, the very first day she'd stepped outside into the sunshine of a Fell's Church summer, something dark and evil and supernatural had started stalking her and her friends.

And as for Stefan . . . God . . . Stefan. What was happening to him?

When she closed her eyes, she saw Caleb flying through the air and heard that horrible, final-sounding crack that Caleb's head had made as it connected with the marble of the mausoleum. What if Caleb never fully recovered? What if this cute, innocent guy, this guy whose parents had died and left him like hers had died and left her, was broken forever because of Stefan?

Stefan. How had he become the kind of person who could do something like that? Stefan, who felt guilty about the animals he took blood from, the doves and rabbits and deer of the forest. The Stefan who she knew at the deepest level of her soul, who she thought kept nothing from her—that Stefan would never have harmed a human being like that.

Elena lay in the bathtub until the water got cold and her tears had stopped. Then she got out, drained the tub, dried her hair, brushed her teeth, put on a nightgown, called good night to Aunt Judith and Robert, and climbed into bed. She did not want to write in her diary. Not tonight.

She switched off the light and lay flat on her back, staring into the darkness—the same blackness, she thought, as Damon's eyes.

Damon had been a monster, she knew—he had killed, although not as blithely as he pretended; he had manipulated people and enjoyed it; he had haunted and hated

Stefan for hundreds of years—but she had also seen the lost little boy he kept locked inside him. He had loved her, she had loved him, and he had died.

And she loved Stefan. Desperately, devotedly, undeniably. She loved the sincerity in his eyes, his pride, his courtly manners, his honor, and his intelligence. She loved that he had rejected the monster that lurked inside him, the one that had driven so many vampires to terrible acts. She loved the sorrow he held—for his past, for his hatred and jealousy of Damon, for the terrible things he had seen. And she loved the hope that always sprang up in him, the strength of will Stefan possessed that allowed him to keep fighting back the darkness.

Beyond all that, she loved Stefan. But she was afraid.

She had thought she knew him inside and out, that she could see clear through to the innermost reaches of his soul. That wasn't true, not anymore. Not since the Guardians had stripped her powers, severing their psychic connection and reverting her back to a normal, human girl.

Elena rolled over and buried her face in the pillow. She knew the truth now. No matter what the Guardians had done for her, she would never be a normal girl. Her life would never be simple. Tragedy and horror would follow her forever.

In the end, there was nothing Elena could do to change her destiny.

"ookies," Alaric said gravely. "Bonnie thinks she could manage to choke down a few cookies. Just to keep her strength up."

"Cookies, got it," said Meredith, rummaging in Mrs. Flowers's kitchen cabinet to find a mixing bowl. She clunked a big china bowl that was probably older than she was onto the counter and checked the refrigerator. Eggs, milk, butter. Flour in the freezer. Vanilla and sugar in the cupboard.

"Look at you," Alaric said admiringly as Meredith unwrapped a stick of butter. "You don't even need a recipe. Is there anything you can't do?"

"Lots of things," Meredith replied, basking in the warmth of Alaric's gaze.

"What can I do to help?" he asked cheerfully.

"You can get another mixing bowl and measure two cups of flour and a teaspoon of baking powder into it," Meredith told him. "I'll beat the butter with the other ingredients in this bowl, and then we can put them together."

"Got it." Alaric found a bowl and measuring cups and started to measure out the items. Meredith watched his strong, tanned hands confidently leveling off the flour. Alaric had gorgeous hands, she thought. His shoulders were nice, too, and his face. All of him, really.

She realized she was ogling her boyfriend instead of stirring, and felt her cheeks color, even though no one was watching her. "Pass me the measuring cups when you're done with them?"

He handed them to her. "I know something scary's going on, and I want to protect Bonnie, too," he said, smiling a little, "but I think she might be milking the situation a little. She loves that everyone's pampering her."

"Bonnie's being very brave," said Meredith primly, then flashed him a grin, "and, yes, she might be milking it."

Matt came down the stairs and into the kitchen. "I think maybe Bonnie should have some tea when she gets out of her bubble bath," he said. "Mrs. Flowers is busy putting protective spells on the bedroom Bonnie chose, but she said she has a mix of chamomile and rosemary that would be good, and to put honey in it."

Meredith focused on mixing the cookie ingredients

together as Matt boiled water and carefully measured dried herbs and honey to make the tea to Mrs. Flowers's exact specifications. When he finally finished fussing over it, Matt picked up the fragile teacup and saucer carefully.

"Wait, maybe I'd better take the whole pot up," he said. As he searched for a tray to carry it on, he asked, "Meredith, are you sure you and Bonnie got everything she might need from her house?"

"She was up there for nearly a half hour. She got everything she wanted," said Meredith, "and if we missed anything, I'm sure Mrs. Flowers has some extras."

"Good," said Matt, his handsome face intent as he picked up the tea tray without spilling anything. "I just want to make sure Bonnie's okay."

He left the kitchen, and Meredith listened to his footsteps heading back upstairs. Once he was out of earshot, she and Alaric both burst out laughing.

"Yes, she's definitely milking it," said Meredith, when she'd stopped giggling.

Alaric pulled her toward him. His face was serious and intent now, and Meredith caught her breath. When they were this close, she could see the hidden flecks of gold in his hazel eyes, and they felt like a secret only Meredith knew.

"I love how you take care of your friend," Alaric told

her, his voice low. "What I love most is that you *know* she's pushing it as far as she can, seeing what you'll do for her, and you laugh, but you're still going to give her whatever she needs." He frowned a little. "No, that's not right. I do love how you see the funny side of it, but what I love *most* is how well you take care of everyone you can." He pulled her closer still. "I guess mostly I love *you*, Meredith."

Meredith kissed him. How could she have worried that Celia would come between them? It was like there had been a mist filling her eyes, making it so that she was unable to see the simple truth: Alaric was crazy about her.

After a minute, she broke the kiss and turned back to the cookie dough. "Get a cookie sheet, would you?" she asked.

Alaric stood still for a moment. "Okay . . ." he said.

Closing her eyes, Meredith summoned all her strength. She had to tell him. She had promised herself she would.

He handed her a cookie sheet and she busied herself by scooping spoonfuls of dough onto it. "There's something I need to tell you, Alaric," she said.

Alaric froze next to her. "What is it?" he asked, his voice wary.

"It's going to sound unbelievable."

He gave a snort of laughter. "More unbelievable than everything else that's happened since I met you?"

"Sort of," Meredith said. "Or, at least, it's specifically

about me this time. I've been . . ." It was hard to say. "I come from a family of vampire hunters. All my life, I've been training to fight. I guess taking care of people is a family trait." She smiled weakly.

Alaric stared at her.

"Say something," Meredith prompted after a moment.

He pushed his hair out of his eyes and looked wildly around. "I don't know what to say. I'm surprised you never told me this. I thought"—he paused—"that we knew each other really well."

"My family . . ." said Meredith miserably. "They made me swear that I would keep our secret. I never told anybody until a few days ago."

Alaric closed his eyes for a minute and pressed his palms against them hard. When he opened them, he looked calmer. "I understand. I do."

"Wait," said Meredith. "There's more." The cookie sheet was full, and she cast about for something else to occupy her hands and eyes while she talked. She settled on a dish towel and twisted it nervously. "Do you remember that Klaus attacked my grandfather?"

Alaric nodded.

"Well, I found out a few days ago that he also attacked me, and stole my brother—the brother I'd never known I had—and took him away and made him a vampire. And he left me—I was only three—some kind of half vampire. A living girl, but one who needed to eat blood sausage and sometimes had . . . sharp teeth like a kitten's."

"Oh, Meredith . . ." Alaric's face was full of compassion, and he moved toward her, hands out. *Toward me*, Meredith noted. *Not away, not afraid.*

"Wait," she said again. "Elena asked the Guardians to change things to the way they would have been if Klaus never came here." She put down the dish towel. "So it never happened."

"What?" Alaric said, staring at her.

Meredith nodded, a helpless, confused smile spreading over her face. "My grandfather died in a retirement home in Florida two years ago. I have a brother—one I don't remember, unfortunately—he got sent away to boarding school when we were twelve and joined the military as soon as he turned eighteen. Apparently he's the problem child of the family." She took a deep breath. "I'm not a vampire. Not even a half vampire. Not now."

Alaric was still staring at her. "Wow," he said. "Wait a minute. Does that mean that Klaus is still alive? Could he come here, come after your family now?"

"I thought of that," Meredith said, glad to address the practicalities. "I don't *think* so. Elena asked the Guardians to change Fell's Church so it was as if Klaus never came here. She didn't ask them to change *Klaus* and his experience. For him, I think, logically, he did come here, long ago, and now he's dead." She smiled shakily. "I hope so, anyway."

"So you're safe," Alaric said, "as safe as a vampire hunter might be. Is that all you needed to tell me?" When Meredith nodded, he reached for her and pulled her back into his arms. Holding her tightly, he said. "I would have loved you with sharp teeth, too. But I'm so glad for you."

Meredith closed her eyes. She had needed to tell him, to know how he would have reacted if the Guardians hadn't changed everything. A great warming gladness spread all through her.

Alaric pressed his lips against her hair.

"Wait," she said once more, and he released her, looking inquisitive.

"The cookies." Meredith laughed and put them in the oven, setting the timer for ten minutes.

They kissed until the buzzer rang.

"Are you sure you'll be okay alone?" Matt asked anxiously, standing by Bonnie's bed. "I'll be right downstairs if you need anything. Or maybe I should stay here. I could sleep on your floor. I know I snore, but I'd try not to, I swear."

Bonnie gave him a brave little smile. "I'll be fine, Matt. Thank you so much."

With one last worried glance, Matt patted her hand awkwardly, then left the room. Bonnie knew he would toss and turn on his own bed, thinking of ways to keep her safe. Probably he would end up sleeping on the floor outside her door, she thought, giving a delighted little wriggle.

"Sleep well, my dear," said Mrs. Flowers, taking his place by Bonnie's bedside. "I have cast all the protective charms I know around you. I hope you like the tea. It's my own special brew."

"Thank you, Mrs. Flowers," Bonnie said. "Good night."

"You are enjoying this *way* too much," said Meredith, who came in next carrying a plate of cookies. She was limping, but had insisted that she didn't need a cane or crutch as long as her ankle was bandaged.

In fact . . . Bonnie took a closer look at Meredith. Her cheeks were flushed, and her usually smooth hair was a little mussed. *I think she's very glad that Celia's gone to UVA*, Bonnie thought with a smirk.

"I'm just trying to keep my spirits up," Bonnie said with a mischievous smile. "And you know what they say: When life gives you lemons, make lemonade. My lemonade is having Matt trying to fulfill my every need. It's too bad we don't have more boys around here."

"Don't forget about Alaric," said Meredith. "He helped make the cookies. And he's downstairs researching everything he can that might be related to this."

"Ah, everyone catering to me, that's what I like," Bonnie joked. "Did I tell you how much I enjoyed the dinner you made? All my favorites . . . it was like my birthday. Or my last meal," she added more soberly.

Meredith frowned. "Are you sure you don't want me to stay in here? I know we've protected the house as well as we can, but we don't really know what we're fighting. And just because the last couple of attacks took place in daylight with the whole group around, it doesn't necessarily mean that's the way they have to be. What if whatever this is can get past our defenses?"

"I will be fine," said Bonnie. Intellectually she knew she was in danger, but oddly, she didn't feel scared. She was in a house with people she trusted, all of whom were focused wholeheartedly on her safety. Besides, she had a plan for the night—something she couldn't do if Meredith slept in the room.

"Are you sure?" Meredith fretted.

"Yes," Bonnie said emphatically. "If something bad was going to happen to me tonight, I'd know in advance, right? Because I'm psychic, and I get warnings about things."

"Hmmm," said Meredith, quirking one eyebrow. For a moment she looked like she was going to argue. Bonnie kept her gaze firm. Finally, Meredith put the tray of cookies on the table by the bed next to the teapot and cup Matt had brought up earlier, pulled the curtains across the window, and looked anxiously around to see what else could be done.

"Okay, then," she said. "I'll be right next door if you need me."

"Thanks, Mer. Good night." As soon as the knob clicked into place, Bonnie lay back in bed and bit into a cookie. Delicious.

A slow smile bloomed on her lips. She was the center of attention now, as if she were a Victorian heroine bravely suffering from some kind of wasting illness. She had been encouraged to pick out her favorite of the boardinghouse's many bedrooms and had chosen this one. It was a charming room with creamy rose-patterned wallpaper and a maple sleigh bed.

Matt hadn't left her side all night. Mrs. Flowers had fussed around her, fluffing pillows and offering her herbal tonics, and Alaric had been conscientiously researching protection spells in all the grimoires he could find. Even Celia, who had never been anything but snippy to her about her "visions," promised before she left to let her know as soon as she found something helpful.

Bonnie turned on her side, inhaling the sweet scent of Mrs. Flowers's tea. Here in this cozy room, it was impossible to feel like she needed protection, that she could be in danger this very second.

But was she? What was the time frame after one's name was called? After Celia's name had appeared, she had been attacked within the hour. After Meredith's had appeared, she hadn't been attacked until the next day. Maybe things were getting more spaced out. Maybe Bonnie wasn't going to be in danger until tomorrow or the next day. Or next week. And Damon's name had appeared before Bonnie's did.

Bonnie's skin tingled at the thought of Damon's name in lake weeds. Damon was dead. She had *seen* him die— and in fact he'd died for her (although everyone else, in their compassion for Elena, seemed to have forgotten that). But the appearance of his name must mean *something*. And she was determined to figure out just what.

She listened. She could hear the sounds of Meredith moving around in the room next door with a steady thumping that suggested she was practicing with her stave, and from down below came the faint voices of Matt, Alaric, and Mrs. Flowers talking in the study.

Bonnie could wait. She poured herself a cup of tea, crunched on another cookie, and wiggled her toes pleasurably under the soft pink sheets. She sort of liked being a supernatural invalid.

An hour later, she had finished her cup of tea and all the cookies, and the house was quieter. It was time.

She climbed out of bed, her too-long polka-dotted pajama pants flapping around her ankles, and opened her overnight bag. While Meredith had waited downstairs at her house, she had pried up the loose board by her bed and taken out *Traversing the Boundaries Between the Quick and the Dead*, a book of matches, a silver knife, and the four candles she needed for the ritual. Now she took them out of her bag and rolled back the rug by the bed so she could crouch on the floor.

Tonight, nothing was going to stop her. She was going to reach Damon. Maybe he could tell her what was going on. Or maybe he was in some sort of danger, in whatever plane dead vampires ended up on, and needed to be warned.

In any case, she *missed* him. Bonnie hunched her shoulders and wrapped her arms around herself for a moment. Damon's death had *hurt* her, not that anyone had noticed. Everyone's attention, everyone's sympathies, had been directed toward Elena. As usual.

Bonnie got back to work. Quickly, she lit the first candle and, dripping wax on the floor to anchor it upright, placed it to her north. "Fire in the North, protect me," she whispered. She lit them in widdershins order: black to the north, white to the west, black to the south, white to the east. When the circle of protection was complete around her, she closed her eyes and sat quietly for a few moments, focusing herself, reaching to find the power at her center.

When she opened her eyes, she took a deep breath, picked up the silver knife, and quickly, without giving herself time to wimp out, cut a gash across her left palm.

"Ouch," she muttered, and turned her hand over,

dripping blood on the floor in front of her. Then she dabbed the fingers of her right hand in the blood and smeared a bit on each candle.

Bonnie's skin tingled painfully as magic rose around her. Her senses honed, and she could see tiny movements in the air, as if flashes of light were appearing and disappearing just out of sight.

"'Through the darkness I call to you,'" she intoned. She didn't need to look at the book; she had memorized this part. "'With my blood I call to you; with fire and silver I call to you. Hear me through the cold beyond the grave. Hear me through the shadows beyond the night. I summon you. I have need of you. Hear me and come!'"

The room went still. It was the stillness of expectation, as if some great creature were holding its breath. Bonnie felt like an entire audience stood around her, suspended in eagerness. The veil between the worlds was about to lift. She had no doubts.

"Damon Salvatore," she said clearly. "Come to me."

Nothing happened.

"Damon Salvatore," Bonnie said again, less confidently, "come to me."

The tension, the feeling of magic in the room was beginning to dissipate, as if her invisible audience were quietly creeping away.

· Yet Bonnie *knew* the spell had worked. She had a funny,

blank, cutoff feeling, like when she was talking on the phone and her carrier suddenly dropped the call. Her call had gone through, she was sure of it, but there was no one on the other end. Only what did it mean? Was Damon's soul just . . . gone?

Suddenly Bonnie heard something. A light breathing, just a smidge out of time with her own.

There was someone right behind her.

The hairs rose on the back of her neck. She hadn't broken the circle of protection. Nothing should be able to cross into that circle, certainly no spirit, but whoever was behind her was *inside* the circle, so close to Bonnie that they were almost touching her.

Bonnie froze. Then slowly, carefully, she put down her hand and felt for the knife. "Damon?" she whispered uncertainly.

A tinkling laugh sounded behind her, followed by a low voice. "Damon doesn't want to talk to you." The voice was honey-sweet, but somehow also poisonous-sounding, insidious and oddly familiar.

"Why not?" Bonnie asked shakily.

"He doesn't love you," the voice said in a soft, persuasive tone. "He never even noticed you were there, unless there was something he wanted from you. Or perhaps if he wanted to make Elena jealous. You know that."

Bonnie swallowed, too afraid to turn around, too afraid

to see who the voice belonged to.

"Damon saw only Elena. Damon loved only Elena. Even now that he's dead and lost to her, he won't hear you calling," the voice lilted. "Nobody loves you, Bonnie. Everyone loves Elena, and that's how she likes it. Elena keeps everyone for herself."

A burning sensation began behind Bonnie's eyes, and a single hot tear ran down her cheek.

"No one will ever love you," the voice whispered. "Not when you're standing next to Elena. Why do you think no one ever saw you as anything but Elena's friend? All the way through school, she was standing in the sunshine and you were hidden in her shadow. Elena made sure of that. She couldn't bear to share the spotlight."

The words rattled inside Bonnie's mind, and suddenly something inside her shifted. The icy terror she'd felt just moments ago had thawed, making way for roiling anger.

The voice was right. Why had she never seen it before? Elena was Bonnie's friend only because Bonnie was a foil for her own beauty, her own sparkle. She had been using her for years without caring how Bonnie felt at all.

"She cares only about herself," Bonnie said, half sobbing. "Why can't anyone see that?" She shoved the book away from her and it knocked over the black candle to her north, breaking the circle. The wick smoked and guttered, and all four candles went out.

"Ahhhh," said the voice in satisfaction, and tendrils of dark fog began to creep from the corners of the room. Just as quickly as her fear had left her, it snapped back. Bonnie spun around, holding the knife, ready to face the voice, but there was no one there—just dark, amorphous fog.

Hysteria welling within her, she got to her feet and stumbled toward the door. But the fog moved quickly, and soon Bonnie was enveloped in it. Something fell with a clatter. She couldn't see more than a few inches. Bonnie opened her mouth and tried to scream, but the fog flowed over her lips, and her scream turned into a muffled moan. She felt her grip on the knife loosen and it dropped to the floor with a dull clank. Her vision grew blurry. Bonnie tried to lift her foot but could barely move.

Then, blinded by the fog, she lost her balance and pitched forward into darkness.

21

When she opened her eyes, Elena found herself in someone's attic. Its wide wooden floorboards and low rafters were thick with dust, and the long room was crowded with objects: a hammock, sleds, skis, boxes with words like *Xmas* or *toddler toys* or *B's winter clothes* scribbled on them in black marker. Oilcloths were draped over larger objects that might be furniture, chairs and tables, by their shapes.

At the far end of the room an old mattress lay on the floor, with an oilcloth crumpled at one end, as if someone sleeping there had been using it as a makeshift blanket and had shoved it off when they rose.

Faint traces of pale light showed around the edges of a small shuttered window at the nearer end of the attic. There was a soft rustling, as if mice were going about their private business behind the shelter of the stored furniture.

It was all weirdly familiar.

She looked back toward the far end of the attic and saw, without the faintest sense of surprise, that Damon was now sitting on the old mattress, his long black-clad legs drawn up, his elbows resting on his knees. He was managing to give the appearance of lounging gracefully despite his awkward position.

"The places where we meet are getting less and less elegant," she told him dryly.

Damon laughed and held up his hands in denial. "You pick the locations, princess," he said. "This is your show. I'm just along for the ride." He paused thoughtfully. "Okay, that's not entirely true," he confessed. "But you do pick the locations. Where are we, anyway?"

"You don't know?" Elena said with mock indignation. "This is a very special place for us, Damon! Full of memories! You brought me here right after I became a vampire, remember?"

He looked around. "Oh, yes. The attic of the house where the teacher was staying. Convenient at the time, but you're right—an elegant setting suits us both much better. May I suggest a nice palace next time?" He patted the mattress next to him.

Elena, crossing the floor toward him, took a moment to marvel at how realistic and detailed her dream was. Each step she took sent tiny puffs of dust up from the floor. There was a slight scent of mildew: She couldn't remember ever having smelled anything in a dream before these visions of Damon.

When she sat down, the mildew smell got stronger. She nestled close to Damon anyway, resting her head on his shoulder, and his leather jacket creaked as he put his arm around her. Elena closed her eyes and sighed. She felt safe and secure within his embrace, feelings she had never associated with Damon, but they were good ones. "I miss you, Damon," she said. "Please come back to me."

Damon leaned his cheek against her head, and she breathed in the smell of him. Leather and soap and the strange but pleasant woodsy scent that was Damon's own. "I'm right here," he said.

"Not really," Elena said, and her eyes filled with tears again. She wiped them roughly away with the backs of her hands. "It feels like I've been doing nothing but crying lately," she said. "When I'm here with you I feel safer, though. But it's just a dream. It won't last, this feeling."

Damon stiffened. "Safer?" he said, and there was a strained note in his voice. "You aren't safe when you're not with me? Isn't my little brother looking after you properly?"

"Oh, Damon, you can't imagine," Elena said. "Stefan . . ." She took a deep breath, put her head in her hands, and began to sob.

"What is it? What's happened?" asked Damon sharply. When Elena didn't answer, just continued to cry, he took her hands and tugged them gently but firmly away from her face. "Elena," he said. "Look at me. Has something happened to Stefan?"

"No," said Elena through her tears. "Well, yes, sort of . . . I don't really know what's happened to him, but he's changed." Damon was looking at her intently, his night-black eyes fixed on hers, and Elena made an effort to pull herself together. She hated acting like this, so weak and pathetic, sobbing on someone's shoulder instead of coolly formulating a solution to the problem at hand. She didn't want Damon, even a dream Damon who was just part of her subconscious, seeing her like this. She sniffled and wiped her eyes with the back of her hand.

Damon delved into an inner pocket of his leather jacket and handed her a neatly folded white handkerchief. Elena stared at it, then at him, and he shrugged. "I'm an old-fashioned gentleman, sometimes," he said, straight-faced. "Hundreds of years of linen handkerchiefs. Some habits are hard to break."

Elena blew her nose and wiped her cheeks. She didn't quite know what to do with the soggy handkerchief—it seemed gross to hand it back to Damon—so she just held on to it, twisting it between her hands as she thought.

"Now tell me about what's going on. What's wrong with

Stefan? What happened to him?" Damon commanded.

"Well . . ." Elena said slowly, "I don't know what's wrong with Stefan, and I don't know if anything happened to change him that you don't already know about. Maybe he's just reacting to your . . . you know." It suddenly seemed weird to refer to Damon's death when he was sitting next to her—impolite somehow—but Damon nodded at her to go on. "It's been hard on him. And he's been even more tense and weird for the last couple of days. Then, earlier this evening, I was visiting my parents in the cemetery . . ." She told Damon about Stefan's attack on Caleb. "The worst part is that I never suspected this side of Stefan existed," she finished. "I can't think of any real reason he had to attack Caleb—he just claimed that Caleb wanted me, and that he was dangerous, but Caleb hadn't done anything—and Stefan seemed so irrational, and so violent. He was like another person."

Elena's eyes were filling with tears again, and Damon pulled her closer, stroking her hair and gently peppering her face with soft kisses. Elena closed her eyes and gradually relaxed into his arms. Damon held her more firmly, and his kisses got slower and deeper. Then he was cradling her head with his strong, gentle hands and kissing her mouth.

"Oh, Damon," she murmured. This was more vivid than any dream she'd ever had. His lips were soft and warm, with just a little roughness to them, and it felt like she was falling into him. "Wait." He kissed her more insistently but, when she pulled away, let her go.

"Wait," Elena repeated, sitting up straight. Somehow she had lain back until she was half reclining across the musty old mattress with Damon, her legs entangled with his. She moved away from him, toward the edge of the mattress. "Damon, whatever's going on with Stefan scares me. But that doesn't mean . . . Damon, I'm still in love with Stefan."

"You love me, too, you know," Damon said lightly. His dark eyes narrowed. "You're not getting rid of me that easily, princess."

"I do love you," Elena said. Her eyes were dry now. She thought she might be all cried out, at least for the moment. Her voice was quite steady as she added, "I'll always love you, I guess. But you're dead." *And Stefan is my true love, if I had to choose between you,* she thought, but did not say. What was the point? "I'm sorry, Damon," she went on, "but you're gone. And I'll always love Stefan, but suddenly I'm afraid of him, of what he might do. I don't know what's going to happen to us. I thought things would be easy now that we're home again, but awful things are still happening."

Damon sighed and lay back on the mattress. He stared up at the ceiling in silence for a moment. "Listen," he said finally, lacing his fingers across his chest. "You've always underestimated Stefan's potential for violence."

"He's *not* violent," Elena said hotly. "He doesn't even drink human blood."

"He doesn't drink human blood because he doesn't *want* to be violent. He doesn't *want* to hurt anyone. But Elena"—Damon reached out and took her hand—"my little brother's got a temper. I know that if anyone does."

Elena shivered. She knew that, back when they were humans, Stefan and Damon had killed each other in a fit of rage over what they thought was Katherine's death. Katherine's blood had been in both their systems, and they had risen again as vampires that night. Their anger and jealousy over a lost love had destroyed them both.

"However," Damon continued, "much as it pains me to admit it, Stefan would never hurt you, and wouldn't hurt anyone else without a real reason. Not without the kind of reason you would approve of. Not these days. He might have a temper, but he's also got a conscience." He smirked a little and added, "An annoying, self-righteous kind of conscience, of course, but it's there. And he loves you, Elena. You're the whole world to him."

"Maybe you're right," Elena said. "I'm scared, though. And I wish you were there with me." She looked at him, as sleepy and confiding as a tired child now. "Damon, I wish you weren't dead. I miss you. Please come back to me."

Damon smiled and kissed her softly. But then he pulled away and Elena could feel the dream changing. She tried to cling to the moment, but it faded and Damon was lost to her again.

"Please be careful, Damon," said Sage, worry lines marring his bronzed forehead.

It wasn't often that the muscular Keeper of the Gates looked worried—or spoke only one language at a time—but ever since Damon had staggered back from death and out of the ashes, Sage had spoken softly and clearly to him in English, treating the vampire as if he were likely to shatter at any minute.

"I usually am careful," said Damon, leaning against the wall of what they called, for want of a better term, the mystical elevator. "Unless I'm being heart-stoppingly brave, of course." The words were right, but to Damon's own ears, his voice sounded off: hoarse and hesitant.

Sage seemed to hear the wrongness there, too, and his handsome face furrowed in a frown. "You can stay longer if you want."

Damon leaned back against the plain white wall. "I have to go," he said wearily, for what felt like the millionth time. "She's in danger. But thank you for everything, Sage."

He wouldn't be here now without Sage. The powerful vampire had cleaned Damon up, given him clothes—stylish black clothes in the right size—and fed him blood and rich Black Magic wine until Damon had been hauled back from the edge of death and realized who he was again.

But . . . Damon didn't *feel* like himself. There was a strange empty ache inside him, as if he'd left something behind, buried deep under the ash.

Sage was still frowning, staring at him with grave concern. Damon pulled himself together and gave Sage a sudden brilliant smile. "Wish me luck," he said.

The smile helped: The other vampire's face relaxed. *"Bonne chance, mon ami,"* he said. "I wish you the very best of luck."

Bilingual again, Damon thought. *I must be looking better.*

"Fell's Church," he said into the empty air. "The United States, the mortal realm. Somewhere I can hide."

He raised a hand in solemn salute to Sage and pushed the elevator's single button.

Elena woke up in darkness. She ran a quick and automatic mental check: smooth, fabric-softener-scented cotton sheets, dim light from the window past the foot of her bed on the right, the faint sound of Robert snoring in his and Aunt Judith's bedroom at the other end of the hall. Her own old familiar room. Home again.

She heaved a deep sigh. She didn't feel quite as mired in despair as she had when she climbed into bed; things were dark, but she could admit there was a possibility they might someday get better again. But her eyes and throat felt raw from crying. She missed Damon so much.

A floorboard creaked. Elena stiffened. She knew that creak. It was the high, complaining whine the floorboard over near her window gave if you stepped right in the middle of it. Someone was in her room.

Elena lay very still, running through the possibilities. Stefan would have announced himself as soon as he heard her sigh. Was it Margaret, quietly wandering in to crawl into bed with Elena?

"Margaret?" she asked softly.

There was no answer. Her ears straining, Elena thought she could make out the sound of slow, heavy breathing.

Suddenly the lamp on her desk was switched on, and Elena was temporarily dazzled by the bright light. She could see only the silhouette of a dark figure.

Then her vision cleared. And at the foot of her bed, a half smile on his chiseled face, dark eyes wary, as if he was unsure of his welcome, stood a figure dressed all in black.

Damon.

22

Elena couldn't breathe. She could vaguely feel her mouth opening and closing, but she found she wasn't able to say anything. Her hands and feet had gone numb.

Damon gave her an almost shy smile—which was funny, because Damon didn't do shy—and shrugged. "Well, princess? You wanted me to be here with you, didn't you?"

As if a rubber band holding her back had snapped, Elena leaped out of bed and hurtled into Damon's arms.

"Are you real?" she said, half sobbing. "Is this real?" She kissed him fiercely, and he met her kiss with equal fervor. He *felt* real, cool skin and leather, the surprising softness of his lips familiar under hers.

"Here I am," he murmured into her hair as he pulled her close to him. "It's real, I promise you."

Elena stepped back and smacked him hard across the face. Damon glared at her and reached up to rub his cheek. "Ouch," he said, and then cracked a narrow, irritating smile. "I can't say that was completely unexpected—I get slapped by women more often than you'd think possible— but not a nice welcome for the long-lost love, sweetheart."

"How could you?" Elena said, dry-eyed now and furious. "How *could* you, Damon? We've all been mourning you. Stefan's falling apart. Bonnie blames herself. I . . . I . . . A piece of my heart *died*. How long have you been watching us? Didn't you care? Was this all some kind of joke to you? Did you laugh when we cried?"

Damon winced. "Darling," he said. "My princess. Aren't you glad to see me at all?"

"Of course I am!" said Elena indignantly. She took a breath and cooled down a little. "But, Damon, what were you thinking? We all thought you were dead! *Permanently* dead, not show-up-in-my-bedroom-a-few-days-later-looking-perfectly-healthy dead! *What's going on?* Did the Guardians do this? They told me they couldn't when I begged them to, that death is permanent for a vampire once it happens."

Damon graced her with a genuine, laughing smile. "Well, you of all people ought to know that death isn't always permanent."

Elena shrugged and wrapped her arms around herself. "They told me that when I came back, it was different," she said in a small voice, her emotions zigzagging all over the place. *Because you're in shock*, a tiny voice at the back of her head said wisely. "Mystical stuff, you know. My time wasn't up. Hey!" She poked him with one finger, perking up. "Are you human now? I was human when I returned."

Damon gave a long, theatrical shudder. "God forbid. I had enough of that when that meddling kitsune made me a mortal. Thank heaven—or whoever—I don't have to go looking for an obliging vampire princess to turn me back this time." He grinned slyly at Elena. "I'm as bloodsucking as ever, darling." He eyed her neck. "Speaking of which, I'm rather hungry. . . ."

Elena smacked him again, though more gently this time. "Knock it off, Damon."

"Can I sit down now?" Damon asked and, when she nodded, settled himself on the foot of her bed and drew her down to sit beside him. Elena looked searchingly into his eyes, then gently traced her hand over his sharp cheekbones, his sculpted mouth, his soft raven hair.

"You *were* dead, Damon," she said quietly. "I know it. I saw you die."

"Yes," he said, and sighed. "I felt myself die. It was horribly painful and it seemed to both go on forever and be over in a few moments." He shuddered. "There was a little bit left of me even then though"—Elena nodded—"and

Stefan told me, told him, to fly away. And you held him—held me—and told me to close my eyes. And then that last little bit of me was gone, too, and even the pain was gone. And then . . . I came back." Damon's dark eyes were wide with remembered wonder.

"But how?" asked Elena.

"Remember the star ball?"

"How could I forget? It was the root of all our problems with the kitsune. It was vaporized when I . . . Oh, Damon, I used my *Wings of Destruction* on the tree on the Nether World's moon. But they destroyed the kitsune's star ball, too, and I had to go to the Guardians to save Fell's Church. The *Wings of Destruction* were . . . like nothing I've ever seen or felt before." She shivered.

"I've seen what you did to that moon," Damon said, smiling slightly. "Would it make you feel better, my lovely angel, if you knew that using your Powers like that and destroying the star ball is what saved me?"

"Don't call me that," said Elena, scowling. The Guardians were the closest thing she had ever seen to real angels, and she did not have fond memories of them. "How did it save you?"

"Do they explain how condensation works in modern schools?" Damon asked with the supercilious expression he always wore when he teasingly criticized her world in comparison to the one he had grown up in. "Is it all sex education, empathy, and second-rate novels now, or do they still tell the children a little about science? I know they've dropped Latin and Greek in favor of theater and consciousness-raising." His voice dripped with contempt.

Elena told herself not to rise to his bait. Instead she folded her hands neatly in front of her in her lap. "I think you may be a few decades out-of-date. But please, O wise one," she said, "assume that my education didn't include the connection between condensation and rising from the dead, and enlighten me."

"Nice." Damon smirked. "I like to see a young woman who is respectful of her elders and betters." Elena cocked an eyebrow at him warningly. "Anyway," he continued, "the liquid *in* the star ball, the pure magic, didn't vanish. It's not that easy to get rid of really strong magic. As the atmosphere cooled, the magic turned from vapor back into liquid and fell down on me, with the rain of ash. I was soaking in pure Power for hours, gradually being reborn."

Elena's mouth dropped open. "Those *sneaks*," she said indignantly. "The Guardians told me you were gone for good, and they took all the treasures we bribed them with, too." She thought briefly of the one last treasure she still had, a water bottle full of the Water of Eternal Youth, hidden high up on the shelf in her closet, and pushed the thought away. She couldn't even acknowledge that hidden treasure to herself for more than a moment, for fear the

Guardians would realize she had it, and she couldn't *use* it . . . not yet, maybe not ever.

Damon shrugged one shoulder. "They do cheat, sometimes, I hear. But it's more likely this time that they thought they were telling the truth. They don't know everything, even though they like to pretend they do. And kitsune and vampires are both a little outside their area of expertise."

He told her how he had woken, buried deep in ash and mud, clawed his way to the surface, and set off across the desolate moon, not knowing who he was or what had happened to him, and how he had almost died again, and that Sage had saved him.

"And then what?" Elena asked eagerly. "How did you remember everything? How did you get back to Earth?"

"Well," said Damon, turning a slight, fond smile on her, "that's a funny story." He reached into an inner pocket of his leather jacket and pulled out a neatly folded white linen handkerchief. Elena blinked. It looked like the same handkerchief he had given her in her dream. Damon noticed her expression and smiled more widely, as though he knew where she was recognizing it from. He unfolded it and held it out for Elena's inspection.

Cradled inside the handkerchief were two strands of hair. Very familiar hair, Elena realized. She and Bonnie had each cut off a lock of hair and placed them on Damon's body, wanting to leave a part of themselves with him, since they couldn't take his body off the desolate moon with them. Before her now lay a curling red lock and a waving gold one, as bright and shiny as if they had just been cut from freshly washed heads, rather than left on a world with ash falling all around.

Damon gazed at the locks with an expression made up of tenderness and a little awe. Elena thought that she had never seen such an open, almost hopeful look from him.

"The Power from the star ball saved these, too," he said. "First they were burned almost to ash, but then they regenerated. I held them and studied them and cherished them, and you started to come back to me. Sage had given me my name, and it sounded right to me, but I couldn't recall anything else about myself. But as I held these locks of hair, I gradually remembered who you were, and what we had been through together, and all the things I . . ." He paused. "What I knew and felt about you, and then I remembered the little redbird, too, and then everything else came flooding back and I was myself again."

He glanced away and lost the sentimental look, smoothing his face into its usual cool expression, as if embarrassed, then folded the locks of hair back inside the handkerchief and tucked it carefully away into his jacket.

"Well," he said briskly, "then it was just a matter of having Sage lend me some clothes, fill me in on what I had missed, and give me a lift back to Fell's Church. And now here I am."

"I bet he was amazed," said Elena, "and ecstatic." The vampire Keeper of the Gates Between Worlds was a dear friend of Damon's, the only *friend* of Damon's she knew of, other than herself. Damon's acquaintances tended to be enemies or admirers more often than friends.

"He was quite pleased," Damon admitted.

"So you just now made it back to Earth?"

Damon nodded.

"Well, you've missed a lot here," Elena said, launching into an explanation of the past few days, starting with Celia's name written in blood and ending on Caleb's hospitalization.

"Wow." Damon let out a low whistle. "But I have to assume the problem is more than my little brother acting like a madman with Caleb? Because, you know, that may be simple jealousy. Jealousy has always been Stefan's biggest sin." He said the last with a smug twist to his lips, and Elena elbowed him gently in the ribs.

"Don't put Stefan down," she said reprovingly, and smiled to herself. It felt so *good* to be scolding Damon again. He really was his own maddening, changeable, wonderful self again. Damon was *back*.

Wait. Oh, no. "You're in danger, too!" Elena gasped, remembering suddenly that he could still be taken from her. "Your name appeared earlier, written in the weeds that were holding Meredith underwater. We didn't know what it could mean, because we thought you were dead. But, since you're alive, it seems you're the next target." She paused. "Unless falling through the surface of the moon was the attack on you."

"Don't worry about me, Elena. You are probably right about the attack on the moon being my 'accident.' But they haven't been very successful attempts, have they?" Damon said thoughtfully. "Almost as if whatever this is isn't trying very hard to kill us. I have a faint inkling about what might be causing this."

"You do?" asked Elena. "Tell me."

Damon shook his head. "It's just a glimmer right now," he said. "Let me get some sort of confirmation."

"But Damon," Elena pleaded, "even a glimmer is much more than the rest of us have been able to come up with. Come with me tomorrow morning and tell everyone about it, and we can all work together."

"Oh, yes," said Damon, with a mock shudder. "You and me and Mutt and the vampire hunter, a cozy group. Plus my pious brother and the little red witch. And the old lady witch and the teacher. No, I'm going to do some more digging on my own. And what's more, Elena," he said, fixing her with a dark stare, "you're not to tell anyone that I'm alive. Especially not Stefan."

"Damon!" Elena protested. "You don't know how absolutely devastated Stefan is, thinking you're dead. We have to let him know you're all right."

Damon smiled wryly. "I think there's probably a part of Stefan that's glad enough to have me out of the picture. He doesn't have any reason to want me here." Elena shook her head in furious denial, but he went on. "It's true. But maybe it's time for things to be different between us. To that end, I have to show him that I can change. In any case, I can't investigate this properly if everyone knows I'm around. Keep quiet for now, Elena." She opened her mouth to object further, but he silenced her with a quick, fierce kiss. When they broke apart, he said, "Promise me for now, and I'll promise you that as soon as I figure this out, you can announce my resurrection to the world."

Elena nodded doubtfully. "If that's what you really want, Damon, and you really think it's necessary," she said. "But I'm not happy about it."

Damon got to his feet and patted her shoulder. "Things are going to be different now," he said. He looked down at her, his face serious. "I'm not the same as I was, Elena."

Elena nodded again, more firmly this time. "I'll keep your secret, Damon," she promised.

Damon gave her a small, tight smile, then took three steps toward her open window. In a moment he was gone, and a large black crow flew out into the night.

23

The next morning, Elena felt light and joyful, as if she was hugging an enormous, wonderful secret to herself. Damon was still alive. He had been in her room last night.

Right?

She'd been through so much, she could hardly trust it. She climbed out of bed, noting that the clouds outside were still pink and gold from the sunrise, so it must be very early. She carefully moved toward the window. She wasn't sure what she was looking for, but she went down on her hands and knees and scanned the floor carefully.

There. A tiny piece of dirt on the squeaky board, fallen from someone's shoe. And there, on the windowsill, the long scratches of a bird's claws. That was proof enough for Elena.

She stood up and gave a funny little hop of joy, clapping her hands together sharply once, an unstoppable grin spreading across her face. Damon was alive!

Then she took a deep breath and stood still, willing her face into blankness. If she was really going to keep this secret—and she supposed she would have to; she'd promised, after all—she was going to have to act like nothing had changed. And really, things were pretty bad still, she told herself. If she thought about the facts, she shouldn't be celebrating just yet.

Damon's return hadn't altered the fact that something dark was after Elena and her friends, or that Stefan was acting irrationally and violently. Her heart sank a little as she thought of Stefan, but still a bubble of happiness went through her. Damon was alive!

And, what was more, he had an idea of what might be going on. It was exactly like Damon at his most infuriating to play this idea close to his chest and not let her know what he was thinking, but still, his glimmer was more hope than anyone else had been able to offer yet. Perhaps there was light at the end of the tunnel after all.

A pebble pinged against Elena's window.

When she looked out, she saw Stefan, shoulders hunched, hands in his pockets, watching her from the lawn. Elena waved to him to stay where he was, threw on jeans, a lacy white tank top, and shoes, and went downstairs to meet him. There was dew on the grass, and Elena's steps left footprints. The cool of dawn was already being replaced by dazzling hot sunshine: It was going to be another sticky Virginia summer day.

As she approached Stefan, Elena slowed down. She didn't quite know what to say to him. Since last night, every time she had thought of Stefan, she had involuntarily pictured Caleb's body flying through the air, the sickening crunch as he hit the marble monument. And she couldn't stop seeing Stefan's savage anger as he had attacked him, although Damon had been sure there must have been a reason. *Damon.* How would she ever keep Stefan from guessing the truth about his brother?

From the pained look on Stefan's face, it was clear he sensed her apprehension. He held out his hand. "I know you don't understand why I did what I did yesterday," he said, "but there's something you have to see."

Elena stopped, but she didn't take his outstretched hand. His face fell a little further. "Tell me where we're going," she said.

"I need to show you something that I found," Stefan said patiently. "You'll understand when we get there. Please, Elena. I would never hurt you."

Elena stared at him. She knew without a doubt that it was true that Stefan would never hurt her.

"Okay," she said, making up her mind. "Wait here for a

minute. I'll be right back."

She left Stefan on the lawn in the early morning sunshine as she retreated into the quiet dimness of the house.
Everyone else was still asleep: A quick glance at the clock
in the kitchen told her it was barely six o'clock. She scribbled a note to Aunt Judith, saying she was going to grab
breakfast with Stefan and would be back later. Reaching
for her purse, she paused and made sure that a dried sprig
of vervain was still tucked inside it. Not that she thought
Stefan would ever do anything to her . . . but it never hurt
to be prepared.

When she came out of the house, Stefan ushered her
into his car parked at the curb, opening the passenger-side
door for her and hovering over her as she fastened her seat
belt.

"How far away is it?" Elena asked.

"Not far," Stefan said simply. Watching him drive,
Elena noticed the worry lines at the corners of his eyes,
the unhappy droop of his mouth, the tension in his shoulders, and wished she could put her arms around him and
comfort him, raise her hand and wipe those lines by his
eyes away. But her memories of the rage on his face the
day before held her back. She just couldn't make herself
reach out to him.

They hadn't driven for long when Stefan turned onto a
cul-de-sac of expensive houses.

Elena leaned forward. They were pulling up to a large white house fronted by a spacious pillared porch. She knew that porch. After junior prom, she and Matt had sat on its steps and watched the sun rise, still wearing their clothes from the dance. She had kicked off her satin sandals and laid her head against Matt's tuxedoed shoulder, listening dreamily to the music and voices coming from the after-prom party in the house behind them. It had been a good night from a different lifetime.

She stared at Stefan accusingly. "This was Tyler Smallwood's house, Stefan. I don't know what you're planning, but Caleb's not here. He's in the hospital."

Stefan sighed. "I know he's not here, Elena. His aunt and uncle haven't been here either, not for several days, at least."

"They're out of town," Elena said automatically. "Aunt Judith talked to them yesterday."

"That's good," Stefan said grimly. "Then they're safe." He cast a worried glance up and down the street. "You're sure Caleb won't be out of the hospital today?"

"Yes," said Elena acidly. "He was too injured. They're keeping him for observation."

Elena got out of the car, slammed the door, and marched toward the Smallwoods' house, not looking back to see whether Stefan was following.

He caught up to her instantly. She cursed his vampiric

speed in her head and walked faster.

"Elena," he said, circling in front of her and forcing her to a stop. "Are you angry that I want to keep you safe?"

"No," she said scathingly. "I'm angry that you almost killed Caleb Smallwood."

Stefan's face sagged with exhaustion and sorrow, and Elena instantly felt guilty. Whatever was going on with Stefan, he still needed her. But she didn't know how to deal with his violence. She'd fallen in love with Stefan for his poetic soul, for his gentleness. *Damon* was the danger-ous one. *Dangerous looks much better on Damon than it does on Stefan*, a dry observing voice at the back of her mind said, and Elena couldn't deny the truth of it.

"Just show me what you wanted me to see," she finally said.

Stefan sighed, then turned and led her up the drive of the Smallwoods' house. She had expected him to go to the Smallwoods' front door, but he cut around the side of the house and toward a small shed in the backyard.

"The toolshed?" asked Elena quizzically. "Do we have a lawn mowing emergency we need to address before breakfast?"

Stefan ignored her joke and went to the shed door. Elena noticed that a padlock that had held the double door shut had been wrenched apart, pulled to pieces. A half loop of metal hung uselessly from the shackle.

Stefan had clearly broken in earlier.

Elena followed him in. At first, after the dew-bright morning outside, she couldn't see anything in the dimness of the shed. Gradually, she realized that the walls of the shed were lined with loose papers. Stefan reached out and shoved the doors wider, letting the sunshine stream into the space.

Elena peered at the papers on the walls and then stepped back with a sharp gasp: The first thing she had been able to make out was a picture of her own face. She yanked the paper off the wall and looked at it more closely. It was a clipping from the local paper, showing her dressed in a silver gown, dancing in Stefan's arms. The caption under the picture read: "Robert E. Lee High School prom queen Elena Gilbert and prom king Stefan Salvatore."

Prom queen? Despite the seriousness of the situation, her lips curled up in a smile. She really had finished high school in a blaze of glory, hadn't she?

She pulled another clipping from the wall and her face fell. This one showed a coffin carried through the rain by pallbearers, grim-faced mourners standing by. In the crowd, Elena recognized Aunt Judith, Robert, Margaret, Meredith, and Bonnie, lips set, cheeks streaked with tears. The caption here read: "Town mourns local high school student Elena Gilbert."

Elena's fingers tightened unconsciously, crumpling the

clipping. She turned to look at Stefan. "This shouldn't be here," she said, a note of hysteria creeping into her voice. "The Guardians changed the past. There shouldn't be any newspaper articles or anything left."

Stefan stared back at her. "I know," he said. "I've been thinking, and the best guess I can make is that maybe the Guardians just changed people's *minds*. They wouldn't see any evidence of what we asked the Guardians to erase. They'd just see what supported their new memories, the memories of a normal small town and of a bunch of ordinary teenagers. Just another school year."

Elena brandished the paper. "But then why is this here?"

Stefan dropped his voice. "Maybe it doesn't work on everybody. Caleb's got some notes scribbled in a notebook I found, and it seems from them as though he's remembering two different sets of events. Listen to this." Stefan scrabbled through the papers littering the floor and pulled out a notebook. "He writes: 'There are girls in town now that I know were dead. There were monsters here. The town was destroyed, and we left before they could get us too. But now I'm back and we never left, even though no one but me remembers. Everything's normal: no monsters, no death.'"

"Hmm." Elena took the notebook from him and scanned through the pages. Caleb had lists there. Vickie

Bennett, Caroline, her. All of them. Everyone who was different in this world than in the other one. There were notes about how he remembered them—how he thought Elena was dead and what was going on now. She turned a few pages, and her eyes widened. "Stefan, listen. Tyler told him about us: 'Tyler was afraid of Stefan Salvatore. He thought he killed Mr. Tanner and that there was something else strange about him, something unnatural. And he thought Elena Gilbert and her friends were tangled up in whatever was going on.' And there's an asterisk referring back to Mr. Tanner being dead in one set of memories and alive in the other." Elena quickly scanned a few pages. "It looks like he focused in on *us* as the cause of the changes. He figured out we were at the center of everything. Because we're the people the most changed—other than the vampire and kitsune victims—and because he knew Tyler was suspicious of us, he's blaming us for Tyler's disappearance."

"Two sets of memories," Stefan repeated, frowning. "What if Caleb's not the only one remembering both realities? What if supernatural beings, or people aware of the supernatural, weren't affected by the spell?"

Elena froze. "Margaret—I wondered if she remembered something. She seemed so upset when she first saw me. Remember how she was afraid I was going to go away again? Do you think she's remembering me dying along with the memories the Guardians gave her?"

Stefan shook his head. "I don't know, Elena. Do you have any reason to think Margaret is anything other than a perfectly normal little girl? Little kids can be very dramatic without needing a reason. Margaret's got a lot of imagination."

"I don't know," Elena said in frustration. "But if the Guardians just covered over the old memories with new ones, that would explain why my old journal was still hidden in my bedroom just where I left it, and everything that had happened up until I left home written in it. So you think that Caleb suspects something is going on because he *is* a werewolf after all?"

"Look," Stefan said, gesturing around the shed.

For the first time, Elena took in the whole scene and its implications. Pictures of her. Pictures of Bonnie and Meredith. Even pictures of poor Caroline, ranging from the haughty green-eyed debutante to a feral half monster, heavily pregnant with Tyler's . . . baby? Pup? Elena realized with a shock that she hadn't thought of Caroline in days. Was Caroline still pregnant? Was she still transforming into a werewolf because she was carrying Tyler's baby? There were, Elena remembered, an awful lot of werewolves in Fell's Church. Powerful, important werewolves, and if that hadn't changed, and if the pack remembered everything, or enough of everything, then they were probably just biding their time.

There were not only clippings but original photographs around the room. She saw a picture taken through the boardinghouse window of herself leaning forward excitedly to talk to Meredith, who was caressing her deadly hunting stave. Based on her outfit, it had been taken right after they picked up Alaric and Celia. Caleb had been not only researching the two sets of memories over the last few months but also spying on Elena and her friends.

Then she noticed something else. In the far corner on the floor was a huge bunch of roses. "What . . . ?" Elena said, reaching for them. And then she saw. A pentagram was drawn around the roses. And encircling the pentagram was a bunch of photographs: herself, Bonnie, Meredith, Matt, Stefan, Damon.

"Those are the same kinds of roses as the one Caleb gave you, aren't they?" Stefan asked softly. Elena nodded. They were perfect, delicate blooms in a dark luscious red that made her want to touch them.

"The rose that started it all," she whispered. "It pricked Bonnie's finger, and her blood spelled Celia's name. It must have come from here."

"Caleb isn't just a werewolf," Stefan said. "I don't know exactly what he did here, but it looks like pretty dark magic to me." He looked at her pleadingly. "I discovered it all yesterday," he continued. "I had to fight him, Elena. I know I scared you, but I had to protect you—and everyone else—from him."

Elena nodded, too stunned to speak. Now she understood why Stefan had acted the way he had. He thought she was in danger. But still . . . she couldn't help feeling sick when she remembered the arc of Caleb's body as he was thrown. Caleb might have attacked them with dangerous magic, but his notes sounded confused and frightened. Elena and her friends had changed his world, and now he couldn't tell what was reality.

"We'd better pack up all of this and bring it back to the boardinghouse," she said briskly. "Are there more notebooks?" Stefan nodded. "Then we'd better look through them carefully. If he cast a spell on us—some kind of curse—it could still be active, even though he's confined to the hospital for now. The spell he used might be in one of the notebooks, or at least we might find some kind of clue as to what it is and exactly what it's doing. And, hopefully, how to reverse it."

Stefan was looking a little lost, his green eyes questioning. His arms were held out very slightly, as if he had been expecting her to embrace him and hadn't remembered to put them down when she hadn't. But for some reason she couldn't quite put her finger on, Elena couldn't bring herself to hug him. Instead, she looked away and said, "Do you have any plastic bags or anything in the car we can use to move it all?"

24

Elena hung up her cell phone as they pulled up to the boardinghouse in Stefan's car. "The nurse at the hospital says Caleb's still unconscious," she said.

"Good," said Stefan. She gave him a reproving glance and he stared back at her in exasperation. "If he's unconscious," he explained, "it'll give us more of a chance to figure out what spell he's cast on us."

They'd filled three fat black trash bags with the papers, clippings, and books they'd found in the Smallwoods' garden shed. Elena had been afraid to disturb the pentagram with the roses and photographs around it on the shed floor, in case that would affect the spell somehow, but she'd taken a couple of pictures of it with her cell phone.

Matt came out and picked up one of the bags. "Bringing over some garbage?"

"Something like that," Elena said grimly, and filled him in on what they'd discovered at the Smallwood house.

Matt grimaced. "Wow. But maybe now we can finally do something about what's been happening."

"How come you're here so early?" Elena asked, following him toward the house. "I thought you weren't coming onto guard duty until ten." Stefan trailed along behind her.

"I spent the night," Matt told her. "After Bonnie's name appeared, I didn't want to let her out of my sight."

"Bonnie's name appeared?" Elena whirled accusingly on Stefan. "Why didn't you tell me?"

Stefan shrugged uncomfortably. "I didn't know," he confessed hesitantly.

"Stefan, I told you to protect Meredith and Celia," she snapped. "You were supposed to be *here*. Even before Bonnie's name showed up, it was Meredith and Celia who were in danger. I was relying on you to watch over them."

Stefan glared back at her. "I'm not your lapdog, Elena," he said quietly. "I saw a mysterious threat that I thought bore investigation. I acted to protect you. And I was right. The danger was more immediate to you than the others. And now we have a chance to piece together the spell."

Elena blinked at his tone but couldn't deny the truth in his words. "I'm sorry," she said contritely. "You're right. I'm glad we discovered Caleb's shed."

Matt opened the front door. They dumped the bags in the hall and went through to the kitchen, where Mrs. Flowers, Alaric, and Meredith were enjoying a breakfast of croissants, jam, fruit, and sausages.

"Celia's gone," Meredith said to Elena as soon as they entered the room. Her tone was casually informative, but her usually cool gray eyes were twinkling, and Elena shared a secret smile with her friend.

"Where'd she go?" Elena asked, equally casually, reaching for a croissant. It had been a long morning, and she was starving.

"University of Virginia," Alaric answered. "She's hoping to get some leads by doing research on curses and folk magic."

"We might have some more information now," Elena announced around a mouthful of deliciously buttery croissant. She explained what they had found in the shed. "We brought all the papers and Caleb's notebooks with us. And here's what he'd laid out on the floor." She pulled out her phone, loaded the picture, and handed it to Mrs. Flowers.

"My goodness," said the old woman. "This certainly looks like dark magic. I wonder what that child thought he was doing."

Stefan snorted. "He's no child, Mrs. Flowers. I strongly suspect he's a werewolf as well as a dark magician."

Mrs. Flowers looked at him sternly. "He's found the wrong way of going about looking for his cousin, that's for certain. But this magic looks rather amateurish to me. If it has worked, it will have been more by accident than design."

"*If* it's worked?" Meredith asked. "I think the evidence suggests that whatever he's done worked."

"Surely it would be too much of a coincidence for Caleb to be trying to cast spells on us *and* for an unexplained curse to be affecting us as well," Alaric noted.

"Where's Caleb now?" Matt asked, frowning. "Does he know you found all this? Do we need to track him down and keep an eye on him?"

Stefan crossed his arms. "He's in the hospital."

There was a little pause as the others looked at one another and decided, based on Stefan's stony demeanor, not to delve deeper. Meredith glanced questioningly at Elena, and Elena nodded slightly to say, *I'll explain later.*

She turned to Mrs. Flowers. "Can you tell what spell Caleb was using? What was he trying to do?"

Mrs. Flowers stared thoughtfully at the picture. "It's an interesting question," she said. "Roses are typically used in love spells, but the pentagram and multiple pictures around it suggest a darker intent here. The roses' unusual crimson color would probably make them more effective. They might be used to evoke other passions as well. My best guess would be that Caleb was trying to control your emotions in some way."

Elena cast a sudden glance at Stefan, taking in his guarded expression and tense shoulders.

"But that's as much as I can tell you for now," Mrs. Flowers continued. "If the rest of you want to look through Caleb's notebooks for clues, Bonnie and I can research the magical properties of roses and what spells they could be used in."

"Where is Bonnie?" Elena asked. Although she'd had the sense that something was missing, she'd only just consciously realized that the petite redhead wasn't among the group in the kitchen.

"Still sleeping," Meredith said. "You know how she loves to sleep in." She grinned. "Bonnie was definitely enjoying being the damsel in peril and having everybody fussing over her last night."

"I thought she was being really brave," Matt said unexpectedly. Elena eyed him. Was he beginning to feel something romantic for Bonnie? They'd be good together, she thought, and was surprised to feel a tiny twinge of possessive anger mixed in with her speculative matchmaking. *Matt has always been yours, after all,* a hard voice whispered to her.

"I'll go up and wake her," Meredith said cheerfully. "No rest for the witches." She swung to her feet and headed for the stairs, limping only slightly.

"How's your ankle?" Elena asked. "You look a lot better."

"I heal fast," Meredith said. "I guess it's part of the vampire-hunter thing. I didn't need the cane by the time I went to bed last night, and this morning it feels almost back to normal."

"Lucky you," said Elena.

"Lucky me," Meredith agreed, grinning at Alaric, who smiled back admiringly. Showing off, she ran lightly up the stairs, leaning only a little on the banister for support.

Elena took another croissant and spread jam on it. "The rest of us should start going through all the papers and things we took from Caleb's shed. Alaric, as you're the only one other than Mrs. Flowers and Bonnie who knows much about magic, you can take his notebooks and I'll—"

She broke off as a scream came from overhead.

"Meredith!" shouted Alaric.

Later, Elena didn't really remember getting upstairs. There was just a flash of shoving limbs and pandemonium as everyone tried to get up the narrow staircase as quickly as possible. At the door of the little cream-and-rose bedroom at the end of the hall, Meredith stood, white-faced and stricken. She turned large panicked gray eyes toward them and whispered, "Bonnie."

Inside, Bonnie's small figure lay motionless facedown

on the floor, one pajamaed arm flung out toward the door. Unlit black and white candles were in a ring behind her, one black candle knocked over. There was a smudge of what looked like mostly dried blood inside the candle ring, and a weathered book lay open beside it.

Elena pushed past Meredith and knelt beside the still figure, feeling at her neck for a pulse. She let out the breath she'd been holding as she felt Bonnie's heartbeat, steady and strong, beneath her fingers.

"Bonnie," she said, shaking her by the shoulder, then gently rolling her over. Bonnie flopped without resistance onto her back. She was breathing regularly, but her eyes stayed closed, her long lashes dark against her freckled cheeks.

"Somebody call an ambulance," Elena said quickly.

"I'll do it," Meredith said, breaking out of her frozen stance.

"We don't need an ambulance," Mrs. Flowers said quietly, gazing down at Bonnie with an expression of sorrow on her face.

"What are you talking about?" Meredith snapped. "She's unconscious! We have to get her help."

Mrs. Flowers's eyes were grave. "The doctors and nurses at the hospital won't be able to help Bonnie," she said. "They might even hurt her by interfering with ineffective medical solutions to a nonmedical problem.

Bonnie's not sick; she's under a spell. I can feel the magic thick in the air. The best thing we can do is to make her as comfortable as we can here while we look for a cure."

Matt stepped forward into the room. His face was aghast, but he wasn't looking at Bonnie's motionless form on the floor. He raised one hand and pointed. "Look," he said.

Near the bed, a tray containing a small teapot, a cup, and a plate had been knocked over onto the floor. The cup had smashed and the teapot lay on its side, tea leaves spilling out in a long, dark curve across the floor.

A curve that spelled out a name.

elena

att swung his gaze in horror between Bonnie's prone figure, the name on the floor, and Elena's pale face. After a few shocked minutes, Elena spun and left the room. Stefan and Matt followed her as Meredith and the others moved to Bonnie's side. Out in the hallway, Elena pounced on Stefan. "You were supposed to look after them. If you had been here, Bonnie would have had some protection."

Matt, trailing Stefan out of Bonnie's bedroom, balked. Elena's teeth were bared, her dark blue eyes flashed, and she and Stefan both looked furious.

"It wasn't Stefan's fault, Elena," Matt protested gently. "Alaric and Mrs. Flowers had set magical protections. Nothing ought to have been able to get in. Even if Stefan had been here, he wouldn't have been in Bonnie's room with her all night."

"He should have been, if that's what it took to protect her," Elena said bitterly. Her face was tight with anger as she looked at Stefan.

Even as Matt stood up for Stefan, he couldn't suppress a glow of satisfaction at seeing trouble between Elena and Stefan at last. *It's about time Elena realized Stefan isn't perfect*, the worst part of him said gleefully.

Mrs. Flowers and Alaric hurried out of the room, breaking the tension between Elena and Stefan. Mrs. Flowers shook her head. "It seems that Bonnie was very foolishly trying to contact the dead, but I don't see how she could have done this to herself. This must be the result of whatever has been endangering you. Meredith is going to stay by Bonnie's bedside for the time being while we investigate."

Matt glanced at Elena and Stefan. "I thought you said that Caleb was out of the picture."

"I thought he was!" Stefan said as they all headed downstairs. "Maybe this is something he started before we fought."

Alaric frowned. "If that's true and it's still going, Caleb himself might not be able to stop it. Even if he died, that wouldn't interrupt a self-perpetuating curse."

Elena strode out to the hall and ripped into the first of the trash bags, her jaw set. "We need to figure out what he did." She dug out a stack of notebooks and shoved them into the others' hands. "Look for the actual steps of a spell.

If we know *how* he did it, maybe Alaric or Mrs. Flowers can figure out how to reverse it."

"The spell book Bonnie was using is one of mine," Mrs. Flowers said. "Nothing in it should have had this effect on her, but I'll examine it just in case."

They each took a notebook and a pile of papers and spread out around the kitchen table.

"There are diagrams in mine," Stefan said after a minute. "There's a pentagram, but I don't think it's the same as the one we saw on the floor."

Alaric took the notebook and peered at it, then shook his head. "I'm not an expert, but that looks like part of a standard protection spell."

The notebook in front of Matt was mostly scribbled notes. *Tanner first death?* it asked. *Halloween? Elena, Bonnie, Meredith, Matt, Tyler, Stefan all present.* He could hear Meredith's feet upstairs, restlessly pacing by Bonnie's bedside, and the words blurred before him. He scrubbed the back of his fist against his eyes before he could embarrass himself by crying. This was useless. And even if there was something helpful in here, he would never recognize it.

"Does it strike you guys as weird," Elena asked, "that Celia was the first one affected by whatever this evil is? There wasn't anything about her in the shed. And she never met Tyler, let alone Caleb. If Caleb was trying to get revenge on us for Tyler's disappearance, why would he attack Celia first? Or at all, really."

That was a really good point, Matt thought, and he was about to say so when he spotted Mrs. Flowers. She was standing stick-straight, staring off past his left ear and nodding slightly. "Do you really think so?" she said softly. "Oh, that does make a difference. Yes, I see. Thank you."

By the time she had finished and her eyes snapped back to focus on them, the others had also noticed her one-sided conversation and grown silent, watching her.

"Does your mother know what happened to Bonnie?" Matt asked her eagerly. He had stayed in Fell's Church fighting the kitsune with Mrs. Flowers when his friends had traveled to the Dark Dimension, and their time as comrades in arms had made him familiar with Mrs. Flowers's casual exchanges with the spirit realm. If Mrs. Flowers's mother had interrupted their conversation, she probably had something useful and important to say.

"Yes," said Mrs. Flowers, smiling at him. "Yes, indeed, Ma*ma* was very helpful." Her face grew serious as she glanced around. "Ma*ma* was able to sense the thing that took Bonnie's spirit. Once it had entered the house, she could observe it, although she was powerless to fight it herself. She's upset that she wasn't able to save Bonnie. She's quite fond of her."

"Is Bonnie going to be okay?" Matt asked, over the others' questions of, "So what *is* it?" and "It's a demon or something, then, not a curse?"

Mrs. Flowers looked at Matt first. "We *may* be able to save Bonnie. We will certainly try. But we will have to defeat the thing that took her. And the rest of you are still very much in danger."

She looked around at them all. "It's a phantom."

There was a little pause.

"What's a phantom?" Elena asked. "Do you mean a ghost?"

"A phantom, of course," Stefan said quietly, shaking his head like he couldn't believe the idea hadn't occurred to him earlier. "There was a town I heard of once back in Italy many years ago, where they said a phantom stalked the streets of Umbria. It wasn't a ghost, but a being created by strong emotions. The story was that a man became so enraged at his unfaithful lover that he killed her and her paramour, and then himself. And these actions released something, a being made out of their emotions. One by one people living nearby went mad. They did terrible things." Stefan looked shaken to his core.

"Is that what we're facing? Some kind of demon created out of anger that will drive people mad?" Elena turned to Mrs. Flowers imploringly. "Because frankly I think this town has had enough of that."

"It can't happen again," Matt said. He was also looking at Mrs. Flowers. She was the only one who had seen the near-destruction of Fell's Church with him. The others had been there for the beginning, sure, but when things got really awful, when they were at their worst, the girls and the vampires had been off in the Dark Dimension, fighting their own battles to fix it.

Mrs. Flowers met his eyes and nodded firmly, like she was making a pledge. "It won't," she said. "Stefan, what you're describing probably was a rage phantom, but it sounds like the popular explanation of what was going on wasn't quite accurate. According to Ma*ma*, phantoms feed on emotions like vampires do on blood. The stronger an emotion is, the better fed and more active they are. They're attracted to people or communities that already have these strong emotions, and they create almost a feedback loop, encouraging and nurturing thoughts that will make the emotion stronger so that they can continue to feed. They're quite psychically powerful, but they can survive only as long as their victims keep feeding them."

Elena was listening carefully. "But what about Bonnie?" She looked at Stefan. "In this town in Umbria, did people fall into comas because of the phantom?"

Stefan shook his head. "Not that I ever heard of," he said. "Maybe that's where Caleb comes in."

"I'll call Celia," said Alaric. "This will help focus her research. If anyone has any material at all on this, it'll be Dr. Beltram."

"Could your mother tell what kind of phantom it was?" Stefan asked Mrs. Flowers. "If we know what emotion it feeds on, we could cut off its supply."

"She didn't know," she said. "And she doesn't know how to defeat a phantom either. And there's one more thing we should take into consideration: Bonnie's got a lot of innate psychic power of her own. If the phantom has taken her, it's probably tapped into that."

Matt nodded, following her train of thought. "And if that's so," he finished grimly, "then this thing is only going to get stronger and more dangerous."

26

The day passed with much research, but with very little in the way of results, which left Elena feeling increasingly concerned for her comatose friend. By the time night fell and Aunt Judith called to wearily inquire whether Elena's family would see her at all that day, they had sorted through the first bag of papers and Alaric had gone over a third or so of what seemed to be the notebook in which Caleb kept the record of his magical experiments, grumbling about Caleb's terrible handwriting.

Elena frowned, flipping through another stack of papers. Looking through the pictures and clippings confirmed that Celia hadn't been among Caleb's planned victims. If the phantom had targeted her first, it must have been because she was rich in whatever emotion this phantom fed off.

"Snippiness," Meredith suggested, but she was careful to say it out of Alaric's hearing.

The clippings and printouts also showed that Caleb was indeed obsessed with Tyler's disappearance, and that he had evidence and memories of two different time lines for the same period—one where Fell's Church had been falling apart and Elena Gilbert had been dead, and one where everything had been *just fine, thanks* in the small Virginia town of Fell's Church, including the continuing reign of the senior class's golden girl, Elena. In addition to Caleb's own double memories, which covered only the summer, Tyler had apparently talked to him over the phone the previous fall and winter about the mysterious events surrounding Mr. Tanner's death and everything that followed. Although it didn't sound from Caleb's notes like Tyler had mentioned his own transformation to werewolf and conspiracy with Klaus, just his growing suspicions of Stefan.

"*Tyler.*" Elena groaned. "Even though he's long gone, he manages to make trouble."

Alaric's examination of the notebook so far had proved that they were right that Caleb was a magic user, and that he was planning to use his magic both to take vengeance against them and to try to locate Tyler. But it hadn't shown how he had summoned the phantom.

And despite Alaric's bringing any likely looking note, incantation, or drawing to Mrs. Flowers for inspection, they had not yet discovered what kind of spell Caleb had been doing, or what purpose the roses served.

Stefan escorted Elena home for dinner, then returned to continue helping the others. He'd wanted to stay with Elena, but she had a feeling her aunt would not appreciate a last-minute dinner guest.

The second Elena stepped through the door, she could feel Damon's lingering presence and remembered how, just hours ago, they had stood upstairs, holding each other. All through the meal, while she told Margaret a bedtime story, and then during her last call to Meredith to check on the rest of the group's progress, she'd thought longingly of him, wondering whether she would see him tonight. That in turn set off pangs of guilt related to Stefan and Bonnie. She was being so selfish, keeping Stefan's brother's return from him, and thinking of herself while Bonnie was in danger. The whole cycle was exhausting, but still she couldn't contain her exuberance that Damon was alive.

Alone in her room at last, Elena ran a brush through her silky golden hair and pulled on the simple cool nightgown she'd worn the night before. It was hot and humid outside, and through her window she could hear the crickets chirping busily. The stars were shining, and a half-moon floated high over the trees outside. She called good night to Aunt Judith and Robert and climbed into bed, fluffing the pillows around her.

She half expected a long wait. Damon liked to tease, and he liked to make an entrance, so he was quite likely to wait until he thought she would be asleep, and then sweep into her room. But she had barely turned off the light when a piece of darkness seemed to separate itself from the night outside her window. There was the faintest scuff of a footstep on the floor, and then her mattress groaned as Damon settled himself at the foot of her bed.

"Hello, love," he said softly.

"Hi," she said, smiling at him. His black eyes glittered at her from the shadows, and Elena suddenly felt warm and happy, despite everything.

"What's the latest?" he asked. "I saw a lot of fuss going on at the boardinghouse. Something got your sidekicks in a tizzy?" His tone was casually sarcastic, but his gaze was intense, and Elena knew he had been worried.

"If you let me tell everyone you're alive, you could be with us and then you'd know everything that's going on firsthand," she teased. Then she grew somber. "Damon, we need your help. Something terrible has happened."

She told him about Bonnie, and about what they had discovered in the Smallwoods' garden shed.

Damon's eyes flamed. "A phantom's got the little redbird?"

"That's what Mrs. Flowers's mother said," Elena

answered. "Stefan told us that he'd known of a rage phantom somewhere back in Italy."

Damon made a little *pfft!* noise. "I remember that. It was amusing at the time, but nothing like what you've been describing. How does this theory of Stefan's explain Bonnie's being taken? Or the appearance of the names when someone is threatened?"

"It's Mrs. Flowers's theory, too," Elena said indignantly. "Or her mother's, I guess. And it's the only one that makes sense." She could feel Damon stroking her arm with the most featherlight touch, and it felt *good*. The hairs prickled on the back of her arms, and she shivered with pleasure in spite of herself. *Stop it*, she thought sternly. *This is serious business*. She moved her arm out of Damon's reach.

He sounded amused and lazy when he next spoke. "Well, I can't blame the old witch and her ghost mother," he said. "Humans mostly stay in their own dimension; they learn only the tiniest piece of what's happening, even the most gifted of them. But if Stefan behaved like any self-respecting vampire and didn't go around trying to be *human* all the time, he'd have a little more of a clue. He's barely even traveled to the Dark Dimension except when he was dragged there to sit in a cage or save Bonnie. Maybe if he had, he would understand what was going on and be able to protect his pet humans a little better."

Elena bristled. "Pet humans? I'm one of those *pet humans*, too."

Damon chuckled, and Elena realized he had said that purposely, to rile her up. "A pet? You, princess? Never. A tiger, maybe. Something wild and dangerous."

Elena rolled her eyes. Then the implication of Damon's words hit her. "Wait, are you saying this *isn't* a phantom? And that you know what it actually is? Is it something that comes from the Dark Dimension?"

Damon shifted closer to her again. "Would you like to know what I know?" he said, his voice like a caress. "There are a lot of things I could tell you."

"*Damon*," Elena said firmly. "Stop flirting and pay attention. This is important. If you know anything, please tell me. If you don't, please don't play games with me. Bonnie's life is at stake. And we're all in danger. You're in danger, too, Damon: Don't forget, your name's been written, and we don't know for sure that whatever happened on the Dark Moon was the attack on you."

"I'm not too concerned." Damon waved his hand disparagingly. "It would take more than a phantom to hurt me, princess. But, yes, I know a little more about this than *Stefan* does." He turned her hand over and traced her palm with cool fingers. "It is a phantom," he said. "But it's not the same kind we saw in Italy long ago. Do you remember that Klaus was an Original? He wasn't sired like Katherine or Stefan or I was; he was never human. Vampires like Klaus consider vampires like us who started out as humans to be weak half-breeds. He was much stronger than us and much more difficult to kill. There are different types of phantoms, too. The phantoms who are born of human emotions on Earth are able to intensify and spur on these emotions. They don't have much consciousness of their own, though, and they never get very strong. They're just parasites. If they are cut off from the emotions they need to survive, they fade away pretty quickly."

Elena frowned. "But you think this is another, more powerful kind of phantom? Why? What did Sage tell you?"

Damon tapped her hand with one finger as he counted. "One: the names. That's beyond the powers of an ordinary phantom. Two: It took Bonnie. A regular phantom wouldn't be able to do that, and wouldn't get anything out of it if it could. An Original phantom, though, can steal her spirit and take it back to the Dark Dimension. It can drain her life force and emotions to make itself stronger."

"Wait," Elena said, alarmed. "Bonnie's back in the Dark Dimension? Anything could be happening to her! She could be enslaved again!" Tears pricked at the corners of her eyes as she thought of how humans were treated in the Dark Dimension.

Damon squeezed her hand. "No, don't worry about that. She's there only in spirit—the phantom will have her in some kind of holding cell; it'll want her safe. I think the worst thing that could happen to her is she'll be bored." He frowned. "It'll sap her life force, though, and that'll weaken her eventually."

"You *think* that being bored's the worst thing that could happen to her . . . oh, at least until it drains all her life force? That's not good enough, Damon. We have to help her." Elena thought for a moment. "So phantoms live in the Dark Dimension?"

Damon hesitated. "Not in the beginning. The Original phantoms were relegated to the Dark Moon by the Guardians."

"Where you died."

"Yes," Damon said caustically. Then he rubbed the back of her hand in a silent apology for his tone. "Original phantoms are kept inside some kind of prison on the Dark Moon, just itching for a chance to get out. Like genies in a bottle. If something broke the prison wall, their ultimate goal would be to make it to Earth and feed on human emotions. After the World Tree was destroyed, Sage said things changed, which would make sense if an Original phantom managed to escape as things shifted after the destruction."

"Why come all the way to Earth, though?" Elena asked. "There're all those demons and vampires in the Dark Dimension."

She could see Damon's smile in the shadows. "I guess

human emotion is extra-delicious. Like human blood is. And there aren't enough humans in the Dark Dimension to make a really good meal. There are so many humans on Earth that an Original here can just keep on gorging on emotion and growing ever more powerful."

"So it followed us from the Dark Moon?" Elena asked.

"It must have hitched a ride with you when you came back to Earth. It would have wanted to get as far from its prison as possible, so an opening between dimensions would have been irresistible."

"And it was freed from its prison when I used my *Wings of Destruction* and blasted the moon?"

Damon shrugged. "That seems to be the most likely explanation."

Elena's heart sank. "So Bonnie's vision was right. I brought this. It's my fault."

He brushed back her hair and kissed her neck. "Don't think of it that way," he said. "How could you have stopped it? You didn't know. And I'm grateful you used the *Wings of Destruction*: That's what saved me, after all. The important thing now is to fight the phantom. We need to send it back before it gets too powerful. If it gets a real foothold here, it can start influencing more and more people. The whole world could be in danger."

Elena half consciously arched her neck to one side so that Damon could get a better angle, and he gently traced the vein on the side of her neck with his lips for a moment before she realized what they were doing and nudged him away again. "I don't understand, though. Why would it tell us who it's going after next?" she said. "Why does it give us the names?"

"Oh, that's not its own doing," Damon said, and kissed her shoulder. "Even the most powerful phantom has to follow the rules. It's part of the spell the Guardians put on the Original phantoms, when they relegated them to the Dark Moon. A safeguard in case the Originals ever escaped. This way, their prey knows they're coming, and it gives them a fair shot at resisting."

"The Guardians imprisoned it," Elena said. "Would they help us send it back?"

"I don't know," Damon said shortly. "I wouldn't ask them if I could help it, though. I don't trust them, do you?"

Elena thought of the cool efficiency of the Guardians, of the way they had dismissed Damon's death as irrelevant. Of the way they had caused her own parents' death. "No," she said, shivering. "Let's leave them out of it if we can."

"We'll defeat it ourselves, Elena," Damon said, and caressed her cheek with his hand.

"Stop it," Elena said. "We have to concentrate."

Damon stopped trying to touch her for a moment and thought. "Tell me about your little friends. Have people been tense? Fighting? Acting out of character?"

"Yes," Elena said immediately. "No one's been acting like themselves. I can't put my finger on it, but something's been wrong since we got back."

Damon nodded. "Since it probably came with you, it makes sense that it would have targeted you and those connected to you as its first victims."

"But how do we *stop* it?" Elena asked. "What do these stories you've heard about the Original phantoms say about recapturing them once they've escaped from their prison?"

Damon sighed, and his shoulders slumped a little. "Nothing," he said. "I don't know anything more. I'll have to go back to the Dark Dimension and see what I can find out, or if I can fight the phantom from there."

Elena stiffened. "It's too dangerous, Damon."

Damon chuckled, a dry sound in the darkness, and Elena felt his fingers run through her hair, smoothing the silky strands, then twisting them, tugging them gently. "Not for me," he said. "The Dark Dimension is a great place to be a vampire."

"Except that you *died* there," Elena reminded him. "Damon, please. I can't stand to lose you again."

Damon's hand stilled, and then he was kissing her gently, and his other hand came up to touch her cheek. "Elena," he said as he reluctantly broke the kiss.

"You won't lose me."

"There has to be another way," she insisted.

"Well, then we'd better find it, and soon," Damon answered grimly. "Otherwise the entire world will be at risk."

Damon was saturated with Elena. Her sweet, rich scent in his nostrils, the throbbing beat of her heart in his ears, the silk of her hair and the satin of her skin against his fingers. He wanted to kiss her, to hold her, to sink his fangs into her and taste the heady nectar of her blood, that vibrant blood that tasted like no one else's.

But she made him go, although he knew she didn't really want to.

She didn't say it was because of his little brother that she pushed him away, but he knew anyway. It was always Stefan.

When he left her, he transformed gracefully into a large black crow again and flew from her bedroom window to the quince tree nearby. There, he folded his wings and shifted from one foot to another, settling in to watch over her. He could sense her through the window, anxious at first, her thoughts churning, but soon her pulse slowed, her breathing deepened, and he knew she was asleep. He would stay and guard her.

There was no question: He had to save her. If Elena

wanted a chivalrous knight, someone who would protect her nobly, Damon could do that. Why should that weakling Stefan have all the glory?

But he wasn't sure what came next. Despite Elena's begging him not to go, heading into the Dark Dimension seemed like the logical next step in fighting this phantom. But how to get there? There were no easy paths. He didn't have the time to journey to one of the gates again, nor did he want to leave Elena's side long enough to travel there. And he couldn't expect to find something as useful as a star ball again by chance.

Plus, if he did get there, being in the Dark Dimension would have special dangers for him now. He didn't think the Guardians knew he had come back from the dead, and he didn't know how they would react when they did. He'd rather not find out. The Guardians didn't care for vampires much, and they tended to like things to stay the way they ought to be. Look at how they had stripped Elena's Powers when she came to their attention.

Damon hunched his shoulders and fluffed out his iridescent feathers irritably. There had to be another way.

There was the slightest rustle underfoot. No one without the sensitive ears of a vampire would have heard it, it was so cautious, but Damon caught it. He snapped to attention and peered sharply around. No one would get to his princess.

Oh. Damon relaxed again and clicked his beak in vexation. *Stefan.* The shadowy figure of his little brother stood beneath the tree, head tilted back, gazing in devotion at Elena's darkened window. Of course he was there, standing by to defend her against all the horrors of the night.

And just like that, Damon knew what he had to do: If he wanted to learn more about the phantom, he'd have to give himself over to it.

He closed his eyes, allowing every negative feeling he'd ever had about Stefan to wash over him. How Stefan had always taken everything Damon wanted, had stolen it, if he needed to.

Damn Stefan, Damon thought bitterly. If his brother hadn't come to town earlier than him, Damon would have had a chance to make Elena fall in love with him first, to be the one to reap the utter devotion he saw in her eyes when she looked at Stefan.

Instead, here he was, second-best. He hadn't been enough for Katherine either; she had wanted his brother, too. Elena, tiger to the kitten Katherine had been, would have been the perfect mate for Damon. Beautiful, strong, wily, capable of great love, they could have ruled the night together.

But she had fallen for his lily-livered weakling of a little brother. Damon's claws clenched the branch he sat on.

"Isn't it sad," a quiet voice beside him suggested, "how

you try and try, but you're never enough for the women you love?"

A cool tendril of fog touched his wing. Damon straightened and looked around. Dark fog was winding around the quince tree, just at Damon's level. Below, Stefan stood unaware. The fog had come for Damon alone.

With a private smile, Damon felt the fog envelop him, and then all was darkness.

27

The next morning was another hot one. The air was so thick and humid that just walking down the street felt unpleasantly like getting slapped with a warm, damp washcloth. Even inside the car with the air-conditioning on, Elena could feel her usually sleek hair frizzing from the humidity.

Stefan had turned up at her house just after breakfast, this time with a list of herbs and magical supplies Mrs. Flowers wanted them to find in town for new protection spells.

As they drove, Elena gazed out the window at the neat white houses and trim green lawns of residential Fell's Church as they gradually gave way to the brick buildings and tasteful store windows of the shopping district at the center of town.

Stefan parked on the main street, outside a cute little café where they had sipped cappuccinos together last fall, shortly after she'd learned what he was. Sitting at one of the tiny tables, Stefan had told her how to make a traditional Italian cappuccino, and that had led to his reminiscing about the great feasts of his youth during the Renaissance: aromatic soups sprinkled with pomegranate seeds; rich roasts basted with rosewater; pastries with elder flowers and chestnuts. Course after course of sweet, rich, heavily spiced foods that a modern Italian would never recognize as part of his country's cuisine.

It had awed Elena when she realized how different the world had been the last time Stefan had eaten human food. He had mentioned in passing that forks had just been coming into fashion when he was young, and that his father had derided them as a foppish fad. Until Katherine had brought a more fashionable and ladylike influence into their home, they had eaten with only spoons and sharp knives for cutting. "It was elegant, though," he'd said, laughing at the expression on her face. "We all had excellent table manners. You'd hardly have noticed."

At the time, she'd thought his differences from the boys she'd known—the scope of all the history he'd witnessed—was romantic.

Now . . . well, now she didn't know what she thought.

"It's down here, I think," said Stefan, taking her hand

and returning her to the present. "Mrs. Flowers said a New Age store has opened up and that they should have most of the things we need."

The shop was called Spirit and Soul, and it was tiny but vibrant, cluttered with crystals and unicorn figurines, tarot cards and dream catchers. Everything was painted in shades of purple and silver, and silky wall hangings blew in the breeze from a little windowsill air conditioner. The air conditioner wasn't strong enough to put much of a dent in the stickiness of today's heat, though, and the birdlike little woman with long curling hair and clattering necklaces who emerged from the back of the shop looked tired and sweaty.

"How can I help you?" she said in a low, musical voice that Elena suspected she adopted to fit in with the atmosphere of the store.

Stefan pulled out the scrap of paper covered in Mrs. Flowers's tangled handwriting and squinted at it. Vampire vision or not, deciphering Mrs. Flowers's writing could be a challenge.

Oh, Stefan. He was earnest, and sweet, and noble. His poet's soul shone through those gorgeous green eyes. She couldn't regret loving Stefan. But sometimes she secretly wished that she had found Stefan in a less complicated form, that the soul and the intelligence, the love and the passion, the sophistication and the gentleness had somehow been possible in the form of a real eighteen-year-old boy; that he had been what he had pretended to be when she first met him: mysterious, foreign, but human.

"Do you have anything made of hematite?" he asked now. "Jewelry, or maybe knickknacks? And incense with . . ." He frowned at the paper. "Althea in it? Does althea sound right?"

"Of course!" said the shopkeeper enthusiastically. "Althea's good for protection and security. And it smells great. The different kinds of incense are over here."

Stefan followed her deeper into the shop, but Elena lingered near the door. She felt exhausted, even though the day had barely begun.

There was a rack of clothing by the front window, and she fiddled distractedly with it, pushing hangers back and forth. There was a wispy pink tunic studded with tiny mirrors, a little hippieish but cute. *Bonnie might like this*, Elena thought automatically, and then flinched.

Through the window, she glimpsed a face she knew, and turned, the top hanging forgotten in her hand.

She searched her mind for the name. Tom Parker, that was it. She'd gone out on a few dates with him junior year, before she and Matt had gotten together. It felt like a lot more than a year and a half ago. Tom had been pleasant enough and handsome enough, a perfectly satisfactory date, but she hadn't felt a spark between them and, as

Meredith had said, "practiced catch and release" with him, "freeing him to swim back into the waters of dating."

He had been crazy about *her*, though. Even after she set him loose, he'd hung around, looking at her with puppy-dog eyes, pleading with her to take him back.

If things had been different, if she had felt anything for Tom, wouldn't her life be simpler now?

She watched Tom. He was strolling down the street, smiling, hand in hand with Marissa Peterson, the girl he had started dating near the end of last year. Tom was tall, and he bent his shaggy dark head down to hear what Marissa was saying. They grinned at each other, and he lifted his free hand to gently, teasingly tug on her long hair. They looked happy together.

Well, good for them. Easy to be happy when they were uncomplicatedly in love, when there was nothing more difficult in their lives than a summer spent with their friends before heading off to college. Easy to be happy when they couldn't even remember the chaos their town had been in before *Elena* had saved them. They weren't even grateful. They were too lucky: They knew nothing of the darkness that lurked on the edges of their safe, sunlit lives.

Elena's stomach twisted. Vampires, demons, phantoms, star-crossed love. Why did *she* have to be the one to deal with it all?

She listened for a moment. Stefan was still consulting

with the shopkeeper, and she heard him say worriedly, "Will rowan twigs have the same effect, though?" and the woman's reassuring murmur. He would be busy for a while longer, then. He was only about a third of the way down the list Mrs. Flowers had given them.

Elena put the shirt back in its place on the rack and walked out of the store.

Careful not to be noticed by the couple across the street, she followed them at a distance, taking a good long look at Marissa. She was skinny, with freckles and a little blob of a nose. Pretty enough, Elena supposed, with long, straight dark hair and a wide mouth, but not especially eye-catching. She'd been nobody much at school, either. Volleyball team, maybe. Yearbook. Passable, but not stellar grades. Friends, but not popular. An occasional date, but not a girl who boys noticed. A part-time job in a store, or maybe the library. Ordinary. Nothing special.

So why did ordinary, nothing-special Marissa get to have this uncomplicated, sunlit life, while Elena had been through hell—literally—to get what Marissa seemed to have with Tom and yet she *still didn't get to have it*?

A cold breeze touched Elena's skin, and she shivered despite the morning's heat. She looked up.

Dark, cool tendrils of fog were drifting around her, yet the rest of the street was just as sunny as it had been a few minutes before. Elena's heart began to pound hard before her brain even caught up and realized what was happening. *Run!* something inside her howled, but it was too late. Her limbs were suddenly heavy as lead.

A cool, dry voice spoke close behind her, a voice that sounded eerily like the observational one inside her own head, the one that told her the uncomfortable truths she didn't want to acknowledge. "Why is it," the voice said, "that you can only love monsters?"

Elena couldn't bring herself to turn around.

"Or is it that only monsters can truly love you, Elena?" the voice went on, taking on a softly triumphant tone. "All those boys in high school, they only wanted you as a trophy. They saw your golden hair and your blue eyes and your perfect face and they thought how fine they would look with you on their arm."

Steeling herself, Elena slowly turned around. There was no one there, but the fog was growing thicker. A woman pushing a stroller brushed past her with a placid glance. Couldn't she see Elena was being wrapped in her own private fog? Elena opened her mouth to cry out, but the words stuck in her throat.

The fog was colder now, and it felt almost solid, like it was holding Elena back. With a great effort of will, she forced herself forward, but could stagger only as far as the bench in front of a nearby store. The voice spoke again, whispering in her ear, gloating. "They never saw you, those boys. Girls like Marissa, like Meredith, can find love and be happy. Only the monsters bother to find the real Elena. Poor, poor Elena, you'll never be normal, will you? Not like other girls." It laughed softly, viciously.

The fog pressed thicker around her. Now Elena couldn't see the rest of the street, or anything beyond the darkness. She tried to get to her feet, to move forward a few steps, to shake off the fog. But she couldn't move. The fog was like a heavy blanket holding her down, but she couldn't touch it, couldn't fight it.

Elena panicked, tried once more to surge to her feet, opened her mouth to call, *Stefan!* But the fog swirled into her, through her, soaking into her every pore. Unable to fight back or call out, she collapsed.

It was still freezing cold.

"At least I have clothes on this time," Damon muttered, kicking at a piece of charred wood as he trudged across the barren surface of the Dark Moon.

The place was beginning to get to him, he had to admit. He had been wandering this desolate landscape for what felt like days, although the unchanging darkness here made it impossible for him to know for sure how much time had passed.

When he had awakened, Damon had assumed he would find the little redbird next to him, eager for his company and protection. But he'd awoken alone, lying on the ground. No phantom, no grateful girl.

He frowned and poked one tentative foot into a heap of ash that might conceal a body, but was unsurprised to find nothing but mud beneath the ash, smearing more filth onto his once-polished black boots. After he'd arrived here and started searching for Bonnie, he'd expected that at any moment, he might stumble across her unconscious body. He'd had a powerful image of what she would look like, pale and silent in the darkness, long red curls caked with ash. But now he was becoming convinced that, wherever the phantom had taken Bonnie, she wasn't here.

He'd come here to be a hero: defeat the phantom, save the girl, and ultimately save *his* girl. *What an idiot*, he thought, curling his lip at his own foolishness.

The phantom hadn't brought him to wherever it was keeping Bonnie. Alone on this ash heap of the moon, he felt oddly rejected. Didn't it want him?

A sudden powerful wind pushed against him, and Damon staggered backward a few steps before regaining his balance. The wind brought a sound with it: Was that a moan? He altered his course, hunching his shoulders and heading for where he thought the sound had come from.

Then the sound came again, a sad, sobbing moan echoing behind him.

He turned back, but his footsteps were closer together and less confident than usual. What if he was wrong and the little witch was hurt and alone somewhere on this god-forsaken moon?

He was terribly hungry. He pushed his tongue against his aching canines, and they grew knife-sharp. His mouth was so dry; he imagined the flow of sweet, rich blood, life itself pulsing against his lips. The moaning came once more, from his left this time, and again he swerved toward it. The wind blew against his face, cold and wet with mist.

This was all Elena's fault.

He was a monster. He was *supposed* to be a monster, to take blood unflinchingly, to kill without a second thought or care. But Elena had changed all that. She had made him want to protect her. Then he had started looking out for her friends, and finally even saving her provincial little town, when any self-respecting vampire would have either been long gone when the kitsune came, or enjoyed the devastation with warm blood on his lips.

He'd done all that—he'd changed for *her*—and she still didn't love him.

Not enough, anyway. When he'd kissed her throat and stroked her hair the other night, who had she been thinking of? That weakling Stefan.

"It's always Stefan, isn't it?" a clear, cool voice said

behind him. Damon froze, the hairs on the back of his neck rising.

"Whatever you tried to take from him," the voice continued, "you were just fighting to even the scales, because the fact is that he got *everything*, and you had nothing at all. You just wanted things to be fair."

Damon shuddered, not turning around. No one had ever understood that. He just wanted things to be *fair*.

"Your father cared for him much more than he did for you. You've always known that," the voice went on. "You were the oldest, the heir, but Stefan was the one your father loved. And, in romance, you have always been two steps behind Stefan. Katherine already loved him by the time you met her; then the same sad story happened all over again with Elena. They say they love you, these girls of yours, but they have never loved you best, or most, or only, not even when you give them your whole heart."

Damon shuddered again. He felt a tear run down his cheek and, infuriated, wiped it away.

"And you know why that is, don't you, Damon?" the creature went on smoothly. "Stefan. Stefan's always taken everything you've ever wanted. He's gotten the things you wanted before you even saw them, and left nothing for you. Elena doesn't love you. She never has and she never will."

Something broke inside Damon at the creature's words,

and instantly he snapped back to himself. How dare the phantom make him question Elena's love? It was the only true thing he knew.

A cold breeze fluttered Damon's clothing. He couldn't hear the moaning now. And then everything went still.

"I know what you're doing," Damon snarled. "You think you can trick me? Do you suppose you can turn me against Elena?"

A soft, wet footstep in the mud sounded behind him. "Oh, little vampire," the voice said mockingly.

"Oh, little phantom," Damon said back, matching the creature's tone. "You have no idea the mistake you just made." Steeling himself to leap, he whirled around, fangs fully extended. But before he could pounce, cold strong hands seized him by the throat and pulled him into the air.

"I'd also recommend burying pieces of iron around whatever you're trying to protect," the shopkeeper suggested. "Horseshoes are traditional, but anything made of iron, especially anything round or curved, will do." She'd passed through various stages of disbelief as Stefan had tried to buy up what seemed like every single object, herb, or charm related to protection in the shop, and now had become manically helpful.

"I think I've got everything I need for now," Stefan

said politely. "Thank you so much for your help."

Her dimples shone as she rang up his purchases on the shop's old-fashioned metal cash register, and he smiled back. He thought he had managed to decipher every item on Mrs. Flowers's list correctly, and was feeling fairly proud of himself.

Someone opened the door to come in, and a cold breeze whooshed into the shop, setting the magical items and wall hangings flapping.

"Do you feel that?" the shopkeeper asked. "I think a storm's coming." Her hair, caught by the wind, fanned out in the air.

Stefan, about to make a pleasant rejoinder, stared in horror. Her long locks, suspended for a moment, twisted their tendrils into one curling strand that spelled out, clearly and chillingly:

matt

But if the phantom had found a new target, that meant Elena—

Stefan whipped around, looking frantically toward the front of the shop. Elena wasn't there.

"Are you all right?" the shopkeeper asked as Stefan stared wildly around. Ignoring her, he hurried back toward the door of the shop, looking down every aisle, in every nook.

Stefan let his Power spread out, reaching for a trace of

Elena's distinctive presence. Nothing. She wasn't in the shop. How could he not have noticed her leaving?

He pressed his fists into his eyes until little stars burst beneath his lids. This was his fault. He hadn't been feeding on human blood, and his powers were sorely diminished. Why had he let himself get so weak? If he had been at full strength, he would have realized immediately that she had gone. It was self-indulgent to give in to his conscience when he had people to protect.

"Are you all right?" the woman asked again. She'd followed him down the aisles of the store, holding out his bag, and was looking at him anxiously.

Stefan took hold of the bag. "The girl I came in with," he said urgently. "Did you see where she went?"

"Oh," she replied, frowning. "She went back outside when we were heading off to look through the incense section."

That long ago. Even the shopkeeper had noticed Elena leaving.

Stefan gave a jerky nod of thanks before striding out into the dazzling sunlight. He looked frantically up and down Main Street.

He felt a wave of relief when he spotted her sitting on a bench outside the drugstore a few doors down. But then he took note of her slumped posture, her beautiful blond head resting limply on one of her shoulders.

Stefan was at her side in a flash, grateful to find her breathing shallow yet steady, her pulse strong. But she was unconscious.

"Elena," he said, gently stroking her cheek. "Elena, wake up. Come back to me." She didn't move. He shook her arm a bit harder. "Elena!" Her body flopped on the bench, but neither her breathing nor the steady beat of her heart changed at all.

Just like Bonnie. The phantom had gotten Elena, and Stefan felt something inside him tear in two. He had failed to protect her, to protect either of them.

Stefan gently slid a hand under Elena's body, cupping her head protectively with his other hand, and pulled her into his arms. He cradled her against him and, channeling what little Power he had left into speed, began to run.

Meredith checked her watch for what felt like the hundredth time, wondering why Stefan and Elena weren't back yet.

"I can't read this word at all," Matt complained. "I swear, I thought *my* handwriting was bad. It looks like Caleb wrote this with his eyes closed." He had been running his hands through his hair in frustration and it stood up in messy little spikes, and there were faint blue shadows under his eyes.

Meredith took a swig of coffee and held out her hand.

Matt passed her the notebook he'd been examining. They'd discovered that she was the best at reading Caleb's tiny, angular handwriting. "That's an O, I think," she said. "Is *deosil* a word?"

"Yes," said Alaric, sitting up a little straighter. "It means clockwise. It represents moving spiritual energy into physical forms. Might be something there. Can I see?"

Meredith handed him the notebook. Her eyes were sore and her muscles stiff from sitting all morning and going through Caleb's notebooks, clippings, and pictures. She rolled her shoulders forward and back, stretching.

"No," said Alaric after a few minutes of reading. "No good. This is just about casting a magic circle."

Meredith was about to speak when Stefan appeared in the doorway, pale and wild-eyed. Elena lay unconscious in his arms. Meredith dropped her coffee cup. "Stefan!" she cried, staring in horror. "What happened?"

"The phantom's trapped her," Stefan said, his voice catching. "I don't know how."

Meredith felt like she was falling. "Oh no, oh no," she heard herself say in a tiny, shocked voice. "Not Elena, too."

Matt stood up, glowering. "Why didn't you stop it?" he asked accusingly.

"We don't have time for this," Stefan said coldly, and strode past them to the stairs, clutching Elena protectively. In silent accord, Matt, Meredith, and Alaric followed him up to the room where Bonnie lay sleeping.

Mrs. Flowers was knitting by her bedside, and her mouth opened into an O of dismay when she saw who Stefan carried. Stefan gently placed Elena on the other side of the double bed by Bonnie's pale and tiny form.

"I'm sorry," Matt said slowly. "I shouldn't have blamed you. But . . . what happened?"

Stefan just shrugged, looking stricken.

Meredith's heart squeezed in her chest at the sight of her two best friends laid out like rag dolls. They were so still. Even in sleep, Elena had always been more mobile, more expressive than this. Over the course of a thousand sleepovers, ever since they were little, Meredith had seen sleeping Elena smile, roll herself more tightly in the blankets, snuggle her face into the pillows. Now the pink-and-gold-and-cream-colored warmth of Elena seemed faded and cold.

And *Bonnie*, Bonnie who was so vibrant and quick-moving, she'd hardly ever kept still for more than a moment or two in her whole life. Now she was motionless, frozen, almost colorless except for the dark dots of her freckles against her pale cheeks and the bright expanse of red hair on her pillow. If it weren't for the slight rise and fall of their chests, both girls could have been mannequins.

"I don't know," Stefan said again, the words sounding more panicked this time, and looked up to meet Meredith's eyes. "I don't know what to do."

Meredith cleared her throat. "We called the hospital to check on Caleb while you were gone," she said carefully, knowing what effect her words would have. "He's been released."

Stefan's eyes flashed murderously. "I think," he said, his voice like a knife, "that we should pay Caleb a visit."

Elena was suspended in darkness. She wasn't alarmed, though. It was like floating slowly under warm water, gently bobbing in the current, and a part of her wondered distantly and without fear whether it was possible that she had never come up out of the waterfall basin at Hot Springs. Had she been drifting and dreaming all this time?

Then suddenly she was speeding, bursting upward, and she opened her eyes on dazzling daylight and gulped a long, shaky breath.

Soulful, worried dark brown eyes gazed down into hers from a pale face hovering above her.

"Bonnie?" Elena gasped.

"Elena! Thank God," Bonnie cried, grabbing her by the arms in a viselike grip. "I've been here all by myself for days and days, or what feels like days and days anyway, because the light never changes, so I can't tell by the sun. And there's nothing to *do* here. I can't figure out how to get out, and there's nothing to eat, although I'm weirdly not hungry, so I guess it doesn't matter. I tried to sleep to pass the time, but I wasn't getting tired, either. And suddenly you were here, and I was so happy to see you, but you wouldn't wake up, and I was getting really worried. What's *going on?*"

"I don't know," Elena said groggily. "The last thing I remember is being on a bench. I think I got caught by some kind of mystical fog."

"Me too!" Bonnie exclaimed. "Not the bench part, but the fog part. I was in my room at the boardinghouse, and this weird fog trapped me." She shivered theatrically. "I couldn't move at all. And I was so cold." Suddenly her eyes widened with guilt. "I was doing a spell when it happened, and something came up behind me and said stuff. Nasty things."

Elena shuddered. "I heard a voice, too."

"Do you think I . . . set something loose? When I was doing the spell? I've been worrying that maybe I might have done so accidentally." Bonnie's face was white.

"It wasn't your fault," Elena reassured her. "We think it's the phantom—the thing that's been causing the accidents—that it stole your spirit so it could use your power for itself. And now it's taken me, I guess."

She quickly told Bonnie about the phantom, then pushed up on her elbows and really looked around for the first time. "I can't believe we're here again."

"Where?" asked Bonnie anxiously. "Where are we?"

It was midday and a sunlit blue sky stretched brightly overhead. Elena was pretty sure it was always midday here: It certainly had been the last time she'd been here. They were in a wide, long field that seemed to go on forever. As far as Elena could see, there were tall bushes growing— rosebushes with perfect velvety black blooms.

Midnight roses. Richly magical roses grown for holding spells only the kitsune could coat onto them. A kitsune had sent Stefan one of these roses once, with a spell to make him human, but Damon had accidentally intercepted it, much to both brothers' dismay.

"We're in the kitsunes' magic rose field, the one that the Gatehouse of the Seven Treasures opens into," she told Bonnie.

"Oh," Bonnie said. She thought for a moment and then asked helplessly, "What are we doing here? Is the phantom a kitsune?"

"I don't think so," Elena answered. "Maybe it's just a convenient place to stash us."

Elena took a deep breath. Bonnie was a good person to be with in a crisis. Not good in the way that Meredith was—Meredith's way was the planning-and-getting-things-done way—but good in that Bonnie looked up at Elena trustingly with big, innocent eyes and asked questions, confident that Elena would know the answers. And

Elena would immediately feel competent and protective, as if she could deal with whatever situation they were embroiled in. Like right now. With Bonnie depending on her, Elena's mind was working more clearly than it had for days. Any moment now, she'd come up with a plan to get them out of here. Any moment now, she was sure.

Bonnie's cold, small fingers worked their way into Elena's hand. "Elena, are we dead?" she asked in a tiny, quavering voice.

Were they dead? Elena wondered. She didn't think so. Bonnie had been alive after the phantom took her, but unwakeable. It was more likely their spirits had traveled here on the astral plane and their bodies were back in Fell's Church.

"Elena?" Bonnie repeated anxiously. "Do you think we're dead?"

Elena opened her mouth to respond when a crackling, stomping noise interrupted her. The rosebushes nearby began to thrash wildly, and there was a great rushing sound that seemed to come from every direction at once. The snapping of branches was deafening, as if something huge was shoving its way through the bracken. All around them, thorny rosebush branches whipped back and forth, although there was no wind. She yelped as one of the waving branches smacked her across the arm, gashing her skin open.

Bonnie let out a wail, and Elena's heart beat double time in her chest. She whirled around, pushing Bonnie behind her. She balled her hands into fists and crouched, trying to remember what Meredith had taught her about fighting an attacker. But as she looked around, all she could see for miles were roses. Black, perfect roses.

Bonnie gave a small whimper and pressed closer to Elena's back.

Suddenly Elena felt a sharp, aching tug rip through her, as if something were being pulled slowly but firmly out of her torso. She gasped and stumbled, clutching her hands to her stomach. *This is it,* she thought numbly, feeling as though every bone in her body were being ground to a pulp. *I am going to die.*

28

No one answered the door at the Smallwoods' house. The driveway was empty and the house looked deserted, the shades pulled down.

"Maybe Caleb's not here," Matt said nervously. "Could he have gone somewhere else when he got out of the hospital?"

"I can *smell* him. I can hear him breathing," Stefan growled. "He's in there, all right. He's hiding out."

Matt had never seen Stefan look so angry. His usually calm green eyes were bright with rage, and his fangs seemed to be involuntarily extended, little sharp points showing every time he opened his mouth. Stefan caught Matt looking at them and frowned, running his tongue self-consciously across his canines.

Matt glanced at Alaric, who he'd been thinking of as the only other normal person left in their group, but Alaric was watching Stefan with what was clearly fascination rather than alarm. *Not entirely normal, then, either,* Matt thought.

"We can get in," Meredith said calmly. She looked to Alaric. "Let me know if someone's coming." He nodded and positioned himself to block the view of anyone walking past on the sidewalk. With cool efficiency, Meredith wedged one end of her fighting stave in the crack of the front door and started to pry it open.

The door was made of heavy oak, and clearly had two locks and a chain engaged inside, and it withstood Meredith's leverage against it. Meredith swore, then muttered, "Come on, come on," redoubling her efforts. The locks and chains gave suddenly against her strength, and the door flew open, banging into the wall behind it.

"So much for a quiet entrance," Stefan said. He shifted restlessly on the doorstep as they filed past him.

"You're invited in," Meredith said, but Stefan shook his head.

"I can't," he said. "It only works if you live here."

Meredith's lips tightened, and she turned and ran up the stairs. There was a brief shout of surprise and some muffled thumping. Alaric glanced at Matt nervously, and then up the stairs.

"Should we help her?" he said.

Before Matt could answer—and he was pretty sure Meredith wasn't the one who needed help—she returned, shoving Caleb down the stairs before her, twisting one of his arms tightly behind his back.

"Invite him in," she ordered as Caleb stumbled to the bottom of the stairs. Caleb shook his head, and she yanked his arm up higher so that he yelped in pain.

"I won't," he said stubbornly. "You can't come in." Meredith pushed him toward Stefan, stopping him just at the threshold of the front door.

"Look at me," Stefan said softly, and Caleb's eyes flew to his. Stefan's pupils widened, swallowing his green irises in black, and Caleb shook his head frantically, but seemed unable to break his gaze.

"Let. Me. In," Stefan ordered.

"Come in, then," said Caleb sullenly. Meredith released him and his eyes cleared. He turned and dashed up the stairs.

Stefan burst through the door like he'd been shot through a gun and then stalked up the stairs. His smooth, stealthy movements reminded Matt of a predator's—of a lion or a shark. Matt shivered. Sometimes he forgot how truly dangerous Stefan was.

"I'd better go with him," Meredith said. "We don't want Stefan doing anything he'd regret." She paused. "Not before we find out what we need to know, anyway. Alaric, you're the one who knows the most about magic, so you come with me. Matt, keep an eye out and warn us if the Smallwoods pull into the drive." She and Alaric followed Stefan up the stairs.

Matt waited for the screaming to start, but it remained ominously quiet upstairs. Keeping one eye on the driveway through the front windows, Matt prowled through the living room. He and Tyler had been friends once upon a time, or at least had hung out, because they were both first-string on the football team. They'd known each other since middle school.

Tyler drank too much, partied too hard, was gross and sexist toward girls, but there had been something about him that Matt had sometimes enjoyed. It was the way he'd thrown himself into things, whether it was the no-holds-barred tackle of an opposing team's quarterback or throwing the absolutely craziest party anyone had ever seen. Or the time when they'd been in seventh grade and he'd gotten obsessed with winning at *Street Fighter* on PlayStation 2. Every day he'd had Matt and the rest of the guys over, all of them spending hours sitting on the floor of Tyler's bedroom, eating chips and talking trash and pounding the buttons of the controller until Tyler had figured out how to win every fight.

Matt heaved a sigh and peered out the front window again.

There was a brief muffled thump from upstairs, and Matt froze. Silence.

As he turned back to pace across the living room again, Matt noticed a particular photo among the neat row of frames on top of the piano. He crossed over and picked it up.

It must have been the football banquet, junior year. In the picture, Matt's arm was around Elena, who he'd been dating then, and she was smiling up at him. Next to them stood Tyler, hand in hand with a girl whose name Matt couldn't remember. Alison, maybe, or Alicia. She'd been older than them, a senior, and had graduated that year and left town. They were all dressed up, he and Tyler in jackets and ties, the girls in party dresses. Elena had worn a white, deceptively simple short dress, and looked so lovely that she'd taken Matt's breath away.

Things had been so easy then. The quarterback and the prettiest girl in school. They'd been the perfect couple.

Then Stefan came to town, a cold, mechanical voice whispered to him, *and destroyed everything*.

Stefan, who had pretended to be Matt's friend. Stefan, who had pretended to be a human being.

Stefan, who had pursued Matt's girlfriend, the only girl Matt had ever really been in love with. Probably the only girl he would ever feel that way about. Sure, they'd broken up just before Elena met Stefan, but Matt might have gotten her back, if not for him.

Matt's mouth twisted, and he threw the photo to the floor. The glass didn't break, and the photo just lay there, Matt and Elena and Tyler and the girl whose name he didn't remember smiling innocently up at the ceiling, unaware of what was heading toward them, of the chaos that would erupt less than a year later. Because of Stefan.

Stefan. Matt's face was hot with anger. There was a buzzing in his head. Stefan the traitor. Stefan the monster. Stefan who had stolen Matt's girl.

Matt stepped deliberately onto the picture and ground it beneath his heel. The wooden frame snapped. The feel of the glass shattering under his foot was oddly satisfying.

Without looking back, Matt stomped across the living room toward the stairs. It was time for him to deal with the monster who had ruined his life.

"Confess!" Stefan growled, doing his best to compel Caleb. But he was so weak and Caleb kept throwing up mental blocks. No doubt about it—this boy had access to Power.

"I don't know what you're talking about," Caleb said, pressing his back against the wall as if he could tunnel into it. His eyes flicked nervously from Stefan's angry face to Meredith, who was holding her staff balanced between her hands, ready to strike, and back to Stefan. "If you just leave me alone, I won't go to the police. I don't want any trouble."

Caleb looked pale and shorter than Stefan remembered. There were bruises on his face, and one of his arms was in a cast and supported by a sling. Despite everything, Stefan felt a twinge of guilt as he looked at him.

He's not human, he reminded himself.

Although . . . Caleb didn't seem all that wolfish either, for a werewolf. Shouldn't there be a little more of the animal in him? Stefan hadn't known many werewolves, but Tyler had been all big white teeth and barely repressed aggression.

Next to him, Alaric blinked at the injured boy. Cocking his head to one side and examining him, he echoed Stefan's thoughts, asking skeptically, "Are you sure he's a werewolf?"

"A *werewolf*?" said Caleb. "Are you all crazy?"

But Stefan was watching Caleb carefully, and he saw a tiny flicker in Caleb's eyes. "You're lying," Stefan said coldly, reaching out with his mind once more, finally finding a crack in Caleb's defenses. "You don't think we're crazy. You're just surprised that we know about you."

Caleb sighed. His face was still white and strained, but a certain falseness went out of it as Stefan spoke. His shoulders slumped and he stepped away from the wall a little, head hanging wearily.

Meredith tensed, ready to spring, as he moved forward. He stopped and held up his hands. "I'm not going to try anything. And I'm not a werewolf. But, yeah, I know Tyler is, and I'm guessing that you know that, too."

"You've got the werewolf gene," Stefan told him. "You could easily be a werewolf, too."

Caleb shrugged and looked Stefan straight in the eye. "I guess. But it didn't happen to me; it happened to Tyler."

"*Happened* to?" Meredith asked, her voice rising with outrage. "Do you know what Tyler did to become a werewolf?"

Caleb glanced at her warily. "What he did? Tyler didn't do anything. The family curse caught up with him, that's all." His face was shadowed and anxious.

Stefan found his tone gentling despite himself. "Caleb, you have to kill someone to become a werewolf, even if you carry the gene. Unless you're bitten by a werewolf yourself, there are certain rituals that have to be performed. *Blood* rituals. Tyler murdered an innocent girl."

Caleb's knees seemed to give out, and he slid to the floor with a muffled thump. He looked sick. "Tyler wouldn't do that," he said, but his voice was unsteady. "Tyler was like a brother to me after my parents died. He wouldn't kill anyone. I don't believe you."

"He did," Meredith confirmed. "Tyler murdered Sue Carson. We negotiated for her to come back to life, but it doesn't change the fact that he did kill her."

Her voice held the unmistakable ring of truth, and all the fight seemed to go out of Caleb. He sank lower and rested his forehead against his knees. "What do you want from me?"

He looked so thin and rumpled that, despite the urgency of their mission, Stefan was distracted. "Weren't you taller than this?" he asked. "Bigger? More . . . put together? The last time I saw you, I mean."

Caleb mumbled something into his knees, too muffled and distorted for even a vampire to hear properly. "What?" Stefan asked.

Caleb looked up, his face smudged with tears. "It was a glamour, okay?" he said bitterly. "I made myself look better because I wanted Elena to want me." Stefan thought of Caleb's glowing, healthy face, his height, his crowning halo of golden curls. No wonder he had seemed suspicious; subconsciously Stefan must have known how unlikely it was that an ordinary human would look that much like an archangel. *No wonder he felt so much lighter than I expected when I threw him across the graveyard*, Stefan thought.

"So you are a magic user, even if you aren't a werewolf," Meredith said swiftly.

Caleb shrugged. "You knew that already," he said. "I saw what you did to my workroom in the shed. What more do you want from me?"

Meredith stepped forward warningly, stave at the ready, her gaze clear and pitiless, and Caleb flinched away from her. "What we want," she said, enunciating every word distinctly, "is for you to tell us how you summoned the phantom, and how we can get rid of it. We want our friends back."

Caleb stared at her. "I swear I don't know what you're talking about."

Stefan prowled toward Caleb on his other side, keeping him off balance so that the boy's eyes flicked nervously back and forth between Stefan and Meredith.

Then Stefan stopped. He could see that Caleb looked genuinely confused. Was it possible that he was telling the truth? Stefan knelt so that he was at eye level with Caleb and tried a softer tone. "Caleb?" he asked, depleting his last remnants of Power to compel the boy to speak. "Can you tell us what kind of magic you did? Something with the roses, right? What was the spell supposed to do?"

Caleb swallowed, his Adam's apple bobbing. "I had to find out what happened to Tyler," he said. "So I came here for the summer. No one seemed worried, but I knew Tyler wouldn't just drop out of sight. Tyler had talked about you, all of you, and Elena Gilbert. Tyler hated you, Stefan, and at first he liked Elena, and then he really hated her, too. When I came here, though, everyone knew Elena Gilbert was dead. Her family was still mourning her. And you were gone, Stefan; you'd left town. I tried to put the pieces together about what had happened—there were some pretty strange stories—and then lots of other weird things happened in town. Violence, and girls going crazy, and children attacking their parents. And then, suddenly, it was over; it just stopped, and it was like I was the only one who remembered it happening. But I also remembered just a normal summer. Elena Gilbert had been here the whole time, and no one thought anything of it, because they didn't remember her dying. Only I seemed to have two sets of memories. People who I'd seen get hurt"— he shuddered at the memory—"or even killed were fine again. I felt like I was going crazy."

Caleb pushed his shaggy dark blond hair back out of his face, rubbed his nose, and took a breath. "Whatever was going on, I knew you and Elena were at the center of it. The differences between the memories told me that. And I figured that you must be connected to Tyler's disappearance, too. Either you'd done something to him, or you knew something about what had happened to him. I figured if I could pull you and your friends apart, something would come out. Once you were set against one another, I'd be able to work my way in and find out what was going on. Maybe I could get Elena to fall for me with a glamour, or one of the other girls. I just had to know." He looked from one to another of them. "The rose spell was supposed to make you irrational, turn you against one another."

Alaric frowned. "You mean you didn't summon anything?"

Caleb shook his head. "Look," he said, pulling a thick leather-bound volume from under his bed. "The spell I used is in here. That's all I did, honest."

Alaric took the book and flipped through the pages until he found the right spell. He studied it, his forehead crinkling, and said, "He's telling the truth. There isn't anything about summoning a phantom in this book. And the spell here fits what we saw in Caleb's workshop and what I've been reading in his notebooks. This rose spell is a fairly low-level discord spell; it would make whatever negative emotions we were feeling—hate, anger, jealousy, fear, sorrow—just a little bit stronger, make us a little more likely to blame one another for anything that went wrong."

"But when combined with the powers of whatever phantom might be hanging around here, the spell would become a feedback loop, just as Mrs. Flowers said could happen, strengthening our emotions and making the phantom more powerful," Stefan said slowly.

"Jealousy," said Meredith thoughtfully. "You know, I hate to admit it, but I was horribly jealous of Celia when she was here." She glanced apologetically at Alaric, who reached out and gently touched her hand.

"She was jealous of you, too," Stefan said matter-of-factly. "I could sense it." He sighed. "And I've been feeling jealous as well."

"So perhaps a jealousy phantom?" Alaric said. "Good,

that'll give us more of a basis for researching banishing spells. Although I haven't been feeling jealous at all."

"Of course not," Meredith said pointedly. "You're the one who's had two girls fighting over you."

Suddenly Stefan felt so exhausted that his legs shook. He needed to feed, immediately. He nodded awkwardly to Caleb. "I'm sorry . . . for what happened."

Caleb looked up at him. "Please tell me what happened to Tyler," he implored. "I have to know. I'll leave you alone if you just tell me the truth, I promise."

Meredith and Stefan glanced at each other, and Stefan raised his eyebrows slightly. "Tyler was alive when he left town this past winter," Meredith said slowly. "That's all we know about him, I swear."

Caleb stared up at her for a long moment, then nodded. "Thank you," he said simply.

She nodded back at him crisply, like a general acknowledging the troops, and led the way out of his room.

Just then a muffled, cutoff shout came from downstairs, followed by a thud. Stefan and Alaric raced after Meredith down the stairs, almost bumping into her as she pulled to a sudden halt.

"What is it?" Stefan asked. Meredith drew aside.

Matt was lying facedown at the foot of the stairs, his arms flung out as though to catch himself. Meredith stepped quickly the rest of the way down the stairs to him and turned him over gently.

His eyes were closed, his face pale. He was breathing, slowly but steadily. Meredith felt his pulse, then shook him gently by the shoulder. "Matt," she called. "Matt!" She looked up at Stefan and Alaric. "Just like the others," she said grimly. "The phantom's got him."

29

I will not die—not again, Elena thought furiously as she writhed in pain, the invisible vise clamping down even harder on her.

Bonnie fell to the grass, even paler than before, clutching her stomach in a mirror image of Elena.

It cannot take me!

And then, just as suddenly as it had started, the deafening roar ceased and the crushing pain lifted. Elena collapsed to the ground, air whooshing back into her lungs. *It's finished grinding bones to make its bread*, Elena thought semihysterically, and almost giggled.

Bonnie gasped loudly, letting out a small sob.

"What was that?" Elena asked her.

Bonnie shook her head. "It felt like something was getting pulled out of us," she said, panting. "I felt it before, too, right before you showed up."

"That pulling feeling." Elena grimaced, her mind whirling. "I think it's the phantom. Damon says that it wants to drain our power. That must be how it does it."

Bonnie was staring at her, her mouth just a tiny bit open. Her pink tongue darted out and licked her lips. "*Damon* says?" she said. She frowned anxiously. "Damon's dead, Elena."

"No, he's alive. The star ball brought him back after we'd already left the Dark Moon. I found out after the phantom took you."

Bonnie made a little noise, a sort of *eep!* that reminded Elena of a bunny, of something soft and small and surprised. All the blood drained out of her face, leaving her usually faint freckles vivid spots against the white of her cheeks. She pressed shaking hands to her mouth, staring at Elena with huge dark eyes.

"Listen, Bonnie," Elena said fiercely. "Nobody else knows this yet. Nobody but you and me, Bonnie. Damon wanted to keep it a secret until he could figure out the right way to come back. So we need to keep quiet about it."

Bonnie nodded, still gaping. The color was rushing back into her cheeks, and she looked like she was caught between joy and total confusion.

Glancing over her shoulder, Elena noticed that there was something in the grass at the foot of a rosebush beyond

Bonnie, something motionless and white. A chill went through her as she was reminded of Caleb's body at the foot of the monument in the graveyard.

"What's that?" she asked sharply. Bonnie's expression tipped over into confusion. Elena brushed past her and walked toward it, squinting in the sunlight.

When she got close enough, Elena saw with amazement that it was Matt, lying still and silent beneath the rosebush. A sprinkle of black petals was scattered across his chest. As she came close to him, Matt's eyes twitched—she could see them moving rapidly back and forth under the lids, as if he was having an intense dream—and then flew open as he took in a long, rattling gulp of air. His pale blue eyes met hers.

"Elena!" He gasped. He hitched himself up onto his elbows and looked past her. "Bonnie! Thank God! Are you okay? Where are we?"

"The phantom caught us, brought us to the Nether World, and is using us to make itself more powerful," Elena said succinctly. "How do you feel?"

"A little startled," Matt joked in a weak voice. He looked around, then licked his lips nervously. "Huh, so this is the Nether World? It's nicer than I'd pictured from your descriptions. Shouldn't the sky be red? And where are all the vampires and demons?" He looked at Elena and Bonnie sternly. "Were you guys telling the truth about everything that happened to you here? Because this place seems pretty nice for a Hell dimension, what with all the roses and everything."

Elena stared at him. *It's possible too many weird things have happened to us.*

Then she noticed the hint of panic on Matt's face. He wasn't unnaturally blasé about what was going on; he was just being brave, whistling to keep up their spirits in this newest danger.

"Well, we wanted to impress you," she joked back with a tremulous smile, then quickly got down to business. "What was going on when you were back home?" she asked him.

"Um," Matt said, "Stefan and Meredith were questioning Caleb about how he summoned the phantom."

"Caleb's not responsible for the phantom," Elena said firmly. "It followed us home when we were here before. We have to get home right away so we can tell them they're dealing with one of the Original ones. It'll be much more difficult for us to get rid of than an ordinary one."

Matt looked at Bonnie questioningly. "How does she know this?"

"Well," Bonnie said, with a hint of the glee she always got from gossip, "apparently *Damon* told her. He's alive and she saw him!"

So much for keeping Damon's secret, Bonnie, Elena thought, rolling her eyes. Still, it didn't really matter if Matt knew. He wasn't the one Damon was keeping the secret from, and he wasn't likely to be able to tell Stefan anytime soon.

Elena tuned out Matt's exclamations of wonder and Bonnie's explanations as she scanned the area around them. Sunshine. Rosebushes. Rosebushes. Sunshine. Grass. Clear blue sky. All the same, in every direction. Wherever she looked, velvety black perfect blooms nodded serenely in a clear midday sun. The bushes were all the same, down to the number and positions of the roses on each one and the distances between them. Even the stems of grass were uniform—all stopping at the same height. The sun hadn't moved since she'd arrived.

It all seemed like it should be lovely and relaxing, but after a few minutes the sameness became unnerving.

"There was a gate," she told Bonnie and Matt. "When we were looking into this field from the Gatehouse of the Seven Treasures. There was a way in *from* there, so there must be a way to get out *to* there. We just have to find it."

They had begun to clamber to their feet when, without warning, the sharp tugging pain struck again. Elena clutched her stomach. Bonnie lost her balance and fell back to a sitting position on the ground, her eyes clenched shut.

Matt gave a choked-off exclamation and gasped. "What is that?"

Elena waited for the pain to fade again before she

answered him. Her knees were wobbling. She felt dizzy and sick. "Another reason we need to get out of here," she said. "The phantom's using us to increase its power. I think it needs us here to do that. And if we don't find the gate soon, we might be too weak to make it home."

She looked around again, the uniformity almost dizzying. Each rosebush was centered in a small circular bed of rich-looking dark loam. Between these circles, the grass of the field was velvety smooth, like the lawn of an English manor house or a really good golf course.

"Okay," Elena said, and took a deep, calming breath. "Let's spread out and look carefully. We'll stay about ten feet apart from one another and go from one end of this rose garden to the other, searching. Look around carefully—anything that's at all different from the rest of the field could be the clue we need to find the way out."

"We're going to search the whole field?" Bonnie asked, sounding dismayed. "It's huge."

"We'll just do one little bit at a time," Elena said encouragingly.

They started in a spread-out line, gazing intently back and forth, up and down. At first there was only the silence of focused concentration as they searched. There was no sign of a gate. Step by step through the field, nothing changed. Endless rows of identical rosebushes stretched in all directions, spaced about three feet from one another, enough room between them for one person to easily pass.

The eternal midday sun beat down uncomfortably on the tops of their heads, and Elena wiped a bead of sweat from her forehead. The scent of roses hung heavily in the warm air; at first Elena had found it pleasant, but now it was nauseating, like a too-sweet perfume. The perfect stalks of grass bent under her feet, then sprang up again, uncrushed, as if she had never passed.

"I wish there were a breeze," Bonnie complained. "But I don't think the wind ever blows here."

"This field must come to an end sometime," Elena said desperately. "It can't just go on forever." There was a sickening feeling in the pit of her stomach, though, that suggested to her that maybe it *could* go on forever. This wasn't her world, after all. The rules were different here.

"So where's Damon now?" Bonnie asked suddenly. She wasn't looking at Elena. She was keeping up the same steady pace, the same careful, systematic gaze. But there was a note of strain in her voice, and Elena broke her own search to glance at her quickly.

Then one possible answer to Bonnie's question hit Elena and she stopped dead. "That's it!" she said. "Bonnie, Matt, I think Damon might be *here*. Or not here, not in the rose garden, but somewhere in the Nether World, in the Dark Dimension." They looked at her blankly.

"Damon was going to try to come here to look for the

phantom," Elena explained. "He thought it followed us home from here when we came back to our own world, so this is probably where he'd start searching for its physical body. The last time I saw him, he told me that he thought he would be able to fight it better from here, where it came from. If he is here, maybe he can help us get back to Fell's Church."

Damon, please be here somewhere. Please help us, she begged silently.

Just then, something caught her eye. Ahead of them, between two rosebushes that looked just the same as any other two rosebushes in the garden, there was the slightest shift, the tiniest distortion. It looked like the heat shimmer that would sometimes appear over the highway on the hottest, most still days of summer as the sun's rays bounced off the asphalt.

No asphalt here to radiate back the sun's heat. But something had to be causing that shimmer.

Unless she was imagining it. Were her eyes playing tricks on her, showing her a mirage among the rosebushes?

"Do you see that?" she asked the others. "Over there, just a little to the right?"

They stopped and peered carefully.

"Maybe?" Bonnie said hesitantly.

"I think so," Matt said. "Like hot air rising, right?"

"Right," Elena said. She frowned, estimating the

distance. Maybe fifteen feet. "We should take it at a run," she said. "In case we have any trouble getting through. There might be some kind of barrier we have to break to get out. I don't think hesitating will help us."

"Let's hold hands," Bonnie suggested nervously. "I don't want to lose you guys."

Elena didn't take her eyes off the shimmer in the air. If she lost it, she'd never find it again, not with the sameness of everything in here. Once they got turned around, they'd never be able to tell this spot from any other.

They all three took one another's hands, staring at the small distortion that they hoped was a gate. Bonnie was in the middle and she clutched Elena's left hand with her thin, warm fingers.

"One, two, three, go," Bonnie said, and then they were running. They stumbled over the grass, wove between rosebushes. The space between the bushes was barely wide enough for three to run abreast, and a thorny branch caught in Elena's hair. She couldn't let go of Bonnie and she couldn't stop, so she just yanked her head forward despite the eye-wateringly painful tug on her hair and kept running, leaving a tangle of hair hanging from a bush behind her.

Then they were at the shimmer between the bushes. Close up, it was even harder to see, and Elena would have doubted that they were at the right spot except for the change in the temperature. It might have looked like a heat shimmer from a distance, but it was as cold and bracing as a mountain lake, despite the warm sun right above them.

"Don't stop!" Elena shouted. And they plunged into the coldness.

In an instant, everything went black, as if someone had switched off the sun.

Elena felt herself falling and clung desperately to Bonnie's hand.

Damon! she cried silently. *Help me!*

30

tefan drove like a maniac all the way back to
the boardinghouse. "I can't believe I forgot to
tell him that his name had been called," he
said for what felt like the hundredth time. "I can't believe
we left him alone."

"Slow down," Meredith told him, trying to hold Matt's
sleeping body steady in the backseat as Stefan whipped
around a corner, tires squealing. "You're going way too
fast."

"We're in a hurry," Stefan growled, yanking on the
wheel to make a hard right. Alaric turned around in the
passenger seat and gave Meredith a panicky look as Stefan
narrowly missed a garbage truck. She sighed. She knew
he was trying to make up for his mistake, for not telling them immediately that Matt's name had appeared in

the herb shop, but killing them all in a race to get home wasn't exactly the solution. Besides, although they probably would have done things differently if they'd known, it might not have changed the outcome for Matt. It wasn't as if their precautions had saved either Bonnie or Elena.

"At least you've got vampire reflexes," she said, more to reassure Alaric than out of any particular confidence in Stefan's driving abilities.

She'd insisted on being the one sitting in the back with Matt, and now she turned her attention to him. She put a restraining hand on his chest so he wouldn't go tumbling to the floor as the car jerked and swerved.

He was so still. None of the twitching and eye movements that usually went with sleep, just the steady shallow rise and fall of his breathing. He wasn't even snoring. And she knew from camping trips as far back as sixth grade that Matt snored like a buzz saw. Always.

Meredith never cried. Not even when the worst happened. And she wasn't going to start now, not when her friends needed her calm and focused to try to figure out how to save them. But if she *had* been the kind of girl who cried, instead of the kind of girl who strategized, she would have been sobbing. And even now, the breath caught in her throat a little painfully, until she schooled herself into impassive calm again.

She was the only one left. Of the four old friends who'd

gone through school and summers and adolescence and all the horrors the supernatural world could throw at them, she was the only one the phantom hadn't captured. Yet.

Meredith clenched her teeth and held Matt steady.

Stefan pulled up and parked in front of the boarding-house, having somehow avoided causing any damage to other cars or pedestrians along the way. Alaric and Meredith started to inch Matt carefully out of the car, looping his arms around their necks and slowly shifting him forward into a half-standing position. But Stefan simply grabbed Matt away from them and threw him over his shoulder.

"Let's go," he said, and stalked off toward the board-inghouse, easily balancing Matt's unconscious body with one hand, not looking back.

"He's become kind of a strange guy," Alaric commented, watching Stefan alertly. The sunshine caught the stubble on Alaric's unshaven chin and it glinted with a touch of gold. He turned toward Meredith and gave her a rueful, disarming grin. "Once more into the breach . . ." he said.

Meredith took his hand, warm and solid in her own. "Come on," she said.

Once they were in the boardinghouse, Stefan clomped straight upstairs to deposit Matt with the other bodies— the other *sleepers*, Meredith reminded herself fiercely.

Meredith and Alaric, hand in hand, turned toward the

kitchen. As she pushed the door open, Meredith heard Mrs. Flowers's voice.

"Very useful indeed, my dear," she was saying, a warm note of approval in her voice. "You've done very well. I'm so grateful."

Meredith gaped. At the kitchen table with Mrs. Flowers, cool and calm and pretty in a blue linen dress, sat Dr. Celia Conner, sipping tea.

"Hello, Alaric. Hello, Meredith," said Celia. Her dark eyes bored coolly into Meredith's. "You'll never believe what I've found."

"What?" said Alaric eagerly, letting go of Meredith's hand. Her heart sank.

Celia reached into a tote bag sitting by her chair and pulled out a thick book bound in ragged brown leather. She smiled triumphantly and announced, "It's a book on phantoms. Dr. Beltram ended up sending me to Dalcrest College, which actually has a very comprehensive collection of texts on the paranormal."

"I suggest we adjourn to the den," Mrs. Flowers said, "where we can be more comfortable, and examine its contents together."

They moved to the den, but Stefan, when he joined them, did not seem any more comfortable.

"Different types of phantoms," he said, taking the book from Celia and flipping rapidly through the pages.

"The history of phantoms in our dimension. Where is the banishment ritual? Why doesn't this thing have an index?"

Celia shrugged. "It's very old and rare," she said. "It was difficult to find, and it's the only book on the subject we're likely to be able to get our hands on, maybe the only one that exists, so we'll have to excuse things like that. These older texts, the authors wanted you to read straight through and really learn about their subject, to understand what they wanted to tell you, not just to find the page you needed right away. You might try looking near the end, though."

Alaric was watching Stefan whip through the pages with an expression of pain. "It's a rare book, Stefan," he said. "Please be more careful with it. Would you like me to look? I'm used to finding what I need in these kinds of books."

Stefan snarled, literally snarled at him, and Meredith felt the hairs along the back of her neck rise. "I'll do it myself, *teacher*. I'm in a hurry."

He squinted down at the text. "Why does it have to be in such ornate print?" he complained. "Don't tell me it's because it's old. I'm older than it is, and I can barely read it. Huh. 'Phantoms who are feeding like vampires on one choice sensibility, whether it be guilt, or despair, or grudge; or lust for victuals, the demon rum, or fallen women. The stronger be the sensibility, the worse be the outcome of the phantom created.' I think we could have figured that out ourselves."

Mrs. Flowers was standing slightly removed from the rest of the group, eyes fixed on empty air, muttering seemingly to herself as she communed with her mother.

"I know," she said. "I'll tell them." Her eyes focused on the others as they stood around Stefan, peering over his shoulders. "Ma*ma* says that time is getting short," she warned.

Stefan leaped to his feet and exploded. "I *know* it's getting short," he roared, getting right up into Mrs. Flowers's surprised face. "Can't your mother tell us something useful for once?"

Mrs. Flowers staggered away from him, reaching out to steady herself on the back of a chair. Her face was white, and suddenly she looked older and more frail than ever before.

Stefan's eyes widened, their color darkening to a stormy sea green, and he held out his hands, his face horrified. "I'm sorry," he said. "Mrs. Flowers, I'm sorry. I didn't mean to frighten you. I don't know what came over me. . . . I'm just so worried about Elena and the others."

"I know, Stefan," Mrs. Flowers said gravely. She had regained her balance and she looked stronger, calm and wise again. "We *will* get them back, you know. You must have faith. Ma*ma* does."

Stefan sat down, turning back to the book, his lips pressed together into a straight line.

Her skin prickling with apprehension, Meredith gripped her stave more tightly as she watched him. When she had revealed to the others that the members of her family were hereditary vampire hunters and that it was now her turn to take on the duty, she had told Elena and Stefan that she would never turn on Stefan, that she understood that he wasn't like other, evil vampires, that he was good: harmless and benign to humans.

She had made no such promises about Damon, and Elena and Stefan hadn't asked her to. They all shared an unspoken understanding that Damon couldn't really be characterized as harmless, not even when he begrudgingly worked with them, and that Meredith would need to keep her options open when it came to him.

But Stefan . . . she had never thought this would happen, but now Meredith was worried that someday she might not be able to keep her promises about Stefan. She had never seen him acting the way he had been lately: irrational, angry, violent, unpredictable. She knew his behavior was probably caused by the phantom, but was Stefan becoming too dangerous? Could she kill him if she had to? He was her friend.

Meredith's heart was racing. She realized that her knuckles had whitened against her fighting stave, and her hand ached. *Yes*, she realized, she would fight Stefan and try to kill him, if she had to. It was true that he was her friend, but her duty had to come first.

She took a deep breath and consciously relaxed her hands. *Stay calm*, she coached herself. *Breathe.* Stefan was keeping himself more or less under control. It wasn't a decision she had to make. *Not yet, anyway.*

A few minutes later, Stefan stopped flipping pages. "Here," he said. "I think this is it." He handed the book to Mrs. Flowers. She scanned the page quickly and nodded. "That feels like the right ritual," she said seriously. "I ought to have everything we need to perform it right here in the house."

Alaric reached for the book. He read the spell, too, frowning. "Does it have to be a blood spell?" he asked Mrs. Flowers. "If it backfires, the phantom might be able to turn it against us."

"I'm afraid it's going to have to be a blood spell," Mrs. Flowers replied. "We'd need more time to experiment to change the spell, and time is the one thing we don't have. If the phantom is able to use its captives the way we think it can, it's only going to get more powerful."

Alaric began to speak again but was interrupted.

"Wait," said Celia, a slightly shrill note in her usually husky voice. "A *blood* spell? What does that mean? I don't want to get involved in anything"—she searched for a word—"unsavory."

She reached for the book, but Stefan slammed his hand down on it. "Unsavory or not, this is what we're doing," he said quietly, but with a voice as hard as steel. "And you're a part of it. It's too late for you to back out now. I won't let you."

Celia gave a convulsive shudder and cringed back in her chair. "Don't you dare threaten me," she said, her voice quavering.

"Everybody calm down," Meredith said sharply. "Celia, no one is going to make you do anything unless you agree to it. I'll protect you myself if need be." Her eyes flew quickly to Alaric, who was glancing back and forth between them, looking worried. "But we need your help. Please. You may have saved us all by finding the spell, and we're grateful, but Stefan's right—you're part of this, too. I don't know if it'll work without you." She hesitated a beat. "Or, if it does, it might leave you as the phantom's only target," she added cunningly.

Celia shivered again and wrapped her arms around herself. "I'm not a coward," she said miserably. "I'm a scientist, and this . . . irrational mysticism worries me. But I'm in. I'll help any way I can."

Meredith, for the first time, felt a flash of sympathy for her. She understood how hard it must be for Celia to continue to think of herself as a logical person while the boundaries of what she'd always accepted as reality collapsed around her.

"Thank you, Celia." Meredith glanced around the room at the others. "We've got the ritual. We've got the ingredients. We just need to gather everything together and start casting the spell. Are we ready?"

Everyone sat up straighter, their faces taking on expressions of stern resolve. As scary as this was, it was good to finally have a purpose and a plan.

Stefan breathed deeply and visibly took hold of himself, his shoulders relaxing and his stance settling into something less predatory. "Okay, Meredith," he said. His stormy green eyes met her cool gray ones, in perfect accord. "Let's do this."

nowing he couldn't perform the ritual on an empty stomach, Stefan hunted down several squirrels in Mrs. Flowers's backyard, then returned to the boardinghouse's garage. Meredith had parked Mrs. Flowers's antique Ford out in the drive, and there was more than enough room to set up everything they needed for the banishment ritual.

Stefan cocked his head at a skittering noise in the shadows and identified the fast-beating heart of a little mouse. The atmosphere might not be a comfortable one, but the spaciousness of the room and its cement floor meant it would be an excellent place to work the spell.

"Hand me the tape measure, please," Alaric said from his sprawled position in the middle of the garage floor. "I need to get this line just the right length." Mrs. Flowers had dug up a box of multicolored chalk from somewhere in the boardinghouse, and Alaric had the book propped open and was carefully copying the circles, arcane symbols, parabolas, and ellipses from its pages onto the smooth cement.

Stefan gave him the tool and watched as he measured carefully from the innermost circle to a row of strange runes near the outermost edge of his drawing. "It's important that everything be precise," Alaric said, frowning and double-checking the ends of the measuring tape. "The smallest error could lead to us accidentally setting this thing loose in Fell's Church."

"But isn't it loose already?" asked Stefan.

"No," Alaric explained. "This ritual will allow the phantom to appear in its corporeal form, which is far more dangerous than the insubstantial thing it is now."

"Then you'd better get this right," Stefan agreed grimly.

"If this all goes as planned, the phantom will be trapped in the innermost circle," Alaric said, pointing. "We'll be at the outermost edge, over there past the runes. We ought to be safe out there." He looked up and gave Stefan a rueful grin. "I hope. I'm afraid I've never done any kind of summoning in real life before, although I've read a lot about it."

Terrific, Stefan thought, but he returned Alaric's smile without comment. The man was doing the best he could.

All they could do was hope it would be enough to save Elena and the others.

Meredith and Mrs. Flowers entered the garage, each carrying a plastic shopping bag. Celia trailed behind them.

"Holy water," Meredith said, lifting a plant mister out of her bag to show him.

"It doesn't work on vampires," Stefan reminded her.

"We're not summoning a vampire," she replied, and went off to mist the outer spaces in the diagram, careful not to disturb the chalk lines.

Alaric stood and started very cautiously hopping out of the huge multicolored diagram, clutching the book in one hand. "I think we're about ready," he said.

Mrs. Flowers looked at Stefan. "We need the others," she said. "Everyone affected by the phantom's powers has to be here."

"I'll help you carry them down," Alaric offered.

"Not necessary," Stefan told him, and headed upstairs alone. Standing by the side of the bed in the little rose-and-cream bedroom, he looked down at Elena, Matt, and Bonnie. None of them had moved since he had placed Matt there.

He sighed and gathered Elena in his arms first. After a moment, he also picked up her pillow and a blanket. At least he could try to make her comfortable.

A few minutes later all three of the sleepers were lying

in the front of the garage, well outside the diagram, their heads supported by pillows.

"Now what?" Stefan asked.

"Now we each choose a candle," Mrs. Flowers said, opening her plastic bag. "One that you feel represents you in color. According to the book, they really should be hand-dipped and specially scented, but this will just have to do. I won't pick one myself," Mrs. Flowers said, handing the bag to Stefan. "The phantom hasn't focused its powers on me, and I don't remember being jealous of anyone since 1943."

"What happened in 1943?" asked Meredith curiously.

"I lost the Little Miss Fell's Church crown to Nancy Sue Baker," Mrs. Flowers answered. When Meredith gaped at her, she threw her hands up in the air. "Even I was a child once, you know. I was strikingly adorable, with Shirley Temple curls, and my mother liked to dress me in frills and show me off."

Putting the astounding image of Mrs. Flowers in Shirley Temple curls out of his mind, Stefan poked through the assortment of candles and chose a dark blue one. It seemed right to him somehow. "We need candles for the others, too," he said. Carefully, he chose a golden one for Elena and a pink one for Bonnie.

"Are you just going by their hair colors?" asked Meredith. "You're such a *guy*."

"You know these are the right colors for them, though," Stefan argued. "Besides, Bonnie's hair is red, not pink."

Meredith nodded grudgingly. "I guess you're right. White for Matt, though."

"Really?" Stefan asked. He didn't know what he would have chosen for Matt. American-flag patterned, maybe, if they had had it.

"He's the purest person I know," Meredith said softly. Alaric raised an eyebrow at her and she elbowed him. "Pure in spirit, I mean. What you see is what you get with Matt, and he's good and truehearted all the way through."

"I suppose so," said Stefan, and he watched without comment as Meredith chose a dark brown candle for herself.

Alaric shuffled through the bag and picked a dark green candle, and Celia selected one of pale lavender. Mrs. Flowers took the bag with the remaining candles and stashed it on a high shelf near the garage doors, between a bag of potting soil and what looked like an old-fashioned kerosene lantern.

They all sat down on the garage floor in a semicircle, outside the diagram, facing toward the empty inner circle, holding their unlit candles. The sleepers lay behind them, and Meredith held Bonnie's candle in her lap as well as her own; Stefan took Elena's, and Alaric Matt's.

"Now we anoint them with our blood," Alaric said.

They all looked at him, and he shrugged defensively. "It's what the book says."

Meredith removed a small pocketknife from her bag, cut her finger, and quickly, matter-of-factly, smeared a stripe of blood from the top to the bottom of her brown candle, then passed the knife to Alaric along with a little bottle of disinfectant. One by one, the others followed her lead.

"This is really unsanitary," Celia said, wincing, but she followed through.

Stefan was very aware of the smell of human blood in such an enclosed space. Even though he'd just fed, his canines prickled in an automatic response.

Meredith picked up the candles and walked to their sleeping friends, crossing from one to the next and raising their hands to make a swift cut and wipe their blood against their candles. Not one of them even flinched. When she had finished, Meredith redistributed the sleepers' candles and returned to her spot.

Alaric began to read, in Latin, the first words of the spell. After a few sentences, he hesitated at a word and Stefan silently took the grimoire. Smoothly he picked up where Alaric had left off. The words flowed off his tongue, the feel of the Latin on his lips reminding him of hours spent with his childhood tutor hundreds of years ago, and of a period when he lived in a monastery in England during the early days of his struggle with vampirism.

When the time came, he snapped his fingers and, with a touch of Power, his candle lit itself. He handed it to Meredith, who dripped a little of the melted wax onto the garage floor at the edge of the diagram and stuck the candle there. One by one, at the appropriate points in the ritual, he lit a candle and she placed it, until there was a little row of multicolored candles bravely burning between them and the chalk outlines of the diagram.

Stefan read on. Suddenly the pages of the book began to flutter. A cold, unnatural wind rose inside the closed garage, and the flames of the candles flickered wildly and then blew out. Two candles fell over. Meredith's long hair whipped around her face.

"This isn't supposed to happen," Alaric shouted.

But Stefan just squinted his eyes against the gale and read on.

The pitch-blackness and the unpleasant sensation of falling lasted for only a moment, and then Elena landed jarringly on both feet and staggered forward, clutching Matt's and Bonnie's hands.

They were in a dim octagonal room lined with doors. A single piece of furniture sat in the center. Behind the lone desk lounged a tanned, beautiful, amazingly muscular, bare-chested vampire with a long, spiraling mane of bronze hair falling past his shoulders.

Instantly Elena knew where she was.

"We're here." She gasped. "The Gatehouse!"

Sage leaped to his feet on the other side of the desk, his face almost comically surprised. "Elena?" he exclaimed. "Bonnie? Matt? What's going on? *Qu'est-ce qui arrive?*"

Usually, Elena would have been relieved to see Sage, who had always been kind and helpful to her, but she had to get to Damon. She knew where he must be. She could almost hear him calling to her.

She strode across the empty room with barely a glance at the startled gatekeeper, pulling Matt and Bonnie along with her.

"Sorry, Sage," she said as she reached the door she wanted. "We've got to find Damon."

"*Damon?*" he said. "He's back again?" and then they passed through, ignoring Sage's shouts of "Stop! *Arretez-vous!*"

The door closed behind them, and they found themselves in a landscape of ash. Nothing grew here, and there were no landmarks. Harsh winds had blown the fine black ash into shifting hills and valleys. As they watched, a strong gust caught at the light top layer of ash and sent it flying in a cloud that soon settled into new shapes. Below the lighter ash, they could see swamps of wet, muddy ash. Nearby was an ash-choked pool of still water. Nothing but ash and mud, except for an occasional scorched and blackened bit of wood.

Above them was a twilit sky in which hung a huge planet and two great moons, one a swirling bluish white, the other silvery.

"Where are we?" said Matt, gaping up at the sky.

"Once this was a world—a moon, technically—that was shaded by a huge tree," Elena told him, walking steadily forward. "Until I destroyed it. This is where Damon died."

She felt rather than saw Matt and Bonnie exchange a glance. "But, uh, then he came back, right? You saw him in Fell's Church the other night, didn't you?" Matt said hesitantly. "Why are we here *now*?"

"I know that Damon's close," Elena said impatiently. "I can feel him. He's come back here. Maybe this is where he began his search for the phantom." They kept walking. Soon they were not so much walking as wading through black ash that stuck to their legs in nasty thick clumps. The mud underneath the ash clung to their shoes, releasing them at each step with a wet sucking sound.

They were almost there. She could feel it. Elena picked up the pace, and the others, still linked to her, hurried to keep up. The ash was thicker and deeper here because they were approaching where the trunk had been, the very center of this world. Elena remembered it exploding, shooting up into the sky like a rocket, disintegrating as it went. Damon's body had lain underneath and had been completely buried in the falling ash.

Elena stopped. There was a thick, drifting pile of ash that looked like it would be at least as high as her waist in places. She thought she could see where Damon had awoken—the ash was disturbed and caved in, as if someone had tunneled out of one of the deeper drifts. But there was no one around except themselves. A cold wind blew up a spray of ash, and Bonnie coughed. Elena, knee-deep in cold, sticky ash, dropped Bonnie's hand and wrapped her arms around herself.

"He's not here," she said blankly. "I was so sure he would be here."

"He must be somewhere else, then," said Matt logically. "I'm sure he's fighting the phantom, like you said he was going to. The Dark Dimension's a big place."

Bonnie shivered and huddled closer to Matt, her brown eyes huge and full of pathos, like a hungry puppy's. "Can we go home now? Please? Sage can send us back again, can't he?"

"I just don't understand," Elena said, staring at the empty space where the great trunk of the tree had once been. "I just *knew* he would be here. I could practically hear him calling me."

Just then a low, musical laugh cut through the silence. It was a beautiful sound, but there was something chilly and alien about it, something that made Elena shudder.

"Elena," Bonnie whispered, her eyes wide. "That's the thing I heard before the fog took me."

They turned.

Behind them stood a woman. A woman-shaped being, anyway, Elena amended quickly. This was no woman. And, like its laugh, this woman-shaped being was beautiful, but frightening. She—it—was huge, more than one and a half times the size of a human, but perfectly proportioned, and it looked like it was made of ice and mist in blues and greens—like the purest glacier, its eyes were clear with just a touch of pale green. As they watched, its solid, icy-translucent hips and legs shifted and blurred, changing to a swirl of mist.

A long wave of blue-green hair drifted behind it, its shape like a gradually roiling cloud. It smiled at Elena, and its sharp teeth shone like silvery icicles. There was something in its chest, though, that wasn't ice, something solid and roundish and dark, dark red.

Elena saw all of this in an instant before her attention was fully riveted on what hung from the ice-woman-thing's outstretched hand.

"Damon." She gasped.

The ice-woman was holding him casually around the neck, ignoring his struggles as he dangled in the air. It held him so easily that he looked like a toy. The black-clad vampire swung out with his leg, kicking at the ice-woman's side, but his foot simply passed through mist.

"Elena," Damon said in a choked, thin voice.

The ice-woman—the phantom—cocked its head to one side and looked at Damon, then squeezed his neck a little tighter.

"I don't need to breathe, you . . . idiot phantom," he gasped defiantly.

The phantom's smile widened and it said in a sweet, cold voice, like crystals chiming together, "But your head can pop off, can't it? That'll do just as well." It shook him a little, and then transferred its smile to Elena, Bonnie, and Matt. Elena instinctively stepped back as the glacier-cold eyes found her.

"Welcome," the phantom said to her in a tone of pleasure, as though they were old friends. "I've found you and your friends so refreshing, all your little jealousies. Each of you with your own special flavor of envy. You've got an awful lot of problems, don't you? I haven't felt so strong or so well-nourished for millennia." Its face became thoughtful, and it began to shake Damon gently up and down. He was making a guttural choking noise now, and tears of pain ran down his face.

"But you really should have stayed where I put you," the phantom continued, its voice a little colder, and it swung Damon casually in a great arc through the air. He wheezed and pulled at its huge hand. Was it even true that he didn't need to breathe? Elena didn't know. Damon wasn't above lying about it if he had a reason, or even for no reason except to annoy his opponent.

"Stop it!" Elena shouted.

The phantom laughed again, genuinely amused. "Go ahead and make me, little one." Its grip tightened around Damon's throat and he shuddered. Then his eyes rolled back until Elena could see only the ghastly, red-veined whites of his eyes, and he went limp.

att watched in horror as the phantom shook
Damon like a rag doll.

Elena spun around to lock eyes with
Matt and Bonnie. "We have to save him," she whispered, a
fierce determination on her face, and immediately took off
running, shoving her way through the piles of ash.

Matt figured that if Damon, with all his vampire
strength and fighting skills honed over the centuries, was
so completely helpless in the hands of this phantom—and
jeez, with the way it was yanking him back and forth now,
his head really *was* going to pop off—then Matt, Bonnie,
and Elena had less than a snowball's chance in hell of making any difference to this fight. The only real question
would be whether the phantom would kill them, too.

And the truth was that Matt didn't even like Damon,

not one tiny little bit. Sure, Damon had helped save Fell's Church from Katherine and Klaus, and from the kitsune demons, but he was still a murderous, sarcastic, unrepentant, cocky, arrogant, nasty, usually unpleasant *vampire*. Damon had undoubtedly hurt more people than he had helped over his long life, even if you generously credited him with saving every single resident of Fell's Church. And he always called Matt "Mutt," pretending that he couldn't remember his actual name, which was completely infuriating. As Damon meant it to be.

Still, Elena loved Damon. For whatever reason. Probably the same inexplicable reason that regular girls loved regular old bad boys, Matt suspected. A dyed-in-the-wool good guy, he'd never seen the appeal himself.

But Elena did.

And Damon was part of the team, sort of, and you didn't leave your teammates to get decapitated by demon ice-women on ash-blanketed moons in other dimensions without at least doing your best to put up a fight.

Not even if you didn't like them at all.

Matt ran after Elena, and Bonnie followed. When they reached the phantom, Elena was already scrabbling at the icy blue hand clutched around Damon's throat, trying to pry its fingers up enough to slip her own underneath. The phantom barely glanced at her. Matt gave an inward sigh at the hopelessness of it all and swung a powerful roundhouse blow toward the phantom's stomach.

Before his fist could connect, his target turned from ice to swirling, intangible mist, and his punch passed right through the phantom. Thrown off balance, Matt staggered and fell into the phantom's now-vaporous torso.

It was like falling into a freezing-cold river of sewage. A numbing chill and a horrible, sickening smell washed over Matt. He pulled back out of the mist, nauseous and shivering but upright. He blinked dazedly around.

Elena was grappling with the phantom's fingers, scratching and yanking, and the phantom watched her with a kind of distant amusement, not the least bit alarmed or discomforted by the girl's efforts. Then it moved, so quickly Matt saw only a blur of bluish green, sending Elena flying, her arms and legs flailing, into a heap of ash. She scrambled to her feet immediately, blood trickling from her hairline, leaving red tracks through the ash that now coated her skin.

Bonnie was trying, too: She'd worked her way around behind the phantom and was hitting and kicking at it. Mostly, her feet and fists swung harmlessly right through the phantom's mist, but occasionally a blow would connect with the more solid ice. These blows seemed like they were totally ineffective, though: Matt couldn't tell whether the phantom had even noticed Bonnie was attacking it.

Veins were bulging out of Damon's face and neck, and he hung from the phantom's hand. The flesh of his neck was white around the stretched tendons. Superpowered strong old vampire or not, Damon was hurting. Matt tossed up a prayer in the direction of whatever saint looked after people pursuing hopeless causes, and threw himself back into the fight.

There was blackness. And then there was pain, and the darkness reddened, then cleared, and Damon could see once more.

The phantom—that *bitch* of a phantom—was holding him by the neck, and her skin was so cold, so cold it burned everywhere it touched him. He couldn't move.

But he could see Elena standing below him. Beautiful Elena, covered in ash, streaked with blood, her teeth bared and her eyes flashing like a warrior goddess. His heart swelled with love and fear. The brave little redbird and the boy Mutt fought beside her.

Please, he wanted to say. *Don't try to save me. Run. Elena, you have to run.*

But he couldn't move, couldn't speak.

Then the phantom shifted her stance and, as Damon watched, Elena stopped her attack and clutched at her stomach, grimacing in pain. Matt and Bonnie were holding themselves as well, their faces pale and strained, their mouths open in screams. With a wail, Bonnie collapsed.

Oh no, Damon thought with a bolt of horror. *Not Elena.*

Not the redbird. Not for me.

Then suddenly, a gusting wind swirled around him, and he was flung from the phantom's grip. There was a roaring in his ears and a stinging in his eyes. Looking around, he saw Bonnie and Elena, their long hair flying around them wildly; Matt, his arms pinwheeling; and the phantom, its glass-green face for once startled instead of knowing.

Tornado, Damon thought vaguely, and then, *Gateway*, and he realized he was being thrown upward, back into the darkness once more.

The wind was howling at a deafening pitch now, and Stefan had to raise his voice to a shout to even hear himself over it. He had to keep both hands clamped down on the book—it was being pulled out of his hands as if something alive and very strong were consciously trying to yank it away.

"*Mihi adi. Te voco. Necesse est tibi parere,*" Stefan said. "Come to me. I summon you. You must obey."

That was the end of the summoning spell in Latin. The next part was the banishing spell, which would be in English. Of course, the phantom would have to actually be there for that part of the spell to be effective.

The wind whipping through the garage grew even stronger. Outside, thunder rumbled.

Stefan watched the innermost circle, deep in the shadows of the garage, but there was nothing there. The unnatural wind was beginning to let up. Panic rose in his chest. Had they failed? He glanced anxiously at Alaric and Meredith, then at Mrs. Flowers, but none of them were looking at him, staring transfixed at the circle.

Stefan looked back into it, hoping against hope. But there was nothing there.

Wait.

There was the faintest movement of *something*, right in the center of the circle, the tiniest flash of blue-green light, and along with it came a chill. Not like the cold wind that had spun through the garage, but more like an icy breath—inhale and exhale, inhale and exhale—slow and steady and *freezing* cold, right from that one spot.

The glimmer widened, deepened, darkened, and suddenly what Stefan was looking at shifted and changed from an amorphous glimmer to a woman. An icy, misty, giant woman tinted in shades of blue and green. Inside her chest was a deep red rose, its stem a solid mass of thorns.

Meredith and Celia let out audible gasps. Mrs. Flowers stared calmly, while Alaric's jaw had dropped.

This must be the jealousy phantom. Stefan had always thought of jealousy as burning hot. Fiery kisses, fiery anger. But anger, lust, envy, all the things that made up jealousy, could be cold, too, and he had no doubt that they had the right phantom.

Stefan noticed all these things about the phantom and

forgot them again in a split second, because it wasn't just the ice-woman who materialized at the center of the circle.

Confused, weeping, staggering, streaked with ash and mud, three humans had appeared there as well.

His beautiful, elegant Elena, caked in grime, her golden hair tangled and matted, lines of blood running down her face. Delicate little Bonnie, tearstained and pale as milk, but with an expression of fury as she kicked and clawed at the phantom. And all-American, always reliable Matt, dusty and disheveled, turning to peer out at them with a peculiarly blank expression, as if simply wondering what fresh hell he'd landed in now.

And then one more person, a fourth figure wobbling and gasping, the last to shimmer into view. For a moment, Stefan didn't recognize him—couldn't recognize him, because this man wasn't supposed to exist anymore. Instead he just felt like a hauntingly familiar stranger. The stranger put his hands to his throat protectively and looked out of the circle, straight at Stefan. Through a bloody, swollen lip and bruised slits of eyes, the ghost of a brilliant smile appeared, and the gears of Stefan's mind slotted into place and began to turn again at last.

Damon.

Stefan was so flabbergasted he didn't know what to feel at first. Then, deep within him, a slow warmth spread with the realization that his brother was *back*. The last piece left of all his strange history was here once again. Stefan wasn't alone. Stefan took a step forward toward the edge of the diagram, holding his breath.

"Damon?" he said softly, wonderingly.

Jealousy snapped its head toward him, and Stefan was pinned to his spot by its glassy cold gaze.

"He came back before, you know," it said conversationally, and its voice chilled Stefan as if ice water had been thrown in his face. "He just didn't want you to know so he could have Elena all to himself. He's been lurking around, lying low, playing tricks like he always does."

Jealousy was undoubtedly feminine, and its cool observational tone reminded Stefan of the little voice that sometimes spoke from the back of his mind, calling out his darkest and most shameful thoughts. Could the others even hear it? Or was it speaking straight into his mind?

He risked a glance around. They all—Meredith, Celia, Alaric, Mrs. Flowers—stood still as statues, staring at Jealousy. Behind them, the makeshift beds lay empty. When the three sleepers' astral forms had entered the circle with the phantom, their bodies must have somehow joined them, making them solid within the inner circle.

"He came to *Elena*," the phantom taunted. "He kept his resurrection a secret from you so that he could pursue her. Damon didn't worry for a moment about how *you* felt about his death. And while you were busy mourning him, he was busy visiting Elena's bedroom."

Stefan reeled backward.

"He always wants what you have, and you know it," the phantom continued, its translucent lips curving in a smile. "It's been true since you were mortals. Remember how he came home from university and stole Katherine away from you? He used all his charms on her, just because he knew you loved her. Even with the small things: If you had a toy, he'd take it. If you wanted a horse, he'd ride it. If there was a piece of meat on the platter between you, he'd take it even if he wasn't hungry, just so you wouldn't get it."

Stefan shook his head slowly from side to side, again feeling *too slow*, like he had once again missed the important moment. Damon had been visiting Elena? When he had cried on her shoulder about his fallen brother, had Elena known Damon was alive?

"But you thought you could trust Elena, didn't you, Stefan?" Elena turned to stare at him, her cheeks pale beneath their coating of ash. She looked sick and apprehensive.

"No, Stefan—" Elena started to say, but the phantom went swiftly on, its words soothingly spoken poison. Stefan *knew* what it was doing. He wasn't a fool. Yet he felt himself nodding, agreeing, a slow red anger rising inside him despite his more rational self's struggle against it.

"Elena kept his secret from you, Stefan. She knew you

were in pain and that knowing Damon was alive would have eased that suffering, but still she kept silent, because Damon asked her to, and what Damon wanted was more important than helping you. Elena's always wanted both of the Salvatore brothers. It's funny, really, Stefan, how you're never quite enough for the women you love. This isn't the first time Elena's chosen Damon over you, is it?"

Elena shook her head, but Stefan could barely see her through the tide of fury and misery rising up inside him.

"Secrets and lies," the phantom went on merrily, with an icy tinkling laugh, "and foolish Stefan Salvatore always a few steps behind. You've known all along there was something between Elena and Damon that you weren't part of, Stefan, and yet you would never have suspected she'd betray you for him."

Damon seemed to snap out of his daze, as if suddenly hearing the phantom for the first time. His brows drew into a heavy frown and he slowly turned his head to stare at it.

He opened his mouth to speak, but at that moment, something in Stefan broke, and before Damon could issue whatever denial or taunt was on the tip of his tongue, Stefan lunged forward with a shout of rage, plunging straight through the chalked diagram. Faster than the human eye could follow, Stefan knocked Damon backward out of the circle and threw him against the far wall of the garage.

33

"Stop!" Elena screamed. "Stefan! Stop it! You'll kill him!"

Even as she said it, she realized that killing Damon might be exactly what Stefan's idea was here. Stefan tore at Damon with his teeth and hands, not pummeling him, but ripping ferally, with fangs and claws. Stefan, his body in a vicious primal crouch, his canines extended, his face distorted by a snarl of animal fury, had never looked more like a bloodthirsty vampire.

And behind Elena as she watched them, that seductive, chilling voice went on, telling Stefan that he would lose everything, just like he always lost everything. That Damon took everything from him and then tossed it carelessly, cruelly aside, because Damon simply wanted to ruin whatever Stefan had.

Elena turned and, too frightened by what Stefan was doing to Damon to have any fear left of the phantom, slammed it with her fists. After a moment, Matt and Bonnie joined her.

As before, mostly their hands just slid through the phantom's mist. The phantom's chest was solid, though, and Elena focused her rage on that, hitting against the hard ice there with as much power as she could.

Beneath the ice of the creature's chest, a rose glowed a rich dark red. It was a beautiful flower, but deadly looking, its color reminding her of poisoned blood. Its thorny stem seemed swollen, thicker than a normal flower's. As Elena stared at it, the glow deepened and the flower's petals opened further, swelling to full bloom. *Is that her heart?* Elena wondered. *Is Stefan's jealousy nourishing it?* She smashed her fist against the phantom's chest again, right above the rose, and the phantom glanced at her for a moment.

"Stop it," Elena said fiercely. "Leave Stefan alone."

The phantom was really looking at her now, and its— no, *her*—smile widened, her glasslike teeth sharp and shiny underneath her misty lips. In the glacial depths of her eyes, Elena thought she caught a chilly but genuine twinkle, and Elena's own heart froze.

Then the phantom turned her attention back toward Stefan and Damon, and, although Elena would never have believed it possible, things got worse.

"Damon," said the phantom throatily, and Damon, who'd been limp and exhausted, eyes clenched shut, passive under Stefan's assault, shielding his face but not fighting back, opened his eyes.

"Damon," she said again, her eyes glittering. "What right does Stefan have to attack you? Whatever you tried to take from him, you were just fighting against the fact that he got everything—your father's love, the girls you wanted—and you had nothing at all. He's a sanctimonious brat, a self-loathing weakling, but he gets *everything*."

" Damon's eyes widened as if in recognition at hearing his own deepest miseries voiced, and his face twisted with emotion. Stefan was still clawing and biting at him, but he fell back a little as Damon snapped into action, grabbing him by the arm and wrenching it. Elena winced with horror as she heard the crunch of something—oh, God—something in Stefan's arm or shoulder breaking.

Undaunted, Stefan only grimaced and then threw himself at Damon again, the hurt arm dangling awkwardly. Damon was stronger, Elena numbly noted, but exhausted; surely he wouldn't be able to keep his advantage for long. For now they seemed fairly evenly matched. They were both furious, both fighting with no reservations. A bestial, nasty snarl came from one of them, shaky, vicious laughter from the other, and Elena realized with horror that she had no idea which sound was coming from who.

The phantom hissed with enjoyment. Elena flinched away from her and, out of the corner of her eye, saw Bonnie and Matt step back, too.

"Don't break the lines!" Alaric shouted from the other side of . . . where were they now, anyway? Oh, Mrs. Flowers's garage—the garage. He sounded desperate, and Elena wondered if he had been shouting for a while. There had been some background noise going on, but there hadn't been a moment to listen to it. "Elena! Bonnie! Matt! Don't break the lines!" he shouted again. "You can get out, but step over the lines carefully!"

Elena glanced down. An elaborate pattern of lines in different colors was chalked beneath their feet, and she, Bonnie, Matt, and the phantom were all together in a small circle in the innermost center of this pattern.

Bonnie was the first one to clearly realize what Alaric was saying. "Come on," she muttered, yanking at Elena's and Matt's arms. Then she picked her way, daintily but quickly, across the floor, away from the phantom and toward their friends. Matt followed her. He had to pause on one foot in a small section and reach with his other foot, and there was a moment when he wobbled, one sneaker almost blurring a blue line of chalk. But he caught his balance and continued on.

It took Elena, still mostly focused on the desperately

grappling figures of Damon and Stefan, a few seconds longer to realize she needed to move as well. She was almost
too late. As she poised herself to take that first step out of
the inner circle, the phantom turned its glassy eyes upon
her.

Elena fled, jumping quickly out of the circle and just
barely managing to stop herself from skidding across the
diagram. The phantom took a swipe at her, but its hand
stopped before crossing above a chalk line, and it growled
in frustration.

Alaric shakily pushed his tousled hair out of his eyes.
"I wasn't sure whether that would hold her," he admitted, "but it seems like it's working. Now, carefully, Elena,
watching where you step, make your way over here." Matt
and Bonnie had already reached the wall of the garage, at
a distance from where Stefan and Damon were locked in
battle, and Meredith had wrapped her arms around them,
her dark head buried in Matt's shoulder, Bonnie nestled
against her side, her eyes as round as a frightened kitten's.

Elena looked down at the complicated pattern drawn
on the floor and started moving carefully between the
lines, heading not for her other friends but for the two
struggling vampires.

"Elena! No! This way!" called Alaric, but Elena
ignored him. She had to get to Damon and Stefan.

"Please," she said, half sobbing, as she reached them,

"Damon, Stefan, you have to stop. The phantom's doing this to you. You don't really want to hurt each other. It's not you. *Please.*"

Neither of them paid any attention to her. She wasn't even sure whether they could hear her. They were almost motionless now, their muscles straining in each other's grip as each tried to simultaneously attack and fend off the other. Slowly, as Elena watched, Damon began to overcome Stefan, gradually pushing his arms aside, leaning in toward his throat, white teeth flashing.

"*Damon! No!*" Elena screamed. She stretched out to grab his arm, to pull him off Stefan. Without even looking at her, he casually, viciously shoved her aside, sending her flying.

She landed hard on her back and slid across the floor, and it *hurt*, the impact jolting her teeth together, banging her head against the cement, white shocks of pain flaring behind her eyes. As she started to get up again, she saw with dismay Damon push through the last of Stefan's defenses and sink his fangs into his younger brother's neck.

"No!" she screamed again. "Damon, no!"

"Elena, be careful," Alaric shouted. "You're in the diagram. Please, whatever you do, don't break any more lines."

Elena looked around. Her landing had sent her skidding through several of the chalk marks, which were now smeared all around her, smudges of color. She stiffened in terror and suppressed a whimper. Was *it* loose now? Had she set it free?

Steeling herself, she turned toward the innermost circle.

The phantom was feeling around itself with its long arms, patting up and down against some invisible wall bordering the circle that kept it contained. As Elena watched, its mouth thinned with effort and it brought its hands together in one spot and *pushed*.

The air in the room rippled.

But the phantom did not manage to break through the circle, and after a moment it stopped pushing and hissed in disappointment.

Then its eyes fell on Elena, and it smiled again.

"Oh, Elena," it said, its voice soft with false compassion. "The pretty girl, the one everyone wants, the one the boys all fight over. It's so very hard being you." The voice twisted, its tone changing to bitter mockery. "But they're not really thinking of you, are they? The two you want, you're not the girl for them. You know why they are attracted to you. Katherine. Always Katherine. They want you because you look like her, but you're not her. The girl they loved so long ago was soft and sweet and gentle. An innocent, a victim, a foil for their fantasies. You're nothing like her. They'll find that out, you know. Once your mortal form changes—and it will. They'll be the same forever, but you're changing and getting older every day; in a few years you'll look much older than they do—then they'll realize you're not the one they love at all. You're not Katherine, and you never will be."

Elena's eyes stung. "Katherine was a monster," she spat out through her teeth.

"She *became* a monster. She started out as a sweet young girl," the phantom corrected her. "Damon and Stefan destroyed her. Like they'll destroy you. You'll never lead a normal life. You're not like Meredith or Bonnie or Celia. They'll have chances at normalcy when they're ready, despite the way you've dragged them into your battles. But you, you'll never be normal. And you know who's to blame for that, don't you?"

Elena, without thinking, looked at Damon and Stefan, just as Stefan managed to shove Damon away from him. Damon staggered backward, toward the group of humans huddling by the wall of the garage. Blood was running from his mouth and streaming down Stefan's neck from a terrible gash.

"They've doomed you, just like they doomed the one they *really* loved," the phantom said softly.

Elena pushed herself to her feet, her heart pounding hard, heavy with misery and anger.

"Elena, stop!" called a powerful contralto voice, filled with such authority that Elena turned away from Damon and Stefan and, blinking as though she'd been woken from a dream, looked out of the diagram toward the others.

Mrs. Flowers stood at the edge of the chalk lines, hands on her hips, feet planted firmly. Her lips were a straight angry line, but her eyes were clear and thoughtful. She met Elena's gaze, and Elena felt calmed and strengthened. Then Mrs. Flowers looked around at the others gathered beside her.

"We must perform the banishing spell *now*," she declared. "Before the phantom manages to destroy us all. Elena! Can you hear me?"

A surge of purpose running through her, Elena nodded and moved back to join the others.

Mrs. Flowers brought her hands sharply together, and the air rippled again. The phantom's voice broke off and it shrieked in fury, shoving at the air around it, its hands meeting resistance sooner, its invisible prison smaller.

Meredith felt urgently around on the high shelf near the garage door, her hands touching and rejecting various objects. Where had Mrs. Flowers put the candles? Paintbrushes, no. Flashlights, no. Ancient can of bug spray, no. Bag of potting soil, no. Some weird metal thing that she couldn't figure out from touching what it might be, no.

Bag of candles. Yes.

"I've got it," she said, pulling it off the shelf and

dumping probably a decade's worth of dust from the shelf onto her own head. "Urgh," she sputtered.

It was a mark of the seriousness of the situation, Meredith thought, that Bonnie and Elena both looked at her, head and shoulders coated in thick dust and spiderwebs, and neither giggled nor moved to brush her off. They all had more important things to worry about than a little dirt.

"Okay," she said. "First off, we need to figure out what color candle Damon would be." Mrs. Flowers had pointed out that Damon was clearly a victim of the jealousy phantom as well, and so would have to take part in the banishment ritual for it to work fully.

Looking at the two vampire brothers still attempting to tear each other apart, Meredith seriously doubted whether Damon would be participating. Stefan either, for that matter. They were solely focused on inflicting as much damage as possible on each other. Still, they would have to get the two vampires back to make the spell work.

Somehow.

Meredith found herself coolly wondering whether, if both Damon and Stefan died, they could safely be counted out of the ritual. Would the rest of them be able to defeat the phantom then? And if they didn't murder each other, but simply continued to fight, endangering them all, would she be able to kill them? She shoved the thought away. Stefan was her *friend*.

And then she determinedly made herself consider killing him again. This was her *duty*. That was more important than friendship; it had to be.

Yes, she could kill them today, even in the next few minutes, if it was necessary, she realized. She would regret it forever if she had to, but she could.

Besides, a part of her mind noted clinically, if things went on as they were now, Damon and Stefan would kill each other, and save her that burden.

Elena had been thinking hard—or maybe zoning out, focused on what the jealousy phantom had said to her, Meredith wasn't sure—and now she spoke. "Red," she said. "Is there a red candle for Damon?"

There was a dark red candle, and also a black one. Meredith pulled both out and showed them to Elena.

"Red," said Elena.

"For blood?" asked Meredith, eyeing the fighters, now only about ten feet away. God, they were both just *covered* with blood now. As she watched, Damon growled like an animal and banged Stefan's head repeatedly against the wall of the garage. Meredith winced at the hollow sound of Stefan's skull slamming against the wood and plaster of the wall. Damon had one hand around Stefan's neck, the other ripping at Stefan's chest as if Damon wanted to gouge out his heart.

A soft, sinister voice was still coming from the phantom. Meredith couldn't make out what it was saying, but its eyes were on the brothers, and it was smiling as it spoke. It looked satisfied.

"For passion," said Elena, and snatched the candle out of Meredith's hands and marched over, straight-backed and head high like a soldier's, to the line of candles Alaric was relighting at the edge of the diagram. Meredith stared after her as Elena lit the candle and dripped a puddle of hot wax to stand it upon.

Stefan forced Damon backward, closer to the others and their line of candles. Damon's boots scraped against the floor as he strained against Stefan.

"Okay," Alaric said, looking at the candles apprehensively, then down at the book. "Each of us will declare the jealousies inside ourselves—the weaknesses that the phantom is able to play on—and cast them out. If we really mean it, if we manage, at least for the moment, to truly and sincerely cast out our jealousy, our candles will go out and the phantom will be weakened. The trick is to really be able to banish the jealousies from our hearts and stop feeding the phantom, and if we all can do it at once, the phantom ought to disappear, or maybe even die."

"What if we can't? What if we try to cast out jealousy, but it doesn't go completely away?" Bonnie asked, her forehead crinkling with worry.

"Then it doesn't work and the phantom stays," said Alaric flatly. "Who wants to go first?"

Stefan slammed Damon down viciously onto the cement floor, a howl of anger coming from him. They were only a few feet from the line of candles, and Alaric stepped between them and the row of tiny flames, trying to shield the candles with his body. Celia shuddered as Stefan gave a low, furious growl and lowered his head to bite at Damon's shoulder. Jealousy kept up a steady stream of venomous chatter, her eyes gleaming.

Mrs. Flowers clapped her hands to get everyone else's attention, her face stern and encouraging. "Children, you will all have to be honest and brave," she said. "You must all *truly* admit to your worst selves in front of your friends, which will be hard. And then you will need to be strong enough to cast these worst selves of yours away, which may be even harder. But you love one another, and I promise we will get through it."

A thump and a muffled shout of rage and pain came from a few feet away, and Alaric glanced nervously over his shoulder at the battle behind him.

"Time is of the essence," Mrs. Flowers said briskly. "Who will go first?"

Meredith was about to step forward, clutching her stave for comfort, when Bonnie spoke up.

"I will," she said falteringly. "Um. I've been jealous of

Meredith and of Elena. I always . . ." She swallowed, and then spoke more firmly. "I sometimes feel like I'm only a sidekick when I'm around them. They're braver than me, and they're better fighters, and smarter and prettier, and . . . and *taller* than I am. I'm jealous because I feel like people don't respect me as much as they do them and don't really take me seriously like they do Elena and Meredith. I'm jealous because sometimes I'm standing in their shadows, which are pretty big shadows . . . metaphorically speaking, I mean. And I'm also jealous because I've never even had a real boyfriend, and Meredith has Alaric, and Elena has Stefan, and because Elena *also* has Damon, who I think is pretty amazing, but who would never notice me when I'm standing next to Elena, because she's all he can see."

Bonnie paused again, and glanced at Elena, her eyes wide and shining. "But I love Elena and Meredith. I know I need to stop comparing myself to them. I'm not just a sidekick; I'm useful and talented, too. And"—she spoke the words Alaric had given them all—"I have fed the phantom of jealousy. But now I cast my jealousy away."

In the semicircle of candles, the flame of Bonnie's pink one flickered and went out. Bonnie gave a little gasp and smiled, half-shamefaced, half-proud, at Meredith and Elena. From inside the diagram, the phantom of jealousy snapped its head around and glared at Bonnie. "Bonnie—"

Meredith started to say, wanting to tell her friend that of course she *wasn't* a sidekick. Didn't Bonnie know how amazing she was?

But then Elena stepped toward the candles and shook back her hair, head high. "I've been jealous of other people in Fell's Church," she declared. "I saw how easy it was for other couples to be together, and after all Stefan and I—and Damon, and the rest of my friends—have been through, and even after we saved Fell's Church and made it normal again, everything just kept on being so *hard* and so *weird* and supernatural. I guess I've been realizing that things aren't ever going to be just easy and normal for me, and that's been tough to accept. When I watched other people and was jealous of them, I fed the phantom of jealousy. I cast that jealousy away."

Elena smiled a little. It was a strange, rueful sort of smile, and Meredith, watching her, thought that, while Elena had cast out her jealousy, she was still haunted by regret for the easy, golden life she'd once had ahead of her and that had probably been taken away forever now.

The candle was still burning. Elena hesitated. Meredith followed her gaze past the line of candles to where Stefan and Damon struggled. As they watched, Damon heaved and rolled Stefan under him, leaving a long streak of blood across the floor of the garage. Stefan's foot brushed the red candle at the end of the line, and Alaric leaped to steady it.

"And I've been jealous of Katherine," Elena said. "Damon and Stefan loved her first, and she knew them before so much happened to change them, to . . . warp them out of who they ought to be. And even though I realize that they both know I'm not Katherine and that they love me for who I am, I haven't been able to forget that they noticed me at first because I look like her. I have fed the phantom of jealousy because of Katherine, and I cast that jealousy away."

The candle flame flickered, but did not go out. Jealousy smirked triumphantly, but then Elena went on. "I've also been jealous of Bonnie." Bonnie's head shot up, and she stared at Elena with an expression of disbelief. "I was used to being the only human Damon cared about, the only one who he would want to save." She looked at Bonnie with tear-filled eyes. "I am so, so glad that Bonnie is alive. But I was jealous that Damon cared enough to die for her. When I was jealous of Bonnie, I fed the phantom of jealousy. But now I cast my jealousy away."

The golden candle went out. Elena looked almost timidly at Bonnie, and Bonnie smiled at her, an open, loving smile, and held out her arms. Elena hugged her tightly.

Other than the grief she felt over Elena's parents' deaths, Meredith had never felt sorry for Elena. Why would she? Elena was beautiful, smart, a leader, passionately loved . . .

but now Meredith couldn't help but feel a pang of sympathy for her. Sometimes it must be easier to live an everyday life than to be a heroine.

Meredith glanced at the phantom. It seemed to be simmering and was now wholly focused on the humans.

Alaric stepped around the candles toward the others, glancing back toward Damon and Stefan. Damon had pinned Stefan painfully against the wall behind Alaric. Stefan's face was twisted in a grimace, and they could hear the scrape of his body against the hard surface. But at least Stefan and Damon weren't endangering the candles for now.

Meredith turned her attention to her boyfriend. What could Alaric be jealous of? If anything, he'd been the focus of jealousy the last week or so.

He reached for Meredith and took one of her hands. "I've been jealous," Alaric said, looking into her eyes. "Of you, Meredith. And of your friends."

Meredith reflexively arched a brow at him. What did he mean?

"God." He half laughed. "Here I am, a graduate student in parapsychology. I've been dying my whole life to prove to myself that there's something more going on in the world than what everybody knows, that some of the things we think of as supernatural are real. And then I come to this small town in Virginia because there are rumors, rumors I don't really believe, that there might be vampires here, and when I get here I find this amazing, beautiful, confident girl, and it turns out she comes from a family that hunts vampires. And her friends are vampires and witches and psychics and girls who come back from the dead to fight evil. They only just finished high school, but they've seen things I've never imagined. They've defeated monsters, and saved towns, and traveled to other dimensions. And, you know, I'm just this ordinary guy, and suddenly half the people I know—and the girl I love— are practically superheroes." He shook his head, looking at Meredith admiringly. "I've fed the phantom of jealousy. But now I cast my jealousy away. I'll just have to deal with being the boyfriend of a superhero." Instantly, the dark green candle went out.

Sealed in the inner circle, the phantom hissed and paced back and forth in the small space like a trapped tigress. It looked angry, but not noticeably weaker.

Celia spoke next. Her face was tired but calm. "I've fed the phantom of jealousy," she proclaimed. "I've been jealous of Meredith Suarez." She didn't say why. "But now I see that it's pointless. I've fed the phantom of jealousy, but now I cast my jealousy away."

She spoke as if she were dropping something into the trash. But still the pale purple candle went out.

Meredith opened her mouth to speak—she was clear

on what she needed to say, and it wouldn't be too hard, because she'd *won*, hadn't she? If it had ever been a battle anywhere besides her own mind—but Matt cleared his throat and spoke first.

"I have . . ." He stumbled over his words. "I guess . . . no, I know I've fed the phantom of jealousy. I have always been crazy about Elena Gilbert, as long as I've known her. And I've been jealous of Stefan. All along. Even now, when Jealousy's got him trapped in this bloody battle, because he has Elena. She loves him, not me. But, well, it doesn't matter. . . . I've also known for a long time that Elena and I together don't work, not for her, and that's not Stefan's fault. I've fed the phantom of jealousy, but now I cast my jealousy away." He blushed and carefully did not look at Elena. The white candle went out, sending a long trail of smoke toward the ceiling.

Three candles left, Meredith thought, looking at the last steady flames. Stefan's dark green, Damon's red, and her own brown. Was the phantom any weaker? From its invisible cage, the Phantom growled. If anything, it seemed to have made the space around itself bigger again, and it was once again pushing at it, seemingly feeling for a weak spot.

Meredith knew she had to keep the confessions going. "I've fed the phantom of jealousy," she said in a strong, clear voice. "I was jealous of Dr. Celia Connor. I love Alaric, but I know I'm much younger than he is, not even in college yet, and I've never really been anywhere or seen anything of the world—the human world, at least—outside of where I grew up. Celia shares so much with him—experiences, education, interests—and I knew he liked her a lot. And she's beautiful and really smart and poised. I was jealous because I was afraid she would take him from me. But if she had been able to take him, that would mean he wasn't mine to keep. You can't steal a person." She smiled hesitantly at Celia, and after a moment, Celia smiled slightly in return. "I cast—"

"Watch out!" Alaric shouted. "Damon! Stefan! Stop!"

Meredith looked up. Damon and Stefan were staggering across the floor of the garage, past the line of candles, past Alaric, who grabbed at them. They broke out of his hold effortlessly without seeming to even notice his touch, shoving against each other desperately, struggling fiercely. Oblivious to anything but their battle, they were getting closer and closer to the phantom.

"No!" shouted Elena.

Damon shoved Stefan backward, and the heel of Stefan's boot scraped across the chalk outlining the small circle that contained the phantom—scraped across the chalk line and smudged it, and the circle was no longer complete.

With a howl of triumph, the phantom was free.

34

We didn't weaken it, not enough!" Meredith shouted to her friends over Jealousy's shouts. The phantom, if anything, appeared stronger as it crossed the garage in one great leap and backhanded Meredith across the face. Meredith felt a searing pain, saw a bright flash of light, and felt herself slam against the wall. Dazed, she staggered back onto her feet.

The phantom was coming toward her again. More slowly this time, with a smile of anticipation.

The spell must be doing something then, Meredith thought groggily, *or it wouldn't care if I finished my part or not.*

Meredith gripped her fighting stave. She wasn't going down easily, not if she could prevent it. Alaric had called her a superhero. Superheroes kept fighting, even when the odds were stacked against them.

She sliced out viciously, expertly, with the end of the fighting stave. All those hours of practice paid off, because the phantom didn't seem to expect the blow, and rather than the stave passing harmlessly through mist, Meredith caught the phantom in its solid form, just above the rose in its chest. The blade at the end opened a deep wound in the phantom's chest, and when Meredith pulled it back for a second blow, viscous green fluid dripped from the end of her weapon.

As she swung again, Meredith's luck ran out. The phantom reached out toward her, its hand moving so fast that Meredith didn't see it until the phantom was holding the other end of the stave. Sharp as the stave was, poisonous as the coating of all those bits of silver and wood and iron were, the phantom held it lightly and easily, and *pulled*.

Meredith went skidding across the garage floor toward the phantom, fast and helpless, and the phantom reached out lazily with its other hand to catch her, a sneer of contempt and anger on its glassy face. *Oh no*, Meredith's internal voice babbled, *not like this. It can't end like this.*

Just before it touched Meredith, though, the phantom's face changed, suddenly blossoming into an expression of confusion. It let go of the stave, and Meredith yanked herself back and caught her balance, wobbling furiously, gasping for breath.

The phantom stared past her, Meredith forgotten, at least for the moment. The phantom's glassy teeth were bared, and there was an expression of terrible rage on its green-tinted face. As Meredith watched, the muscles in its icy-solid arms seemed to strain, then dissolve to swirls of arm-shaped mist, then solidify again, still in the same tense stillness. *She can't move*, Meredith realized. She turned to look behind her.

Mrs. Flowers stood straight and tall, her blazing blue eyes fixed on the phantom. She held out her hands in front of her, her face set in strong, determined lines. Several strands of her gray hair had escaped from her bun, standing out in all directions as if caught by static electricity.

Mrs. Flowers's lips moved soundlessly, and, as the phantom strained to move, Mrs. Flowers strained, too, looking as if she was struggling to support something cripplingly heavy. Their eyes, cool intent blue and glacier-clear green, were locked together in silent battle.

Mrs. Flowers's eyes were steady, but her arms were shaking violently, and Elena didn't know how much longer the older woman would be able to hang on and keep the phantom under control. Not long, she suspected. The battle with the kitsune had taken a lot out of Mrs. Flowers, and she hadn't recovered fully yet. She wasn't ready for a new fight.

Elena's heart was thumping like crazy, and she couldn't stand to look at the bloody figures of Damon and Stefan on the other side of the garage, because the one thing she knew she couldn't do right now was panic. She needed to be able to *think*.

"Meredith," Elena said crisply, with such a tone of authority that her friends all turned away from watching the struggle between Mrs. Flowers and the phantom to look at her. "Finish your part of the ceremony."

Meredith looked at Elena blankly for a moment and then snapped into gear. That was one of the many wonderful things about Meredith: She could always be relied upon, no matter what, to pull herself together and get on with the job.

"I have fed the phantom of jealousy," Meredith said, looking down at the floor where her brown candle still burned, "but now I cast my jealousy away."

Meredith's words rang with truth, and the candle went out.

The phantom flinched and grimaced, flexing its fingers angrily. The deep red of the rose in its chest dulled to a dark pink for a moment before flushing back to crimson. But . . . it didn't seem like it was defeated; it seemed merely irritated. Its eyes never left Mrs. Flowers's, and its ice-sculpted muscles still were straining forward.

Almost all the candles were out. Only two flames were

flickering, from the blue and red candles, only two victims feeding the phantom with their jealousy.

So, with almost all its victims torn away from it, shouldn't the phantom be *weaker*? Shouldn't it be sick and struggling?

Elena turned to Alaric. "Alaric," she whispered. "What did the book say? Shouldn't the spell be starting to kill the phantom by now?"

Alaric was watching the silent showdown between Mrs. Flowers and the phantom again, his own fists clenched and his body straining as if he could somehow lend Mrs. Flowers his strength, and it took a little time—*time we don't have*, thought Elena furiously—for him to drag his attention to Elena. When he did and she repeated her question, he turned a more analytical gaze on the phantom, and a new worry dawned in his eyes.

"I'm not entirely sure," he said, "but the book did suggest . . . the book said something like, 'Every word truly spoken by its victims, each dark emotion willingly rejected, will draw back to them the life the phantom has stolen from their thoughts and deeds. The creature will crumble with every honest word spoken against it.' It could be just rhetoric, or maybe the person who wrote down the spell had heard about the ritual without seeing it performed, but it sounds . . ." He hesitated.

"It sounds like the spell ought to be killing the phantom

by now," said Elena flatly. "It sounds like this isn't working right."

"I don't know what's going wrong," said Alaric unhappily.

The world shifted and everything snapped into focus.

"I do," said Elena. "It must be because this is an Original, not an ordinary phantom. We didn't create it with our emotions, so we can't destroy it just by taking them away. I think we're going to need to try something else."

Stefan and Damon were still locked in combat. They were both bloody and battered. His hurt arm dangling at an unnatural angle, Stefan moved as though something inside him had been damaged, but they were both still attacking each other viciously, Stefan no less than Damon.

Elena reasoned that they must be fighting on their own initiative now. The phantom, absorbed in its battle with Mrs. Flowers, was no longer muttering poisonous encouragement to them. If Damon and Stefan weren't being seduced by Jealousy's voice, maybe they could be persuaded to listen to someone else. Elena, trying not to catch the phantom's attention, eased her way toward the fighters.

Damon was bleeding from his neck and a long cut on his head, and the skin around both his eyes was bruising up. He was limping, but he was clearly gaining the upper hand. Stefan, circling warily now just out of arm's reach, was not only curled forward to protect whatever was injured inside him but had a long strip of torn skin hanging from his cheek.

Damon was grinning savagely at him, moving closer with every shift of his feet. There was an alertness to Damon's eyes that spoke only of the predator within, of his joy in the hunt and in the kill. Damon must have forgotten in the pleasure of the fight who he was battling, Elena told herself. He would never forgive himself, once he *was* himself again, if he really seriously hurt Stefan, or even killed him. *Although*, something inside her whispered, *part of him has always wanted this.*

She shoved the thought aside. *Part* of Damon might want to hurt Stefan, but the real, whole Damon did not. If there was anything that fighting the phantom had shown her, it was that the dark emotions everyone hid in their depths weren't all of who they really were. They weren't their true selves.

"Damon," she shouted. "Damon, think! The phantom is influencing you! It's making you fight." She heard her voice rise pleadingly. "Don't let it beat you. Don't let it destroy you."

Damon didn't seem to hear her, though. He still wore that feral smile, and prowled a little closer to Stefan, edging him farther and farther toward the corner of the garage. Pretty soon Stefan would be trapped, boxed in and unable to run.

And, catching a glimpse of the defiant expression on Stefan's poor, battered face, Elena realized with a sinking heart that Stefan wouldn't run, even if Damon gave him the chance. The part of Stefan that hated Damon was in control of him now.

Stefan bared his teeth in a ferocious snarl. Damon pulled back his fist to deliver a powerful blow, his canines extending in anticipation of drinking his brother's lifeblood.

More quickly than she had ever moved before, at least as a human, Elena flung herself between them as Damon's fist swung forward. Eyes squeezed closed, she threw her arms wide to protect Stefan and awaited the impact.

Damon was moving so fast by the time she jumped in front of him that momentum was carrying his whole body forward. With his inhuman strength, it was a punch that would break her bones and crush her face.

But Damon stopped in time, as only a vampire could. She could feel the rush of displaced air from the blow, even the brush of his knuckles against her face, but there was no pain.

Gingerly Elena opened her eyes. Damon stood poised, coiled to strike, one arm still raised. He was breathing hard, and his eyes glittered strangely. Elena returned his gaze.

Was there a tiny bit of relief shining in Damon's eyes? Elena thought so. The question was, was it relief that he had stopped himself before he killed her, or that she had stopped him from killing Stefan? Surely Damon could have thrown her out of the way by now and attacked Stefan again, if that was what he really wanted.

Elena took a chance and reached out toward Damon's fist, folding those battered knuckles within her own smaller hand. He didn't resist as she lowered his fist to his side, passively allowing himself to be moved.

"Damon," she said softly. "Damon, you can stop now." His eyes narrowed and she knew he could hear her, but his mouth was tight and fierce, and he didn't answer.

Without letting go of Damon's hand, Elena turned toward Stefan. He was close behind her, his eyes fixed on Damon. He was panting rapidly, and he wiped the back of his hand absently against his mouth, smearing blood across his face. Elena reached out and took his hand, sticky as it was with blood.

Damon's hand tensed in hers, and she glanced at him to see he was staring at her other hand, the one that was holding Stefan's. Stefan saw where Damon was looking, too, and the corners of his swollen mouth drew up in a bitter little smile.

Behind them, the phantom snarled as it fought Mrs. Flowers's power. It sounded louder, fiercer.

"Listen," she said urgently, looking from one brother to the other. "The phantom's not focusing on you now, so you can think for yourselves. But Mrs. Flowers won't be able to hold her for long. So you need to do it; you need to start thinking *now*, instead of just acting. I need to tell you . . . um." She cleared her throat uncomfortably. "I never told you this, but when Klaus was keeping me prisoner, after Katherine's death, he used to show me . . . images. Memories, I guess, Katherine's memories. How you both were with her, back when you were human. When you were young and alive and loved her. How *much* you loved her. I hated it, seeing how real that love was. And I knew that you noticed me at first only because of the love you had for her then. It's always bothered me a little bit, even though I know your love for me now is deeper."

Both brothers were looking at Elena now, and Stefan's lips parted to speak. Elena shook her head briskly and went on. "No, let me finish. It's bothered me *a little bit*. It hasn't destroyed me, and it hasn't changed what I feel . . . for either of you. Because I also know that you might have noticed me for Katherine's sake, but that once you got past it, you both saw *me*, Elena. You don't see Katherine in me anymore."

She had to venture into dangerous territory now, so she proceeded cautiously, trying to lay out her argument with logic and sensitivity. "So, I know that, right? But when the phantom spoke to me, it dredged up that old jealousy and made it burn inside me again. And the other things the phantom said to me are partly true, too. Yes, I'm jealous

sometimes of girls with"—she smiled despite herself—
"normal love lives. But in my most centered moments, I
know I wouldn't want to be them. What I've got is amazing, even if it's hard." Elena swallowed. "And so I know that
what the phantom said to you is partly true. You're jealous
of each other. You're angry about things from the past, and
you're upset that I love both of you. But I also know that's
not *all* there is. It's not the most important thing, either.
Not anymore. Things have changed since the days when
jealousy and anger were the only emotions between you.
You've worked together, and you've protected each other.
You've become brothers again."

She gazed into Damon's eyes, searching for a response.
"Damon, Stefan was *devastated* when he thought you were
dead. You're his brother, and he loves you, and he didn't
know what to do with you gone. You're a big part of his
life—past and present. You're the only one who's been
there with him throughout his history."

She swung to look at Stefan. "Stefan, Damon didn't
hide from you the fact that he was alive because he wanted
to make you suffer, or to be free of you, or whatever the
phantom was convincing you of. He wanted to be able to
come back in a way and at a time that he could show you
things were going to be different. That he was capable of
changing. And you were the person he wanted to change
for. Not me. You. You're his brother and he loves you, and

he wanted things to be better between you."

Elena paused for breath, and to gauge what effect, if any, her speech was having on the brothers. At least they weren't currently trying to kill each other. That had to be a good sign. They stared at each other now, their faces unreadable. Damon licked the blood from his lips. Stefan reached up and carefully ran his free hand over the torn skin on his face and chest. Neither one said a word. Was there a connection left between them? Damon was looking at the cuts on Stefan's neck with an almost soft expression in his black eyes.

Elena let go of them and threw up her hands. "Fine," she said. "If you can't forgive each other, then just think about this. The phantom *wants* you to fight. It wants you to kill each other, to hate each other. Your jealousy is what's feeding it. One thing I know about you—about *both* of you—is that you've never given your enemies anything they wanted, not even if it would have saved you. Are you going to give in to what this phantom, this manipulative monster, wants? Is it going to control you, or are *you* going to control you? Does either of you really want to murder your brother for someone *else*?"

At the same exact moment, Damon and Stefan blinked.

After a few seconds, Stefan cleared his throat awkwardly. "I'm glad you're not dead after all," he offered.

The corner of Damon's mouth twitched. "I'm relieved

I didn't manage to kill you today, little brother," he answered.

Apparently, that was all they had to say. They held each other's eyes for a beat longer, then turned to Elena.

"So," said Damon, and he was beginning to smile, a wild, reckless smile that Elena recognized. Damon the unstoppable, Damon the antihero, was back. "How do we kill this bitch?"

Mrs. Flowers and the phantom were still locked in their silent, almost motionless battle. Mrs. Flowers was beginning to lose ground to the phantom, though. The phantom's stance was wider; its arms had spread out. It was gradually gaining the power to move, and Mrs. Flowers's hands and arms were shaking with strain. Her face was pale, and the lines of age around her mouth seemed deeper.

"We have to hurry," Elena said to Damon and Stefan. They skirted around Mrs. Flowers and the phantom, and joined the others who, white-faced and wary, were watching them approach. In front of them, only two candles still burned.

"Stefan," Elena said. "Go."

Stefan stared down at the dark blue candle still burning on the floor of the garage. "I've been jealous of everyone lately, it seems," he said, the shame evident in his tone. "I've been jealous of Matt, whose life seems so simple and good to me, who I know could have taken Elena out of the shadows and given her the uncomplicated life she deserves. I was jealous of Caleb, who seemed like the kind of golden boy who would be a good match for Elena, so much so that I distrusted him even before I had reason to, because I thought he was after her. And especially, I was jealous of Damon."

His gaze left the candle and settled on his brother's face. Damon looked back at him with an inscrutable expression. "I suppose I've always been jealous of him. The phantom was telling the truth when she said that. When we were alive, he was older, faster, stronger, more sophisticated than I was. When we died"—Stefan's lips curled up in a bitter smile of remembrance—"things only got worse. And, even more recently, when Damon and I found we could work together, I've resented how close he was to Elena. He has a piece of her that I'm not a part of, and it's hard not to be jealous of that."

Stefan sighed and rubbed the bridge of his nose between his thumb and forefinger. "The thing is, though, I love my brother. I do." He looked up at Damon. "I love you. I always have, even when we were at our worst. Even when all we wanted to do was kill each other. Elena's right: We're more than the bad parts of ourselves. I have fed the phantom of jealousy, but now I cast my jealousy away."

The blue candle flickered and went out. Elena was

watching the phantom closely, and saw the rose in its torso dull for a moment. The phantom flinched and snarled, then renewed its struggle against Mrs. Flowers's spell. As it gave a powerful twist, the older woman staggered backward.

"Now!" Elena muttered quietly to Damon, looking at him meaningfully and wishing more than ever that she had her powers of telepathy. *Distract her,* she hoped her eyes said.

Damon nodded once, as if to say he understood her message, then cleared his throat theatrically, drawing every eye to him, and picked up the dark red candle, the last one burning in the line. He dabbed a line of his blood down its length and spent a few seconds posed with his head lowered pensively, his long, dark eyelashes brushing his cheeks. He was milking the moment for every drop of drama.

Once every eye was fixed on him, Elena touched Stefan and indicated for him to help her approach the phantom from either side.

"I have been jealous," Damon intoned, staring down at the flame of the candle he held. He flicked his eyes up quickly at Elena, and she nodded encouragingly.

"I have been jealous," he repeated, frowning. "I have coveted that which my brother has, over and over again."

Elena slipped closer to the phantom, coming up beside it on its right side. She could see that Stefan was inching nearer on its left.

Mrs. Flowers saw them, too. Elena could tell, because the older woman raised her eyebrows fractionally and began to mutter her spell more loudly and fiercely. Damon's voice rose, too, everyone in the room competing for Jealousy's attention, to keep it from noticing Stefan and Elena's machinations.

"I don't need to go into every single detail of my past," Damon said, his familiar smirk appearing on his battered face, a smirk that Elena found oddly reassuring. "I think there's been enough of that here today. Suffice it to say there are things I . . . regret. Things that I would like to be different in the future." He paused dramatically for a moment, his head thrown back proudly. "And so I admit that I have fed the phantom of jealousy. And now I cast jealousy *out.*"

In the moment that Damon's candle went out—and thank God it *had* gone out, Elena thought; Damon was apt to cling to his worst impulses—the rose in the phantom's chest dulled again to a dark pink. Jealousy snarled and wobbled ever so slightly on its feet. At that same instant, Stefan lunged for the cut across the phantom's chest and got his hand inside it, inside the phantom's torso, and grabbed for the rose.

A gout of green, viscous fluid spurted from the wound as Stefan squeezed the rose, and then the phantom screamed, a long, unearthly howl that made all the humans flinch. Bonnie clapped her hands over her ears, and Celia moaned.

For a moment, Elena thought they were going to win that easily—that by attacking the rose at the phantom's heart, Stefan had defeated it. But then the phantom steadied itself and, with a huge flexing of muscle, pulled suddenly out of Mrs. Flowers's control, and in one smooth motion ripped Stefan away from its side, his hand coming empty out of its chest, and threw him across the garage.

Stefan hit the wall with a muffled thump, slid to the floor, and lay still. Evidently exhausted by her battle with the phantom, Mrs. Flowers also sagged backward, and Matt rushed to catch her in his arms before she hit the ground.

The phantom smiled slowly at Damon, showing its sharp teeth. Its glacier-clear eyes glittered.

"It's time to go, Damon," Jealousy said softly. "You're the strongest one here. The best of all of them, the best of anyone. But they'll always fawn over Stefan, the weakling, the brat, your useless baby brother. No matter what you do, no one will ever care for you the way these mortals do for him. The way everyone, for hundreds of years, has always cared for Stefan. You should leave them behind. Make them suffer. Why not leave them in danger? They'd do the same to you. Elena and her friends traveled through dimensions, faced slavery, braved the greatest perils, to save *Stefan*, but they left you lying dead, far from home. They came back here and were happy without you. What loyalty do you owe them?"

Damon, his face in shadow now that all the candles were out, gave a dark, bitter little laugh. His black eyes gleamed in the dimness, fixed on the phantom's clear ones. There was a long silence, and Elena's breath caught in her throat.

Damon stepped forward, still holding his candle. "Don't you remember?" he said, his voice cool. "I cast you *out*."

And with superhuman quickness, before anyone could even blink, he lit his candle again with a flick of Power and threw it, straight and true, directly into the phantom's face.

35

Elena leaped backward as the phantom caught fire. She was so close that the heat of the flames burned her cheeks, and she could smell her own hair smoking.

Shielding her face with her hands, she eased her way forward as silently and sneakily as she could, closer and closer to the phantom. Her legs shook, but she willed them still and steady.

She was consciously *not* letting herself look at or think about Stefan's body crumpled on the floor of the garage, in the same way she had kept herself from looking at Damon and Stefan's fight when she needed to think.

Suddenly a burst of flames shot into the air, and for one dazzling second, Elena dared to hope that Damon had done it. The phantom was *burning*. Surely no creature of ice could withstand that.

But then she realized that the phantom was not only burning. She was also laughing.

"You fool," the phantom said to Damon, in a soft and almost tender voice. "You think fire can hurt *me*? Jealousy can burn hotter than fire as well as colder than ice. You of all people should know that, Damon." She laughed her strange clinking laugh. "I can feel the jealousy, the anger that burns in you all the time, Damon, and it burns so hot I can smell the hatred and despair that live in you, and your little petty hurts and rages are meat and drink to me. You clutch them to you and pore over them like treasure. You may have succeeded in casting out a tiny piece of the multitudes of hurts that burden you, but you'll never be free of me."

Around the phantom's feet, tiny blue lines of flame ignited and spread quickly across the floor of the garage. Elena watched in horror: Were these burning traces of oil left by Mrs. Flowers's ancient car? Or was it simply the phantom's maliciousness made solid, spreading fire among them?

It didn't really matter. What mattered was that the garage was on fire, and while the phantom might be impervious to the flames, the rest of them weren't. Smoke filled the musty space, and Elena and her friends began to cough. She covered her nose and mouth with her hand.

Streaking past Elena, Damon snarled and leaped for

the phantom's throat.

Even in their current dire situation, Elena couldn't help admiring Damon's speed and grace. He collided with the phantom and knocked it to the floor, then recoiled, protecting his face with his leather-clad arm. *Fire*, Elena remembered with a frisson of terror. *Fire is one of the few things that can kill a vampire.*

Her eyes watered from the smoke, but she forced them to stay open as she moved closer, circling around behind the phantom, who was back on its feet. She could hear her friends shouting, but she concentrated on the fight.

The phantom was moving more awkwardly than it had been earlier, and did not immediately attack Damon. Through the flames, Elena could see that thick greenish fluid was still trickling down its solid torso from the wound Meredith had given it. Where the liquid touched the flames, they flickered with a greenish blue tint.

Damon lunged for the phantom again, and it flung him off with a shrug. Snarling, they circled each other warily. Elena skittered around behind them, trying to stay out of Damon's way, trying to see how she could help.

A crackling from across the room distracted Elena for a second, and she glanced back to see fire climbing the far wall, reaching for the wooden shelves set around the room. She missed seeing what exactly happened next, but suddenly Damon was skidding across the floor on his back, an angry red burn glowing on his cheek.

He was up again in a second and prowling back toward the phantom, but his eyes had a slightly wild glint to them that made Elena nervous. Even injured, the phantom was stronger than Damon, and, after his long fight with Stefan, Damon's reserves must be waning. He was growing reckless. Elena gathered her courage and moved closer to the phantom again, as close to the flames as she could stand. The phantom glanced back at her for a second and then away, focusing on the stronger threat.

It sprang forward to meet Damon, its fiery arms spread wide and a savagely joyous smile on its face.

And suddenly Meredith was there beside Damon. She looked solemn and pale as a young martyr, her lips tight and her eyes wary, but she moved as fast as lightning. Her stave sliced through the air almost too quickly to see, leaving another long cut across the phantom's stomach. The phantom howled, and the flames on its torso hissed as more greenish fluid gushed from the wound.

But the phantom remained upright. It snarled and reached for Meredith, who danced rapidly backward, just out of range. Meredith and Damon exchanged a wordless look and moved to flank the phantom, one on either side, so that it couldn't watch both of them at once. Damon cuffed Jealousy, a short, intense blow, and pulled back a reddish, blistering hand. Meredith swung her stave again, nearly catching the phantom on the arm but instead cleaving only a wisp of smoke.

There was a crash as a burning shelf collapsed onto the floor. The smoke grew thicker. Away from the fight, Elena could hear Bonnie and Matt coughing.

Elena moved closer still, again coming toward the phantom from behind, safely out of Meredith and Damon's way. The phantom's heat was like a bonfire.

Meredith and Damon were moving in tandem now, as smoothly as if they had rehearsed, dancing in and back, sometimes catching the phantom with a blow, more often passing through a curl of smoke or mist as the phantom transformed its parts from solid to airy shapes.

A voice rang out. *"Impera te desistere."* Mrs. Flowers leaned against the supporting arms of Matt and Alaric. But her eyes were clear and her voice was steady. Power crackled in the air around her.

The phantom slowed only slightly in its fight, perhaps no more than a half second behind in its thrusts and transformations. But this was enough to make at least a little difference. More of Damon's and Meredith's blows landed, and they were able to dodge a few more of the phantom's.

Was it enough, though? The phantom flinched when a punch hit home, and it bled horrible green goo where the stave cut it, but it was still steady on its feet as Meredith and Damon hacked and choked in the smoke and stumbled away from the flames. The rose in Jealousy's chest pulsed a steady dark red. Elena exhaled in frustration and immediately began to cough again. The phantom wasn't staying in one place long enough for Elena to get a good shot at grabbing the rose-heart.

Meredith sliced at it with her fighting stave, and this time the stave slid through smoke, and the phantom grabbed the stave in one hand, swinging Meredith toward Damon. Colliding, they both fell heavily to the ground, and the phantom, still slightly hobbled by Mrs. Flowers's spell, strained toward them.

"I've envied Meredith for her brains!" shouted Bonnie. Her face was smudged with smoke and tears, and she looked incredibly small and fragile, but she was standing straight-backed and proud, yelling at the top of her lungs. "I know I'll never be as good at school as she is, but that's okay. I cast my jealousy out!"

The phantom's rose dimmed to a dark pink for a moment, and it staggered ever so slightly. It glanced at Bonnie and hissed. It was only a tiny pause in the phantom's advance, but it was enough for Damon to spring to his feet. He stepped in front of Meredith, shielding her as she clambered up. Without even looking at each other, Meredith and Damon began circling in opposite directions again. "I've been jealous that my friends have more money than I do!" Matt shouted, "but I cast the jealousy out!"

"I envy the way Alaric truly believed in something unproven, and turned out to be right!" Celia yelled. "But I cast it out!"

"I've envied Elena's clothes!" Bonnie cried. "I'm too

short to look good in lots of things! But I cast that out!"

Damon kicked at the phantom, pulling his smoldering leg back quickly. Meredith swung her stave. Mrs. Flowers chanted in Latin, and Alaric joined her, his low voice in counterpoint to hers, reinforcing her spell. Bonnie, Celia, and Matt kept shouting: dredging up small jealousies and hurts that they were probably usually hardly aware of, casting them out to pepper the phantom with tiny blows.

And for the first time, the phantom looked . . . baffled. It swung its head slowly from one to another of its opponents: Damon stalking toward it, fists raised; Meredith, her stave swinging surely as she watched the phantom with a cool and considering gaze; Alaric and Mrs. Flowers reciting strings of Latin words, hands lifted; Bonnie, Matt, and Celia shouting confessions as if they were throwing rocks at it.

Jealousy's glassy eyes passed over Elena without really seeming to notice her: Standing still and quiet among the entire hubbub, she was not a threat.

This was the best chance Elena was going to get. She nerved herself to move forward, then froze as the phantom turned toward her.

Then, miraculously, Stefan was there. He grappled at the phantom's back, throwing one arm around its neck as the flames licked at him. His shirt caught fire. The phantom, briefly, was pulled backward past Elena, its torso toward her, unprotected.

Without hesitation, Elena plunged her hand into the fire.

For a moment, she barely felt the flames, just a gentle, almost cool touch against her hand as the flames flickered around her. *Not so bad*, she had a moment to think, and then she felt the pain.

It was pure and agonizing, and dark fireworks of shock went off behind her eyes. She had to fight to overcome the almost irresistible instinct to pull her hand back out of the fire. Instead, she groped at the phantom's torso, searching for the cut Meredith had made just above its rose. It was slippery and smooth, and her hand fumbled. *Where is it? Where is it?*

Damon had thrown himself into the flames alongside Stefan, yanking at the phantom's arms and neck, keeping its torso clear for Elena, preventing the phantom from ripping free and throwing her across the room. Meredith beat at Jealousy's side with her stave. Behind her, her friends' voices rose in a babble of confessions and spells as they did their part to keep the phantom off balance and disoriented.

At last Elena's hand found the cut and she *pushed* inside. It was icy cold in the phantom's chest, and Elena yelped at the contrast—the cold was excruciating after the heat, and the flames still licked at her wrist and arm. The freezing liquid inside the phantom's chest was so thick, it was like feeling through gelatin. Elena shoved and reached, and the phantom screamed with pain.

It was a horrible sound and, despite all that the phantom had done to her and her friends, Elena could not help flinching in sympathy. A moment later, Elena's hand closed on the rose's stem and a thousand thorns pierced her burned flesh. Ignoring the pain, she pulled the rose out of the freezing liquid, out of the fire, and staggered backward, away from the phantom.

She didn't know what she'd expected to happen, exactly. For the phantom to melt like the Wicked Witch of the West, perhaps, leaving nothing but a puddle of vile greenish water. Instead, the phantom stared at her, its mouth open, its pointed, shining teeth on full display. The tear in its chest had expanded, and fluid oozed rapidly, like an untended faucet. The flames burned low and green where the liquid tracked down its body and dripped to the floor.

"Give it to me," Stefan said, appearing at Elena's side. He took the rose from her hand and ripped at its petals, now fading to a lighter pink, and scattered the petals into the fire burning up the sides of the garage.

The phantom watched with a stunned expression, and gradually its blazing fire thinned to smoke, its solid form slowly vaporizing. For a moment, a smoky, malevolent image hung in the air before them, its eyes fixed sullenly upon Elena. And then it was gone.

amon was the first to move, which didn't surprise Elena. His leather jacket scorched, long burns running across his face and arms, he staggered past the others through the fire and threw open the garage door. Outside, thunder rumbled overhead and a heavy rain was falling.

Despite the rain, the garage was burning ferociously, flames licking their way up the sides of the small building and across the roof. As they all stumbled outside, Meredith, coughing, turned her face up to the rain. Matt and Alaric supported Mrs. Flowers and placed her in the driver's seat of her car. Elena held her hands out, letting the driving rain wash away the soot and soothe her burns. The rest of her friends milled around not far from the burning garage, still stunned.

"Oh, *Damon*," said Bonnie. She paused to cough and wheeze for a few seconds, then leaned carefully toward Damon, avoiding his injuries, and kissed him on the cheek. "I'm so happy you came back."

"Thank you, redbird," Damon said, patting her on the back. "Excuse me for a second; I need to take care of something." He stepped away and caught Elena by the hand.

In the distance came the wail of sirens, signaling the advance of fire trucks and police cars drawn by the fire.

Damon pulled Elena toward the dark shadows under a tree near the house. "Come on," he said. "You need blood now." He felt his throat with charred fingers, then drew a fingernail against one of his veins. His leather jacket was practically destroyed, just rags and ashes hanging from him, and the long burns on his face and body were still red and raw-looking, but already better than they had been a few minutes before.

"I could do that," said Stefan, approaching them and leaning against the wall of the house. He looked tired and bedraggled, but his injuries, too, were already healing. "Elena's always welcome to my blood."

"You can definitely pitch in. But that's a bad injury she's got," said Damon matter-of-factly, "and you don't have the Power to heal it right now."

Elena had been trying not to look at her right hand.

Although she couldn't really move it, it didn't hurt much anymore. Which was probably a bad sign, actually. Did that mean the nerve endings were dead? A quick, anxious glance down at her hand made her stomach churn. Even that tiny glimpse showed her horribly blackened and reddened flesh and peeling skin and—God—she thought she'd seen a glimpse of bone beneath the flesh. She let out a low, involuntary whimper.

"Drink," said Damon impatiently. "Let me fix it before they come and drag you off to the burn unit." Elena still hesitated, and Damon sighed and turned to Stefan again. "Look," he said, his voice softening, "it's not always about Power. Sometimes the blood is just about taking *care* of someone."

"I know that," Stefan replied, blinking tiredly at him. "I just wasn't sure that you did."

Damon's mouth twisted in a wry smile. "I'm an old man, little brother," he said. "I know a lot of things." He turned back to Elena. "Drink now," he insisted, and Stefan smiled reassuringly at her.

Elena nodded at Stefan before pushing her mouth tightly against Damon's neck. The second she tasted his blood, Elena became wrapped in warmth and the pain in her hand stopped. She no longer felt the unpleasant cold drumming of the rain on her head and shoulders, the icy trickle of water down her body. She was cozy and safe and loved, and time had stopped just long enough for her to catch her breath.

Damon? she thought, and reached out to his mind with hers. He answered her without words, but with a wave of affection and care, of undemanding love. Through the haze, Elena realized there was something new here. . . .

When she and Damon had allowed their minds to touch in the past, she had often sensed that Damon had been holding back a part of himself. Or, on the rare occasions when she got past the inner barriers he'd thrown up against intruders, she'd found hurt and rage, a lost child chained to a rock.

Now Elena sensed only love and peace as she and Damon melted into each other. When she pulled back from him at last, it took her a moment to return to the real world. Stefan was no longer next to them. It was raining still, cold water running through her hair, over her shoulders, down her neck and arms and body. Her hand ached and was still badly burned, but it had healed to the point of needing ointment and a bandage rather than surgery.

A couple of fire trucks and police cars pulled into the drive, lights blazing, sirens screaming. Closer to the garage, she saw Meredith abruptly drop Stefan's arm, and Elena realized Meredith had been drinking from his wrist.

She realized vaguely that she would have been shocked by this only a few hours ago—she would have assumed Meredith would shy away from touching the blood of *any* vampire, and Stefan had always reserved his blood for

Elena as part of the connection only they shared—but she couldn't work up any real emotion about it now.

It felt like all the barriers between their group had broken down. Whether this new state of things lasted or not, they were all one for now. They'd seen the worst of one another. They'd told the truth and come out the other side. And now, if Meredith needed to be healed, of course Stefan would give her his blood. It would be the same for any of them.

The firemen jumped from their truck and unrolled the hoses. As they turned their attention to putting out the fire, a couple of uniformed police officers and a man who must be the fire marshal walked purposefully toward Mrs. Flowers, Matt, Alaric, Celia, and Bonnie, all of whom were now huddled in the car. Meredith and Stefan headed toward them, too.

"Why didn't they help her into the house?" Elena wondered aloud suddenly, and Damon turned a blank gaze of surprise on her.

"I have no idea," he said slowly. "It never even occurred to me that we could go inside. I guess everyone felt like they should be out here to watch it burn. Make sure the phantom doesn't come out."

"It's like we were at the end of the world," she said softly, thinking aloud. "Even the boardinghouse seemed so far away that it just wasn't part of the picture. Now that other people are here, the world is starting to turn again."

Damon *hmmm*ed noncommittally. "We'd better get over there," he said. "I think they could use some help." Mrs. Flowers's voice was raised indignantly, although Elena couldn't make out the words. As she trailed after Damon she smiled to herself: Since when had Damon cared whether anyone, except Elena herself, could use some help?

As they got closer, Elena could see that Mrs. Flowers had gotten out of the car and assumed her best expression of dottiness and eccentricity, blue eyes wide, arms akimbo, as Alaric held an umbrella over her head.

"Young man!" she snapped at the fire marshal. "What are you trying to imply by asking why my car wasn't parked in the garage? Surely I have every right to distribute my possessions anywhere I like on my own property! What sort of world do we live in where I am penalized, where I am judged for not following conventions? Do you dare to suggest that I might have had some advance knowledge of this fire?"

"Well, ma'am, it's been known to happen. I'm not suggesting anything, but the matter has to be investigated," said the fire marshal stolidly.

"What're all these kids doing here?" one of the police officers asked, shooting a glance around. His eyes lingered on Damon's burned leather jacket and the raw skinless patch on Stefan's cheek. "We're going to need to talk to all of you," he said. "Let's start by getting your names and addresses."

Stefan stepped forward and held the officer's eyes with his. "I'm sure that won't be necessary," he said softly, compellingly. Elena could feel him using his Power. "The garage burned because it was struck by lightning in the storm. No one was here except the old lady in the house and a few of her guests. Everything's so straightforward and simple, there's no need to question anyone."

The officer looked puzzled and then nodded, his face clearing. "These storms can cause a lot of property damage," he replied.

The fire marshal snorted. "What are you talking about? Lightning didn't strike anywhere near here."

Stefan shifted his gaze to the fire marshal. "There's nothing to bother investigating. . . ." But the spell was broken, and now all three men were looking at him with suspicion.

Stefan's Power wasn't going to be strong enough to use on all three, Elena realized, and he wouldn't be able to convince even one of them if the men were all together, awakening one another's doubts. Stefan's face was drawn and tired. He had fought a long battle—more than one, actually. And Stefan was never strong in Power, not when he didn't drink human blood. If he'd been worrying over her and preparing to fight the phantom, it had probably been days since he had had even more than a few swallows of animal blood.

Damon stepped forward. "Sir?" he said politely. The

fire marshal looked at him. "If I could speak to you privately for a moment, I'm sure we can clear this up."

The marshal frowned but followed him to the back porch of the boardinghouse, the second police officer tagging along. Under the porch light, they faced Damon, at first suspicious. Gradually, as he spoke to them, their shoulders relaxed and they began to nod and smile.

Stefan spoke softly to the other officer again. He'd be able to handle influencing one person alone, Elena knew, even in his current state.

Meredith and Bonnie had gotten into the backseat of Mrs. Flowers's ancient automobile—so old that Elena suspected it might predate Mrs. Flowers herself—and were deep in conversation, while Alaric and Celia continued to support Mrs. Flowers under the umbrella as she listened to Stefan's conversation with the police officer, Matt hovering nearby.

Elena walked quietly past them and slipped into the back of the car with Bonnie and Meredith. The door shut with a satisfyingly heavy clunk, and the black leather bench seat creaked and groaned under her.

Bonnie's red curls were soaked straight, wet tendrils hanging down over her shoulders and sticking to her forehead. Her face was smudged with ash and her eyes were red, but she gave Elena a genuinely happy smile. "We won," she said. "It's gone for good, isn't it? We did it."

Meredith was solemn yet exultant, her gray eyes

shining. There was still a smear of Stefan's blood on her lips, and Elena stifled the urge to wipe it away for her. "We did win," Meredith affirmed. "You both did so amazingly. Bonnie, it was really smart of you to start casting off jealousies as fast as you could. It kept the phantom off balance. And Elena . . ." She swallowed. "Plunging into the fire was so brave of you. How's your hand?"

Elena held out her hand and flexed the fingers in front of them. "The incredible powers of vampire blood," Elena said lightly. "Very useful for the aftermath of a battle, right, Meredith?"

Meredith flushed at Elena's teasing, then smiled a little. "I don't know," she said. "It seemed silly *not* to use all our . . . advantages. I feel better already."

"You were terrific, too, Meredith," Bonnie said. "You fought like you were dancing. Graceful and strong and beautiful and so supertough, the way you used your stave."

Elena agreed. "I never could have gotten the rose if you hadn't cut the phantom."

"I guess we're all terrific," said Meredith. "The first meeting of the Robert E. Lee High School Alumni Mutual Admiration Society is now called to order."

"We'll have to get Matt in and tell him how wonderful he is," Bonnie said. "And I guess Stefan also counts as an alum, right? I think now that the world's changed, he might have graduated with us." She yawned, showing a small pink tongue like a cat's. "I'm just worn out."

Elena realized she was, too. It had been a very long day. A very long *year* since the Salvatore brothers had come to Fell's Church and life had changed forever. She slumped down in the seat and rested her head on Meredith's shoulder. "Thank you for saving the town again, both of you," she said sleepily. It seemed important to say it. "Maybe tomorrow we can start working on normal again."

Meredith laughed a little and hugged them both. "Nothing can defeat our sisterhood," she said. "We're *too good* for normal." Her breath hitched. "When you were both taken by the phantom," she said quietly, "I was afraid I had lost you forever. You're my sisters, really, not just my friends, and I need you. I want you to know that."

"Abso*lute*ly," Bonnie said, nodding feverishly. Elena reached out for both of them. The three friends squeezed one another tightly in a laughing, slightly tearful group hug.

Tomorrow would come, and maybe *normal*—whatever that was at this point—would come, too. For now, Elena had her true friends. That was a lot. Whatever happened, that would be enough.

37

The next morning found them all back at the boardinghouse. After the previous night's rain, the sunshine had a fresh quality to it, and everything felt bright and damp and clean, despite the smell of smoke that permeated the boardinghouse and the charred remains of the garage that could be glimpsed through the windows of the den.

Elena sat on the couch, leaning against Stefan. He traced the burn lines, nearly entirely faded, on the back of her hand. "How do they feel, heroine?" he asked.

"They hardly hurt at all, thanks to Damon."

Damon, on the other side of Stefan, gave her a brief, blinding smile but said nothing.

They were all being careful of one another, Elena thought. She felt—and she thought everyone else probably did, too—like the day looked: shining and freshly washed, but slightly fragile. There was a lot of quiet murmuring back and forth, exchanged smiles, comfortable pauses. It was like they had completed a long journey or a difficult task together, and now it was time to rest.

Celia, dressed in pale linen trousers and a silk dove-gray top, elegant and poised as always, cleared her throat. "I'm leaving today," she said when they all looked up at her. Her bags sat neatly on the floor beside her feet. "There's a train to Boston in forty-five minutes, if someone will drive me to the station."

"Of course I'll take you," Alaric said promptly, getting to his feet. Elena glanced at Meredith, but Meredith was frowning at Celia in concern.

"You don't have to go, you know," she told her. "We'd all like it if you stayed."

Celia shrugged expressively and gave a little sigh. "Thank you, but it is time I get going. Despite the fact that we destroyed a priceless rare book and I will probably never be allowed on the Dalcrest campus again, I wouldn't have missed this whole experience for the world."

Meredith grinned at her and raised one eyebrow. "Even the brushes with death?"

Celia raised an eyebrow of her own. "Was there a part that wasn't a brush with death?"

They laughed, and Elena was grateful to see that the

tension between them had evaporated.

"We'll be glad to have you anytime you want to come back, dear," Mrs. Flowers said to Celia earnestly. "I will always have a room for you."

"Thank you," Celia said, looking touched. "I hope I can come back and see you all again someday." She and Alaric left the room, and soon the rest of them heard the sounds of the outside door shutting and a car starting up.

"Good-bye, Celia," Bonnie chirped. "She turned out to be okay in the end, though, didn't she?" She went on without waiting for an answer. "What are we going to do today? We need to have an adventure before summer ends."

"You haven't had enough adventure yet?" Matt asked her disbelievingly from where he was sprawled on a rocking chair in the corner.

"I mean a *fun*, summery kind of adventure," she said. "Not all doom and gloom and battles to the death, but fun-in-the-sun stuff. Do you realize we've got only about three weeks before it's time to start *school* again? If we don't want our only real memories of this summer in Fell's Church to be one disastrous picnic and a horrific battle with a phantom, we'd better get started. I vote we go out to the county fair today. Come on!" she urged them, bouncing in her seat. "Roller coasters! Fun houses! Fried dough! Cotton candy! Damon can win me a big stuffed animal and take me through the Tunnel of Love! It'll be an adventure!"

She fluttered her eyelashes at Damon flirtatiously, but he didn't take her up on her teasing. In fact, he was gazing down into his lap with a strained expression.

"You've done very well, children," said Mrs. Flowers approvingly. "You certainly deserve some time to relax."

No one answered. Damon's tense silence was filling the room, drawing everyone's eyes to him. Finally, Stefan cleared his throat. "Damon?" he asked cautiously.

Damon clenched his jaw and raised his eyes to meet theirs. Elena frowned. Was that *guilt* on Damon's face? Damon didn't do guilt—remorse wasn't one of his many qualities. "Listen," he said abruptly. "I realized . . . while I was making my way back from the Dark Dimension . . ." He stopped again.

Elena exchanged an anxious glance with Stefan. Again, stammering and having trouble finding the words to say what he wanted to say were not typical of Damon.

Damon shook his head and collected himself. "While I was remembering who I was, while I was barely alive again, and then while I was getting ready to come back to Fell's Church, and everything was so painful and difficult," he said, "all I could think of was how we—how *Elena*—had moved heaven and earth to find Stefan. She wouldn't give up her hunt, no matter what obstacles she faced. I'd helped her—I'd risked everything to do so—and we were success-ful. We found Stefan and we brought him home, safe and sound. But when it was my turn to be lost, you all left me on that moon alone."

"But Damon," said Elena, reaching out to him, "we thought you were *dead*."

"And we did try to move heaven and earth to save you," Bonnie said earnestly, her big brown eyes filling with tears. "You *know* that. Elena tried everything to bribe the Guardians to get you back. She almost went crazy with grief. They just kept saying that when a vampire died, he or she was gone for good."

"I know that now," Damon said. "I'm not angry anymore. I haven't been angry about it for what seems like ages. That's not why I'm telling you this." He glanced guiltily at Elena. "I need to apologize to all of you."

There was a tiny collective gasp. Damon just didn't apologize. Ever.

Elena frowned. "What for?"

Damon shrugged, and the ghost of a smirk passed over his face. "What not for, my princess." He sobered. "The truth is, I didn't deserve saving. I've done terrible things to you all as a vampire, and even when I became human again. I fought Meredith; I endangered Bonnie in the Dark Dimension. I endangered all of you." He looked around the room. "I'm sorry," he said to everyone, a note of sincerity and regret in his voice.

Bonnie's lips trembled; then she threw her arms around

Damon. "I forgive you!"

Damon smiled and awkwardly patted her hair. He exchanged a solemn nod with Meredith that seemed to indicate that she also forgave him—this time.

"Damon," said Matt, shaking his head. "Are you sure you're not possessed? You seem a little . . . off. You're never polite to any of us but Elena."

"Well," said Damon, looking relieved at having gotten the confession off his chest, "don't get used to it. *Matt.*"

Matt looked so startled and pleased that Damon had called him the right name for a change, instead of "Mutt" or nothing at all, that Damon might as well have given him a present. Elena saw Stefan give his brother a sly, affection-ate nudge, and Damon elbowed him back.

No, she wouldn't get used to it. Damon, temporarily drained of his jealousies and resentments, was as beautiful and intriguing as ever, but a heck of a lot easier to get along with. It wouldn't last, but she could enjoy it for now.

She took a moment to really look at them, the Salvatore brothers. The vampires she loved. Stefan with his soft dark curls and sea green eyes, his long limbs and the sen-sitive curve of his mouth that she always longed to kiss. Sweetness and solidity and a sorrow she'd had a hand in lightening. Damon, leather and silk and fine chiseled fea-tures. Mercurial and devastating. She loved them both. She couldn't be sorry, couldn't be anything other than sincerely, wholly grateful for the fate that had thrown them in her path.

But it wouldn't be easy. She couldn't imagine what would happen when this new comfort and friendliness between the brothers, between all of them, ended. She didn't doubt that it would dissolve. Irritations and jealousies were just a part of life, and they would build up again.

She squeezed Stefan's hand in hers and smiled past him at Damon, whose dark eyes warmed.

Inwardly, she sighed a little, then smiled more widely. Bonnie was right: College was just around the corner, a whole new adventure. Until then, they should take their pleasures where they could find them.

"Cotton candy?" she said. "I can't remember the last time I had cotton candy. I'm definitely up for Bonnie's idea of adventure."

Stefan brushed his lips against hers in a kiss that was as sweet and light as cotton candy itself, and she leaned into the comfort of his arms.

It couldn't last. Elena knew it. But she was very happy. Stefan was himself again, not angry or fearful or grieving, but himself, the one she loved. And Damon was alive, and safe, and with them. All her friends were around her.

She was truly home at last.

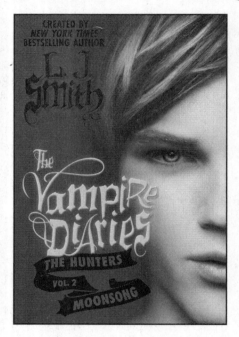

Undyingly Romantic

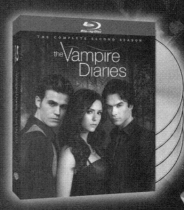

the Vampire Diaries
THE COMPLETE SECOND SEASON

INCLUDES FEATURETTES, DELETED SCENES, COMMENTARIES AND GAG REEL
OWN IT NOW ON BLU-RAY AND DVD

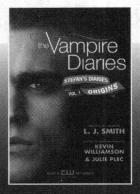 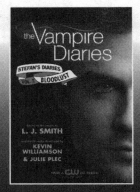 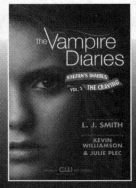